THE WALKING DEAD

THE WALKING DEAD

GERALD SEYMOUR

THE OVERLOOK PRESS
WOODSTOCK & NEW YORK

This edition first published in the United States in 2008 by
The Overlook Press, Peter Mayer Publishers, Inc.
Woodstock & New York

WOODSTOCK:
One Overlook Drive
Woodstock, NY 12498
www.overlookpress.com
[for individual orders, bulk and special sales, contact our Woodstock office]

NEW YORK:
141 Wooster Street
New York, NY 10012

Cataloging-in-Publication Data is available from the Library of Congress

Manufactured in the United States of America
ISBN 978-1-59020-005-6
10 9 8 7 6 5 4 3 2 1

For James

Prologue

To Whom it may Concern: In the event of my death or incapacity, will the finder of this Diary please facilitate its safe delivery to my sister, Miss Enid Darke, 40 Victoria Street, Bermondsey, London, England. Many thanks. Signed: Cecil Darke.

14 September 1936
Well, this is the start. The top of the first blank page. It will not be a literary work because I do not have the intelligence or education for that, but it will be a record – I hope – of my journey. I am going to fight on a foreign field, and I cannot say how many days or weeks or months I will be filling this notebook, or where this journey will lead me.

If the handwriting is poor – and this is a personal testament so, should I survive, it will not be read by any other living soul, except Enid – that is because the train is rocking on the track, and I have little room in which to write as we are all packed tight in our carriage, as tight as sardines in a tin.

I am twenty-one years old, and my clean new passport lists my occupation as 'bank clerk'. I am thinking of the shock and confusion on the face of my supervisor, Mr Rammage, when I handed in my resignation last Friday, with immediate effect. So predictable, his reaction. Said sternly, 'Why are you leaving us, Darke?' To go abroad, Mr Rammage. 'Oh, going off on a holiday, are we? Don't expect that your desk will be waiting for you. Don't think I'll be holding your place vacant for you – plenty of likely lads to take your position. For employment, these are difficult times, and to walk out on work with prospects and security is – frankly – extraordinarily stupid.' I understand, Mr Rammage. And then, with sarcasm: 'And are you prepared, Darke, to enlighten me as to where – abroad – you intend to travel to?' To Spain, Mr Rammage. 'That is not extraordinarily stupid, that is deluded idiocy. To get involved in that war, Communists and Fascists viciously massacring each other – a war that is none of your business and where you have no cause to be a part – is simple lunacy. I don't believe you have any military experience . . .' There will be people who will teach me what I need to learn. 'I was, Darke, at the Somme and at Passchendaele. It's not like they say, those who sit behind the lines. It is a thousand times worse. To fight modern warfare is beyond imagination. God, please, watch over you . . . Now, clear your desk and be gone.' I cleared my desk, and I was gone, and I swear there was a tear in Mr Rammage's eyes.

Neither Dad nor Mum came to Victoria to see me off, but Enid did. She gave me this notebook and she had had my name stamped in gold on its cover – that was very sweet and loving of her – and with it was a half of a hob loaf and a quarter of cheese. We kissed, and when the train left I leaned through the window and waved back to her. Then the packet boat to Calais, then to Paris by train.

In two days we were at the Gare d'Austerlitz, and were marshalled on to Train No. 77, which they call the Train of Volunteers. We went south through the afternoon, evening and night, and we left France after Perpignan. Now we are on the line to Barcelona. The mountains of the Pyrenees are behind us. I have spent one pound, three shillings and fourpence in Paris, and have but two pounds ten shillings in my wallet. Yet, because of where I go and why, I feel myself a rich man.

I have started out in my Sunday suit, best shirt, cap, and raincoat, with my boots all shined up, but now I feel overdressed, so I have taken off cap and tie and loosened the stud on my collar. The stubble is thick on my chin – which would horrify Mr Rammage.

I believe that I am the youngest of the volunteers in this carriage, and I am the only Briton. There is a German, Karl, who speaks a little English, but none of the others do. I am grateful to Karl: without his help I would not be able to communicate with my fellow travellers. They are from Germany and Italy. They are all, through Karl, interested to know about me because I am different from them. They are refugees from their own countries because they are members of the CP – sorry, the Communist Party – and at best they would be locked up by the Fascist regimes in Berlin and Rome. At worst they would be executed. From them, there is surprise that I am not a member of the CPGB, and they say that I have a home to go back to, but they do not, and they are bewildered that I am coming to Spain to fight alongside them.

They have called me 'the idealist', which is flattering. They tell me that it is time Fascism was fought, and that the battlefield is Spain, where democracy must survive or face annihilation all over Europe. Did I know that? I must have or I would still be at my desk with Mr Rammage peering over my shoulder and criticizing untidiness in my ledgers. I suppose I knew it was important to travel to this war and play my part, but to be told that I am 'the idealist' brings a little glow of pride to my chest. I have told them that Mr Rammage, last Friday, said this conflict was none of my business, and each in turn has shaken my hand and congratulated me for understanding that it was the duty of all principled men to come to Spain and fight for freedom. I feel humble to be with these men, and humble also that I know so little of politics. But I have not told them that beside my 'idealism' as a warrior against Fascism, and the need to drive back the barbarians of militarism, there was another factor in my joining up. I craved adventure . . . I look to find excitement and be a better man for it.

There is no food on the train, but a man comes round with buckets of water for us to drink from, and the queues to reach the lavatories take an age, but in this company the hardships do not seem to matter.

We are now, Karl says, an hour out from Barcelona. I have never before been abroad, and my father has never been out of London, except for annual excursions to the coast at Ramsgate. In London it was cold and wet: autumn was starting. Here, the sun beats on the train windows, and we are slowly cooking because we are squashed so close . . . I have stopped writing for a few minutes and just stared out. There are fields that are yellow and dry, with horses and carts in them, and women are bringing in the last of the harvest. There are only women working. As we go by, they stop their work, stand straight and raise a clenched fist in salute to us – and all the men, in all the carriages, shout back at the top of their voices, in Spanish, 'They shall not pass.' Already, just from sitting in the train, I know that that is the slogan of those I will fight with. It brings a shiver to me – 'They shall not pass' – not of fear but of pride.

Chapter 1: Thursday, Day 1

It was as if he had been brought to a camel market. All of his life since he had gained the first clouded images of memory, he had stood and watched such markets. And now they were thirteen hundred kilometres behind him, separated from him by the wilderness of the Kingdom's deserts and by the knife-edge crests of the Asir mountains. There, between the mountains and the shining sea, was the village that was his home.

The beasts of burden – camels, hobbled at the ankle, and mules lined up, standing listlessly, tethered to a rope running between two posts – were well respected by the travelling Bedouin and the itinerant merchants who came to buy. In the extremities of the desert's temperatures, brutal heat by day and chill air at night, or on the passes through the mountains that led to the Yemen border, a tribesman or trader would suffer death by dehydration or exposure if he had bought unwisely at the market. It was the skill of those men that their experience guided them towards paying only for animals in which they could place total trust. The new wealth of the Kingdom, in the cities beyond the mountains where there were wide highways and the oil wells with their networks of pipes, had not penetrated the Asir mountains. He came from the part of the

Kingdom that had not shared the affluence of the petroleum deposits, and where old ways still continued. Where he had lived, there remained a use for animals that could be trained to fulfil a given purpose, and such animals were chosen and haggled over in the markets.

A good beast was prized and the arguments over its value could last from early morning sunrise to dusk when the market closed. The best beast would see the bidding for its ownership disputed.

Thirteen hundred kilometres distant, Ibrahim Hussein's home was an hour's walk from the town of Jizan by camel or astride a mule, and a five-minute drive in his father's Mercedes saloon. The house was beyond the view of the Corniche and the Old Souk. But from an upper window, from the bedroom that his sisters shared, the highest turrets of the Ottoman Fort could be seen. It was inside the compound of the Interior Police barracks, but he did not believe there was a tagged file about him on their computers. Behind the fort, nestling on low ground alongside the compound's walls, was the market where camels and mules were brought for sale. He was near to completing the twenty-first year of his life, and if his ambition was fulfilled he would not reach his next birthday.

There were a dozen of them. They sat where they could find shade, against the rear wall of a single-storey building constructed of concrete blocks and roofed with corrugated-iron sheeting. Ibrahim had his back against the concrete, and the others made a small, tight circle facing him. With his youth and inexperience, he had never travelled outside the Kingdom; he could not have said where the rest had started their journey, but some were darker than him, some had sharper features and some had a more sallow, pale skin. They had all been told that they were not to talk among each other, most certainly not to ask for names, but Ibrahim assumed that most came from Yemen and Egypt, Syria and Pakistan. He was not stupid and had good powers of deduction. Two sat awkwardly, shifting continually to be more comfortable. He thought them from Europe, unused to squatting where there was no cushion. The instruction not to talk had been given with curt authority, and they all sat with their heads bowed. Common to them all, the bright light of their Faith burned in their eyes.

They waited.

In front of Ibrahim, but distanced from the group by a few paces, four men stood in a huddle – the potential buyers. At first, as if the market had opened in the relative cool of the early morning, the four had minutely examined each in the group, remarking on them. But that was long past. Now, they talked quietly, but their attention was on the sandscape on the far side of the building. Behind them, two pickups were painted with light and dark yellow camouflage markings. The front cab roof had been cut out of both, and a machine-gun was mounted above the windscreen.

Ibrahim had expected that each of them would be welcomed, that they would pray together. But they had been ordered to sit still and hold their silence.

He saw the men react and, for the first time, smile in anticipation. They were all dressed in drab olive uniforms and their faces were masked by the folds of the *khaffiyehs* wrapped round their heads. Pistols hung from webbing belts in holsters. He heard a vehicle approaching, its engine straining in the sand where there was no track.

He thought it was the vehicle they had waited for, and that the business of the market could now begin.

Beyond the concrete building, it stopped. The men went to meet it. He heard laughter and shouted greetings.

Ibrahim, and all of those sitting in the faint shade of the wall, was in the state of the living dead. He was between being a young man with a future, two years into his studies in medicine, and a martyr who would be greeted and shown a place at God's table. He knew of the rewards offered to the *shahidas* because they had been listed to him at the mosque in Habalah by the *imam*, who had been his gate-keeper, his recruiter, who had made possible the start of his journey to Paradise.

The man they had waited for was tall and erect and seemed to carry no spare weight on his body. He moved loosely on his feet. His boots were coated with sand, as was the uniform he wore with its intricate camouflage patterns. More sand clung to the straps that came down from his shoulders to his belt. Grenades were festooned from them, and an assault rifle hung from his right shoulder rocking against the pouches on his chest that held spare magazines. The sand caked his balaclava into which slits had been crudely cut. The eyes, fierce and unwavering in the intensity of their stare, fastened on the group, never left them. Ibrahim felt their force bead on his body, and tried to give himself courage. He clasped his hands tightly together, hoping that the shake in his fingers would not be seen. He felt as naked as if a surgeon's knife had cut him open.

A strangely shrill and high-pitched voice – Ibrahim did not recognize the Arabic dialect that was spoken – ordered the group to stand. They did. As he pushed himself upright, he felt the stiffness in his knees. He tried to stand tall. The man moved away from the group, waved aside the other men, and placed himself some fifty paces from the building.

A second order was given. In turn, the living dead were to walk towards him, stop, turn, walk back, then sit. His finger jabbed towards one of those whom Ibrahim believed to have come from Europe.

They were pointed to. They walked forward, stopped, turned, went back and sat. Some hurried, some dawdled, some moved hesitantly, some tried to throw back their shoulders and stride, and some shuffled. Ibrahim's turn came, the last but one. He did not know what was expected of him.

Perhaps he was too deeply exhausted. Perhaps the ache in his legs and hips dulled his thoughts. He started, drifting over the dirt, not feeling the roughness of stones and debris under the soles of his trainers. He walked as if he sought only to be closer to his God, and he could not help the smile that came easily to his lips. He did not know how he should walk, or what the man with the mask of sand-crusted black material, with the twin gems of his eyes, wanted from him. He came close enough to the man to scent the old sweat beneath the tunic, and the smile held. The sun, blisteringly hot, beat on him as he turned. He went back to the shade.

He was about to sink down against the building's wall, when the shout arrowed into his back.

'You! Do not join them. Sit apart from them.'

He watched one young man get to his feet and move slowly from the wall, confusion settling on the immature mouth, then despair. He thought the young man believed himself rejected. He faced the four older men. Deference was written on their faces. He gestured with his filthy calloused hand towards the hunched-down group. He believed he had found the youth he wanted.

He observed from a distance. The rest of the group was split into four parts. Three would go to Mosul in the north, two to Ar-Ramadi, one to Baquba, and five to Baghdad. Each one, wherever he was taken, would spend between one and three days in transit, then one more day in briefing for his target. The next day they would be in a car weighted down with explosives, or a lorry, or be on foot with a belt or waistcoat against their stomach or chest under a full flowing robe. Within a week, at most, all would be dead and the remains of their corpses would be scattered against the walls and roofs of houses and office blocks, on the pillars of flyovers and in the court-yards where policemen gathered to be recruited or to draw their pay. The names of some would be known later from videos broadcast on websites, and the names of others would be lost in eternity. The enemy called them 'suicide-bombers' and feared their dedication. For himself and his fellow fighters, they were useful tactical weaponry, valued for the exactness with which a chosen target could be destroyed.

He was listened to, as he should have been. It was said now by those who reported to the resistance clandestinely, while holding down positions of importance in the regime of the collaborators, that no photograph of him existed but that already a price lay on his head – dead or alive – of a million American dollars, that he was identified in files only by the name he had given himself. He was the Scorpion.

His attention roved between the future and the present. The future was the enormity of the mission on which he was now embarking, and it would take him to a continent that was beyond his previous experience; the message had come from the Tribal Areas of Pakistan, from old men who were fugitives. The present was the open expanse of sand grit, where the only mark of human habitation was the single-storey building of concrete blocks, which was thirty kilometres from the mid-point of the road that ran for nine hours of driving between the Saudi desert communities of Hafr Al-Batn, to the south-east, and Arar, which was north-west; where he sat, ate and talked he was not more than a kilometre from the border.

He saw the misery in the face of the young man, saw him blink away tears. He went to him. He squatted beside him. 'What is your name?'

A choked response: 'Ibrahim, Ibrahim Hussein.'

'Where are you from?'

'From Asir Province, the town of Jizan.'

'Do you have work in Jizan?'

'At Jeddah, in the university, I am a student of medicine.'

The sun had started to slip from its zenith. Soon, perhaps, small rats or rabbits would emerge to scurry on the sand having scented the crumbs of the bread they had eaten. Later, maybe, as the greyness of dusk approached, foxes would track them.

'We do not move before darkness. There is danger here, but greater danger if we travel in the light . . . Are you strong?'

'I hope to be. Please, am I rejected?'

'Not rejected, but chosen.'

He saw again the fullness of the smile, and relief broke on the young man's face.

He went to his own vehicle, and lay down full length in the sand, his head against the forward off-side tyre. Beneath the balaclava he closed his eyes and slept in the knowledge that the cool of dusk would wake him. More than the present, the images of the future sidled into his mind, and the part in it that a young man would play because he walked well.

'The laws of justice permit a jury to be reduced from twelve persons to ten. With ten of you the trial may still proceed. Regretfully, we have lost two – first, through tragic bereavement, and second, by this sad accident today in which your foreperson has fallen on the way into the building and has, I am informed, suffered a fractured bone in her leg . . . I am sure you will all join me in expressing our sincerest sympathy to your colleague. But now we must move on.'

When he had been told in his chambers of the wretched woman's tumble, Mr Justice Herbert had cursed softly, but to himself, not in the view or hearing of the bailiff.

'We have now been together for a day less than nine weeks and I anticipate that three more weeks, at a maximum, will enable us to reach a conclusion and you to find the defendants guilty or not guilty of the offences with which they are charged.'

He was a careful man. Sitting as judge in court eighteen at Snaresbrook on the eastern extremity of metropolitan London, Wilbur Herbert was renowned for his weighted words . . . He had no intention of letting the trial, Regina v. Oswald (Ozzie) Curtis and Oliver (Ollie) Curtis, slip from his grip, and no intention that his words now could justify any subsequent appeal by defence counsel for the overturning of a guilty verdict.

'We will adjourn, I hope briefly, so that you may go back to your room and choose a new foreperson. Then we will resume.'

He spoke softly. It was his belief that a lowered voice caused jury members to lean forward the better to hear him and held their attention. They were a run-of-the-mill crowd, neither remarkable nor unremarkable but typical, and he thought the case against the Curtis brothers was unlikely to tax them with complications. Should he tell them to be certain to have a bottle of aspirin conveniently adjacent should any relative show signs of sickness? No, indeed not. A momentary titter from a relaxed jury, valuable as it was, denigrated the majesty of the Bench. He believed that majesty important to the process of justice.

'A few minutes only, I hope, for your choice of a new foreperson, and then we will continue . . . The matter of flowers is in hand.'

He gathered his robes closely against his stomach, rose and left the court. He was damned if this case would slide from under him – and slide it would if court eighteen lost just one more of those jurors.

A bitter little argument had divided the room. Trouble was that both Corenza and Rob had wanted the job, and both had trumpeted their claim. Important, was it, to be foreman, forewoman or *foreperson* of a jury? Both had obviously thought so. What they had in common – Corenza, the toff, and Rob, the pompous idiot – was the dislike they generated among the remaining eight jurors. Deirdre, Fanny and Ettie had gone with Corenza, as Glenys's successor, while Dwayne, Baz, Peter and Vicky had supported Rob. Himself? Well, he didn't give a damn, and he'd used his casting vote to give Rob, an officious, pedantic prat, the job that the imbecile seemed to yearn for.

They were back in court now, and the whole morning had been given up to the dispute; the judge had looked to be biting his lip to control his irritation at time lost. Jools hadn't given a toss, and had enjoyed another cup of coffee from the machine in their room.

He was 'Jools' to his colleagues of nine weeks. Actually, everyone who knew him well – and the few who loved him, some who despised him, and the many who were casual in his life – called him Jools. Formally, he was Julian Wright: husband of Barbara, father of Kathy. He was Julian to his parents, and Mr Wright, occasionally, to his pupils. He enjoyed the nickname, Jools, and believed it gave him a certain welcome raffishness. Now, because they had all had to move chairs, he sat between Ettie and Vicky; the rearrangement of their places was because Rob had eased into Glenys's seat, extreme left of the lower tier, nearest the judge . . . Ettie had a powerful scent on her, dabbed on her wrists and neck, but the whiff of Vicky's perspiration was richly attractive.

Of course they were guilty.

It was the first time that Jools had sat on a jury. Not bad to have reached the age of thirty-seven and never before received the brown envelope with the demand that he present himself to Snaresbrook Crown Court for duty as a juror on a Monday morning in February. His initial reaction had been, as he realized now, typical. He hadn't time for it, he was in work, he had responsibilities. He'd telephoned the given number and explained, rather forcibly, that he was deputy head of the geography department at a comprehensive, and had a classroom schedule stretching through the coming term into the summer – but the woman at the far end of the line hadn't taken a blink of interest. She had said that, unless there were more pressing demands on his time, he should pay more attention to his civic responsibilities and be at Snaresbrook on the appointed day.

Jools had gone to his head teacher, believing that there he would find support, that a letter would be written on the school's headed paper stating that he could not be spared from his curriculum obligations. He had been brushed away with a cryptic 'We'll just have to get a temporary replacement in. Personally, I'd give my right ball to be out of this place for a month or two. Consider yourself fortunate, Jools. The education authority will pay your salary, you won't be out of pocket. You'll be envied by each one of us – an escape tunnel from this *stalag* is how I'd regard it. Relax and enjoy the ride. But, please, try not to get one of those long ones.' His retaliation had been, when a milling mass of prospective jurors was gathered in a cold, airless waiting room, to volunteer for any case, regardless of how much time it would take up, and he had said to the bailiff, with an earnest lilt in his voice, that he regarded his obligations to society as of paramount importance. His reward was to be free of a classroom of juvenile yobbery where geography counted only as a route map to the nearest fast-food outlet, or the way to the park where blow-jobs were on offer for peanuts, or the road to . . . On his last Friday afternoon, he'd turned in the doorway of the staff common room and announced that it might be some time before he met up with them all again. The remark had been greeted with indifference, as if nobody cared whether he was there or not.

Not only was it the first time he had sat on a jury, it was also Jools's induction to the daily working life of a Crown Court. The legal profession hardly stretched themselves – God, they didn't. The hours weren't fierce. With pomp and circumstance the judge entered court eighteen at ten thirty in the morning, broke for lunch at a quarter to one, resumed at two fifteen, and called a halt usually at a quarter past four and certainly not later than half past. At the drop of a wig, the barristers were on their feet and seeking to make legal arguments that necessitated the jury evacuating to their room, sometimes for hours. When the court was in session, with full steam up, the barristers' questioning of witnesses was as slow as paint drying.

If the padding had been cut away, the business of the court could have been completed in a week or less. Herbert, up there in the clouds with angels for company, seemed to have little interest in prodding witnesses and lawyers from a jog to a run. Jools had had much time to ponder on the courtroom pace, nine weeks of it . . . Most of the others took full notes, as Mr Justice Herbert did, in longhand on the lined pages of A4 refill pads. Corenza was on her second, Rob was on his third, and Fanny wrote in short headline bursts on scraps of paper. Jools did not do notes. He could see no reason to.

They were guilty.

He rarely looked at them. The brothers sat away to his right shoulder. They faced the judge, were behind their legal team and the prosecution's, and were flanked by prison guards. They were in their mid-forties, with wide chests pushing against their suit buttons and muscling bulged in the sleeves. They had clean shirts for each day of the hearing, and the type of quiet tie that a senior civil servant – or a top administrator in the education authority – would have chosen; he assumed that the ties had been nominated, along with the executive suits and daily changed shirts, by their defence people to make a 'good impression' on the jury. There was no way that a suit costing what Jools took home in a month would fool him. On their wrists were heavy gold chains, and he thought that under the laundered shirts and the fall of their ties there would be heavier gold necklaces. When he did look at them, sharp side-of-eye glances, he could see their intimidating bulk, and the cold arrogance of power in their faces. All right, all right, he would admit it – to himself: they frightened him. There were fathers who came to the school to complain when their child was suspended or sent home, fathers who clenched their fists and spat anger. Fathers frightened him, but not as much as the brothers did. The trouble was that each time he stole a look at them – having been drawn to do so, moth to a flame, compulsion – they seemed to sense it: their heads would twist and their eyes would fasten on to him, leech secure. He would turn away fast and look at his hands or shoelaces, the judge or the court reporter. But always, when he looked right, there was the moment when they trapped him and he felt the fear. He knew what they'd done, had heard in crawling detail of their entry into the jewellery shop, had listened to the stumbling recall of witnesses terrorized by the guns and the certainty of violence if they'd resisted. The fear made him shiver.

He cursed silently. Now he must find a new eyeline, somewhere else in court eighteen, to focus on. The elder brother, with a springy step, was being escorted by twin minders from the dock to the witness box, and from there would face the jury. Jools gazed at Mr Justice Herbert's nose, and the mole on its left side; he did not know where else it was safe to look.

He had never told his wife that eye-contact with the brothers frightened him. He was no hero, and Babs would have told him so. He had never before tasted the sourness of danger, and when this trial was complete he doubted he ever would again.

There were no snow-capped mountain peaks here, no caves above the iceline where hunted men hid. There were no tracks on which sure-footed couriers brought reports for evaluation and took away messages laced with hate that demanded execution. There were no cliffs against which old men would stand, leaning on sticks for support and holding rifles to guarantee their power, to denounce a sprawling society they loathed.

There were no deep-rutted roads along which armoured vehicles edged, and helmeted men, sweating in bulletproof vests, peered over the sights of machine-guns for an unseen enemy.

Nothing of this town showed the possibility that it might become a front-line outpost in the new war. Normality ruled in Luton. That afternoon, the Bedfordshire town, thirty miles due north of central London, had a population of a few hundred short of 170,000 inhabitants. It boasted a major automobile factory and an airport patronized by tourists flying out on cheap charter flights. The town had been named – and had angrily rejected the title – 'Britain's crappiest', with the 'worst architecture in the country' and 'wrist-slittingly moribund nightclubs'. But front line Luton was not.

In St George's Square, sandwiched between the town hall and the shopping centre, drunks and hooded kids had taken occupancy of the benches and were sprawled over them. They, and the shoppers who skirted them warily, the office workers who came out to smoke in spite of the rain, the council's cleaners emptying overfilled rubbish bins, and the youngsters trooping into the public library off the square to use the computers, did not concern themselves with the war. Why should they? For what reason might they consider them-selves threatened and labelled as legitimate targets? All thought themselves safe from terror. Months before, detectives had broken down doors and taken away handcuffed men. A year and a half before a vehicle had been left at the railway-station car park by four men who had taken a train to London to kill themselves and fifty others . . . Too long ago, best forgotten.

To the men and women of the town, the war was confined to tele-vision screens, distant beyond comprehension. But confined inside the boundaries of the town resentment simmered in ghettos of Asian immigrants – where a few Muslim radicals awaited the call to *jihad* . . . The town that sprawled on either side of the river Lea did not, could not, know it.

*

When the girl had first arrived, punctual to the minute, the farmer's wife had thought her pretty. When she had come closer, the woman saw the livid scar on the girl's forehead, running laterally, and the second shorter one, vertical on her left cheek.

The farmer's wife tried not to stare. She thought the scars were from a car accident, a head striking a windscreen.

'I hope I am not late. Have not kept you?' the girl asked.

'Not at all, no. You're on the dot.'

The girl was probably in her early twenties; the woman glimpsed her hands and saw no wedding ring. Sad for her: with such disfiguring wounds, the girl would have difficulty in finding a husband with whom to raise a family . . . She was Asian, but her accent was local. The farmer's wife hesitated as to whether Oakdene Cottage should be let to an ethnic-minority group, then killed the thought. She would let the cottage to the girl for a month, payment in advance, not to champion racial tolerance but because – the books of Oakdene Farm showed it – she and Bill needed the cash.

'Come on in, my dear, and look round.'

'Thank you, but I am sure it will be very satisfactory.'

'And how many will you be?'

'Eight in all. It is for our family. Some are coming from abroad.'

'Well, it'll be a bit of a squash. Only four bedrooms – did I say that?'

'It is not a problem. I think it will be excellent.'

The farmer's wife said quickly, 'And that will be, for a month, eleven hundred pounds, paid in advance.'

A young man was left sitting in the car that had brought the girl. She would have been pretty, with a good figure under her jeans and light windcheater and striking dark hair to her shoulders, but for those hideous injuries. They went inside, and the farmer's wife fussed through the details of the kitchen and its appliances, the bathroom hot water, the bedrooms and their linen, the dining room, crockery and cutlery stores, but she thought the girl only vaguely interested, which surprised her.

'It's ideal,' the girl said. She was at the doorway, gazing out over the fields and the emptiness of the Bedfordshire farmland. She would have heard rooks calling and the engine of Bill's distant tractor. 'So quiet, perfect for my family.'   .

22

'And if you don't want quiet, Luton's only five miles . . . Either my husband or I will pop down and do the grass, see that you're settled.'

'No need. We'll do it. You can forget we're here. We will enjoy looking after your lovely cottage. We'll see you when we leave.'

'You're sure?' She had enough to be getting on with at the farmhouse, and Bill did on the land, not to come down the quarter of a mile on the side track to cut the grass.

'Absolutely sure, thank you.'

The deal was done. The girl was driven away up the long, bumpy track to the main road.

Only when she had gone, and the farmer's wife had gunned her Land Rover, did she realize that she was ignorant of the girl's name and had no address for her. But she did have a letting for a month when there were no other takers for Oakdene Cottage, and eleven hundred pounds in fifty-pound notes rammed into her trouser hip pocket. She wondered why an Asian family should wish to stage a reunion in such a remote corner of the county, but only for a moment. Then she was considering how to prioritize eleven hundred pounds in cash, none of it for declaring.

He looked up from his screen. Its content rarely held him after his lunch break. After his two sandwiches and an apple, taken in a plastic box to the park at the back of the building, he was usually enveloped in tiredness. Now he was wondering – as his mind wandered – whether he could slip down to what he called 'the heads', lower himself on to the lavatory seat and get in a ten-minute doze that would help him through the remainder of his working day . . . Dickie Naylor scowled.

The bloody woman was eyeing his territory already. Through the open door of his cubicle, he saw that Mary Reakes was gazing into his space, and he fancied he recognized covetousness in that look. Not that his cubicle had much to offer: a desk with a screen on it, a fishing-line tangle of cables beneath, his upright swivel chair, a lower upholstered seat for a visitor, a floor safe alongside two filing cabinets that each had a padlocked bar running vertically over the drawers, a side-table with a coffee machine and a couple of plastic water bottles. There was precious little else, except wall charts of holidays to be taken by the few staff who answered to him, and the roster for their night-duty obligations, a photograph of a cricket team proudly holding up a pathetically small silver cup and one of his wife in the garden, pictures of sour-faced bearded men were pinned to a board.

She would have to wait. After that evening, at the end of a dreary, damp April day, the cubicle would be the work home of Dickie Naylor for eleven more working days. Then she could have it – was welcome to it. On that Friday evening, two weeks away, he would carry his few personal items out of the cubicle, swipe his card for the last time at the main door, then hand it to the uniformed staff for shredding. He would walk away along the Embankment – sniff for a last time at the tang of the river – from the building that was officially known as Thames House, occasionally Box 500, and to him was Riverside Villas. The new regime in the carpeted suites of upper-floor offices, grander temples than his cubicle, would have marked down the title 'Riverside Villas' as a sign of an old man's disrespect for the modern world that was shortly to be shot of him. To them, it was a fine block and commensurate with the Service's fledgling importance as a front-line arm of the War on Terror. To Dickie Naylor it was a pretentious edifice.

When he went, closing the door on his cubicle, he was damned sure that Mary Reakes – who was destined to succeed him as head of section – would be on his old ground before he had reached the Underground station. But, until then, he would make her wait, right to the minute of his last departure.

She was half his age. She had sexless bobbed hair, her face was half masked by powerful spectacles, and she dressed in black trouser suits. She had a degree, which he did not, and . . . She did not look away. She held his eyes and challenged him. Her attitude was clear: he was a 'veteran', his shelf-life had expired and the sooner he was gone the better. The word 'veteran' would not have slipped her tongue with either affection or respect. 'Veteran' meant worthless, an impediment to progress . . . He smiled sweetly to her through the open door.

He had never been, and he could recognize it, the brightest star in the heavens. At best he had been conscientious, a dogged plodder, and he had probably risen a grade higher in the hierarchy than his abilities warranted. He had been thought of as a 'safe pair of hands'.

In two weeks he would see in his sixty-fifth birthday; then retirement to Suburbville in Worcester Park. There, he was Richard to his neighbours – but at Riverside Villas he was Dickie to all, from the director general on high to the basement garage guards at the bottom of the pecking order. He had long valued the familiarity as a badge of trust from the tribe he belonged to.

In the dog-days of a career that had run since his recruitment to the Service on New Year's Day 1968, he could not look back on those thirty-nine years of fielding the material that crossed his desk and point to any single moment when his intervention had altered the flow of events, which was ample cause for the resentment he harboured as Mary Reakes peered through his wide-open door, raked her eyes over his ground, the clock ticked and his work role ebbed.

He had been given, in the chaotic days after Nine-Eleven, a small department to run that was intended to search for an impending attack on the United Kingdom by foreign-based, overseas-born suicide-bombers. Down the corridor a huge, expanded section dealt with the domestic-based threat, but he presided over a backwater. And after eleven more working days he would preside over nothing.

There had been few in the crematorium chapel. And fewer had come along afterwards to the garden room of the pub. Most of the patients from the nursing-home who had attended the service had ridden back by minibus in time for lunch.

He was there because his mother had made the arrangements. He had told her that he had an hour free but no longer because after that he was rostered for evening duty. He stood close to her, and when she moved among the twenty or so who had walked from the chapel after the curtains had closed during the last quick three-verse hymn, he followed her.

His mother was a small, neat woman and David Banks towered over her.

If she had not made the arrangements, the gathering would not have happened; he owed it to her to be there – it was a son's loyalty. But the family had long split, he knew no one, and he had been by far the youngest in the chapel and was now in the garden room. He hovered a half-step behind his mother, as if he needed to guard her and she was his Principal. It was his way, not purposely but from instinct and training, to watch over her; it was unlikely that he realized his gaze played over the faces of the elderly who murmured quietly as though one of them, in a best but now poorly fitting dark suit, might threaten her. She had never remarried after his father had died and he tried to see her as often as work permitted, but it was not often enough. She lived a hundred miles from London on the Somerset and Wiltshire borders and he was locked into a life in the capital. For the last three and a half years men of his professional skills had been larded with overtime requirements and extra duties.

He was a detective constable, an authorized firearms officer, in demand to the extent that most evenings he went back to his bedsit in a west London attic reeling from exhaustion. But he tried, moving in her wake, to smile with warmth when he was introduced to distant relations of whom he had heard vaguely but never met. He shook hands, was careful not to squeeze hard and heartily on skeletal fingers. The talk drifted around him but he heard little of it. His mind was away, the funeral of Enid Darke subsumed by thoughts of where he would be that evening and the previous day's briefing on the risk to the Principal posed by the man's presence in the capital on a three-day visit.

An old man came to his mother's side – and it was the policeman's reflex that he stiffened because a stranger had approached her. Banks ground his fingernails into the palm of his hand as if that might relax him.

He could not hear them but sensed the earnestness of the man's words to his mother, and she had leaned closer to hear better. Nor could he see what was passed from the jacket pocket into his mother's grasp. The man did not draw breath, and talked with a faint, whistling reediness. And then he was gone, tottering in the direction of the bar and the steward, and Banks saw him grapple shakily with a further schooner of sherry. His mother held what she had been given in both hands, turned to her son and grimaced.

'What was all that about?' He spoke from the side of his mouth, his eyes roving again.

Her voice was low, confidential and conspiratorial. 'Rather interesting, actually. His name's Wilfred Perry. He lived next door to

Great-aunt Enid in some ghastly tower block in east London – he's still there. Eight months ago, or whenever she was moved out and taken to the nursing-home, she knocked on his door early in the morning. She couldn't look after herself any more and needed care. She told him that she had only one item that was precious and she wanted it taken care of, then passed on in the family. She gave it to Mr Perry – why not to one of her family he doesn't know, and I don't. If he'd fallen off the twig before she did, God knows what would have happened to it. Anyway, I've got it. But it's for you – why you? Someone must have told him that you were family, but also that you were a policeman.'

She passed her son a small leather-covered notebook.

He took it. 'What am I supposed to do with it?'

'Read it, I suppose, and keep it. It's family and it's history, so he said – and Great-aunt Enid had made him promise that it would be given to the younger generation of the family. He's done that, ful-filled his obligation.'

The leather had been black once. It had long lost any lustre, was chipped at the edges; across the open side of it a dark stain had smeared down and on to the paper sheets. An elastic band, wound over it twice, held it together. He peered at it and saw the faintness of what had once been gold-embossed lettering. 'So, who was Cecil Darke?'

'According to Mr Perry, Cecil was Great-aunt Enid's elder brother. Sorry, David, I haven't heard of him. She gave it to Mr Perry with that elastic band round it, and he never opened it, never looked to see what was inside.'

Banks saw, across the garden room, that Wilfred Perry – the man who had kept a promise – had set his empty schooner back on the steward's table, and was reaching for another, which was filled. He looked at his watch. 'I have to go, Mum, in a couple of minutes. You'll get a taxi? It's something I can't be late for.'

'You'd better open it, David. I mean, on her funeral day, you should see what was important to her.'

'Yes, Mum – but I can't hang about.'

He peeled off the elastic band, and the spine of the notebook cracked as he opened it. He saw handwriting, barely legible, on the cover's inside ... God, but he did have to shift himself ... and he read aloud but softly so that only his mother shared with him: 'To Whom it may Concern: In the event of my death or incapacity, will the finder of this Diary please facilitate its safe delivery to my sister, Miss Enid Darke, 40 Victoria Street, Bermondsey, London, England. Many thanks. Signed: Cecil Darke.' There was a date on the facing page, then close-set writing. It would take his full concentration to decipher it. He snapped the notebook shut, twisted the elastic band back over it and dropped it into his pocket.

'Got to dash. Good to see you, Mum, and you look after yourself.'

'Thanks for coming. You will read it, won't you? I suppose it's part of us.'

'I will, when I've time.'

He pecked her cheek and was gone. He ran through the thin rain across the car park, and the notebook bounced in his pocket lightly against his hip. Later, when he was working his shift, a Glock 9mm pistol, with a loaded magazine of eleven bullets, would – should he run – be flapping against that hip.

Chapter 2: Thursday, Day 1

When he saw them loaded into the two pickups, Ibrahim felt a sense of loss. He had been with them since the previous evening. He did not know their names, where they had come from, what they would be leaving behind them, but in those few hours of chaotic trauma – for all of them – they had been his brothers.

New masters had selected them and now determined into which of the pickups they should climb. The fighting men, those who had made the choices and had seemed to weigh their value, barked instructions and gestured them forward. None was helped over the tail gates: they were left to struggle up. When they were all on board, crouched and half hidden by the sides of the vehicles, Ibrahim fought the stiffness in the joints of his legs and stood. The engines had started, and he heard the clatter of the mounted machine-guns being armed – an alien sound – and he wondered if he should wave in farewell to them.

Their laughter came to him over the gravel roar of the straining engines, as if now they were old friends, but distanced from him who would not travel with them.

None looked at him, none noticed him, so he did not wave.

The farewell that was seared in his mind was in front of him. The fighting men left the engines running and the machine-guns armed, and walked briskly to the man Ibrahim thought of as the Leader, *his* leader. Each in turn hugged him and their lips brushed the cheeks obscured by the balaclava. Those men had no joy, no happiness, and the kisses were perfunctory, without cheer or laughter. He sensed the difference between the fighting men, and his new-found leader, and the brothers crushed close in the pickups. They broke away, but each held the Leader's hand tight for a moment longer than was necessary, as if that farewell was more meaningful, as if a little of the danger and threat, risk and uncertainty was communicated between them. The pickups edged away across the sand, like the dhows going from the harbour at the end of the Corniche. Then, as the dhows did when they were outside the harbour wall, they increased speed, and the engines throbbed with power.

He watched them go.

For a few seconds the vehicles were lost behind the walls of the building. When he saw them again they were moving fast. He saw them bounce across the raised heap of sand where the single strand of barbed-wire was buried. To the right and to the left, the wire was raised and hung from rusted posts of iron, but at the point of the track it had been lowered. The wire was the frontier. He did not know, when they were taken into Iraq, why he had been left behind. He watched the two billowing clouds of sand thrown up by the back wheels of the pickups for as long as he was able, long after his eyes failed to find them, and long after the sound of the engines had dispersed in the quiet of the desert.

He felt the chill of the coming evening. He had not noticed it the previous night because then the bodies of his brothers had been pressed close to him.

The Leader was a remote figure, pacing in the sand and staring back often into the last of the light from the sun's setting. Often, he peered in the gloom at the watch on his wrist, then looked up to scan the far horizon where a quarter of the sun's circle, blood red, teetered on the desert's limit. Ibrahim did not dare to interrupt him ... Instead he thought of his home and his family.

Ibrahim Hussein's father sold electrical goods from a business one street behind the Corniche in the town of Jizan. His father, and Ibrahim recognized it, was dominated by melancholy. His wife,

Ibrahim's mother, had died four years before from peritonitis; she should not have done – but the incompetence of the medical staff at the clinic, and their panic in crisis, had killed her. His father was a prosperous man in his community and drove the latest model of Mercedes saloon, but inescapable depression ruled his life. Ibrahim, the medical student at university, had identified his father's symptoms as readily as he knew of the incompetence at the clinic when his mother had died unnecessarily. Like a lost man, with only the ignored company of his daughters, his father padded the corridors and living room of the family home, forswore his fellow traders and spoke only of the profit and loss from the business in the street behind the Corniche. Before Ibrahim's mother's passing, his father had mourned two sons.

Aged only three at the time, Ibrahim could not now recall the news coming to the family home – brought by an *imam* – of his eldest brother's death in the Jalalabad region of Afghanistan. Now he knew that he had been caught without cover on a track that traversed a cliff slope. Often, the image came to his mind. His eldest brother, escorting a supply train of mules, on a bare path with a cliff face above and below him, had been spotted by the pilot of a Soviet gunship helicopter: cannon fire and rockets had killed him, his fellow *jihad*ists and their beasts.

He could remember well enough the death of his middle brother – the news had been brought to his father by the same *imam*. It had been on a sweltering day two months after the invasion of Afghanistan by the Americans, when every air-conditioner in the family home had been turned to full power, that the *imam* had reported the loss of Ibrahim's middle brother, killed near Kandahar with others of the 055 Brigade by the carpet-bombing of the giant B52 aircraft. His middle brother had followed Ibrahim's eldest brother into the ranks of the foreign fighters who had struggled to resist the invasion of Afghanistan, first by Russians and then by Americans. His middle brother had taken cover in a concrete-roofed bunker, which the explosive had collapsed; he might have been killed outright, or left trapped to suffocate slowly in the dust-filled darkness. It was not known.

A complex web of emotions had brought Ibrahim Hussein to this illicit border crossing, used by fighters and smugglers, where a track crossed from the Kingdom into Iraqi territory. At their heart was his feeling for his father, and the wish to give his parent cause for pride that would lighten his acute depression. And it was for revenge, to strike back at evil forces, and to show the world the determination of a young man's Faith . . . His mother had died because the Kingdom's rulers starved Asir Province of resources, and those corrupt rulers cohabited with the *kaffirs*, the unbelievers. His eldest brother had died in defence of a Muslim land raped and invaded by unbelievers. His middle brother had died at the hands of the worst of the unbelievers. He believed his own death, his own martyrdom, would liberate his father from melancholy.

He could barely make out the body shape of his leader against the darkening horizon. Then, far away and near to where the sun had been, he saw two pairs of pinprick lights. Now, the Leader came, shadowy as a wraith, towards him, and stood at his side. The hand rested on Ibrahim's shoulder, and he felt the reassurance of its power squeezing his collarbone and the ligaments there.

The voice was soft, the words spoken almost with gentleness: 'I told you, you were not rejected but were chosen.'

He nodded, unable to speak.

'Chosen for a mission of exceptional value, for which you are honoured and respected.'

'I hope to fulfil the trust placed in me.' Pleasure coursed through him.

'It is a mission that requires from you a degree of unique dedication.'

'You have the promise of my best . . .'

The Scorpion ground his fingers harder on to the boy's bone. It was difficult for him, in his exhaustion, to play-act either kindness or concern for a medical student who had declared himself in love with death. But it was important to hold his belief.

'It is a mission that demands of you total obedience to the instructions with which you will be provided. Are you capable of obedience?'

'I believe so.'

'Please, listen carefully to everything I tell you.'

'I will do so, my leader.'

Under the balaclava, his mouth froze out a brief smile. He heard

32

the boy's adoration and admiration for him, but did not seek it. The boy sought praise. He could give it if necessary, however false.

'Without dedication and obedience, the mission for which you are chosen will fail. If it fails, that is a great victory for our enemies.'

'I have dedication and I have obedience. I seek the chance to demonstrate them.'

Another boy with bright eyes, his Faith gleaming . . . What made him different from those in the two pickups speeding across the darkened Iraqi sands towards distribution points was the ability to walk well. His judgement had been made after he had seen them stride towards him: some had been awkward or heavy in their step; some had looked to the side and flinched when they came close to him; some had been hesitant to the point of almost tripping. This boy had a good step, had not hurried, had not looked around him, had walked as he would have on a pavement at home. That had dictated the choice made by Muhammad Ajaq – the name lived only in the recesses of his mind. The name that existed in the intelligence files of his enemy, and on the lips of those with whom he fought, was the Scorpion – and now, he grimaced, he was the Leader.

'Ibrahim, do you have military training?'

'None. My brothers did. My eldest brother was martyred fighting the Russians in Afghanistan. The other was martyred in the war against the American invaders of Afghanistan. I seek to match their dedication, to be worthy . . .'

They all mouthed this shit. All the boys recruited by the gate-keepers in the mosques – of Riyadh and Jeddah, Damascus and Aleppo, Sana'a and Aden, Hamburg and Paris – spoke of the roots of their commitment. He was not a martyr, had no wish for suicide, and thought those who did were fools and deluded . . . But he needed them. They were the lifeblood of the war he fought. They took his opportunities of attack into defined areas of exactness that were otherwise unreachable. No shell, rocket or bullet fired from whatever distance had the same accuracy as a martyr bomb, or created matching devastation and fear. So he lived with the shit. He massaged the boy's shoulder and talked softly – as if the boy was his equal.

'What you need to know, we will teach you.'

'So that I may achieve success for my mission. Thank you.'

'Have you been prepared in the matter of resistance to interrogation?'

He felt the boy flinch. 'No.'

Of course, the gate-keeper would not have talked of capture, of torture, of the failure of battery-powered circuits. The possibility of failure would have weakened the boy's commitment. Sometimes a back-up electrical circuit was built into the car bomb, or the bomb in the belt, so that it could be remotely detonated from a distance if dedication died or a device would not ignite. Sometimes a sniper with a long-barrelled Makharov watched the advance of a bomber through a telescopic sight and would shoot to kill if will or circuit failed. A boy, this one or any of those now riding in the pickups towards the cities of Iraq, would know too much of recruitment and transport routes, safe-houses and the personnel who commanded their mission – he would talk if he was captured alive and tortured to make rivers of pain. But Ibrahim Hussein could not be followed with a telescopic sight when he travelled to his target.

He said, 'We put great trust in you, and you should trust us for our skills. Everything that can be prepared has been – but disaster can come from a sunlit morning, from a clear sky, without warning. There are successes, there are setbacks. I will not hide anything from you, Ibrahim.'

The lights, far away, became clear and the engines' sounds swelled as they approached. It was his tactic that the mention of failure, disaster, should be aired only at the end before they parted.

'Huge courage is asked of you. We believe of you that the courage will be found. They will use electrodes on your genitals, they will inject drugs into you, they will beat you with clubs and iron bars. You will be denied sleep. Shrieking noise will be played in your ears, and they will question you . . . and at the end you will face execution if you are still in this region or a lifetime of imprisonment if you are far from here. We will all be praying for your resolve, your bravery. Our ability to continue the struggle will depend on the courage we believe you have. God will be watching over you. Take a place with your eye on a crack in the ceiling, on a join of plaster between tiles on a floor, on a bar in the window, on what has been scratched on the floor and stay silent. Stay silent for a week. Give us time to dismantle and move. A week – do you promise me?'

34

He heard the small, stuttered answer: 'I will, a week, I swear it.'

'Whatever the pain?'

'Because I will be thinking of God.'

He cuffed the boy. He made that speech to all the boys sent across the frontier to him by gate-keepers, and they all swore to stay silent for a week . . . A day would be enough. He eased his hand off the boy's shoulder.

Two vehicles came close and braked, scuffing up sand. He told the boy, Ibrahim, that he must listen to what was ordered of him, do what he was told to do, give trust and not falter in his Faith. Through the mouth gap of his mask he kissed the boy's forehead. Then he led him to a Chevrolet truck. In the flash of the interior light, he saw the boy's face momentarily, the struggle with fear, then he slammed the door and the truck drove away.

From the second vehicle, a Dodge, he took a holdall that had been lying on the wide back seat, where he had known it would be. He stood in the sand between the Dodge and the truck with the machine-guns that had brought him, laid down his assault rifle, peeled off the webbing that held the magazines, dragged up his mask, unlaced his boots and kicked them off. He dropped his combat trousers to his ankles, stepped out of them, and stripped off the tunic. He lifted the laundered white robe from the holdall, passed his arms through the sleeves and wriggled into it. Within a minute he had passed from being a soldier at war, a commander in conflict, to a businessman of stature. The uniform, the boots, the webbing harness and the assault rifle went to the driver who had escorted him from the battlefields of Iraq. Within another minute, that driver was on his way back over the sand hump that covered the single strand of wire. Within a third minute he was driving away in the Dodge. He remained a soldier, but had exchanged one battlefield for another.

In two hours, the Scorpion would be at a remote desert airstrip, used by contractors who drilled in search of mineral deposits, where a twin-engined Cessna aircraft would be waiting for him. He did not doubt that all arrangements would be delivered as promised. His belief was total in the organizational skills of the Base now controlling him, and in the Cessna he would find the documentation for the new identity to be used in his onward travel.

Yet he felt, so rare for him – even in the worst moments of combat

– a little tremor of nerves. He had no Faith to comfort him, as the boy had. The nerves in his gut were because he journeyed to a foreign battlefield, on to ground he had not fought over before, and he had no knowledge of the quality of those who would fight beside him.

She knew the name of the driver, and more of him than she should have.

At Faria's direction they had twice circled the village after leaving the cottage. The driver, Khalid, had taken her back up the track from the cottage she had rented from the farmer's wife. On the far side of the village there was a sprawling, recently built housing estate, a bolt-hole escape for the middle classes who had abandoned the town that was her home; small detached brick houses were set behind pocket-sized front gardens. Faria understood the reason for their exodus from the streets where she and her community lived. The school in the town she had left six years earlier had then had 84 per cent Asian pupils; now she had read in the local paper that the figure had crept to 91 per cent. The new residents of the village distrusted the influx of migrants from the sub-continent, and had run from them. They would have whispered among their own, those who had fled from Luton, of the ghettos in their old town, of an alien state within a state and Muslim dominance as justification for uprooting their families.

She knew that the driver, Khalid, was twenty-three and came from Hounslow, in west London. She had told him to circle the village so that she might see where there was a shop selling fruit and vegetables, where there was a doctor's surgery, in case she needed it, and a dentist. She knew that Khalid had been a worshipper at a mosque near to his home, where he lived with his parents, and that he had been recruited a year and a half before, after meetings in the evenings at an upper room in the mosque. She knew that he had been ordered to leave the mosque, not to associate again with friends there, and to await a call. She knew that his father worked as a security guard in a bonded warehouse complex at Heathrow, and that his mother cleaned the offices of the Qantas airline . . . They had sat in the car, a Honda Accord bought for cash at auction, in front of a pub and had watched the traffic flow through the village, and they had sat in a lay-by up the lane from which the cottage's track ran and seen the farmer's wife leave by Land Rover. After less than two hours in his company, she now knew that Khalid worked as a mini-cab driver in Hounslow, for a company owned by his uncle, and that his parents believed he had taken two weeks' leave for a holiday with cousins from Manchester. She knew all the lies of his life, and was horrified at the babble beating in her ears – and she knew that the cause of it was fear.

Of herself, she had told him nothing.

The driver's eyes were on the road, flickering between the windscreen and his mirrors, but he talked as a tap dripped. 'Did they ask you? You know what I mean.'

'It is not important what they asked me. You should not talk of it.'

'If men come from abroad, important men, an attack is planned – yes?'

'I don't know what is planned.'

'What I believe, if an attack is planned and important men are coming it will be a martyr attack – so did they ask you?'

'What I was told, what I was not told, should not be talked of.'

At the time of her own recruitment the need for total secrecy had been emphasized, with nothing shared even in the privacy of her family. She did not know how to silence his torrent.

'I am saying it will be a martyr's attack – have you been asked if you would do that?'

'You should drive, not talk.'

'You know what happens to a martyr? I saw it on a website. If he has a vest or a belt, his head comes off. The head is taken off. It is how they knew which were the martyrs on the trains in London. They had no heads. In Tel Aviv, they found the head fifteen feet from his body, on a table, and he was still smiling. It was on the website.'

'Do you want me to tell you to stop? Shall I get out and walk?'

'It is not for me. I will help, I will drive and—'

'And you will talk – and by talking you will put all of us at risk,' Faria snarled.

'Do you think they would force one of us to do it, make it impossible to refuse? Could they do that? I support the struggle but—'

'Stop.'

The traffic flowed round them. If he had slowed, cars, vans and lorries would have swerved to overtake on the inside. He could not stop and she knew it.

'It is not just me they might ask, but you . . . Would you?'

'What I will tell you is this. Tell you once. The important people, when they arrive, I will tell them to dismiss you.'

'You have to think of what you would do if you were asked. There were videos from the struggle in Palestine. Women were used. In Palestine the word for them is *shahida*. Arafat called them his "army of roses". Women were martyrs who carried the bombs. Arafat said to them, "You are my army of roses that will crush Israeli tanks." Have you not thought of what might be asked of you?'

Her ears were closed to him. Faria could not answer; neither could she threaten again to denounce him for cowardice, for lack of faith, for talking and putting them all into a marksman's sights or a prison cell. She stared from the window and the car brought her towards the town's centre. She had thought that as a stranger to the town he might find it difficult to locate the street that was her home when he came to pick her up, so she had told him, when he had called the mobile, to meet her at the extremity of the station car park. That mobile now lay embedded in the silt of the river Lea that divided the town. Faria had thought, before he had talked through the history of his life, that he could drop her close to home . . . The looseness of his talk frightened her. At the next set of lights, she swung open the door and was gone. She never looked back at him.

Have you not thought what might be asked of you? Faria had. In her room, at night, she had wrestled with that thought, sweated and been unable to sleep. She had read that in Palestine the funeral of the small pieces of a woman martyr was a 'wedding with eternity'. She could picture in her mind the photograph of the calm face of the *shahida* Darine Abu Aisha, who had gone to the bus station at Netanya, killed three and injured sixty. A friend had said of her, 'She knew that her destiny was to become the bride of Allah in Paradise.'

She did not know what she would say if it were asked of her.

'A police officer, in sworn testimony, described you, Mr Curtis, as a "main man", and meant by that, Mr Curtis, that you were a major criminal. Was he right or wrong?'

The defence barrister, in court eighteen, used a low lectern in the front row of the lawyers' territory between the judge's bench and the dock, now occupied only by Ollie Curtis and the minders.

'I can say quite honestly, sir, that the description of me is wrong. It is a lie, a fabrication.'

It was possible for Jools Wright to watch the barrister but not to permit his eyes to waver to the left, into a field of vision that included Ozzie Curtis in the witness box.

'I want to be quite sure of this. You are telling m'lord and the members of the jury that you are not a big player in the criminal underworld?'

'What I am saying, sir, is utterly truthful. I am not a big player, not a major criminal, not a main man.'

Jools watched the barrister ask the questions and listened to the answers. He thought that Ozzie bloody Curtis wriggled like a maggot on a hook.

'You are in fact, Mr Curtis, a businessman and a legitimate trader?'

'That's right, sir, dead right.'

'I'm asking this because I think the jury will expect to hear your answer to the allegations made by the police, in evidence, that you associate with criminals, are in fact at the heart of a web of thieving and violence.'

'Maybe I meet criminals, but not intentionally. In business, buying and selling, I meet many people. Honestly and truthfully, though, I don't go round asking guys whether they've done bird. They sell to me and I sell to them. That's about it.'

'Now – and this is most important, Mr Curtis – a Crown witness has said, again on oath, that she can positively identify you as being in the allotment nurseries, and behind a lock-up shed, as you changed from a boiler-suit into more normal clothing, then dumped the boiler-suit, rubber gloves and a face mask in a brazier that was already lit. Was that witness correct in her identification or mistaken?'

'Absolutely mistaken. She got it wrong. I wasn't anywhere there – and it's lies if people say I was.'

'Possibly a lie, Mr Curtis, but more probably a genuine mistake.'

'Whichever, I wasn't there.'

Jools could remember that witness better than any of the Crime Squad detectives who had given evidence and better than any of the forensics experts and the one who had said the men in boiler-suits and masks caught by CCTV inside the shop had identical physiques to the accused brothers. The witness had been small in build, plain-faced and with an ugly cold sore at her mouth, not more than twenty-two years old, probably younger – and she had been so certain. Jools had believed her. He would have staked his life on her.

The defence barrister was a tall, bowed man, with a hawk nose and a casual stance – his weight was taken by the lectern on which his notes were laid out – and he was dressed in crumpled striped trousers and waistcoat, and a tatty old robe that might have been slept in. Not for a night but a month. Jools thought that the studied indifference was part of the barrister's well-practised art. Confronted by the eye-witness, he had started out with bogus sincerity in challenging her, but received no satisfaction. He'd gone through the quiet, sneering phase and still failed to shake her. Then he'd barked. Eyeball contact and courtesy slipped away, and flat statements demanding that she contradict what she had already stated. He'd not broken her. She was as strong after four hours of ruthless cross-examination as she had been when she'd started in the box. Jools had thought her so gutsy. Himself, he couldn't have turned in such a per-formance, and he'd gone home that evening, after she'd finished, and told Babs about the girl's courage in the face of her ordeal. All of them in the jury room had believed her.

'And where were you, Mr Curtis, at the time the jewellery shop was robbed by armed men who threatened the lives of the staff and who wore boiler-suits, rubber gloves and face masks? Could you tell the jury where you were?'

'Down at my mum's, sir. She's not well.'

'She has, I believe, a medical history of diabetes mellitus, Mr Curtis.'

'That's what they call it. I look after her, and Ollie does. I was with my mum and so was he.'

He heard a little snigger from Corenza. Ettie murmured to Baz that Curtis must have been watching too many police soaps on TV. Peter grunted scornfully. Yes, it was a pretty old one – sick mum, loving and dutiful sons playing carers.

'So, we can be very clear on this. At the time that this criminal enterprise was under way, you were more than twenty miles away with your mother . . . and a witness who says otherwise is mistaken?'

'Right. Yes.'

The judge intoned, 'I think this a good moment to adjourn.'

After he was gone, and the Curtis brothers with their minders, Jools and the rest were led out by their bailiff. He wondered, going to the door sandwiched between Fanny and Dwayne, whether the accused men realized they were scuppered, knew they were on a conveyor-belt to a guilty verdict.

'What do you reckon?'

'You want it straight up, Ozzie?'

'Straight up? Course I bloody do.'

'Then I have to say that you're shafted – and I can see no different outcome for Ollie. Both of you, well and truly shafted.'

As a hard-working solicitor who represented a superior strata of the criminal classes – if they had the resources to pay for his services, and pay substantial sums – Nathaniel Wilson had a potent reputation. A serious facet of it, alongside his willingness to beaver away all the hours of the day and week on behalf of his clients, was frankness.

'You can't see any way out?' A cloud had settled over the elder Curtis brother's face. They were dinosaurs, from a world long extinct. Armed robbery, waving handguns in the faces of the staff at a jeweller's – it was the stuff of fossils.

The solicitor shrugged. 'We'll try, your brief and I. If there was going to be a happy ending I'd be the first to tell you . . . and I'll be the first to tell you when you're going down.'

Ozzie Curtis turned to his younger brother. 'Be a good lad, do us a Dolly.'

Singing, good cadences, burst from Ollie's mouth. Nat Wilson thought the younger brother must be the hero of every pub karaoke night he patronized. Dolly Parton bounced off the cell walls. 'I Will Always Love You' filled the space from the mesh-covered ceiling light to the scarred floor tiles on to which they flicked cigarette ash. No way that any detective from the Robbery Squad would deliberately bug the confidentiality of a meeting between a legal representative and his clients, but there *might* just happen to be an old wire going to a device fitted into the cell bars, or the light casing, or the panic button. And that old wire *might* just lead to a tape-recorder that happened to be loaded. So Ollie Curtis sang 'I Will Always Love You' and placed his back so that it covered the cell door's spy-hole, and Ozzie Curtis leaned close from the mattress bed on which he sat to Nat on the hard chair. 'It's as bad as that? We're shafted?'

'Not looking very clever – not just my opinion but the brief's as well. Goes right back to that star, the little bitch, because we didn't shift her, and you could see the jury believed her. They lapped her up. I watched them again this afternoon. I have to tell you, Ozzie, we didn't score any points with them. They're getting bored, want it over, want to get their lives back, and when they're bored they're not open to argument . . . Sorry, you're going down.'

Every client of Nathaniel Wilson knew of his loyalty to them. They paid well for his commitment to causes beyond the hopeless, and because he never gave them the crap they might want to hear. He worked from behind a battered door in east London's Hackney, and lived with his wife in the flat above. Nathaniel and Diane, who did the books, the paperwork and the filing, grossed in excess of a quarter of a million a year. They were hugely wealthy but had no extravagant tastes; they took an annual fortnight's holiday on the Isle of Wight in a guesthouse, and in their wills everything they owned was destined for the People's Dispensary for Sick Animals.

'That stuff about Mum . . .'

'Didn't cut any ice. I watched their faces. A complete contrary re-action, like it was so obvious, so manufactured. One even laughed to herself. We're not getting to them.'

He heard Ollie starting again, back on the first verse of 'I Will Always Love You', and perhaps his voice or his enthusiasm was fail-ing because Ozzie had swung towards him and lifted his arms, gestured that more was wanted and louder.

Ozzie Curtis's mouth was less than an inch from Nathaniel Wilson's right ear. 'If you're right, and I'm not saying you're wrong, we need Benny in on the act.'

Nathaniel Wilson's breath hissed as he sucked it in between nar-rowed lips. 'That's fighting talk, Ozzie.'

'For fuck's sake, if I'm going away for an eighteen or a twenty – I'm bloody going to go down fighting.'

'And not long to set it up.'

'You said three weeks for this to run.'

'I said, Ozzie, the trial will be complete within three more weeks, not a day more and likely less.'

'So we need Benny, need him on the move now.'

Seldom a demonstrative man, Nathaniel Wilson raised his eyebrows and let a frown furrow his forehead. For a moment he seemed to lose the odour of the cell, and the smell of Ozzie Curtis's body lotion. 'Not with the time that's available – and he'd have to drop everything else. It won't come cheap.'

Ozzie's chin jutted in defiance. 'Nothing about me is cheap – too fucking right it isn't.'

'You'd be looking at a hundred for an acquittal, and seventy-five for a retrial.'

'Not a problem. Get Benny. You do that, Mr Wilson.'

'If that's what you want.'

'Can't see another option – I want it. Hey, Ollie, shut that fucking row.'

The singing died. Nathaniel Wilson stood, lifted his briefcase and rang the bell beside the door. He smiled at the guard who unlocked it, then said that his legal consultation was complete. As he stepped out into the corridor he saw two detectives lounging at the far end, the bastards, and he was happy that Ollie Curtis was an uncrowned karaoke champion.

He went out of the court building, into the growing dusk. In half an hour, inside a security ring of guns, the brothers would be leaving for HMP Belmarsh and another night on remand. In an hour he would be making a first contact with Benny Edwards, with the promise of big bucks to attract the man's interest – and his own fee would be ratcheting up. He faced spending his old age in a cell alongside the brothers, and being struck off all Law Society lists, if it became public knowledge in the Robbery Squad that Nathaniel Wilson was, on behalf of clients, in touch with the man better known as the Nobbler.

29 October 1936
We are still at Albacete. I have written little of the first days here because we are worked hard and with all that is fitted into each day there seems little

time to put down on paper my thoughts and experiences, but the commandant is away this afternoon and we have been allowed time off.

At Albacete, a good-sized town inland from the coast and Valencia, we are housed in the old barracks of the Civil Guards. I do not see any point in writing a diary dictated by self-censorship. When we arrived here the building was in a quite disgusting state – not just filth but worse. Government forces took the barracks from the Civil Guards, but they did not just put the defeated men into a prison cage: they <u>killed</u> them. The Civil Guards who surrendered were then massacred. My German comrade who was on the train with me, Karl, told me that the first of the International Brigade volunteers to arrive here after the slaughter were his fellow countrymen. These Germans were so horrified with what they found that they cleaned the barracks. They scrubbed its walls and floors to cleanse it of blood, bones and flesh. They even found dried-out brain matter from the Civil Guards who had been bludgeoned. Then they painted over the worst of the stains with whitewash.

The same slogan is now written on those walls. Where I sleep there is 'Proletarios de todos Paises! Unios!' (Spanish); 'Proletarier Lander, vereinigt euch!' (German); 'Proletari di tutti i Paesi, Unitevi!' (Italian); and 'Workers of the World, Unite!' So, from the walls around me, I am already something of a linguist! I am also shown the truly international quality of the struggle to turn back the tide of Fascism.

The commandant at Albacete is André Marty. He is Spanish or French, I don't know which, and comes from the Pyrenees. He has a white moustache, is short but with a big stomach. I have never spoken to him. He is not a man you approach. He has a bad reputation. Discipline here is enforced with what I suppose would be called 'an iron fist'. Discipline is everything and is enforced with brutal beatings – some volunteers have died from their injuries. I have never before seen beatings of such ferocity, and they are done by men we call the 'commissars': they wear a uniform of black leather jackets and blue berets and have heavy pistols hanging from their polished leather belts. We avoid them.

I had thought I would be trained in the arts of modern warfare at Albacete. It is not so. Most of the time we drill in the square, and are shouted at by the commissars if we are not in step, or punched or kicked. In the day we drill for hours. In the evenings we go to political lectures, which are compulsory. If a volunteer is late for a lecture, or goes to sleep, he is taken outside and beaten. We are learning about Communism and the sacrifices that the Soviet state has made in support of the working-class people of Spain. I want to know what some of the older men call 'fieldcraft' and the tactics of fighting, and how to use a rifle, but there are no rifles here and what I am being taught is the politics of the struggle.

We live on a diet of beans cooked in vegetable oil. We do not see meat or fresh vegetables. Some volunteers have collapsed on parade because they have dysentery and are weak.

But I must not be negative. (I think if it were known what I have written this evening my negativity would earn me a beating from the commissars!) I came here of my own free will. I could still be at my desk with my ledger in front of me, Mr Rammage at my shoulder. I could be at the kitchen table with Mum dishing up from the stove. I am here, and it was my decision to travel to this war. And, whatever the conditions in the barracks at Albacete, I am determined to play my part as a foreign soldier in a foreign land, and stand in defence of a cause I believe in.

The best news of the last week is that I have found two new friends. Daniel is from Manchester and is three years older than me; he was a road-building labourer when he could find work. Ralph is a year younger, and should have been starting his first term at the University of Cambridge to study history, but he came here instead. On the parade-ground we march together, in the lectures we sit together, and their palliasses are on either side of mine. We watch out for each other and share everything. I have never been to Manchester or Cambridge, and they know nothing of a room full of clerks' desks in a bank. With them at my side I know – yes, know – that I will be able to fight with courage.

We have not been told when we will go to the front and stand against the Army of Africa – they are Riffian tribesmen and the battlecry when they advance is 'Viva la Muerte', which means 'Long Live Death' – but the rumour is that they are advancing towards Madrid and that they do not take prisoners.

With friends beside me, when the time comes, I shall not be afraid.

'Stand by, Delta Group. Principal on the way.'

Banks jerked upright in the passenger seat of the car. First reaction, to slide a hand inside his suit jacket, down to his belt and the pancake holster, feel the cold, hard shape of the Glock. Second, to drop the weathered leather-covered notebook into the jacket pocket where it would lie on the folded black tie he had discarded after leaving the funeral. Third, to reach for the door handle and prise it back.

'Delta Group. Principal with you in a half-minute.'

Their car was parked over double-yellow lines. For the protection officers of the Delta Group traffic restrictions were of no importance; neither did it matter that the nearside wheels were on the pavement. In front of them stood the black limousine, weighed down with armour plating, in which the Principal would be taken away, and forward was the car that would be driven ahead of the limousine. Already the motorcycles were easing past them to take up the position where they could clear traffic hold-ups from the passage of the convoy.

There was a pecking order of importance in the Delta Group. Foremost on the pyramid's pinnacle were the officers of the Royal and Diplomatic Protection team – Delta 1 and Delta 2 – who would have had a table inside the hotel's restaurant, but not eaten with the Principal's own people. Half-way up the pyramid were the men – Delta 3, Delta 4, Delta 5 and Delta 6 – who had loitered outside the restaurant door in the foyer and in the kitchens. At the bottom were the drivers, and the guys who sat in the front passenger seats: David Banks was Delta 12. He stood on the pavement, his back to the hotel's revolving doors, and made his body into a barrier to prevent late-night pedestrians, perhaps spilled out from a theatre, a film or a meal, obstructing the passage of the Principal.

'Delta Group. All clear?'

'To Delta One. Bring him through.'

He heard the bleak, controlled voices in his ear. He opened his arms, held them wide apart and blocked the pavement. A tourist in a Burberry raised a camera, but Banks shook his head and the lens was lowered. It was the power he had. Power came from proximity to a rated Principal. He twisted his head, at speed, and saw the Minister, the man they protected, scurry across the pavement and disappear into the limousine. Banks walked backwards briskly, and when he was level with the car's door, he ducked down and inside, and they were gone into the late-evening traffic.

Banks almost resented the interruption of the Principal's departure from the hotel. He'd been using a small torch to decipher the faded pencil writing in the notebook. He had read of the journey across

France and into Spain and, within a few minutes, had been captivated by the story written seven decades earlier by a relative he had not heard of before. When the Principal had been hustled from dinner to the car, he had known a moment of irritation at being snatched away from the drill yard, the straw-filled bedding and the brain-spattered walls – but, more important, he had begun to feel, just, that he walked in Spain's sunshine with the humility and bravery of Cecil Darke.

The motorcycles cleared a way for them. He could see the top of the Principal's close-cut grey hair through the limousine's back window. The Principal was the Minister for Reconstruction in Baghdad and the carpet had been rolled out for him in London, where he had come to beg and borrow resources. The word was that he would go home with little more than a few asinine meetings under his belt and a few decent meals in his stomach. The Principal was a prime target in Baghdad; there, he would have been at risk every time he stuck his toe outside his front door, but how was he a target here? Only a target if the information was trumpeted to Al Qaeda's office in Iraq that the Minister for Reconstruction was arriving at 8.35 p.m. at a particular hotel restaurant in a particular street (see attached map), would be entertained by an under-secretary at Overseas Development, then head off again at 10.47 p.m. Al Qaeda, Baghdad, did not have an army of floaters drifting round the West End with primed bombs, loaded handguns and, maybe, an armed rocket-propelled grenade-launcher, all on the lookout for the faint chance of being in the right place at the right time.

No, it was not about the threat.

Yes, it was all about the show.

As David Banks saw it, the size of the escort of Protection Officers was an indication to the Principal of the respect in which his hosts held him. Little on offer in resources and funding, but the compliment of two cars riding front and back of the limousine and a small army of well-dressed men to open and close doors. It was flattering, and it bred self-esteem, and Banks knew that the dread of every home-brewed politician who had held a sensitive office of state was to get the heave from Downing Street or the electorate and have protection removed overnight.

Along with the flattery of the Principal went similar doses of feel-good for the Protection Officers. They were an élite. They rubbed shoulders with the movers and shakers of government, and the biggest and best that came in from overseas. They had the privileged access that dictated they were party to little mutters of gossip and the tantrums of the great and mighty . . . But David Banks was different, which was why he was an outsider and anchored at the bottom level of the pyramid.

'Hey, Banksy.' It was Delta 6, the sergeant, leaning forward from the back.

'Yes.' He didn't turn, kept his eyes on the pavements they sped past: might be an outsider but didn't think his commitment to his work could be faulted.

'Just a little problem. We like to look the part in this team. It's your shoes, they've got mud on them. That's not good, Banksy – don't let it happen again.'

He could have said he'd been to a family funeral, and that the mud had come from a crematorium garden where he and his mother had laid flowers, but he held his peace.

Chapter 3: Tuesday, Day 6

'They are not before the court, Mr Curtis, but the case for the prosecution is that you were aided in this robbery by friends.'

'I don't have those sort of friends, sir.'

Maybe it was because the air-circulation plant was on the blink or switched off, but warmth seemed to have invaded court eighteen. Jools Wright had noticed that a bead of sweat had formed on the defence barrister's forehead. He'd followed it, watched the tiny rivulet it made from the forehead down between the shaggy eyebrows, then its passage under the bridge of the spectacles and along the nose. By the nostrils a drip had formed, had gathered in size and weight, and fallen – wow! – right on to the barrister's papers. Jools lifted his gaze back to the man's forehead and waited for the next rivulet to flow.

'Do you deny that among your friends, Mr Curtis, there is what we would call an "armourer"?'

'Never heard of anyone called that.'

The word he would have used to his *students* to describe the atmosphere in court was soporific: dictionary definition, 'inducing sleep'. He'd lost track of the growing size of the latest drip accumulating on the barrister's nose because his eyes had closed. Jools felt his head droop. His chin banged against his chest, then rested on his open-necked purple shirt. So hard to stay awake . . . and why should he bother? The damn man in the box was lying through his teeth.

'The weapons carried, allegedly, by you and your brother when – as the prosecution says – you were involved in this violent theft, were identified from witness reports as a military Browning 9mm automatic pistol and a Smith & Wesson revolver, a Magnum . . . Do you have, Mr Curtis, among your friends, an armourer, someone who could have supplied such fiendish weapons?'

'No, sir.'

'Have you ever touched, handled, aimed, threatened with a Browning 9mm pistol or a Smith & Wesson revolver?'

'Absolutely not, sir. God's truth, I have not.'

Head down again, not bothering to lift it. They'd been shown, four weeks before – it might have been five – photographs of the pistol and the revolver; a detective, with a litany of firearms experience behind him, had described the killing power of such weapons . . . Not going to think about the weapons because that area of the case, in Jools's mind, was closed. He was going to think about Hannah.

'And you can state categorically that you have no friends who hire out such weapons, Mr Curtis?'

'I've a lot of friends . . . People seem to adopt me, like I'm an uncle to them – but I don't know nobody who supplies shooters. Personally, sir, I wouldn't touch nothing like that.'

'And, Mr Curtis, at the time of the robbery – as we established last week in your evidence under oath – you were with your mother who has a serious diabetic condition.'

Lovely Hannah. Sweet, delicious, sweaty Hannah. Brilliant, gorgeous Hannah—

There was a sharp, grating cough beside him. Jools's head jerked up. He blinked. Corenza coughed again, and gave him a savage glance. Should he concentrate? To shake off the desire to sleep, he locked his fingers together and cracked the joints, then wriggled his toes, looked down and saw the movement in his striped socks below the straps of his sandals. For the trial's first week he'd worn a suit and black shoes, for the second week he'd dressed in an open shirt, sports jacket and brogues. Now, as if to stamp his individuality, he'd reverted to work gear, and that, at the comprehensive, was jeans and sandals. He rather relished the individuality . . . No, nothing to be gained from earnest concentration – Hannah was what he coveted.

'That's right.'

'I think we've nailed that little point down. You know of no individual who is paid to hire out deadly weapons, nor have you ever handled such weapons, in particular a Browning automatic pistol or a Smith & Wesson revolver. You confirm that?'

'Never, sir, that's correct.'

He'd heard it said in the staff common room, with the inevitable accompanying snigger, that men usually chose a mistress who was the spitting image of the wife back home. Barbara, the wife, had short-cut fair hair and so did Hannah, the mistress. Both had good hips, and both were endowed with breasts that could be snuggled in the palms of his hands . . . so similar. But – big but – one slept with her back to him and the other – God was kind – didn't expect to sleep at all in a long night. He had not been able to get to Hannah last weekend: Kathy's school concert, back row of the recorders, had denied him the well-worn excuse utilized to get him eight hours in Hannah's bed.

'Thank you. Now we're going to move on. Right, Mr Curtis, do you know what a "bag man" is?'

'I believe I've heard that expression.'

'What does a "bag man" do? What's his speciality? I doubt the members of the jury know.'

'Well, he's a money guy, isn't he? He takes care of the money.'

Sheets pulled back, the light left on as Hannah liked it. Hannah crouched beside him and the carpet covered with her scattered blouse and skirt, bra, tights and knickers. Hannah stroking him so gently. God, she was bloody marvellous . . . Babs didn't do sex except on his damn birthday or if he'd managed to lower half a bottle down her, and that was rare. He squeezed his eyes shut.

'Most members of the jury, I assume, use a bank to take care of their money, so where does a bag man enter the equation?'

'Criminal money. A bag man looks after thieved money, money from drugs deals, that sort of money.'

'Mr Curtis, among your circle, is there a bag man? A man who handles and launders the monies gained from criminal enterprises?'

51

'Not that I know of, sir. As a reputable businessman, I wouldn't associate with such persons, sir.'

He felt spent, exhausted, as he did when Hannah slid off him.

'It's a big ask, Nat. You could say that it's a very big ask.'

'Yes, Benny, but it has the potential of being rather a well-paid big ask.'

Nathaniel Wilson saw a quick smirk cross Benny Edwards's lips. They were in a café's annexe; the main area was nearly empty so they had the overspill to themselves. A colleague of the Nobbler's lounged in the doorway, blocking entry. Friday had gone by, and the weekend, and this week's Monday, but the Nobbler had been at his pad in a village outside Fuengirola and he had a tan that shouted he went there often.

'And the trial's near run its time?'

'The jury will be out within two weeks, and I don't reckon they'll be taking long.'

'Open and shut?'

'More shut than open. They're going down. There's no time to be wasted.'

'Not an easy one.'

'They're looking at big stretches, but not looking forward to them . . . I can't see there's a cat in hell's chance of getting an acquittal, but with the jury down to ten I reckon that nine to one against means a retrial. Only bit of luck we've had is two jurors dropping down the tube. A retrial could be a year away, or a year and a half, and all that time I'd be yapping for bail and might just get it. What's more important is the chief prosecution witness, just a bit of a girl, up for it now but might not be in eighteen months. She's had a witness liaison officer assigned and been moved to a safe-house – she's had a witness protection scheme team. For another eighteen months, with the cost of that, I reckon they'd cut her adrift because the cost'll hurt them. She might just go off the boil if she didn't have liaison and protection in tow, might find her enthusiasm dwindling – and, not my business of course, she might show up where she's spotted or her family might be induced to lean on her . . . That's all in the future. What's for now is to ensure the jury's hung this time round, can't reach a guilty verdict. What do you think, Benny? Are you up for it or not?'

52

They were a mile from the Snaresbrook complex. Nathaniel Wilson had walked over and, after his lengthy association with players in serious and organized crime and a lifetime of sitting in court listening to police evidence, he had good perceptions of the arts of close surveillance. At one moment he had been sitting on the bench behind the barrister, the next he had been gone – as if needing a comfort call – and he'd been walking hard to be clear of the place. Only if he'd given a telegraphed warning, and looked furtive, would there have been the possibility of a tail. He'd done the routines including two dog-legs in side-streets and was happy enough that his security was intact. The business needed total secrecy if the Nobbler was to have a chance.

'I don't come cheap, Nat.'

'But your reputation says you're the best, Benny, and no one's expecting you to do it for charity rates.'

'Those blaggers, are they dumb? I thought blagging, going into jewellery shops waving guns, went out with the Ark. Why don't they do coke, smack, like everyone else?'

'See that as beneath them. I think it's the adrenaline rush . . . No, don't ask me. They make a healthy living from whatever they do, pleasantly healthy. I'm not authorized to bargain, but I'm permitted to offer – take it or leave it – the sum of fifty K win or lose on a retrial and paid up front, a further twenty-five K paid in the event one juror becomes the Great Persuader and it's an acquittal. Then there would be, also up front, twenty-five K as an inducement should it be a carrot rather than a stick. How does that sound?'

'That's all cash?'

'Cash and handed over on trust.'

'Handed over when?'

'Tomorrow – it's in place.'

'When I'm satisfied I don't argue.'

A hand snaked across the table, took the solicitor's, shook it gently, and the reverberation of the deal's conclusion slid through Nathaniel Wilson, as the implications invaded his whole body. Why? Why get involved? Something about perceived slights from established lawyers in the distant past, something about sneered and curled lips when he was young, had had suit trousers with a shiny seat, and had put together a basic law degree at night classes and from correspondence courses. Truth to tell, he had some admiration for the criminal classes, their *esprit*, their limited code of honour, even their bloody-minded – arrogant and obstinate – determination to breach the system: it was not something he often thought of. He leaned closer across the empty coffee cups. 'I've done some notes on the jury. There's five males and five women – does the sex matter?'

He made a show of ignorance that was not justified. Nathaniel Wilson had not used Benny Edwards as a Nobbler before but he'd been on defence teams who had, and he could recognize that they now moved on to high-risk territory. Yes, he knew very well what the answer would be to his question.

'Carrot and stick, right? I don't like using women. Dangle the carrot, but women aren't that interested in cash – they don't worry about the mortgage arrears, and don't give a stuff if the credit card's stacked with debt. Wave the stick and women are likely to throw the big wobble, tears and screaming, shrieking and howling, and then it's all gone out of control. No, men are the better bet . . . Five, you say?'

That morning, in court, before he slid off his seat, Nathaniel Wilson's note-taking had not involved the evidence given by Ozzie Curtis. Instead he had jotted down a description of each juror and their clothing. He pushed the single sheet of paper across the table. The Nobbler scanned it. His finger rested on the new foreman for a moment, then eased on down the sparse pen-portrait of the Afro-Caribbean, the young, keen one, the moaner who looked to have a permanent ache in his ear or his tooth, then to the one who could barely stay awake and wore a purple shirt with bloody sandals. When he'd read it, absorbed it, the Nobbler took a cigarette-lighter from his pocket and burned the paper, leaving the flakes to fall into the table's ashtray. Then he gave a first name and an address to which, the next day, a suitcase of banknotes should be delivered.

Nathaniel Wilson hurried back to court eighteen.

Eight more full working days to go.

Sitting in his small, closed-in territory, as though he were a sub-sistence farmer with minimal ground, Naylor's mind scraped over the wretched, irritating little spat before he had left home that morning. The sniped exchange with Anne weighed on him.

'Dickie, you're just a sore-headed bear and making a fuss about the inevitable. For Heaven's sake, everyone has to retire and pack it in. Daddy accepted it – and started a new life – and so can you,' she'd said, exasperated.

Her father's new life, and he'd responded churlishly with it, had been three mornings a week on a south-coast links course and membership of the golf club's catering committee. It had gone downhill from there. Unwisely, he'd commented that he wanted more from the future than worrying about the price of breaded cod fillets served up in a golf club bar and whether tartare sauce should be served in a bowl or from sealed sachets. She'd retaliated that her father had carried a burden of greater responsibility when he'd finished than Dickie had ever been given, and he'd flounced away to the cupboard under the stairs for his raincoat and umbrella. He'd been bending to pick up his briefcase from its place under the hall table when she'd punched him, verbally, in the flab of his stomach.

'Oh, I forgot – Mary in your office rang yesterday, quite slipped my memory.'

'I was sitting a dozen feet from her all day. What did she want that she couldn't have said to me?'

'God, you're in a foul mood. Mary – she seems a sweet girl – rang, behind your back, to talk about the leaving bash they're giving you, and what you'd like as a present. The DG can't make it, and the deputy DG is on leave, but one of the assistant DGs hopes to be there . . . Anyway, your present. Well, I said that we had clocks littered all over the house, and didn't want another. I also said that we had a perfectly good cut-glass drinks set and no room for more of the same. I suggested a greenhouse, not a big one, but where you can grow tomatoes in the summer and keep the geraniums and fuchsias in the winter, somewhere you can potter. That's what you're getting – Mary thought it an excellent idea. There'll be vouchers for it.'

He should have gone on out through the front door, after kissing Anne's cheek, and should have started out on a brisk walk to the station. He'd turned. Said malevolently, 'And what did Daddy have, bloody golf clubs?'

'You know he did.'

'And was the director general at his bash to make the speech and hand them over?'

'You know he was.'

Then, too late, he'd tried to do the kiss but her head had turned away and his lips had pursed against thin air. He'd snorted and gone. It had been a cross he'd carried since his first day with the Service, thirty-nine years before, that his father-in-law had not only been an iconic counter-intelligence figure with legendary status and the right to take an early-evening sherry or gin with successive DGs, but had put a word in an ear that had ensured his son-in-law was recruited for employment as a junior general-duties intelligence officer. He had never matched the importance in the Service carried by Anne's father – but only when he goaded her was he reminded of his failings. Her father, before heading off to the golf links, had tracked traitors, the pathetic, dangerous creatures who had sold out their loyalty to their country and passed military secrets to the agencies of the Soviet Union. Those creatures had gone to the Old Bailey for high-profile trials and inordinately long sentences of imprisonment. Dickie Naylor, after thirty-nine years' hacking at anything thrown down on his desk, had never rivalled her father's favoured position. The proof of it for all to see: the top cats would not be at his party, and he would be getting a flat-pack greenhouse – if he were ever able to assemble it – for tomatoes and frost-endangered plants. All arranged by Mary Reakes.

So little time left, and what made it worse – hardest to accept – was that there was bugger-all, sweet damn all of nothing, for him to look back at and feel a shimmer of pride in. He was a journeyman. He had failed at nothing but succeeded at less, and a week on Monday would see him wrestling with the sections of a greenhouse, and no one would have noticed his going. He snorted annoyance. There was nothing on his computer screen now that had not been there the day before.

The section he headed, overseeing Mary Reakes who had officer rank and four women who did not, had twin responsibilities in Riverside Villas. It was tasked with identifying the possible arrival into the United Kingdom of a suicide-bomber of foreign origin, and – considered of greater importance and therefore greater threat – the arrival of what the neighbouring sister 'Firm' in Ceauşescu Towers across the river called a 'co-ordinator' and the residents of the Villas described as a 'facilitator'. Since Nine-Eleven and the formation of his section, neither had appeared on the horizon . . . Dickie and Anne had not been blessed with children, therefore were denied grand-children. There would be no small boy to sit on his knee and ask, 'What did you do in the war, Gramps?' and get the answer, 'Nothing, darling, because on my watch the bloody enemy never came.' Plenty to tell the kid, who didn't exist, if he had been following the money trails of that enemy's credit-card frauds, which financially supported their planning; too much to tell, if he had been setting up informants in mosques and *madrassa* schools where the principles of the Koran were taught and the texts learned by heart; or he could have talked of the computer records of those youths from north London or the west Midlands who shuffled passports and took flights to Karachi or Rawalpindi . . . Nothing to recount and nothing to speak of, and Dickie Naylor's time was slipping away.

He rehearsed what he would say, turned away from his screen and dialled home. He apologized, curtly and awkwardly, stuttered through it.

Naylor heard her: 'Don't be silly, nothing to be sorry for. Everyone has to do it, retire and start a new life, as I said. You just caught me as I was going to the supermarket – it'll be nice, you being able to come with me.'

He grimaced, and replaced the receiver.

In a room high in the principal building inside the protected complex of the American Embassy in the Saudi Arabian capital of Riyadh, Cindy read aloud from the situation reports that had come through on the teleprinter. She had a fine voice, and Joe Hegner listened. In his mind he played pictures of the carnage she described from the flimsy, neatly bullet-pointed sheets.

```
SitRep, Task Force Olympia, Northern Command, Mosul:
Triple car-bomb attack in our Area of Responsibility.
Attack One: Target was a Contractors' Convoy. Attack
Two: Target was the Follow-Up reaction of Coalition
Forces, 300 metres from first strike. Attack Three:
Target was approach to Coalition base as reaction
forces returned. Casualties include 2 civilian secu-
rity guards from convoy, KIA. 3 Coalition Forces
```

from Follow-Up, KIA. 8 Iraqi civilians at Coalition
base, KIA. WIA in 3 attacks not yet available but
expected as 'substantial': Message Ends.

Without interruption, Joe Hegner heard her as she stood in the open doorway and read to him. He knew the men who worked as civilians and guarded the electricity-supply engineers, or who came in to fix the sewage plants, or who tried to keep the oil flowing through the pipelines that crossed the desert sands. With them, a bad bet for life insurance, were their guards. Many of the guards were from the old apartheid days of South Africa, some were prematurely retired paratroops and special forces from the UK; more were from the Midwest states of America and had left behind broken relationships and mounting debts. They could earn, for riding shotgun in armoured SUVs with the contractors, five thousand US dollars a week. They had, as a stereotype, shaven heads, muscles pumped up by weights and steroids, and skin covered with the permanence of crap-done tattoos ... and now two were dead. Later that day, from the safety of an office in Johannesburg, London or Los Angeles, an email or a telegram would be winging to an abandoned family, and in a few days a bag would be packed with the censored contents of a locker, the porno magazines not included. In the evening, Budweisers and slugs of Jack Daniel's would be downed by the survivors, and toasts made ... Joe Hegner liked them as free spirits, liked them well. He felt it more keenly because his experience of Mosul had scarred him.

SitRep, Central Command, Ar-Ramadi: Double vehicle-
bomb attack. Liquid gas tanker driven at improvised
defences at Police Barracks, followed by car used as
rescue and medical help reached site of tanker
strike. Killed and Wounded casualties not yet
assessed, but will be categorized as 'heavy' among
police personnel and civilians: Message Ends.

His shoes off, Joe Hegner had his feet on the desk, and there was a hole in the heel of his right sock, but there didn't seem time, these days, to call up a driver assigned to the Bureau and the necessary security people and travel downtown to get new pairs. His stick was propped against the desk edge. Many times he had been into police barracks, and he had good friends among the newly recruited officers. He had a rapport with them that verged on love. Most Iraqis living in the goddamn Triangle preferred to go short, see their family half starve from privation, rather than risk signing up and taking the American dollar, but a few were prepared to break the mould of fear. They had such damn awful equipment – shitty vehicles, shitty weapons and shitty barricades round their barracks – but they seemed so cheerful when he was over there, one week in four. For seven days in every month he was out of the embassy in Riyadh, holed up in the protected Green Zone on the Tigris river that split Baghdad, and before he caught the flight back to the Saudi capital, he would make damn certain – even if he had to get there inside the armour-plated walls of a Main Battle Tank – that he visited police-men in their barracks. There were Agency boys in the Green Zone, and agents from the Bureau, but they never moved off their asses and never went to meet the men at the real front line. He seemed to hear the keening wail of widows, brothers and mothers, as the bodies of policemen were identified – what was left of them, after the explosion of a liquid fuel tanker. He knew Ar-Ramadi as a place of rare hatred, of particular cruelty.

```
SitRep, Central Command, Ba'quba: Single suicide-
bomber attack. Target was an Iraqi Army recruitment
centre — suicide-bomber had joined end of queue and
detonated explosives when challenged. Casualty figure
not known, but will be 'large': Message Ends.
```

Thoughts formed in Joe Hegner's mind, and they ran alongside the images he held of the days when he had lived in the rarefied atmosphere of the Green Zone, before his hospitalization, before his convalescence, and before it was confirmed that he could work out of the embassy in Saudi Arabia . . . A queue outside a grimy building that was set back from concrete blast barriers and sandbag parapets. A line of young and middle-aged men watching uneasily behind them as they shuffled forward with painful slowness. A table with three clerks sitting behind it and a wad of application forms, riffled by an early-morning breeze. A man joined the far end of the line, and perhaps he smiled, as if at peace, and perhaps his clothing was too bulky for the size of his shoulders or the shape of his head, and perhaps the sweat ran on his forehead when the sun was not yet high, and perhaps those in the queue smelt the scent of danger and started to run back, and perhaps a security guard – paid a pittance – had had the courage to charge towards the sweating, overweight, smiling man. But a hand was inside the robe. A finger was on a switch. A bomb detonated. A body disintegrated and many other bodies were mutilated . . . He knew those young men. They were the secondary field of Joe Hegner's expertise.

SitRep, Central Command, Baghdad: Attack on garrison (Coalition Forces) at Abu Graib detention complex. Reports still incoming. At least 5, repeat 5, suicide-bombers involved in vehicles and on foot, alongside insurgent ground forces using 88mm mortars, RPG launchers and 50mm calibre machine-guns. Neither enemy casualties nor Coalition Forces casualties yet known or confirmed, but there are reports of at least two KIA from 101st Infantry: Message Ends.

He winced at the catalogue of disaster. He was not thirsty but sipped water from a plastic beaker as if that might moisten his dried, cracked lips. Joe Hegner never interrupted Cindy when she read aloud for him. The two unconfirmed Killed in Action soldiers might be sturdy white boys from Montana, where Hegner had been reared, or tough young black guys from Alabama, where he had done early years in his Bureau career. Each one, whatever part of his country they came from, was a wound to him. Part of that wound came from emotion, but more was from the failure of his professionalism. He was contemplating the scale of the attack on the gaol perimeter, estimating how many insurgent fighters had been deployed, considering the enormity of the use of five suicide merchants, pondering on the supply line – on a scale that Wal-Mart would not have sniffed at – of death volunteers his enemy could muster into line.

'That it?'

'Yes. Nothing else, thank God. That's what we have.'

'About as bad as it gets.'

'What are you thinking, Joe?'

It was the way they habitually worked. After she'd read to him, and he had assimilated what she'd told him, she would feed him anodyne questions that had the purpose of stirring the analytic juices in his mind. They had been together in Riyadh from three months before the launch of the invasion, had been together in the Green Zone from a week after the occupation of Baghdad to the December day in 2004 at the mess hall in the garrison camp at Mosul, and together once his convalescence had started in the Frankfurt military hospital. She had stayed at his side on his return to Riyadh. It was not a master-and-servant relationship – him an agent and her from the personal-assistant pool – or a relationship touched by sexual attraction, or unrequited affection, but had the stamp of elder brother and younger sister. He would have sworn that without her he would have been a finished, spent man; she would have said that meeting Josiah Hegner was the only meaningful event of her life. What hurt her most was that she was no longer permitted, by diktat of the Bureau, to fly with him for that one week in four when he returned to Iraq: then she lost the opportunity to watch over him. He was in his fifty-second year, and disfigured; she was thirty-four and attractive, but unavailable to any of the embassy staffers who pitched attention towards her. She waited for his answer.

'It's the scale of it that tells the story.'

'Five strikes in different locations and all within an hour of each other.'

'That's eleven in one sixty-minute slot, and five in just one strike.'

'Like they've a line of them backed up, and no shortages.'

'All co-ordinated. All put together by a single individual who controls them and wants to send a message to us. He is more important, so much more, than the fodder he's pushing forward. It's all about the co-ordination – it's about one man.'

In the old days in Riyadh, in his embassy office where an armed marine-corps guard stood sentry at the door, he had plastered the walls with photographs of the first men who had been identified as leaders of the insurgency. They were all gone. And 'one man's' image could not have gone on to the wall anyway because that man had neither a name that could be given him, nor did a photograph exist.

'But, Joe, you know who he is.'

'Yes. Yes.'

'It's the Twentyman, Joe. What are you thinking?'

'I've got a sense, almost a scent – but like he's signing off and moving on. Does that sound stupid, giving him that name? Christ, there ain't anything laughable about that bastard . . . but it's what he is, the Twentyman. He's the only guy who could do eleven suicides in an hour, four locations but – and this is my sense – it's as if he's heading for a rest or for new territory. Can't say which, but it has to be him – know nothing about him, only his quality. Has to be the Twentyman. I feel it.'

The flight was called, the departure of a KLM air-liner to Amsterdam.

He rose from the bench where he had waited for the announcement.

Ibrahim Hussein had been chosen, so the man he thought of as the Leader had told him, because he walked well. In front of him, inside the number four terminal of the King Khalid International Airport, lay an open expanse of shining floor, and he strode across it, not looking back to see if his last escort watched him go. He had been driven from the desert, then taken to a house in a slum quarter of the town of Qatif to sleep dreamlessly, then brought to the airport. In all of that time, and with each of the escorts, he had not been offered conversation, and he realized it was intended that he should not know who had handled and moved him. That morning he had been given a new pair of jeans, a yellow T-shirt, a leather jacket and trainers. He had a lightweight rucksack hooked over his arm, and on his head was an 'I Love NY' cap with a broad, extended peak to hide part of his face from the terminal's ceiling cameras. In the airport car park he had been passed an envelope containing a passport and a single sheet of scribbled writing that described a family history and justified the visa entry for the Netherlands on the passport's second page; he had been given time to read the sheet, then it had been taken from him and dumped in a rubbish bin. Already he marvelled at the care for detail that had been employed. At one moment, as the flight was called, his last escort had been at his side; at the next, the escort was no longer there. His target was the departure gate and, as was expected of him, he walked purposefully towards it. He heard the shout from far behind him. A name was called: not the name on the passport he held tight in his hand. The shout came again. He did not break his stride and as the departure gate yawed open automatically and swallowed him, the shout was repeated: 'Ibrahim? Is that Ibrahim Hussein? Are you Ibrahim—'

The gate closed and shut out the sound of the shout.

Across continents and time differences another flight was called. The charter for Sun Tours would fly a cabin of Spanish tourists from Barcelona to the English airport at Stansted.

He could not fault the arrangements in place for him, or the cover supplied by his travel documents. He was not Muhammad Ajaq, or the Scorpion. He would make the final leg of his journey with a Spanish passport, and the light olive skin of his cheeks and hands – not European and not north African – would be explained in the passport he now carried by a father's origin in Valencia and a mother's in the Moroccan city of Tetouan. He obeyed orders given to him three months before, but with them had come a labyrinth of planning of which he had no criticism. At every travelling stage he had been met, treated with the courtesy and respect to which he thought himself entitled, and money had been provided. Rendezvous arrangements had been flawlessly in place. The previous day he had been driven by a man, who asked no questions and made no idle conversation, into the mountains to the north-west of Barcelona, and there he had met a cell of Basque fighters from the Euzkadi ta Askatasuna, two men and a woman. Near to the town of Irurzun, overlooking it, in a shed where winter animal fodder was stored, he had been shown and then had purchased fifteen kilos of PTEN explosives in one-kilo sticks; he had paid twenty thousand American dollars, and four commercial quarrying detonators were added to the package.

He had thought the men good and strong, the woman pretty – there had been a moment when her hand had rested on his thigh as she made a point of emphasis, and excitement brimmed in him – and there had been trust. If he was captured and talked, they would be destroyed, and if they were taken and went down under interrogation, he would be broken. The woman had limped, and had said, matter-of-factly, she had been tortured long ago, which had clinched the trust for him. He had left them, the men wrapping him in bear grips, the woman kissing him full on the mouth, and carried away the fifteen kilos of explosives with the detonators, in waterproof paper sealed with masking tape.

With the parcel in the car's boot, the driver had negotiated narrow, winding roads and brought him to the port of Castro Urdiales. There, he had sat in a café and sipped coffee with a florid-faced Englishman, who had failure written at his mouth and defeat in his eyes. The price, without haggling, was agreed at twenty-five thousand American dollars, and the parcel had been slipped from its place on his knees under the table into the grasp of the Englishman, and the money was given over. From the near-empty café's window, he could see the grey skies over the harbour and the spray climbing over the outer groyne. The launch was pointed out to him – it nestled against a pontoon but shook in the swell.

He had been taken back, through the night, towards Barcelona, and in the dawn, with rain in the air, near to a station on the city's railway, he had suggested that the driver might wish to relieve his bladder after the long drive. Then he had come behind the man, taken his throat in his hands and strangled him. He had torched the car and left the body in undergrowth at the end of an uncleared track; the killing was to protect his identity. He had taken the train, with the day's early commuters, and after two changes had reached the airport, and forgotten the man who had driven him.

As he presented his ticket – best to travel in a tourist mass because with a group the scanning of passports at his destination would be slack – a ground hostess smiled at him, and he smiled back, but his eyes were on the bursting cleavage under her blouse.

She giggled and he laughed, as if he was going on holiday, took back his ticket, walked on and was buried in the flow of tourists.

He thought the package was drugs – heroin from Afghanistan or cocaine from Colombia – and Dennis Foulkes didn't give a damn. He was broke, and likely to be formally bankrupted. The cash stashed in a plastic bag in a galley cupboard would be enough to hold off the creditors, and protect his proudest possession.

She was the *Joker of the Pack*, and Dennis Foulkes loved her with passion. The money paid to him would hold off the inevitability of their parting. She was a motor-cruiser with two Volvo 480 h.p. engines that gave her a maximum speed, in good conditions, of thirty-three knots. She was a little over thirteen metres from bow to stern, with a beam of fractionally more than four metres. Inside those specifications were a cockpit, a saloon, a galley and dinette, three master staterooms – two of them en-suite – and crammed into every corner of her hull were the luxuries of wealth . . . He had had wealth. Money had dripped off him when he had run a prospering Rover car dealership, and he had not heard the warning sirens – eye off the ball – because he had just shelled out £265,000, paid without a loan, and he had taken the berth at the Kingswear marina on the south Devon coast, and had thought his business could run itself.

What a bloody fool. The car factory had collapsed in insolvency, what was in his showroom couldn't be given away, and he had not seen it coming. House gone – repossessed when the mortgage could not be met. Wife gone. All he had to remind him of what he had once been was the *Joker of the Pack*, which boasted the best electronic navigation systems, cocktail cabinets in solid wood, carpets and a bed in the biggest master stateroom that he could have shagged three little beauties in and not felt it a crowd. He did chartering. Any sod who'd pay could get a ride across the Channel, and he wasn't too proud to do day trips to Plymouth in the west or Lyme Regis to the east. He was for hire, and each pound or euro he was paid helped to keep his love under his feet. And if there were no punters, too early in the season, just a package wrapped in waterproof paper and bound with masking tape – stacked at the back of the galley cupboard – Dennis Foulkes wasn't losing sleep. The nightmare in his life was that his creditors at the bank or the mortgage company would hear of the *Joker of the Pack*, send in the bailiffs and flog her off dirt cheap to settle against the million, might be two, that he owed the bank and the building society – but a drip of cash showed willing and would keep them off his bloody back . . . Necessity, and love, dictated that he had made no judgements on the man who had sat with him in the café overlooking the harbour at Castro Urdiales.

The *Joker of the Pack* shuddered under him in the crested waves of a force six, might be seven, and he was far out in the Bay of Biscay and on course for a landfall sighting of the French coast at the Île d'Ouessant and then the run, God willing in calmer waters, across the Channel and into the Dart estuary.

He reflected, hanging on to the wheel as she bounced on the swell and water cascaded on to the bridge's windows, that the girl who had come tripping down the pier at Kingswear to arrange all this hadn't seemed the type tied into drugs importation. The guy had, cold sort of bastard for all his smiling, and he'd left a taste of fear behind him that was still in Dennis Foulkes's throat – but he'd thought her a nice girl. A pity about that awful bloody scar on her face.

He kept her shoulders and back always in view. Jamal was beside her, but it was the woman on whom he concentrated his attention.

A hundred and fifty yards behind her and Jamal, it was hard for Syed to follow her, but he had the skills. Syed's home, where he lived with his parents and where he worked in the kitchen of a fast-food kebab store, was north-west London, Hanger Lane, but the skills he now used had been learned on the teeming streets of Peshawar. Pakistan was where he had travelled two years before, aged nineteen, to visit family, and there he had been recruited. He had been putty in the hands of those who had noted him: four months before he had flown to the homeland of his father and mother, his elder brother had been attacked on a late-night bus, punched and kicked unconscious by white yobs – why? Because his brother was a Muslim, Asian, a 'bastard bloody Paki', the family had spent weeks travelling to and from the West Middlesex Hospital to see a young man who, for three days, had lingered close to death with tubes and drips keeping him alive. His brother was now recovered in body, but seldom left his Hanger Lane home. For what had been done to him, Syed had no regrets at having accepted the advances of the recruiters.

In Peshawar he had been trained in the arts of following a man or woman and remaining unnoticed. Ahead of him, the woman guided Jamal through the streets in the centre of the town and into the wide square, where the first buds were on the trees, and led him towards

66

the steps up to the shopping centre. Using what he had been taught in Peshawar, Syed was in place to satisfy himself that the woman had no tail on her. If there had been a tail from the security people, he would have spotted the signs from as far back as a hundred and fifty yards. He would have seen men pass women and move forward without acknowledging a colleague, and men or women lift their hands to speak into their wrists, and the loitering of those men and women with newspapers who did not read the columns of print. They had believed him an excellent pupil in Peshawar, and told him so . . . It was the first day that Syed had met others from the group, and the first time since his return from Pakistan that he had been called forward. He thought, his initial impression, that the woman believed she owned too great an importance with them, that she was flawed by the scar that marked her out and would make her remembered, but those decisions had been taken by others.

They climbed the steps to the shopping centre. From that distance, a hundred and fifty yards from it, he hated the place, and his thoughts were of avarice, its corrupting influences and ostentation. He saw the woman and Jamal skirt a gang of white youths. His brother would be avenged, his Faith protected, when the man came from abroad and they struck the target that was given them.

Looking for opportunities on Luton's streets was how Lee Donkin spent his days and evenings. Then, if he had found some and could buy, he spent his nights nodding out in the arms of injected heroin.

The best opportunities, and he had experience to back his opinion, were about in mid-morning: women pushing prams and buggies along the Dunstable Road, the Dallow Road or the Leagrave Road on their way to the town's shopping centre. Going to spend, weren't they? Cash in their purses, hadn't they? Never going to fight, were they? Lee Donkin, nineteen years old, fed his addiction with mugging and bag-snatching, and if the victim went down on to the pavement that was their fault for being fucking stupid and resisting, wasn't it? He had spiked hair, bleached white blond, but it was too distinctive when he worked and then he had his black hood over it. What made Lee Donkin most proud was the knowledge that he was a considerable statistic in the offices of the town's police station, among the detectives in the anti-street-theft team, but he had not been successfully prosecuted since he was sixteen when he had served thirty months in a young offenders' institution. Now, he reckoned, he was too smart for them. He was small and short but that was deceptive: his wiry body rippled hard muscle ... He had an opportunity. A woman, not old but using one of those hospital sticks and bad on her feet, was ahead: she'd just missed a bus into town and was going to walk. She had a handbag hooked on her elbow, and he closed on her. Alongside that section of the pavement was the school playing-field over which he could leg it when he'd done her.

The hand of Lee Donkin slid into his pocket as his pace increased, as he came nearer to her, and he used his thumb to prise off the little leather sheath that covered the blade of the knife.

8 November 1936
This is the beginning. It is what I have come for.

Albacete is behind us. I have woken as if from a nightmare, and that was the barracks at Albacete.

It has been an incredible day and I have felt such pride at being here. I have little time to write because, free from the nightmare, I will need all the sleep tonight that it is possible to have. Tomorrow I – Daniel and Ralph with me – will fight and be tested.

We were brought in buses last night to Madrid – and with every mile further from Albacete our spirits rose, and there was much singing in many languages. Our turn came and Daniel led our bus in 'It's A Long Way To Tipperary', and by the third time round we had everyone, Poles, Germans and Italians, whistling with us and even trying the words. We had a few hours' sleep in a park, under clear skies.

This afternoon we were formed into squads – platoons and companies – and most of us were issued with rifles. They are old and French, from the Great War, and each man given one had ten rounds of ammunition. I do not understand why we did not have more military training at Albacete: instead our brains are bulging with political stuff from the commissars. I have a rifle and so does Ralph, but not Daniel. We were marched up a main road in Madrid, like Regent Street in London, that is called the Gran Via. It was incredible.

At first the pavements of the Gran Via were empty, except for long queues at bread shops, but as we marched up the middle of the road people emerged and waved to us, or clapped and cheered. I marched as best I could, with my rifle on my shoulder, and felt such pride, and my good friends were either side of me, and there were near to two thousand of us. We were a magnificent sight, and those citizens of Madrid recognized the gesture we had made in coming to help them. A woman shouted – I know it because Ralph translated for me: 'It is better to die on your feet than live on your knees.' And many yelled what we had heard when we first came to Spain: 'They shall not pass.'

Later, when we came to the top of the Gran Via, we heard very clearly the noise of the artillery barrage falling on the forward positions, and none of the three of us sang any more. It was so close and so deafening. There, the roadside was at first deserted, but people must have heard the stamp of our marching boots, and they appeared from barricaded doorways and cheered us with such enthusiasm, as if we were their saviours and would drive back Los Moros, the Moorish troops of the Army of Africa . . . Of course we, of the XIth International Brigade, will drive them back from the Caso di Campo.

As we reached the trenches, the second line, where we will spend the night, I asked Daniel how he would be able to fight if he did not have a rifle. He said, very calmly, 'Don't you be worrying about it, Cecil. I expect one of the brigadiers will drop one and I will pick it up.' At first I did not understand what he meant. Now I do. The shelling is continuous, but I am sure we will get used to it and will sleep.

I have seen wounded men carried back through our second line, and I try to look away. What I have seen is ghastly – it is better not to look at those men. Strange, but I feel more anxiety for Ralph and Daniel than for myself – enough of that!

Tomorrow we fight – I hope God will look after my brothers in arms, and me – and the day after tomorrow we are going to have a party*! – Ralph and Daniel have promised it, because it will be my birthday.*

He held the notebook in front of his eyes and lingered on each sentence, every pencilled word. Voices were in his ears, but Banks ignored them, and the card game . . . That morning, the Delta team had been, in the dawn light, down the motorway in convoy – with the sirens going and the motorcycles ahead – to Heathrow, to deposit the Minister for Reconstruction. They had waited with him until it was time for his flight to Amman, the first leg of his journey home to Baghdad.

The team – less the Royal and Diplomatic guys – were now in the canteen of the police station at Vincent Square, a usual watering-hole when they were stood down and killed time before the next briefing. The talk at the far end of the table, which slid past Banks, was of clothing kit, a tour of the business end of Downing Street organized by a Special Branch sergeant, and a new modification to the Heckler & Koch's telescopic sight . . . The only image of the morning that had lasted with Banks was the insistence of the Minister – going home to bloody Baghdad – that he should shake their hands individually, thank them one by one. God, and they weren't bullet-catchers: none of the Delta team would have chucked his body into the line of fire to save the poor bastard. The plane had barely started its taxiing run before they had been on their way back for the canteen, cards and chaff talk.

'Hey, Banksy, what you got?' He was with Cecil Darke, far away. 'Banksy, are you in this world or out of it?'

What he missed most was his inability to fashion a picture of Cecil Darke. He could not put a face or features to his great-uncle. Did not know whether he was tall, as David Banks was, whether he was well-built with broad shoulders, as David Banks was. Dark- or fair-haired, or shaven bare at Albacete, did not know. As a substitute, while he read, he imagined a short young fellow – fourteen years younger than himself – with a pale complexion, and probably a concave, shallow chest, with clothes or a uniform that hung on him as they had on the scarecrows Banks's father had erected on new-sown fields. There would have been thin shoulders, pulled back with pride, weighed down by the old French rifle as he'd gone up the Gran Via. But it was only Banks's imagination, a poor substitute for knowing.

'Anyone home, Banksy?'

He tried to think what he believed in. What would have made David Banks – a detective constable who had never gone for the sergeants' exam – travel to join someone else's war? Couldn't imagine it. What would have made David Banks – divorced from Mandy, resident in an Ealing bedsit – go into a secondary line and think about sleep under shellfire rather than the dawn when he would charge over open ground? Couldn't comprehend it.

'Banksy, don't mind me saying it, what's the matter with you?'

Perhaps they were bored with the merits of various brands of thermal socks, or the self-esteem that came from a Downing Street tour and access to the Cabinet room, or the added magnification of the latest gunsight . . . He closed the notebook and saw the printed, faded, gold-leaf name. He knew so little of the man whose name it had been, and who, in the morning, would face an enemy and fight.

'It's a diary,' Banks said quietly.

'What's so special about it – makes us not interesting enough?'

Banks said, 'It was written by my great-uncle seventy years ago.'

'And . . . So . . . ? The way it's been stuck in your hands it might be a Tablet brought down from the mountain.'

Trying hard to control his irritation, Banks said, 'My great-uncle, aged twenty-one, packed in his job in London and went to Spain for the Civil War. He was a volunteer in the International Brigades and—'

'One of the great losers, a fucking Commie?'

His head rose to face Deltas 6, 8, 9 and 11. 'He was not a Communist,' Banks said evenly, through his teeth. 'He was an idealist. There is a difference.'

They came at him as if in an avalanche, and boredom was gone. It was sport.

Delta 6: 'Come off it, they were all reds, Soviet-supplied and Soviet-funded, controlled by the Comintern, recruited by the Communist Party of Great Britain.'

Delta 8: 'Just a load of wankers interfering in another dog's fight.'

Delta 9: 'What you could say, your great-uncle was yesterday's terrorist – like any of those bastards from outside going into Iraq, exactly the same, to slot that Principal who's on his way home. What you reckon, Banksy?'

The notebook was in front of him, with its worn leather cover and its faded gold-printed name. At that moment, David Banks could have grinned and shrugged and even laughed – could have pushed himself up off the hard chair and asked who needed another coffee or tea, how many sugars, could have defused it. But the blood ran warm in him. He was tired to the point of exhaustion and his temper surged. 'You lot are talking right out of your arses.'

'Oh, that right, is it?' Sport over, conflict joined. 'That's not very pretty, Banksy.'

He was an Authorized Firearms Officer. He had been given the highest responsibility a policeman held: the right to carry a lethal weapon. He was not allowed the personal luxury of anger. But all that had gone clean out through the canteen's window. No apology, no backing off. Banks stared up at the ceiling, which was a mistake.

It was Delta 11 who saw the opportunity of advantage and took it. Beyond Banks's main eyeline, fast as a snake, Delta 11 came past two empty chairs, and had the notebook in his fist. Banks's reaction was a clawing grab at Delta 11's sleeve, but he couldn't hold it. Delta 11 sank again on to his chair.

'Right, let's have a look – let's see what the Commie's got to say for himself.'

It had begun as a lark, then gone serious.

Banks was up – his chair fell back behind him – along the length of the table and his right hand snatched at the back of Delta 11's neck while the left dived for the notebook. His left wrist, with his watch on it, brushed Delta 11's earlobe, and the little metal angle holding the strap in place nicked the flesh. Banks had the notebook in his hand as the first drop of blood hit the table. Only a nick, just a scratch, but there was blood on the table. He spun on his heel and went back to his chair at the end of the table. Then he could have apologized, and maybe thrown his handkerchief to Delta 11.

Banks said, 'Actually, my great-uncle was an idealist and prepared to make sacrifices for those ideals, a brave and principled man.'

Delta 9 mocked, 'And what would make him any different from the foreign suicide-bombers in Iraq and their "sacrifices"? Come on, I'm listening, Banksy.'

Without thinking, without weighing, Banks spat back, 'It's perfectly possible that such men there are brave and principled, and though I don't agree—'

For a moment the silence hung, and the enormity of his statement, which contradicted the culture of Protection Officers, billowed in him. He saw their huddle re-form, and he heard, wafting low towards him, the debate resume on whether useful thermal socks could be bought for less than twenty pounds – and he was shut out.

Regret was not in David Banks's nature, or humility. And his great-uncle, Cecil Darke, had made no compromises.

He dropped the notebook into his jacket pocket, and went to sit at a far table – where there was no blood from a nicked ear – away from the clatter of conversation.

Chapter 4: Thursday, Day 8

He used the Isosceles stance, and fired.

About all that David Banks knew of the ancient Greek language was 'Isosceles', and most of what he knew about geometry was of a triangle with two sides of equal length. He felt the jolt of the mechanism's recoil, and from the side of his eye saw the cartridge case discharged. His feet were apart and his toes level; his knees were slightly bent and his arms were punched out; his back was straight; the triangle was from his head to his fists holding the pistol and back to his belt. He realized immediately that his shot would be rated poor, as were most of those he had fired before – counted the trigger squeezes and knew his magazine was exhausted.

He shouted, 'Out.' He went down on to one knee, because the training dictated that a marksman should reduce the size of the target he offered when he was taken from the equation, and was slipping out the empty magazine and replacing it with a loaded one. Around him he heard a chorus of similar yells: 'Out.' Then the clicks, metal scraping on metal, as the others and he worked the safety catches forward. He stood and was breathing hard; he shouldn't have been.

He was apart from the rest, as if outside a tribal fence, not invited in and not making the effort to approach them. Maybe the instructors who oversaw them, or the invigilators who checked the target sheets and awarded the marks for 'pass' or 'fail', had been told that he was beyond the pale as far as the rest of the Delta team were concerned, or maybe they hadn't noticed.

An instructor came to him, not to the others. They were rated as 'pass', but if an instructor came straight up to a marksman it indicated 'fail'. Must have been three years since he had last been confronted by an instructor, wearing an expression of puzzlement and disappointment, to be told that his score was below the forty-two points out of fifty that were required.

'You been out on the piss last night, Banksy? Trouble is, you're giving me a problem.' The voice was quietly confidential, but the others would have known. 'My problem is that I cannot fudge the score. You're not just one down, you're seven. I can't remember you having had difficulty before – well not in the last three years. You're on thirty-five. You'll have to repeat it after the Alley work – sorry and all that.'

He heard, and was meant to, a staged whisper from the knot of the tribe and thought it was Delta 7. 'Not on the piss, more likely worrying about the survival of a 'rather brave and principled man' and therefore screwing up.'

They unloaded their pistols, handed over the live magazines, pulled on waterproof trousers and oiled jackets, tugged their caps low on their foreheads and walked in the rain to what was called, at the range, Hogan's Alley. It was the time for simunition, plastic bullets fired from pistols with their tips holding fractional quantities of red and black paint. The bullets would spatter a marking of the hit point, but would not break a man's skin. New magazines and pairs of eye-protectors were handed out. The way the team formed up in a queue to go down the Alley, Banks was left at the end and would shoot last. In front of him he could see a tiny nick – sandwiched between a coat's collar and the side of a cap – on an earlobe . . . Too bloody obstinate to apologize, not that there was anything to apologize for. Shooting in the Alley did not count in the areas of 'pass' and 'fail', but doing badly would be noted by the instructors and go on his report.

The Alley was designed to beat the 'complacency syndrome'. It was an open-air corridor flanked by imitation house fronts built of plywood and paint-daubed, with doors and open windows. It was designed as nearly as possible to replicate the 'real thing'. Between the house fronts were beaten-up cars, most without tyres. The Alley was where a marksman, an Authorized Firearms Officer, tested his reactions; no one could order him when to fire – it was his decision and his responsibility if he fouled up and a mistake, in the 'big and nasty world out there', brought a charge of murder down on his shoulders. A senior instructor stood back and had a console in front of him under a clear plastic sheet that kept the rain off the switches; cables led from it across the grass and the mud to either side of the Alley. The way to avoid a mistake was not to fire, never to fire, unless his own life was threatened and not his Principal's, but the Alley showed up that lack of determination.

He waited his turn. Where he stood, at the tail of the queue, he could not see the shapes, human figures of cardboard, that would appear in windows, doorways and from behind the cars. Judges were walked up the Alley, and magistrates, and those sour-faced bastards from the Independent Police Complaints Commission who investigated every fatal shooting by a police officer. A few learned the difficulties of making the nano-second decision on whether to shoot or not, but most didn't . . . and that was why David Banks was there. His self-regard demanded it. It was what he did well, his purpose in life – until that morning when he'd shot like an idiot. Daft, but the ongoing shit with Mandy . . . their loathing of each other after the divorce was finalized, the word being passed to him that she was shagging a uniform sergeant from West End Central, the acrimony over the division of wedding presents and their old household's contents, his firm-held belief that the estate agent had colluded with her to mark down his split on the sale of the Wandsworth terraced house and her screaming denial . . . The shit with Mandy had never, in eight separate shooting assessments, caused him to fail.

Reading the diary had. Last night, lying on his unmade bed, with the plastic trays of the microwaved meal for one – vegetable curry, the only one left in the freezer, and pilau rice – on the carpet beside his pillow, he had been into combat on the fields of the Caso di Campo. He had heard machine-gun fire, artillery fire, tank fire and mortar fire, and he had learned that one-third – Cecil Darke's

76

estimate – of the XIth International Brigade were dead or wounded when the dusk had mercifully covered the open ground. His great-uncle had come through the day, as had the friends who were his brothers. On the bed, Banks had lived it – the atrocity of the wounds, the agony of the deaths, the naked fear and the collapsed relief of those who were not hurt or dead on that foreign field. Bloody hell! What was a nicked earlobe when set against those casualties, dead and injured? The only soldiers he had met, men who were combat-trained, were those from Hereford – Special Forces guys – quiet as the grave, focused, trained and easy on their feet. But he did not know the man, without military experience, who had led him by the hand, through a notebook's pages, to the Caso di Campo and hell.

His turn, and the instructor waved him forward.

The Alley opened ahead of him.

No brothers beside him, no brigade around him, he started his walk and his hand was close to the pancake holster under his opened coat, and the rain slid down from the peak of his cap. OK, OK, a target was expected: he had the Glock out of the holster, and the sweat or the rain made his hand wet and his grip loose. His heart pounded. Anyone who'd said, 'Only an exercise, my old mucker, doesn't matter', was talking shit. He was a third of the way in and the silence surged. They would all be watching, their eyes needling into his back . . . Then—

A figure snapped upright in a doorway, and he swung, went Isosceles and had the safety off. His finger lay on the trigger stick, and he saw the shape of a woman, and against her chest, down his Glock's V sight and needle sight, was a life-size image of a held baby. He had not fired the paint bullet that would have 'killed' the baby and maybe the woman too.

There was stiffness in his legs and the pistol was a lead weight. He was on his own, isolated. The tribe was quiet behind him: a titter would have broken their prized code of 'professionalism', their totem god. The woman had been to his left – half-way down the Alley. To his right, a figure was thrown up in a window frame. A man: chest in the sights, finger on the trigger, starting to exert the pressure, then seeing, blurred, the man's empty hands with the palms exposed. He had not fired and the man lived. Went on, past more doors and more windows, more broken cars.

He was near the end of the Alley. Fatal, with only a few steps to the end, to relax. He summoned the dregs of his concentration. The car on the left. Two figure shapes jerking upright from either side, their bodies half hidden by the two doors. Saw, a flashed moment, that the shape – male – nearest him held a plastic supermarket shopping-bag. Saw, a lightning fast moment, the far man had a lifted and aimed handgun. Double tap. Two shots fired. A splurge of red paint on a lower chest, and second on the shoulder above the lung space and below the shoulder's bones. Two rivulets ran down the cardboard. He reached the end of the Alley.

When he looked back up it, only the instructors stood there.

He was told he had done well, that three of the others in the Delta team had killed innocents and that two more had fired on 'bad guys' but had missed their targets.

Banks went back to the range with the senior instructor. He learned that the rest of the Delta team had decamped to the canteen. He did not ask, so did not learn, whether they had watched him shoot – but he felt a small glow of satisfaction in the knowledge that three faced a possible murder charge, and two more were dead – and he knew, from that feeling deep inside his mind, that he would not, ever again, make the effort to be assimilated back into the tribe.

On the range, with the senior instructor watching over him, he made his authorization to continue carrying a weapon safe, secure. He scored forty-eight out of fifty, and the senior instructor slapped his back cheerfully, then told him not to be a pillock again and waste everyone's time.

When he'd finished they weren't in the canteen. They were sitting in the minibus that would ferry them back to London. The engine kicked into life when he was barely inside, and there was no query as to how he'd done, passed or failed, but the message was there: that he was a pain for delaying them all.

He heard, said in the front, with a camp accent intended to mimic him, '. . . "perfectly possible that such men there" – Iraqi suicide-bombers, bloody foreigners – "are brave and principled, and though I don't agree . . ." What fucking crap.'

His eyes closed, Banks shut them out.

*

He came off the Eurostar, and was a 'clean skin'. Not that Ibrahim Hussein, the youngest and only surviving son of an electrical-goods dealer in the extreme south-west of the Kingdom of Saudi Arabia, knew that phrase. His knowledge of the covert world of his enemies was as limited as were the inches of rain falling in a twelvemonth on the great desert, the Rub' al Khali, the hostile expanses that he had traversed at the start of his journey and that he would not see again. The importance of keeping his identity as 'clean' as the scrubbed skin on his cheeks was beyond his experience.

What he had learned already was the extent of the tentacles of the organization he believed he now served, and would serve with his life.

He wore the same jeans and trainers as he had at the airport in Riyadh, but his T-shirt was different and showed a reproduction of Jan Asselyn's *The Threatened Swan* on his chest. He had been told to leave his leather jacket loosely open when he went through the immigration checks at the London terminal. It had been explained to him that the T-shirt, and its motif, created an image of European intellect. He walked from the train towards the descending escalator stairs. His faith in the organization brimmed. There were no doubts.

On arrival at Schiphol in Amsterdam, he had been met and taken by train to a town thirty-five minutes away. He had been asked by his escort not to look at its name on the station platform, and he had not. He did not register the name of the street to which he was driven. The whole of the previous day he had been alone in an upstairs room, with just two visits to the bathroom, and his food had been left on the rug outside the door. Late that evening a voice had called for him to leave his passport on the bed when he left. Early that morning he had been walked to the town's square where a taxi waited for him. He had sat in the back and the driver had not spoken to him. The only contact had been to point out an envelope of brown paper left on the seat he was to occupy. He had found a Canadian passport in the envelope, a rail ticket that listed a return journey in nine days, and a sheet of paper describing the life history of the young man named in the document. While they drove on the highway south he had memorized his new biography. The taxi had turned into the Belgian town of Lille and dropped him at the main railway station. There was no farewell from the driver, only fingers flicking persistently until he had lifted up the sketched-out biography and handed it forward. On the train, at departure, his passport had been examined by a policewoman and returned to him without comment.

He stepped on to the moving stairs.

It amazed him how many, already, had helped his journey, and the preparation that so far had been given to that journey. He did not know that, inside the organization, more care was given to the acquisition of reputable travel documentation than to the gaining of weapons, the forging of networks and the gathering of cash resources. He descended, and between the sheer sides of the escalator, there was no escape. Ibrahim Hussein had no wish to flee – but if he had there was no possibility of it. The escalator dragged him down towards the subterranean concourse. He saw policemen, huge, their bodyweight enhanced by armour, carrying automatic weapons, but if they saw him they did not notice him.

As he had been told to, he headed towards the sign and the cubicles for Commonwealth passports. A kaleidoscope of thoughts hit the young man, who was a second-year student at the university's school of medicine, and dazed him. He had entered, almost, the fortress of his enemy: had breached, almost, their walls with the same ease that he might have entered the Old Souk of Jizan or his father's shop behind the Corniche. He was surrounded by his enemy and their soldiers, but it was as if he was invisible to them. It was where he would strike against those who abused his Faith, and would avenge the martyrdoms of his brothers . . . A hand reached forward, a bored face gazed into his. 'Please, we don't have all day. Your passport, sir.'

He offered it. The page of details was scanned into a machine, then the pages were flipped.

'The purpose of your visit, sir?' A tired question.

He said, as instructed, that it was tourism.

'Well, if the weather ever lifts, you'll enjoy your stay, sir. The place is empty so you won't have to queue for the Eye or the Tower. Don't let all the guns put you off. Actually, it's pretty safe here.'

His passport was given back to him. He found himself carried gently towards the last gates by the hurrying crowds from the train. A man, whose bag struck Ibrahim's heel, stopped to make profuse apologies, then dashed on. The last gates were open, and he took the final strides to enter the enemy's fortress.

'That's him.'

'I saw it.' A dry gravelled reply. 'The Threatened Swan has flown to us.'

'Not only flown, but landed.'

'What I say, this is a moment of danger.'

'There have been many moments of danger, but you are right to tell me of it and I recognize it.'

Below Muhammad Ajaq and the man standing beside him, the only one in the whole of his world to whom he entrusted his life, was the well of the Waterloo terminal where passengers came to board the Eurostar for a journey through the tunnel to Europe, or to leave it. They were at the top of wide steps, where their view would not be blocked. With Ajaq was the man he called, with honest respect, the Engineer. Because of the cold in the streets outside the station, and the rain glistening on the pavements, both could have their collars turned high, scarves at their throats and caps on their scalps. When they left the station they would expand their collapsed umbrellas. They knew of the cameras. Each would have been certain that his face was hidden from the lenses.

'It is good, *The Threatened Swan*, easy to see.'

'And good also because it has the look of a virgin's innocence, but it is defiant, which means it has determination.'

The Engineer chuckled, Ajaq took his arm and their laughter melded.

'I said to you that he walked well.'

'He has a good walk.'

'The rest were shit.'

'Shit and gone,' the Engineer said. 'Used and gone. But is it only a picture on a shirt of *The Threatened Swan* that has defiance? Is *he* determined enough? Is he strong?'

'I'll twist his arm out of its socket, or break it, to make him strong and able to walk . . . You've seen enough?'

'He has the shoulders and chest to take the vest . . . I have seen enough.'

Beneath them, the young man had dropped his bag on to the ground by his feet. He looked around him, waiting for the approach. Both Ajaq and the Engineer did the drills familiar to them. They watched for tails, for the surveillance people. To both men, the obvious and unspoken concern was that the youth who was a 'walking dead' had been identified, had been allowed to go on and enter a network. But they saw no tails from their vantage-point, no surveillance. It was this obsession with detail that had kept them alive and loose in the Triangle to the west of Baghdad.

'Have you seen yet the one who meets him?'

'No. He will be here, I am sure – but I cannot do everything.'

'Already, my friend, you have more burdens than one man should carry,' the Engineer said sombrely.

They walked away, and the postcard from the Rijksmuseum of Amsterdam, of a painting created three and a half centuries before, of a swan with webbed claws apart, wings raised to fight and neck twisted in anger, was torn into many pieces and dropped on to a coffee shop table.

The morning was not yet finished, but the day had already been long. The meeting at the coast, the extraction of the packet from the boat's kitchen, the retrieval of monies, the settling of the matter of the boat's driver, more than five hundred kilometres of driving with the Engineer at the wheel and the return to the capital – he was drained. Ajaq needed to sleep before he met the young man. When he had slept he would have the charm and the mesmerizing gaze in his eyes that would calm the one who wished for martyrdom. And the Engineer, also, needed sleep because his fingers must be nimble and supple for the circuits and the wiring.

For part of Muhammad Ajaq there might have been, here, a sense of homecoming. Half of his heritage, his blood, was here. He hated that half . . . That blood had fashioned him, made him what he was.

They walked in the rain away from the station.

The body floated face down. It was wedged under the slats of the pontoon at the far extremity of the marina's spider legs. The pontoon rested on large plastic drums that gave it buoyancy and also prevented the body being carried by tide or current from under the pontoon. It was beside the berth of a luxury launch that, when the boating season for weekend sailors started, would be the same centre of envied attraction as it had been since the *Joker of the Pack* had first been moored at Kingswear. Unless a member of the marina's permanent staff or a yachtsman came along that far pontoon, then stopped and peered directly down through those slats, the body might remain undiscovered for several days. If Dennis Foulkes was not seen for a week or two that would not have been remarkable, and his absence from the *Joker of the Pack* would arouse no suspicion. The launch, tethered to the pontoon, was closed up and none of the portholes or bridge windows gave a view into the galley. An opened bottle of whisky lay on the tiled floor, which was stained below it. When the body was found and retrieved, and the hatches forced open, an impression would be left of a lonely man drinking to a state of intoxication, then coming on deck, losing his footing, slipping, falling – and drowning. A subsequent post-mortem would find whisky traces in his stomach tubes, and marina water in his lungs, no marks of violence on his skin. A forensic search of the launch would identify no other individuals as having been present in the galley on the night of Dennis Foulkes's death: they had worn disposable rubber gloves. The CCTV camera at the marina's gate would not show the arrival of individuals and their walk through the reception area: they had come by dinghy on a route beyond the reach of the lens. A sniffer dog, with an excellent nose, trained by the police or Customs, might have located the faint traces of explosives in a galley cupboard: the chance of such a dog being used, when the scenario of the cadaver's death was so obvious, were minimal. The killing had been done with care.

Its legs and arms splayed out, zebra stripes of light on its back, the body lay – unfound and unmourned – under the pontoon's slats, the last tied knot of a conspiracy's small loose end.

He saw him, could not miss him. The leather coat was open and the white of the swan was clear and prominent on his chest. Ramzi recognized the bird: they glided on the Derwent river, which split the city that was his home, and made nests on an island close to the bridge that linked the shopping centre to the main bypass round Derby and the county cricket field. It had been in the evening paper, last month, that white kids had thrown stones from the bridge's parapet at the swans' nests with the intention of breaking the eggs, and his mother had said it was disgraceful behaviour. Ramzi crossed the concourse, remembered what he had been told to say and came close to the young man from behind his shoulder.

Ramzi said, 'Is that the work of the painter Asselyn?'

There was a short gasp, a fraction of hesitation, the turn of a brain's flywheel, then the smile. 'It is the work of *Jan* Asselyn . . . Yes, Jan Asselyn.'

He saw relief split across the young man's face. He had been told that he should use no names and that conversation should be limited to the briefest exchange. But the relief at the approach, the successful exchange of the coded greeting and the response killed his intentions. 'I am Ramzi, and I am sorry to have been late. Please, when we meet with others do not say that I was late.'

'My name is Ibrahim. I won't speak of it.'

Ramzi hugged him. Ramzi was heavy to the point of obesity, but he used weights and reckoned his bulk gave him authority. He had been recruited twenty-one months before at a cultural centre in the Normanton district of the city after announcing his determination to be a part of the armed struggle against the oppression of Muslims – in Britain, Chechnya, Kashmir, Iraq, anywhere. He had been told then that his value to the armed struggle dictated he went home, never returned to the cultural centre, and 'slept' till he was woken. He had not believed that the terms of his recruitment represented inadequacy, but held the opinion that his talents would be employed in a strike of major proportions. Roused from sleep a week earlier, he had assumed the role of 'muscle' in the cell that was coming together. Once, before the call, and long ago, Ramzi had boasted that his destiny was martyrdom. In his bear grip, he felt the frailty of the young man, Ibrahim, the prominent bones of his shoulders and the slightness of his arms. For a moment he thought of their destruction.

Ramzi towered over him. 'We should go. We are going to walk. It is quite a long way but there are cameras on the buses and trains. We will seem to part now – cameras are watching us. I will be ahead of you and you will follow . . .'

'Why do the cameras matter?' The question was asked with simplicity, in good but accented English, and seemed to demand honesty.

Ramzi had been told by the woman – who knew everything, who had arrogance – that the cell had been woken and afterwards would return to a second long sleep. The cameras were important because after the strike the cell would disband and wait for a call to reactivate them, their identities safeguarded.

Ramzi said limply, 'It's what I was told.'

Ramzi hugged him again, tighter, heard the breath hiss from the young man's mouth. He broke away and strode off up the stairs to the station's main concourse. At the top – and he should not have – he turned and looked down. He saw the confusion and, almost, pleading in the young man's face, as if he had expected bonding within a brotherhood but was abandoned; he saw the swan on the young man's chest, between the flaps of his leather jacket – was that jacket big enough to hide a belt or a vest? It was a good jacket – and he thought of the birds that had been stoned on their nests in the Derwent river. He lengthened his step.

In that step there was lightness. He could boast of his determination to be a martyr for God, and know he was not chosen. He was in the rain, leaving the station, and his follower would be tracking behind him.

'It is what I saw.'

'But what you say you saw is impossible.'

'I saw it, I promise that to you.'

'A person cannot be in two places at the same time,' Omar Hussein said, and chuckled. 'You are wrong. He is in Sana'a.'

'I saw your son, my nephew, at the King Khalid airport in Riyadh. Omar, I have known him all of his life.'

'Did you see his face?'

'I saw his back, but I have seen him walk – from the front and the side and the back – all of his life and mine.'

'Our country has a population in excess of eight millions. Do you not consider, my brother, that one other boy can walk like Ibrahim, if seen only from the back? He is in Sana'a to see cousins, from his mother's family, and in a week he returns to go back to the School of Medicine. Is that not good enough for you?'

'I saw him. The flight was called and he went to the gate. Only one flight was boarding. The flight was the Dutch airline, and was for Amsterdam. I do not lie, brother, and I know my nephew's walk.'

'It is impossible.'

'It is what I saw.'

Doubt crept now into the mind of Omar Hussein. Eleven days before he had been told by his son, Ibrahim, of a journey to Sana'a, the principal city of Yemen, to visit cousins from the family of Omar's beloved and missed wife. Now, his brother who had a sharp mind that was not dulled with age, as his own was, declared with certainty that the boy had lied to his father and sisters and had travelled to Riyadh, then caught an aeroplane to Europe.

'I shall telephone him,' Omar Hussein said, attempting a decisive response.

In the living room of that prosperous home were the fruits of his labours: a wide-screen television with cinema-standard speakers, video and DVD attachments, electric fans that purred softly to shift the day's heat, and a state-of-the-art cordless phone. He picked it up from its cradle, punched into its gargantuan memory, waited and listened, then asked. An answer, in Sana'a, was given him. His lips pursed. 'They have not seen him. They have not been told to expect him.'

'I can only tell you what I saw, brother.'

Again, Omar Hussein delved into the memory of his telephone, and rang his son's personal mobile. He was told that its owner was unavailable and was requested to leave a recorded message. The days of the last week had flown past with stock checks at the shop and with representatives calling on him to sell new models. A father realized now how long it had been since he had spoken to a son, and how there had been no phone calls. He led his brother up the wide stairs of the villa.

He found the door to his son's bedroom locked, put his shoulder to it and could not break it open. He felt tears of frustration welling. But his brother was stronger, fitter, and crashed his weight into the door. It swung open, and his brother half fell through it. Omar came past him, steadied him, and looked round the room.

It was so tidy. The room was that of a twenty-one-year-old boy and normally shoes, clothes, books for studying and magazines littered the floor. Everything had been left so neat. He saw the two photographs on the wall, the glass of the frames gleaming, of his elder sons, both dead. The loss of them was a misery of which he rarely spoke but always felt. There was a vase of flowers on a table under the photographs, but the water had been sucked out in the room's heat and the blooms had withered. His son's mobile phone was on the bedside table, switched off. Now Omar Hussein believed what his brother, who had the eyesight of a hunting Lanner falcon, had told him – and he understood. The weight of it crushed him.

'What should I do?'

'To protect him, and to safeguard your daughters and yourself, there is only one choice open to you.'

'Tell me.'

'It is just possible that he can be intercepted and stopped . . . I think more of you and of your daughters. Times, Omar, have changed. They are no longer martyrs, they are terrorists. When his name is released and when the television shows what he has done, you will be hounded by the police, by every agency. You will be seen – because you reported nothing and because you are from Asir Province, which they say is a 'hotbed' of terrorism – as an accomplice to an atrocity. The families of those who flew into the Towers, and most of them were from Asir, are now disgraced, ruined. You may endure it, you probably can, but do you wish that on your daughters? I think you know what you should do.'

Omar Hussein, his head hung, said, 'If I did nothing my wife, if she were able, would curse me.'

An hour after his brother had left the villa, and in response to Omar Hussein's telephone call to the Ministry of the Interior police, whose compound was around the walls of the Ottoman fort in Jizan, an unmarked Chevrolet car drove up to his front door.

Two men of the *mabaheth* sipped coffee with a frightened father and took notes of what he said concerning a missing son who was far away and lost.

'A nice little runner, Miss.'

She walked a fourth or fifth time round the Ford Fiesta. She had left the yard at its wheel and they had done a short circuit round the side-roads off the main route to the motorway, and Avril Harris had not found fault. It was her finances that caused her to hesitate at this last hurdle. She was twenty-five years old, a nurse in A and E at Luton's main hospital where she earned a pittance for the responsibilities heaped on her, and her last car – with a hundred and fifty-one thousand on the clock – had died on her. No young woman in her right mind would come off night duty and rely on finding a taxi or getting a late bus across the town. The town at night was a battlefield of violence, and she did not need the local paper to tell her so: in A and E, on night duty, she fielded the victims. She had seen, from different dealers, four other cars but this Fiesta – seventy thousand miles done – priced at nine hundred pounds seemed the best value. It shone, the seats were clean, and she did not have her father there to check the tyres and pose better questions. She asked for a discount and saw the pain on the dealer's face as he offered it for eight fifty, 'final price – a give-away'. She rooted in her handbag for that amount in cash, and a half-full tank was thrown in. She signed the papers, got in and turned the ignition.

At the lights blocking the Dunstable Road, at the hospital turn-off, she had to pull up, and her new joy echoed with the report of the Fiesta's backfire. For a moment she was dazed by the intensity of the noise. Then there was an impatient hoot behind her because the lights had changed, and Avril Harris drove on, swung to the right and headed for A and E's staff parking area.

The team was in place and it waited, like a hunting pack for prey at a waterhole, for the business of court eighteen to be finished for the day.

With the collusion of Nathaniel Wilson, criminal solicitor, who had slipped away in the lunch adjournment with a description of the clothing worn by a single juror – as requested before the day's proceedings were under way – the prey was identified.

Three men on foot and the drivers of two mass-produced, unremarkable cars made up the strength of the team. The target was described as bearded, a little over average height, with longish, brown hair, grey flashes at the temples, wearing a green anorak, designer jeans that were probably imitation, bought off a market stall, and heavyweight leather sandals; he would have a navy blue rucksack carried on one shoulder. A piece of cake, couldn't be missed.

The Nobbler himself, Benny Edwards, was not with them. He would come on to the scene when a dossier of the target's identity had been fashioned, not before. He could rely on these men to fulfil the preparatory work because they were the best in this field. The services they provided, through Benny Edwards, were much sought after. He only employed the best, and his own reputation was supreme over his rivals'. The five men, whether on foot or at a car's wheel, had skills in the arts of surveillance that kept them on a par with any unit that might have been put on to the roads or pavements by the Serious Crime Directorate of the Metropolitan Police; those skills had been refreshed by the recruitment the previous year – a source of considerable pride to the Nobbler – of a detective sergeant from the SCD who had suffered problems with his claims, written down and signed for, on overtime sheets. The prime difference between Benny Edwards's men and the Directorate's was in communications. He used pay-as-you-go mobile phones that were ditched and changed usually after two days' use, three maximum, and they used complex networks of digitally enhanced radios that could not be broken into, but the difference in effectiveness was minimal. Where they were equals – the Nobbler's people and the Directorate's – was in street craft. His men could follow and track; they could put a target in a 'box', a 'trigger man' having initially identified him or her, and not be 'burned'. Never, not once, had men paid by Benny Edwards been spotted while walking or driving as a tail.

When court eighteen finished for the day, when Mr Justice Herbert's clerk had yelled, 'All rise', and the jurors were led back to their room to shrug on their coats, the solicitor would hurry into the Snaresbrook corridor and dial a number, let it ring four times, then cut the connection, unanswered.

The team, activated, would follow wherever the target led them.

'So, Mr Curtis, you would have the jury believe that you are the unhappy victim of what would be, in effect, a conspiracy of lies by the prosecution's witnesses. The conspiracy, which you claim has put you before the court, involves sworn – and therefore perjured – evidence from a young woman who is sure she saw you, evidence from the owner and staff working in the jewellery shop, evidence from reputable police officers of which several have commendations on their records for outstanding conduct . . . and they all lied. I am being blunt, Mr Curtis. That seems to be the defence you are offering to these very grave charges. I see you shrug. I take that as the answer you are providing. They are all lying. You alone are giving the members of the jury the truthful version of events. No more questions.'

Jools saw the theatrical roll of the barrister's shaggy eyebrows, as if the whole thing was a game. But not a bloody game to anyone who had been in that shop and who had faced the open barrel of a pistol and a revolver: Jools didn't think it was a bloody game. His eyes followed Ozzie Curtis's back as the horrible bloody man was taken from the witness stand to the dock – could look at him then because the damned intimidating eyes gazed the other way.

He heard the judge: 'We've had a long and concentrated session, and I don't think we should start with the evidence of Mr Ollie Curtis before the morning. Ten thirty tomorrow.'

The clerk sucked in breath to make herself better heard: 'All rise.'

Another day gone.

Actually, quite a good day – one of the best.

A day of good entertainment . . . not in court but at the lunch break.

A wholesome spat, if he did not feature in it, always entertained Jools Wright. The argument, materializing from nowhere, had been worthy of one of those bickering catfights in the staff common room. The dispute had featured Rob, the foreman, and Peter, the moaner. The first complaint Peter had thrown at Rob had involved the quality of the rice pudding served to them: was it not Rob's function, as jury foreman, to lodge the matter with the catering manager? Rob had said, 'You want a damn nanny? Well, you can find one for yourself. My job, as leader of the jury, is with the case we're hearing, not wet-nursing you and your bloody dietary groans.' Seconds out. No holding. Blows above the belt, please. A good clean fight, gentlemen. The bailiff had rung the bell, end of the round, and called them back. But it had been good spectator sport, and the pleasure of it had lasted Jools Wright through the afternoon as Ozzie Curtis had wriggled and lied and pleaded loss of memory through the prosecution barrister's final and impeccably polite onslaught.

He loved a catfight, claws and teeth, when he was a spectator.

Didn't love the ones at home.

Couldn't abide them when he was the receiver and Babs on the attack.

She didn't do teeth, claws and insults. She hit with endless silences, occasional tears, and her ability to move around in a room as if he did not exist and had no place in the house. Perhaps she knew, perhaps she didn't know, of Hannah and the weekends, but it was not spoken of. Nor had their financial state, getting worse, been recently discussed. Tears were in another room. Weeping usually followed his bald statement that he would be going to see 'Mum and Dad' for the weekend because 'they're not getting any younger and it's the right thing to spend what time I can with them before they're gone'. He had no intention of leaving home, couldn't bloody well afford it. He was, he didn't deny it to himself, a low-life, a deceiver, a man who did not deserve trust – and he lived for the days when he was gone early through the front door and on his way to court eighteen, and for the weekends when Hannah shagged him. Could have been worse . . .

From the locker allocated to him, he took his green anorak and zipped it over his shirt, then slid the navy rucksack on to his shoulder. Because he had enjoyed his day, Jools called cheerfully from the jury-room door, ''Bye, everybody. Have a nice evening. See you all tomorrow.'

He noted it as one of those daft afternoons when the sun shone between darkened clouds. It lit the brightness of his shirt and high-lighted the gaudiness of his socks, but he had to pull up the anorak's hood to protect his hair from the shower. The socks might get really wet if the rain came down any heavier. He lengthened his stride down the Snaresbrook driveway and hoped he wouldn't be kept waiting at the pedestrian lights across the main road. Then there'd be the charge in the open up the hill to the station.

He knew nothing of counter-surveillance procedures, nor had any reason to wish he had been taught them. He did not look behind him as he went for his train, and would not look beside him and along the platform when he waited for it.

Jools Wright was in ignorance of the world in which he moved, an innocent, and would have been bemused had he been told that the price of innocence could be costly.

Chapter 5: Thursday, Day 8

He left his room, checked that the door's lock had fastened, and slipped soft-footed down the corridor. In his recent life, that of the Scorpion, Muhammad Ajaq had slept some nights in the homes of wealthy merchants or professional men, some nights in the compounds of the leaders of minor tribes, some nights in the sheds used by herdsmen under the palms by the banks of the Euphrates river, some nights in the cover of dried-out irrigation ditches, some nights on the sand with a blanket round him and the stars for company. But, he had never slept in a hotel.

Ajaq knew nothing of hotels.

Going down the corridor, he was refreshed by sleep. It was his ability to rest where he could find it, and dreams did not disturb him. He had not used the bed in the room – in compound guest wings, in a shed, a ditch or in the open air he lay on the floor or on a carpet or on fodder or in the dirt. It was his belief that on a floor or on the ground his reactions would be faster: he would wake more quickly if a threat gathered round him. The room was on the first floor of the building, at the back and overlooking a walled yard, and he had kept the window up, and would have gone out through it if danger had come close. From his sleep, he felt strong, alert.

His tread was light, but the boards under the carpet squealed as he went.

He paused at the door, stiffened, as if he had no taste for what he must now do . . . Then he tapped on the wood panel where paint had flaked off.

'It is your friend. Please, let me inside.'

A footfall came to the door, then stopped. He imagined the boy's fear, but did not know for how many hours he had been in the room without contact. He watched the door's edge, heard the click of the lock and saw the door open, but a chain held it. The room was darkened, no light on. Then the boy was staring back at him. Relief flooded the face. The chain was unhooked.

The bed was rumpled where the boy had lain on it and a copy of the Koran was on the pillow. The leather jacket was discarded on the thin, shoe-worn carpet. Ajaq could smell the fast food, and could make out the stains at the boy's mouth. He went inside and closed the door behind him, threaded his steps over the carpet and round the bed, then drew back the curtains. Light from a street-lamp beyond the yard wall seeped inside.

Ajaq sat on the floor. Its hardness, through the carpet, pinched his buttocks, and he waved for the boy to come and take a place beside him. He pushed aside the little tray in which the food sauces still lay, the paper bag and some clothing. The boy lowered himself, nervously, and their bodies were close.

'You travelled well?'

'I did, my leader, and always there were people who helped me.'

'You remember when we met?'

'I remember.'

'What did I say to you?'

'You asked me who I was and where I was from and what I did – was I strong?'

'And you told me?'

'I hoped to be strong. You said I was chosen. You said that you looked for a man who walked well and that I did.'

'And before you left me, to begin your journey, I said?'

'You told me that I was chosen for a mission of exceptional value, for which I would be honoured and respected. Without my dedication and obedience the mission would fail and that would make a great victory for our enemies . . . I told you of the martyrdom of my brothers, and I said that I would seek to equal their dedication and be worthy . . .'

'You remember it well.'

Ajaq knew that it was necessary to keep those in love with death, the volunteers, in the company of others who shared their certainty so that the will for martyrdom was not permitted to dribble away. With others around him, it was harder for a man to trip away from the boasts he had made, or the promises . . . But the boy, Ibrahim, had seen eleven others bounce away in the back of two pickups and had now been effectively alone for seven full days, seven nights. Did the strength to continue still exist? He had to know. Perhaps his own life, certainly his freedom, depended on the answer. In Iraq, where he had fought and where a price of many thousands of American dollars rested on his head, others would have decided whether strength had gone. Himself, he cared as little for the individuality of a martyr as for a shell loaded into a breach or a mortar missile into a tube or a bullets' belt into a machine-gun . . . but here there was no other man to make that decision for him. Ajaq was not in Iraq but in a first-floor room of a cheap, rundown hotel to be found in a network of side-streets close to the Paddington terminus in London. He forced himself, and it was an effort, to play-act sincerity.

'Are you strong, Ibrahim?'

'I promise it.'

He took the hands of the boy, his long, sensitive fingers, and held them locked in his own fists, which were calloused and rough, those of a fighting man.

'You know of the haughtiness of Britons?'

'I do.'

'And you know of the aggression of the Crusaders, who are British?'

'I do. I have been told it by the *imam* at our mosque in Jizan.'

'Because you have been chosen from many, you are privileged. Ibrahim, you walk at the front of our struggle, God's struggle. The British are a people of corrupt unbelievers and you will teach them a lesson that will be long spoken of among the faithful followers of God. For what you will do, you will be taken to the table of God. Already there are the men who were your brothers on earth, with whom you were before I chose you. They are at the table, they keep a place for you and their welcome awaits you. You will have their respect for what you will have done and where you will have been. And I believe that young women of great beauty, in the gardens of Paradise, also await your coming. There you will be honoured – and you will be honoured on earth, wherever the Faith exists. Your name will be sung, your photograph will be shown, and your name and your photograph will fortify the courage of so many . . . Ibrahim, to sit at God's table and to lie in the gardens of Paradise is only for the strongest. Are you among them?'

'I hope to be.' Emotion, sincerity, played on the boy's face.

The agenda of revenge of Muhammad Ajaq had little to do with a table set with fruits and a fable of women who fucked endlessly behind shrubs in gardens. Because of the blood in his veins, and the lightness of his skin's texture, he had answered the call and had journeyed to the heartland of an enemy. He was the product of the seed of his father, that blood and that skin pallor. His father – he knew it now but had not known it for the many years of his childhood – was William Jennings, from Yorkshire in northern England, an engineer who had worked on the building of modern sewage plants in Jordan thirty years before. His father, the bastard Jennings, had seduced his mother, who was a secretary at the ministry in Amman that oversaw the modernization of Jordan's infrastructure. His father, Jennings, had been repatriated before his mother could no longer hide her pregnancy. She had gone back to her home – in the north of Jordan, near to the town of Irbid – with her disgrace and her shame, had borne the boy-child and suckled him, had left him in her room and gone. On a winter's morning, his mother had walked out into the desert sands, had stripped off her clothes and lain down naked so that hypothermia would claim her life quickly. She had died there and her skeleton – stripped of flesh by scavenging foxes – had not been found until the spring came. He had been brought up through childhood by his grandparents, his mother's family. On his nineteenth birthday, in the hour before he left home in Irbid by bus for the paratroops' training depot in the south, he had been told of his father's flight and his mother's death . . . and at that moment his character had been fashioned. Hatred ruled him, not God and not Faith.

95

'You have to stay strong, Ibrahim, to justify the trust placed in you.'

'I will.'

He believed him. He did not think it would be necessary to use the hoax, with honeyed words, of a 'delayed time switch'. Some of the volunteers, so others told him, would buckle as they approached the day when they would walk or drive to their target. Those who showed weakness were given the lie by the Engineer that they should reach the target, then dump a bag or park a car, and press the switch: they had a minute, or five minutes, to run before the explosion. There was, of course, no 'delayed time switch', and it was an unsatisfactory procedure. He believed the boy sought martyrdom and, without deception, would achieve it.

He ran his fingers through the boy's hair, left him and returned quietly to his room.

Left alone, Ibrahim listened to the stirring sounds of the building beyond the door, the street beyond the window and the yard's walls.

He still sat on the floor.

A harsh noise, new, filled his ears and eddied in the darkness around him.

Ibrahim fought the noise, tried to rid himself of it. He held the palms of his hands over his ears. He thought of the table and his brothers, of the empty chair and the place set for him, but he could not lose the noise.

It disgusted him.

It was above him.

Bedsprings squealed with growing intensity and a faster beat. What he knew about sex, about the physical matter of copulation, had been learned from textbooks in the library of the School of Medicine. He had never talked of it with his father, or – of course not – with his sisters: his parents' bedroom, when his mother was alive, had been at the far end of the villa from his own room and solid walls would have blocked out the sounds of lovemaking. Above him, over the now swaying lightshade, there was a thin layer of plasterboard, then planking, a similarly worn carpet, a bed with springs that sank and rose and howled. He had the image, and it had been hard in his mind since the *imam* had talked of it, of the young women who waited for a martyr in the gardens of Paradise, and their nakedness, but – in his mind – when he advanced on them and bent to touch them, there was always a distraction that snatched them away. He had never touched a woman. Boys who had been with him at the university, or at school in Jizan, had talked endlessly of women, even told stories of prostitutes they had paid in the cities, but Ibrahim had thought they lied.

It fascinated him.

Before he went to the gardens, where virgins waited for him, he would never know the feeling of a woman's body. His hands' palms were tighter against his ears. He summoned the image of his father, whom he loved, and called to him shrilly in the night. From a great distance, his father seemed to smile on him. He heard his father speak of pride in his youngest, the same pride he had spoken of when the eldest and the middle sons had been reported dead in the *jihad* against the infidels of Russia and America. He saw his father sitting in the deep-cushioned chair in front of the wide-screen television with the cinema-standard speakers, and thought his father blessed him for his courage.

There was a cry overhead, a groan and silence, and the swing of the lightshade slackened. He let his hands fall from his ears and rejoiced: he had his father's pride.

'It is what his father told us today.'

'Why'd he call your people?' Hegner asked softly.

'Because of love and because of fear.'

'Wouldn't he have felt proud of his boy's actions?'

'Pride perhaps in former times, at the loss of two sons, but not in the loss of a third, all that remains to him . . . and fear now at the consequences of silence.'

Of all the Americans, of the Bureau and the Agency, working from the Riyadh embassy, only Joe Hegner would have had that late-evening call from the head of counter-intelligence in the Kingdom. Only Hegner had the status, the reputation and the friendship to have been invited to come in the darkness to the Mabatha interrogation centre, south of the capital city. Only this dogged zealot from the Federal Bureau of Investigation would have had a limousine chauffeur drive him behind privacy windows out of

Riyadh, past the Ministry of Interior complex and through the high gates of what staffers at his embassy called the 'Confession Factory'. He sat now in a comfortable chair beside the senior man in that section of the *mabaheth*, with a cocktail of fruit juices at his elbow.

'I am exceptionally grateful for this information you offer me.'

'It is natural, Joe, that it should be given you.'

'And already I have a scent on this.'

'The nose, Joe – and I say it with respect – is the best.'

He had access where for others of the Bureau and the Agency none existed. He had never concerned himself with the reasons that it was given him, because that would have been time wasted, and he thought time too precious. The trust had existed before he had gone on permanent posting to Baghdad and the insurgent war in Iraq, but had been cemented when it became known – after his injuries – that at the end of his immediate convalescence he had demanded to be posted back to the Kingdom. The trust had borne fruit. On his last visit from Washington, the director of the Bureau had spent forty-eight hours inside the embassy compound, kicking his heels, then been fobbed off with junior functionaries. A month before that, the director of the Agency – in spite of hourly telephone demands from subordinates – had not been granted an audience for three days. The door opened for Joe Hegner, and the carpet rolled out.

'I thought, Joe, you would wish to know of this matter.'

'I do, sir, and I appreciate it.'

A wish and an appreciation – of course. The speciality of Joe Hegner was in the collection of information on the strategies of recruitment, and the tactics employed for them, of suicide-bombers. He learned and in return he gave back a conduit route by which sensitive information from the *mabaheth* was funnelled back to the Bureau analysts at the Edgar Hoover Building. So different from the days before Nine-Eleven, but the muscle on those aircraft had been from the Kingdom: men from the Kingdom had carried the box-cutter knives that had terrorized cabin staff and flight-deck crews. The funnel was important to the counter-intelligence officers and reduced the suffocating pressure of criticism flowing from DC. He had been told, but it mattered little to Joe Hegner, that his reports were in the Oval Office within forty-eight hours of being filed. He had small regard for praise, and only the barest interest in the stature he had achieved. His hand rested loosely on the handle of the stick that lay against his thigh.

'I'm sorry to say, and I know you won't take me the wrong way, but you folks have failed to stop the flow of suicide-bombers recruited here, and failed to lock down your borders.'

'We know it, Joe.'

'You are the prime source of these kids.'

'Joe, we know it.'

'You've waited till the eleventh hour, but finally you're trying to arrest these boys.'

'We are trying, Joe, and that is the truth.'

'I've got to be honest with you, I'm not sure the "trying" is good enough.'

For such a riposte, any other man from the Bureau or the Agency would have been shown the door, booted out of the gate with a kick four-square in the ass, and would have had to trek back across the desert towards Riyadh's distant lights and illuminated towers. Joe Hegner was not 'any other man'. Hegner lived off plain-talk, always had. Folks spoke plain and simple where he came from. A man kept his conversation plain and simple, or he walked alone, in the bit of Montana that was north of the intersection at Forsyth of Route 12 and Route 94 and close to Big Porcupine Creek. The nearest town was at Ingemar where his grandfather had been the community blacksmith, and his father had run a hardware store. Hegner had lost most of his plain-talk when he'd gone, first of his family, to the university in Helena – and lost some more during a marriage now also gone, during induction and subsequent postings with the Bureau ... but he'd regained it while lying in inked darkness after his injury. His Saudi contacts in the *mabaheth* were at professorial level with obliqueness, innuendo and subtlety of language, as obscure as mirrored walls, but they listened to him.

'Your government, its policies, they are the recruiter.'

'Well, that's one on the money and I'm not going to argue.'

'A twenty-one-year-old medical student, Joe, has told his family he is visiting cousins in Sana'a, and in fact he is travelling to Europe, with a false passport and a false name on the airline's manifest . . . What am I telling you?'

'You are telling me to listen for one heck of a bang – a big, big bang. We will hear the bang unless – where he's travelling to – they get their act together fast. More important they get real lucky, and fast. You got a different take on it?'

'I am hearing you, Joe.'

'They're gonna need a sack of luck large enough to keep a Bedu's camel happy for a month in the Rub' al Khali. I'm going to ship this on. Right?'

'Disperse it where it should be thrown.'

'Gotcha. Hope we have the time.' At the last, Joe Hegner was fulsome in courtesy. He said gruffly, sincerely, 'I thank you, sir, for your trust in me.'

The head of counter-intelligence of the *mabaheth* in the Kingdom kissed Hegner's cheek. His arm was taken and he was guided to the door with a sympathy that did not embarrass him. He paused there while those who would lead him back to his limousine came from an outer office.

He asked, 'What do you make of the kid's father telling you what he knew? He a patriot or . . . ?'

'A frightened man, Joe, or a parent wanting his son to live. As yet, I do not know. We flew him here this afternoon to talk to him. To drain him, Joe. I have no interest in the father, except what he can tell me of his son. I am concerned only with his son, with Ibrahim Hussein.'

'That's good. That's real good.'

Heavily, on his stick, Joe Hegner went out into the night, and the inner walls of the Mabatha Interrogation Centre were behind him. From the darkness, the shadows in which he lived, he heard the limousine door opened. He had that bad feeling. It was the one the Shin Bet officers in Israel talked about when he visited Tel Aviv, and the tortured Americans in Baghdad. A bomber was on course for a target. A boy with a dream of Paradise stalked close to a place of martyrdom. Where'd he go? Where was the kid headed?

He was sagging but the chain that held him did not permit him to fall to his knees.

Two men, alternately, thrashed the back of Omar Hussein with an iron bar and a pliable rubber truncheon. The cell in which he was suspended had a floor space of less than three metres by less than two. He had now defecated and urinated in his underpants. He could not protect his back from the blows, and when he screamed the bar and the truncheon hit him with greater power. He could smell his own filth. He thought he had done right . . . He screamed at the pain, hoped only for unconsciousness, and cursed his son.

The questions came . . . When had he first known? Who had recruited his son? What was the target of his son? Was not the whole of Asir Province a snake's nest of dissent, a foxes' den of violence against the Kingdom? Did he support his son's belief in murder? The answer was a single croak inside the hood over his old head: he knew nothing, *nothing*.

And then his tormentors left him.

Again, muffled by the hood, he screamed the curse against his son.

He had been working late, was in no hurry to be home after the early spat with Anne and, for a break, he had slipped out of Riverside Villas and walked to the park at the back. He shared a bench with a pathetic creature, sodden with a bottle of full-strength cider and destitute, but Dickie Naylor was ignored, left alone with his thoughts and his lit pipe.

When six more working days were done, Naylor would never again sit in the evening quiet of St John's Gardens. He had learned the value of coming to the park and sitting under the high plane trees when the world, his world, collapsed around him. And here he could smoke a pipe and be free of the tobacco police.

It had been a burial ground. He fancied that he, and the vagrant, sat with phantoms long deceased. That did not bother him, was actually something of a comfort; he could cope with the past and inevitability. Three and a half centuries before that spring evening, and the ebb of his working life, the cemetery had been full and an extra yard deep of topsoil had been carted in so that new graves could be dug on top of the old. An enterprising solution to a capacity problem. He had sat here, with the same pipe stem clamped in his teeth, on the evening of Nine-Eleven.

On that September day, some had rushed round the offices and corridors of Riverside Villas, acting the parts of whirling dervishes, or clutched paper sheets, or had mobiles pressed to their ears and called for meetings, or rifled for files from the archive. Dickie Naylor had watched the frenetic action, then walked to the solitude of St John's Gardens and smoked, using the quiet to ponder. He had returned and said, 'This day will turn out to be as significant as that of the first of September sixty-two years ago when the battleship *Schleswig-Holstein* fired the first shells at the Polish garrison of the Westerplatte at Danzig.' He did not flatter himself that any had listened. A month later the new·section was formed to monitor for the arrival of suicide-bombers into the United Kingdom and he had been nominated as second in charge. After a year Freddie had gone, retired to golf or tomato-breeding, and Naylor had taken his place and occupied his cubicle. The tick of his own retirement clock had started.

But the new topsoil dumped on the garden had created its own problems. Solutions always bred consequences, Naylor believed. The shallow graves, not excavated deeply enough for fear of disturbing the already interred, had provided scope for body-snatchers. 'Block one hole and another appears', he would have said, if the vagrant had asked him. By 1814, what was now St John's Gardens had been patrolled by armed guards, carrying not cudgels but primed pistols, and the hospitals were denied the cadavers they needed for dissection tutorials.

He had come here, to the same bench, on the day that jargon now called Seven-Seven. That day, Riverside Villas had been stunned and quiet. 'God, it's bloody well reached us – *us*,' he'd heard an ashen-faced branch director murmur. The building's business was compartmentalized. An officer was supposed to know his own area of study, but not of investigations in hand adjacent to his desk. 'Need to bloody know' was the mantra of the Villas. By mid-morning on Seven-Seven that sacred rule was shredded. A verdict of failure had consumed the building. The guards on the big doors to the basement car park, the canteen cooks and the director general in a lofty suite of offices would have known it. There hadn't been a damn whisper of what was going to happen. Four guys, with clean skins, had walked through all the beavering efforts of detection with which the Service was charged. Naylor had come to the gardens that lunchtime, eaten a sandwich and thought that the illusion of all-seeing competence manufactured in the Villas was gone. He had come back in, swiped his card, taken the lift up, tramped down his corridor and an officer had asked him, 'What the hell should be our response, Dickie?'

And Naylor had said what was obvious to him: 'We should all pedal a bit harder.'

By order of Lord Palmerston, at some date in the 1850s, the burial ground had been closed, the gardens had been laid out, a fountain built in the centre and the plane trees planted. It was the best place Dickie Naylor knew . . . God's truth, he'd miss it.

Charity did not come often to him, but on an impulse he took the half-emptied tobacco pouch from his pocket, laid it in the vagrant's lap and smiled. He wished him a good evening, and was on his way.

He padded into the outer office. The new carpets, from last year's refurbishment, muffled his footsteps. She was at his door.

Mary Reakes was not aware of him. She had, damn it, a colour chart in her hand. He could see it over her shoulder, the chart a client used to choose a decoration scheme. It showed squares of pastel shades, and he thought she'd probably end up daubing the cubicle in bloody magnolia.

'In a hurry, are we?' He tried the old acid but had never been good at it.

She didn't have the decency, he reckoned, to spin round and blush. It was as if he was sick with a plague, and the funeral people were round his bed, measuring him up.

'It's only six bloody days, can't you wait that long?'

She didn't do embarrassment. 'Thought you'd gone home, Dickie.'

'Well, I can tell you I'll be here to the last minute, last hour, last day of my employment. Then the reins will be passed and you can have your painters in, but not a minute before.'

An obsession with history dominated the life of Steve Vickers, and what delighted him most was the opportunity of sharing it with others – not a history of kings and queens, not the great cultural, political and social earthquakes of the United Kingdom's past: history for him was the development of the town, Luton, that was his home.

'I am asking you, ladies, to look up and study the clock in the tower. Are you all with me?'

Disappointingly, only a dozen or so were, but if there had been only three souls, he would have persisted with the tour.

'The tower above our town hall – yes, it dominates the main square, St George's Square – was built in 1935 and 1936, and opened by the Duke of Kent. I'll come to the clock in a moment but, excitingly, the building has a story of its own . . .'

He beamed around him. It was necessary, Steve Vickers believed, to share his enthusiasm if he was to hold an audience. The weather was cool, darkness settled over the building's roofs, but the rain had held off. Only two of his original party had slipped away. Not bad . . . A not ungenerous disability pension from Vauxhall cars' Research and Development Unit, after he had been invalided out with persistent migraine attacks, allowed him to devote his life to the town's historic past. Now he had with him a Women's Institute group from a dozen miles away, shivering but standing their ground.

'They had to put up a new town hall because the previous one was burned down by an angry mob. Yes, believe me, in this town a mob was sufficiently enraged to storm a police line – just where we're standing now – break down the main door and set fire to the building. Order was not restored until regular troops were brought in from Bedford . . . and that happened in 1919 and it was called the Peace Riot. Former soldiers, then demobbed, couldn't get work and the celebration of the armistice caused their fury. That day was probably the last on which significant violence hit the town – and long may the quiet last.'

He had heard, at his reference to the Peace Riot, a faint titter of amusement, sufficient to sustain him. The following Wednesday he was booked to escort a group from the Townswomen's Guild around Hightown, on the other side of the river, where the hat-making industry had been the country's largest a century ago. On the Saturday after that he would be back, early in the morning, with sixth-form students and any others who cared to attend, in St George's Square. Communicating raw history was a joy to him.

*

Through the car's passenger window, she saw a man bob his head as money was passed from purses.

Faria recognized him. With his old coat, the wool hat down on his forehead and the sheaf of papers in his fist, she had seen him often enough with his little tour groups. For a moment she thought it sad that so few accompanied him – but it was only a fleeting thought because the business in hand was shopping and on her knee was the list she had been given of items to be bought. A police car pulled out behind the car and passed them, and the policewoman, who was the passenger, eyed her. She said quietly to Jamal, 'Don't worry, they're not for us. They're for druggies and drunks. The town is bad with all levels of abuse. It's the corruption ... There are no guns here. The town is not protected.' A little shiver went through her but she thought Jamal hadn't seen it. She had neatly ticked off each item on the list, and now she needed only the hardware store, which never closed before ten, to buy the soldering iron. They followed the police car, and the road took them away from the guide and his party past the steps to the shopping arcade. She knew it was the target but not when it would be hit.

Without thinking – she had dedication but not professionalism – she broke a rule. She turned to the young man beside her who was so young and had smooth skin, not her scars. She asked, 'When it's done, what will you do?'

'Go home as soon as I am released to my father's shop in Dudley. After the end of the holiday, I will go to London and my college, at London University. I am nineteen, I am doing first-year business studies. I was identified at the mosque in Dudley because I spoke up for the three boys from Tipton, which is close to where I live, who were barbarically imprisoned by the Americans at the concentration camp of Guantánamo, and tortured. The government did nothing to help them. The government is the lackey of the Americans. I tell you, Faria, I am disappointed I was not chosen. I would have done it, worn the belt or the waistcoat. They told me I was more valuable alive, but that is confusing to me. How can doing reconnaissance be more important than dying as a martyr? But I am obedient. I will go to London and hope that I have proved my value and will be called again ... Is this the shop?'

'I apologize for asking the question. Please, forgive me. This one, yes.'

He braked and pulled the car close to the kerb.

She went with her list towards the shop's open door. Behind her, in the car, she left the youth with the pretty face, the small stunted body, the heavy spectacles and the first fluff of a moustache: she wondered if the girls at the college, white-skinned or Asian failed to notice him, if the story of the virgins in the gardens of Paradise stirred him. She could not kill it – a small, fast excitement ran in her at the thought of virgins. In the shop, Faria asked for a soldering iron and knew to what purpose it would be put.

The table had barely been cleared. Kathy had gone, charging up the stairs to her room, homework and music. The mats were still on the table, and the water glasses, but the silence of the meal was over. The envelopes were dumped in front of Jools, where the crumbs from the pudding had not been wiped away.

He stared at them. Babs had thrown them down, then retreated to the sink and was running water into the bowl.

Some of the envelopes were three months old, some had come that week. One must have come today. Babs had taken his plate off the mat, gone to the drawer where brown envelopes festered and flipped them so that the oldest were at the top.

Bills, final demands and threats.

The household finances of Jools Wright were a disaster. Bank accounts overdrawn, credit cards leaking interest charges, gas, electricity and water all unpaid. There was an abuse-laden hand-written note from the man who had repaired the chimney flashing.

No point going to the drawer where the envelopes accumulated and getting out the cheque book, his or hers, because any cheque he wrote would bounce high. Even the damned piggybank, only for two-pound coins and the summer holiday, was empty because it had been rifled for last week's supermarket run: he had counted out a pocketful of coins while the woman had stared bleakly at him and the queue building behind him had fidgeted in irritation.

The house was the trouble. Her parents had put down the deposit for them, and the mortgage had been based on Babs going back to work when Kathy started school. But Babs didn't work any more, citing stress. The mortgage ate what he earned. He was blamed for her stress. Couldn't argue with it. Didn't argue with it. He'd not made head of department, wasn't on a high-achiever bonus, and above-inflation salary increments were a thing of the past. He looked down at the bills, shuffled and restacked them, then laid them out across the table.

'Well, I don't know what to bloody do with them, short of robbing a bank.'

'Which you'd probably cock up,' came the whiplash from behind him.

'In fact, where I am, I'm hearing of some very professional people and they screwed up clearing out a jewellery shop. They had guns and I don't – so robbing a bank isn't exactly a starter. And since we never have a sane, civilized conversation—'

'That would be a start. I'm stuck here. I've that drawer shouting at me each time I pass it. I daren't open it. I suppose you want me to go to Mum and Dad, tell them how useless you are and beg on my bended knee for them to go and draw what we owe from their building society. Well, I won't. Will not.'

'I'm a bit short, my love,' Jools liked irony, big doses of it, 'of ideas.'

'It's all right for you, sitting in that bloody court. Precious little or nothing to think about. I'm here when they come through the letter-box.'

'I know exactly what I'll do.'

He took the top envelope, contents printed in red, from the gas company.

He held it up in what he thought was a dramatic gesture.

He ripped it into four pieces and dropped them on to the table.

Then the electricity, then the water. He heard the squeal of shock from the sink. Then the builder's note. He went to work at his task with intense enthusiasm, as if it was sex with Hannah and the squeals hers. Then the credit-card notices of accrued interest. Then the bank's letters that referred him to amounts outstanding and the likely punitive outcome of that situation. The torn pages flaked on to the table.

Drama complete. Curtain down on theatricals. Methodically Jools picked up each piece of paper from the letters, statements and envelopes and clasped them in both hands. He went to the front door, opened it awkwardly, because he had no intention of leaving a paper trail behind him, and strode down the few feet of the front path.

At the wheelie-bin, he used his elbow to lift the lid and, into its mouth, he dropped what he thought of as junkmail, then let the lid fall back. He remembered what he had read, graffiti, on a London wall long ago: *There is no problem so big or complicated that it can't be run away from.*

He left Babs in the kitchen and Kathy with her music, and went to bed. His daughter was at the back of the house, deafened, his wife was in the kitchen, crying, and he would soon be asleep and past caring. End of problem. So simple.

'Go for it,' the voice murmured. 'Get it before they bring the kitchen stuff out – don't want it all covered with bloody food.'

The door of a darkened car opened quietly. Soft shoes scurried forward. A shadow skirted the light pool from a street-lamp. A wheelie-bin's lid was lifted and a hand groped down. Paper rustled as it was snatched up. The lid was eased back into place. A car door was opened and torn sheets of printed paper and pieces of brown envelope were dropped into a plastic bag. A vehicle drove out of the street. A pencil torch shone into the bag.

'Benny'll be well chuffed with this lot. Looks like we got his Crown Jewels.'

Christmas Day, 1936
Well, most certainly different from last year. Dad's not carved the goose and Mum's not dished up the spuds, but we're doing what we can.

It's not much.

No misunderstandings. I am not complaining. My decision to come here, and the same goes for Ralph and Daniel, but it is different. We are allowed no celebration. The political officer – he's Russian – says that Christmas is a festival for Fascists and that it has no place in our lives. He's a hard man (hard enough last week to shoot a deserter, an Italian, who had been brought back to our company: made him kneel and shot him with a revolver in the back of the neck, then went for his lunch – that hard) and we would not want to anger him. But Ralph said we had to do something. He tore down some *ivy off a tree and wove the leaves into a bit of a decoration, and that was our tree. Daniel – he is <u>wonderful</u> on the scrounge – found three apples, and we ended up giving them to each other, but Ralph's was rotten at the core.*

We could not – because the political officer would have heard us – sing carols, but we told each other about our last Christmas at home. At Ralph's there were servants and he's promised that next Christmas, if we've won and we're home, Daniel and I will be invited. (I wouldn't accept, of course, because I'll want to be with Mum, Dad and Enid.) But talking passed the time and made us feel better.

The best thing about today was that we were not under fire. God, tomorrow (Boxing Day) we will be. The Fascists are Catholics and they've observed a ceasefire since last midnight. Our artillery has not. We've lobbed shells on to them, but they haven't replied. They will, with interest, and it'll be awful tomorrow. We've heard them, from their trenches, singing hymns, and I had a turn on sentry in the morning and through a periscope one of the Germans made I saw the priests walking in the open, with full robes on, to their forward positions. They sang really well, which means it isn't the heathen Army of Africa opposite us right now.

Daniel – I said he was good on the scrounge – has hidden in our dug-out a half-bottle of wine. He took it a week ago from the political officer's bunker. We are going to drink it tonight, then bury the bottle. It's going to be our real Christmas treat, and the next treat – while we are drinking – will be to make a wish. We've talked about it, what we're going to wish.

I don't know whether the others will allow it, but I want to have two wishes for Christmas. <u>First</u>, I'm going to wish that never again will I have a big live rat run over my chest when I'm trying to sleep: they're so bold. Give them half a chance and they'll cuddle in your armpit for warmth. If they're on your face you can feel the claws on their feet, and they're fat because they live in no man's land and eat . . . (well, you know what they eat). <u>Second</u>, I'll wish we had proper uniforms. We have woolly caps, jerkins, breeches, long socks and boots that kill your feet, but that isn't sufficient to keep out the cold. (Last night, and half the week before, we all slept together, on the same palliasse, using all our blankets, and we were still cold.) Those are my wishes. <u>Daniel</u> says he's going to wish for a whole battalion of German girl volunteers to come into our section of the line and be alongside us. <u>Ralph</u>'s wish is that we all come through this and stay alive and unhurt – Daniel and I aren't sure whether he's allowed that as a wish.

I've too many wishes. I'd like to know that Mum, Dad and Enid are well.

Also, I'd like to hear from the Poetry Group: did their party go as well as it did last year and did they remember me and did anyone, because of me, read some Sassoon or Owen or Rosenberg? Rosenberg's poem, 'On Receiving News of the War', was the one I recited this morning to Ralph and Daniel – it was read last April at the group – and I said it to them: 'Red fangs have torn His face./God's blood is shed./He mourns from his lone place/His children dead.' Daniel told me that if the political officer heard that he would label me a Fascist and it would be down on my knees with a cocked revolver for company. I think Ralph was near to tears. Without them, their brother-hood, I don't know that I could survive. But no retreat is possible.

To retreat is to desert. To desert is to die.

I have to stop now because Daniel is digging under the palliasse for the bottle. Hurrah!

I find many confusions confront me. I have come to help the Spanish people achieve freedom and democracy. Alongside me, in this struggle, are Poles and Italians, Germans and Russians. More British are coming and Americans will soon join us. There are no Spanish fighters near us. (Perhaps they are in other sectors, but they are not alongside the International Brigades.) The only Spaniards I see are those in the trenches beyond the wire and no man's land, with their priests, and they are trying to kill me. Too much confusion for me to understand.

Soon Christmas will be finished, and their shelling will start again. I am too tired to be afraid and Daniel's wine will ensure we sleep. I wish Christmas lasted for ever, for a whole year.

'You have a moment, Banksy? In my office? Please.'

Banks turned, gazed at the inspector's smiling face. 'Of course. Be right up.'

He waited for the footsteps' retreat, then rolled his eyes and asked the armourer, 'What's he doing still here?'

'Been on the prowl, finding something to do. Look, he even did the ammunition dockets, checked them through. Must be a mid-life crisis . . . OK, sign here.'

He did, and heaved his bulletproof vest, his ballistics blanket, magazines and the Glock on to the counter. The armourer checked them and lifted them on to the racks behind. A line of men from Delta's team was behind him, but he might as well not have been there. If he had looked for signals in their faces as to why an inspector had hung around late into the evening, then asked for him, he would have failed to find them. It had been another session in the close art of ostracism, as if he was no longer a part of them. He'd done his job, made damn certain there could be no criticism of his work, but he had not been spoken to. He had sat in the back of the second escort vehicle and had read the diary while their Principal and his wife had had their Covent Garden evening. He'd thought it the most miserable bloody Christmas he'd ever heard of, and worse than anything Dickens had described. His own Christmases, since Mandy had gone, had been back at home with his mother and he'd never told her that he was at the top of the volunteers' list for working Christmas Eve and Boxing Day; but he had driven down to his mother for lunch and left when it was barely decent, enjoyed the empty roads, and had a packet of new handkerchiefs and a new shirt to show for it. He saw that the isolation clinging to him had been noted by his friend, the armourer, and there was anxiety, but no one could help him and, right now, after what had been said, he wanted no help. He would fight his own bloody wars.

He eased past the line of Delta men and no eye met his.

Banks went in search of the inspector in his office. Why – in US Marine Corps Vietnam-speak – would a Rear Echelon Mother Fucker have stayed late, then called him in? What did the REMF want of him? He knocked lightly.

'Ah, Banksy, good of you. Bit difficult this.'

'How can I help?'

'Is everything all right? I mean, I've eyes in my head. Are there problems in Delta?'

'Not that I know of.'

'Are you sure, Banksy, nothing you want to tell me of?'

'Can't think of anything.'

'What about the atmosphere in Delta, you and colleagues?'

'It's fine ... If you don't believe me, ask around and see what answers you get. Will that be all?'

'I will. Don't want any niggles in a good team. Thanks, Banksy, and safe home.'

He went out into the night. He was an intelligent man but too racked with exhaustion to recognize that deflecting the enquiries of the REMF, his inspector, was not clever. He walked briskly towards the station and the late train home to his bedsit where all the company he would have would be in the lined pages of a notebook, scrawled with pencil writing, each entry harder to read than the last. It was not clever because he had put himself on to a track and did not know where it would take him.

Chapter 6: Friday, Day 9

He thought the judge was watching him. He was tense. Sweat ran down the back of his neck. Jools Wright gnawed at the problem engulfing him.

The judge seemed to break away from his laborious writing down of key points of evidence and glance up. His eyes roved across the well of court eighteen, his concentration fractured and his frown spreading, then came to rest on Jools – not on Corenza, Deirdre or Baz.

The evidence droned on: Ollie Curtis's turn in the witness box where he had been all day, lying, twisting and evading. But Jools had heard little of the wriggling denials. His problem was larger, causing him to squirm in the plastic chair. Once, Peter had turned in his seat and said soundlessly – but lip-readable: 'Can't you sit still for five minutes?' He could not, and the problem loomed bigger ... Late-night shopping. He always went with Babs, after school finished on a Friday, to do the late-night shopping.

He tried to smile at Mr Justice Herbert, as if that would free him from the beady surveillance.

In the box, Ollie Curtis hadn't the stature of his brother, didn't create the same aura of intimidation but was still a formidable creature. It was a diabolical tissue of lies to suggest that two hand-guns had been brought by a woman, unidentified, to the shop's front door in a pram for him and his brother to retrieve from under a sleeping baby, then return to the same hiding-place when he and Ozzie had sprinted clear. He had been – injured innocence swam on his face – with his mother at the time of the robbery . . . Of course she could not come to court to testify: she was old, ill, and there was a doctor's certificate to prove it. Questions and answers wafted over Jools's head, because it was Friday, and Friday was late-night shopping, and there was the not-so-small problem of the increasingly imminent check-out.

'You state categorically, Mr Curtis, that you were not there?'

'Honest and truthful, I was not.'

Neither question nor answer was written down on Mr Justice Herbert's pad, but his eyeline was fixed on its target, and Jools's smile had failed to divert it.

The judge said, with studied resonance, 'I think we'll call it a day. Thank you, Mr Curtis. I have never believed that good justice is made when those before the courts are tired. You will be refreshed, Mr Curtis, by the weekend break before you resume your evidence on Monday morning . . . It has been a punishing week, not just for Mr Curtis but for all of us. There is something else I would like to say before we go our differing ways – in fact, to emphasize – and that is for the members of our jury . . .'

He paused. Jools stared back at him and the smile was frozen off his face. What's the old pedant up to? Recall of evidence was lost. The problem of late-night shopping was gone.

'We have been together a long time now and I am heartened by the commitment that you all, on our jury, have shown. It would be easy now for you, ladies and gentlemen, as we approach the final stages of the trial, to feel more relaxed about the strictures I have placed on you than you might have felt a month or two months ago. But, the guidance I gave you when we started these proceedings remains as important now as it was then. You might feel that a conversation with family or friends on the details of the case before you could not harm any of the participants. You would be wrong, members of the jury. I urge you most strongly not – I repeat, *not* – to discuss any aspect of the trial with any person who is not a colleague on the jury, and then only in the assured privacy of your jury room. Is that, Mr Foreman, understood by you and all of those with you?'

Their foreman, Rob, looked down the row beside him, then twisted to see behind him. Heads nodded. Bizarre, and bloody unnecessary, but the judge had not addressed his remarks to Rob, Dwayne, Fanny or Ettie, only to Jools. He jutted his chin, and could have shouted, 'Don't pick on me, friend. I know what's expected of me. I'm voting guilty as charged.' But didn't. Who was he going to talk to? Not much chance of him having a conversation with Babs while pushing the trolley at late-night shoppin , getting closer to the checkout . . . no bloody chance. Hardly going to be spieling through the evidence with Hannah – in bed, Saturday night, thank God – was he? Rob, the officious prat, bobbed his head and bobbed it again: all understood. It was because the end was in sight that the judge had raised it. Not going to be easy, when it was over, to go back into the groove with the little thugs of year nine, and the statistics of the grain harvest in the Midwest and the consequences of the melting polar icecap.

'That's it, then. Have a good weekend – but remember not to discuss these matters with any third party, with nobody. My father was on the Atlantic convoys in the Second World War and he told me of the poster on the gates at Liverpool docks. 'Loose Lips Sink Ships.' Never forgotten it. So, no "loose lips" because these are matters only for you.'

Jools filed out of court. He wished his colleagues well, then ran for the station. He did not look beside or behind him.

Now Benny Edwards was hands on and had taken responsibility.

Two other rubbish bins had been checked out, and one of the males on the jury had been followed to his parents' home. Then the father had come back and been seen to wear that white shirt with the discreet straps on it that meant he was a uniformed police-man and off duty. Needn't have bothered, because they had the target, the best one – maybe the only one.

That morning, Benny had pulled on the latex gloves and sifted through a treasure trove of bills, demands and statements. A bonanza moment in his career of nobbling, he reckoned.

While he had been reading through the financial mess that was the

life of Julian Wright, his photographer had been at work with a
discreet little digital job – but that was for later.

He was up close to what he called the 'Tango'. He was always
thorough and that was the basis of his reputation, which justified the
charges he made on clients. The Tango and the wife had been
through Fruit and Vegetables and were half-way down Cereals, and
he was four trolley lengths behind them. There were others of his
team in the coffee-shop beyond the checkouts, and another at the
main doors, so a box had been formed round the Tango. It was all
good, the way it should be done. Benny Edwards need not have been
there, up close, but it was his tactic to observe before he moved on
the approach run. This was confirmation, and he'd never reckoned
that what another guy told him had half the value of being there,
watching for himself and learning.

They had the right Tango, no question. The Tango gave them a
chance. Too many failures, too many convictions, and the reputation
he valued would slide. Too many jerks banged up in Belmarsh,
Whitemoor or Long Lartin, and the price he could charge went on
the slide. He had chosen well, could see it. The Tango's finances were
a disaster, and worse. She'd pick something off the shelf – last one
had been a branded cornflakes packet – and dump it into the trolley
that he pushed behind her. She'd go on, and the Tango would shove
it back on the shelf and take instead the supermarket's own product,
which might save twenty pence. Penny-pinching was good news,
because with just the two options – the carrot and the stick – there
looked to be a useful chance of making the carrot do the work. Less
messy than the stick. Because he was there, and tracking them in the
box, he reckoned – would have bet big money on it – that the Tango
would do the business.

They'd switched aisles. They were through Detergents, had done
bottom-of-the-range bread, had picked up only packets of sausages,
mince and burgers – what Benny Edwards wouldn't have fed
his dog on – from Meats, and they were at the start of the
Beverages/Alcohol section. Her eyes lingered on wines, Bulgarian
and the least expensive, and he'd seen but not been able to
hear the short, snapped exchange between the Tango and his
wife, and she hadn't put a bottle into the trolley. Then she'd marched
to the checkouts and joined a queue, leaving him to trail behind.

It was all for Ozzie and Ollie Curtis. Two bulky packages were nestling in the rafters of Benny Edwards's home: one held fifty thousand in fifties, and the other was half of that. It was all for Ozzie and Ollie's freedom. Well, they were a legend, a throwback to the past. Hadn't moved on from the times of the east London gangs – all that shit about hitting wages vans, bullion warehouses, banks *and* a jeweller's, if there was enough tasty stuff inside the safe. Benny Edwards didn't do conscience and he didn't do morals. He did drugs importers if they had the cash, up front, to pay him. The brothers, blaggers, were history. Just about everyone he dealt with had gone over to drugs, and he'd learned that the trade bred deceit and double-cross: the drug dealers were shites, they had no bloody *honour*. Funny thing, but that was what the brothers had, honour. But he doubted he could do more for them than get a hung jury, which would cost them a whole big mountain of money. Worse, drugs importers would grass up an associate, and would look for the security of sliding information on rivals to the police. No way the Curtis brothers would do down an associate to get leniency, and they'd never pass information to the Serious Crime Directorate. Honour was an old-world thing, and when he'd finished with the blaggers Benny Edwards doubted he'd ever meet it again.

Where he stood, he could see them, the Tango and the wife, at the checkout. The plastic bags were filled. The Tango was into his hip pocket, had the wallet in his hand and seemed to be wondering which of his cards to use. Chose one, it was swiped, and the girl shook her head. Took out a second, offered it, had it rejected. Back into the hip pocket and the cheque book was produced. Benny Edwards had seen the bank statements and didn't rate the Tango's chances. Which was when the wife intervened. She had her purse out of her bag, then a wad of notes in her fingers. He saw surprise splash on to the Tango's face, like the poor bastard hadn't known she had that money. He heard her say, loud enough to share with the queue, 'I went to my mum this morning, told her I'd married a tosser who couldn't earn a proper wage, was too lazy or too stupid.' He saw the Tango flinch, and no other shopper met his eye. God, that was out of order. The Tango was loaded with plastic bags and stormed towards the doors before she'd taken her small change.

They traipsed away from him towards a bus stop. He used his mobile and broke the box round them. The approach would be in the morning, when the wife had softened the Tango some more and made him pliant. His usual line, which he used when it was a carrot job, played on his lips: 'There are no consequences, no kick-backs. You do me a favour and I do you a favour, and we forget about it. I promise, it'll be like it never happened ... Except that the financial worry in your life is removed. Believe me, nothing will be different.' That was what Benny Edwards would say to the Tango and it was all true: nothing would be different.

In the first shower of London's evening, Ajaq walked the pavements. He cut across great squares and passed the seats of government and power. He went alongside the black-painted barriers of concrete that protected buildings from the approach of a car under their walls, a car that might have been low on its chassis under the weight of a half-tonne of fertilizer explosive. He was so far from his home, and so close to his blood. Great edifices towered over him. He passed policemen, made huge by the bulletproof vests under their top coats and noted their readiness to shoot: magazines loaded, a finger laid on a trigger guard, a machine pistol hung from the shoulders ... but they did not know him. They were at the mouth of an Underground station, watching the surge of the crowds that pitched down the steps. They were in doorways. They were behind the gates that shut off a cul-de-sac, and Ajaq knew it was the workplace of a great enemy, the Americans' lap-dog.

It was confirmation of the tactical decision he had already taken.

The centre of the city, where its authority lay, was hunkered down as if it awaited the inevitability of attack. Barricades and guns were its defence. He thought of it as the Green Zone, Baghdad, where the Americans lived with their allies and collaborators and where security was tightest. It amused him to walk among them, to feel the brush of bodies against his. There was, and Ajaq recognized it, a particular and peculiar thrill when he moved in the heartland of an enemy and was not known; he was merely a face in the crowd, anonymous.

The decision had been his and had been made four weeks before he had started out on his journey. It had not been queried by those who had created the organizational web in which he now crawled. The decision was that the protected city, its ministry buildings, its sprawled labyrinth of train tunnels, its guards and weapons should be ignored. He had chosen to strike where the forces of his enemy were weakest. He thought of an underbelly that was soft, where a knife could dig deep, and where panic would be greatest. The decision had been committed to a handwritten note, a fine nib fashioning the coded characters on two sides of a single sliver of cigarette paper, which had been taken by courier across frontiers and boundaries to the cave or the compound in the Tribal Areas where the leaders of the base existed. He had never met them. The Engineer had, but Muhammad Ajaq had not. No counter-command had been issued, and every aspect of their planning was effective, had earned his admiration. He assumed that those men, the leaders, would sit each evening with a battery-powered radio or television downloading the satellite and would flick the channels, listening for news of his success.

He went past the parliament building and a massive clock struck the hour. He came to a garden and passed into it through a gateway. He crunched along a gravel path and approached a floodlit statue of coal-black figures, who stood in submission but with dignity – as if they were beaten but not defeated; he read that they were *The Burghers of Calais*, and that the sculptor was Rodin, but he did not know what 'burghers' were or where Calais was. There was an image of pride about those men that stayed with him as he crossed the garden, came out on to the pavement and went past a great grey stone building where lights burned in every window. Two men came out of its swing-door entrance and stepped in front of him, which made him check his stride, but there was no apology that he was impeded and no acknowledgement of him – as if he did not exist.

'I tell you, Dickie, you don't know how lucky you are. It's going to get worse – couldn't be a better time to be getting out. Did you say a greenhouse?'

He heard them, took no note. What filled his mind was telling the Engineer – when he met him the next day – what he had learned and the sights he had seen.

They had confirmed his decision. Muhammad Ajaq started out on his lonely walk back to the hotel.

A table had been brought into the room and sheets of old newspaper were laid across it. On the newspaper he had placed what had been bought for him the previous evening from his list. Reaching him were the smells of cooking, not the scents of the Arab food with which he was familiar, but the odour of an Asian curry; he could eat it but would not enjoy it. That door was closed and the curtains of the room given him were pulled tight across.

In the centre of the table, across the middle of a fold in the newspaper, he had placed the artefact of his trade: the stack of explosive sticks that had been retrieved from the cupboard of a boat's kitchen. The slim, shiny detonators lay at the edge of the table. Between the sticks and the detonators and over the rest of the newspaper were what he would need for the construction of the device: a loose waistcoat of cotton fabric and straps cut from a towel, a packet of heavy needles and a reel of thick thread, big batteries for a flashlamp torch, coils of multi-coloured wire, a soldering iron, a paper bag of two-inch nails, another of carpet tacks, a small plastic sack of screws, washers, bolts and ball-bearings, and a button switch from the flex of a table light. He could have fashioned the device with greater intellectual skill, but thought it unnecessary.

In his own country, far away and behind him, he built devices of ever-increasing sophistication. He could booby-trap a dead body and cause it to explode when the medical crews came from the Shi'a hospital. He could use mercury tilt switches that would detonate a device in a car parked close to a barracks, and the vehicle would explode as troops opened its doors. He could place culvert bombs under a road and have an infrared beam flare across the tarmac to catch a Humvee or armoured personnel carrier. He could spend many hours at his work, if his target was an enemy explosive and ordnance disposal officer . . . or he could spend a minimum of time and still create havoc, chaos and fear. But with every creation, clever or simple, he followed a basic rule of survival and used differing techniques of wiring, positioning of detonators and loading of a vehicle or waistcoat. He left no repetitious signature. All that was constant in his work was the devastation in the aftermath.

The name given him by his father was Tariq, but to all with whom he fought he was the Engineer. He doubted that a photograph of his head and shoulders existed in the headquarters of the intelligence buildings at the airport, but there a ghost's image of him would exist. He loathed his enemy, and where he could find them, he killed them, and that would have created, in their air-conditioned suites, respect.

He came from the Triangle town of Fallujah.

His wife, three children, and his mother had perished in the rubble of the assault on Fallujah, and he had never seen or prayed at the rough, quickly dug graves in which they were buried. His father – insane from the bombing, shelling, shooting and grief – now lived in a world of devastated silence at the home of his brother; he had never visited him. He carried no photographs of that family, only the memory of them and his hatred of those who had killed them and broken his father.

In Iraq, alongside the graves of his family, there were many hundreds more; he and his hatred were responsible for them.

The Scorpion had asked him to travel far from his home. 'For what reason? Am I not more valuable here?' The Scorpion had spoken of the 'underbelly' and its softness. 'I accept it. I will go with you. The underbelly attracts me.' Why did it attract him? 'The town of Fallujah was an underbelly. The home of my wife, my children, my mother and father was an underbelly. They should learn what was done to us in their name. They should be hurt where they are soft.'

The hands that had laid out the items he would meld together in a killing device were thick and pudgy inside thin surgical gloves. He was in his forty-fourth year, was built like a bull, had rippling muscles. He smoked cigarettes and drank alcohol. He had not prayed since the deaths of his family, and before that only on the holiest of festivals to please his mother. He had fought in the Iranian war on the front of the Faw peninsula, had been in the humiliation of the retreat from Kuwait, and had reached the rank of major in a battalion of the Republican Guard, specializing in ordnance, when the Americans had launched, four years back, their campaign of Shock and Awe. Then his unit had dispersed in confusion. He had joined the fledgling insurgency and had met the Scorpion. He valued the day of their meeting, under the searching gaze of aircraft circling overhead. In a sewer ditch, with bombs falling and missiles, with death close, they had met ... The fingers matched the bulk of his body yet they were nimble and he could control their movement to the most subtle degree. The devices he made – if handled correctly – always worked, *always*, and many hundreds of graves, and more graves in the cemeteries of America, were filled as proof of his fingers' delicacy.

He would not see the underbelly target, he had no need to. When the youth with the swan on his chest walked to the target, Tariq – the Engineer of destruction – would be long gone, far from his work.

Bent over the waistcoat, grinning to himself, thinking of where the straps would be sewn, how much thread was necessary to hold the weight of the sticks, what length of wire would run from the batteries to the button switch, how easy to make the detonation for the boy, he heard the light rap at the closed door.

Concentrating, his mind filled with problems and solutions, he murmured, 'Wait – a moment.'

And he did not realize that he had spoken in Arabic.

The door opened. He felt a draught against his cheek. He saw the girl. Anger sprawled through him. 'Get the fuck out. Close the door.'

But she did not, was rooted, and her mouth was sagging open as if in shock. He could not hide what was laid out on newspaper across the table – the explosives, the detonators and what she had brought him.

'You never come in here. Never.'

She stammered, a tiny voice, that food was ready.

'And tell the rest of them. You, they, any of you *never* enter my room.'

She fled. The first of the tears had welled in her eyes – and she was gone. She hadn't closed the door. He went to it, kicked it viciously. Paint was dislodged by his toecap and flaked to the carpet. The door slammed. In a Triangle town or in Mosul or Salman Pak to the south, if a foot-soldier had come into his room and had seen the detail of his work, the Engineer would have shot him. Straight out into the yard, ankles kicked away, hair grabbed, pistol cocked and trigger pulled – shot dead. She, they, saw his face each time he emerged from the room allocated to him. He did not know them, there were too many of them – and they had not earned his trust.

For the first time since he had left all that was familiar to him – as he peeled off the gloves – he felt a sense of unease.

But he left the room, locked the door after him and went to the table. The girl, red-eyed, set a bowl of spice-scented curry before him and his mind drifted to the weight that the waistcoat would carry, the thinness of the shoulders and chest that would be inside it.

Ibrahim paced. He had not been out of the room for the whole of the day and into the evening. No explanation had been offered to him, not by the Leader, whom he had not seen since the huge hands had taken his fingers and held them with gentleness, and not by the fat one, Ramzi, who brought him food that was each time more foul than the last.

He had thought that by now – nine days since he had been chosen in the desert – he would be walking closer to God, in the company of those who were his brothers. The room had not been cleaned since he had come and the sign to tell staff not to disturb him hung outside on the door handle. He could only pace and pray. What comfort he could find, other than when he faced the window and prayed, was in the memory of the photographs in his room at home, on the far end of the Corniche in Jizan, of his eldest brother and his middle brother. Did they wait for him, beside God, in Paradise? Would he find them? His solitude strained the strength of his Faith. He heard laughter and shouting, a television's music, from the rooms above and below him; lavatories were flushed and water sprayed from shower heads. His eyes shut, he walked the number of strides on the carpet that the walls allowed . . . Would they know him?

When the building was quiet, and the street beyond the hotel's yard, the television was off and he had sunk, exhausted but dressed, on to the narrow bed, Ramzi came. 'You all right, friend? Of course you are, why wouldn't you be? We move on tomorrow to where . . . Well, you know. It's a nice place you're going to, pretty, and close to . . . You are all right, aren't you?'

'See the TV at lunchtime, the news? More bloody trouble, more heartache, more bombs in Iraq – you see it? If they hadn't screwed up in the Tora Bora, none of it would be going on now. I told them then, but they didn't want to know. Those days in Afghanistan were a window of opportunity, but they didn't snatch it – and, Christ, they're paying a price. I told them . . .'

The stool at the left end of the bar was George Marriot's. Only a brave man, or a total idiot, among the regulars would have claimed it on a Monday, Wednesday or Friday evening, when Gorgeous George stomped down from his home and came to the pub in the village that was half a dozen miles north of Luton. On GG's nights, even if the darts team was at full strength and playing at home, or the golf team had been lowering a few after a competition, and the bar heaved, that stool was never taken. It was his, where he drank whisky chasers and pints of ale.

'They had two choices, the Yanks had, didn't they? At Tora Bora, they could have left it to us, that's the Northern Alliance people who'd hired me, or they could have done the whole damn thing themselves. He was there, you see, Osama was. He was all ready for picking off. My people and me, we could have done it – maybe even the Yanks on their own could have. Osama was bottled up. What did the Yanks do? Well, worst of two worlds. We had to wait while they took their time and lifted a block force in. Too long hanging about and Osama broke the trap. Typical Yanks. We were all itching to go, but the Yanks wouldn't have it, not till they were ready. Yank trouble was that they wouldn't take casualties. And Osama was long gone by the time they'd put their act together. If we'd had him then, God, wouldn't life be different?'

Some in the pub, particularly any with the misfortune to be within earshot of the stool, thought of Gorgeous George as sad; to others he was a 'loony'; to most he was the Rose and Crown's resident five-star bore. Many would have claimed to know by heart the story of the failed Tora Bora operation, and the net through which Osama bin Laden had slipped to safety across the Pakistan border – and he had been a freelancer and a bounty-hunter, the CIA had loved him, the British spooks had called him a genius of a guerrilla fighter, and he'd been up the mountains with his tribesmen within a spit of Osama, but the Yanks hadn't let him do the business until they'd put their own men, Special Forces and 101st Airborne Division troops, into the block position.

'Fierce country, you see. Mountain precipices that were razor sharp. Total cover so's you couldn't see the Al Qaeda fighters till you were damn near standing on them. Worse than anything we'd had in Oman. My people, me – and I wasn't a spring chicken, was forty-seven then – we could have hacked it, but we had to wait for the

124

Yanks . . . You know the 101st Airborne? Well, they couldn't handle the ground. They couldn't walk in there like we did. Had to have the CH-47 choppers lift them in when they finally moved. Where's the surprise with that? It was criminal letting Osama get clear. I said to a colonel of the 101st that we were up for it, my tribesmen and me – wouldn't have it. Had to be Yanks that got the big man's head. So what happened? Nobody got him. The Yanks told us that if we moved before they gave the say-so they'd bomb us. At that time, I'm telling you, we weren't more than a day's hike from the cave where Osama was holed up. Bloody wicked, and look at the consequences.'

No one in the saloon bar of the Rose and Crown believed a word of it. The tales dripped over the regulars' heads – all a fantasy, of course, but harmless. The general opinion was, most likely, he'd not been south of Bognor Regis. He was humoured, and he did no harm other than bend ears, was as much a part of the fabric as the horse brasses on the walls.

'Everything that happens today, these kids blowing themselves up – the suicide people – it comes from me and my tribesmen not being allowed forward in the Tora Bora. I doubt Osama was more than four miles from us – a day's hike in that country, if you're fit. We'd have cut his head off. It would have been close-quarters fighting, rock to rock, enemy at fifteen paces, but we'd've had him and sawn off his head. You kill a snake by cutting off its head . . . Suppose I'd better be gone, or Sister will be fretting.'

He slid off the stool and braced his weight on the surgical sticks. The crowd parted for him and he hobbled out. When GG, or Gorgeous George, or George Marriot, had first arrived in the village, moved in with his sister in the last cottage on the Hexton Road, come to the pub and taken the stool, they'd seen how badly he walked. Even with the aid of the sticks, his progress was painful to watch. Many had offered to drive him home and been ferociously refused. It would take him the best part of an hour, in the moon's light or in rain, defiantly edging along the road with his sticks, to reach his sister and the little two-bedroom cottage, with roses on the wall, that was their home.

Always, when he stood in the door, the landlord would shout across the bar crowd, 'Safe home, GG. See you next week.'

*

'Would you like to take a chair, Banksy?'

But David Banks was wary. To be called in on successive evenings by the REMF, his inspector, broke the pattern of life in protection. He shook his head, didn't care if that wasn't the polite response. And he wouldn't be calling the inspector by his given name, Phil, which was usual. He stood by the door and was trying to puzzle out why, late on a Friday evening and Delta just coming off a hotel run with a Principal, the Rear Echelon Mother Fucker didn't have a home of his own to go to.

'Please yourself, Banksy. You remember our little chat last night?'

He lied, but casually, 'Vaguely, sir.'

'Then I'll refresh your memory. I asked you if the atmosphere was good on Delta. You said it was fine. You went on that if I wasn't satisfied with that answer I should ask around, speak to the others. You remember that?'

'I do now, sir.'

'Well, I did just that.' There was the earnestness that was well practised in a veteran of policy meetings. It itched correctness. 'Banksy, I value *esprit* in a team.'

'Don't we all, sir?'

'A close team works well, Banksy. A divided team does not.'

'Sir, you won't find me arguing with you.'

He was, at heart, a country boy, from the border farmlands where the counties of Somerset and Wiltshire joined. The spring of his childhood had been happiness, and every summer evening and every day of the school holidays he had ridden with his father in the tractor's or the combine's cab.

'Right, I'll spell it out from what I can tell. I understand that Delta is *not* working well – and, most certainly, is divided.'

He said quietly, but with flint hardness, 'I'd say you've been listening to gossip, sir, ill-informed gossip.'

'I'm being patient, Banksy, trying to be reasonable – and you playing the dumb bugger isn't helping. All right, all right, you can have it straight. I'm told you're on the outside of your team following your striking of a colleague, a blow that drew blood. I cannot think of much that is more serious than that.'

'You won't find me snitching, sir – and you shouldn't believe everything you hear.'

A hand slapped on to the desk. 'That's offensive, Banksy, bloody rude and unworthy of you. You struck a colleague and, as a result, blood was spilled. That's what I hear.'

'I have no comment to make, sir, *except* that what you may have been told is a parody of the truth.'

He had been with his father, on a November weekend, ploughing a field into which wheat would be sown. He hadn't noticed the pain that creased Henry Banks's face, had only been alerted by his last little gasp as the tractor had slewed off course. At nine he'd known how to halt it – and that his father was gone. He'd run a half-mile across sodden fields, mud caking on his boots, to the nearest farm-house and had made the call for an ambulance, then gone back to the tractor and sat holding his father's hand till the crew had come. When his father's corpse had been taken away, he had walked two miles home, and had told his mother when she came back from work. It was the day he never spoke of, but it was inside him and always with him. It had shaped him.

'In denial, is what you are. You disappoint me, Banksy. I admit it, I'm surprised at your response. Well, I've put a deal of work into this. I have better places, right now, to be than here – at this God-awful hour – with you playing semantics.'

'Then, sir, why don't you go home?'

'Banksy, you're trying me . . .' Again the smile was used, but was not sufficient to disguise growing frustration. 'There was some horseplay in the canteen, some mucking about. You lost your temper, which is not something to be expected of an AFO. An Authorized Firearms Officer is supposed to have emotions, sudden anger attacks, well buckled down and under complete control. I'm looking at a failure on your part, and the failure led you to strike a colleague on the ear, and hard enough for it to bleed. True or false?'

His father had been a tenant, and their farmhouse had been reclaimed by the landlord. His mother had moved into a bungalow near the town of Frome. Mother and son lived off a small annuity and from her wages as a counter-staff librarian. He had applied to join the Metropolitan Police the day after he had finished school, a modest achiever but dogged in carrying the academic workload. London was about as far as it was possible to get from the fields,

127

hedgerows and wildlife around him where the heart-attack had taken his father.

'With respect, sir, you were not there. You are ignorant of what happened and why.' He spoke as if to a child who had strayed far from his remit. 'I suggest that the matter is best left alone, and that you go home.'

'At this precise moment you are outside the culture of the team. The team is united against you by a count of eleven to one, and the one is you. Don't interrupt me and don't come up with another stonewall of what I'm saying. If you want it in your face I'll put it there. You're looking at the edge of a precipice. I have negotiated—'

In shock that was genuine and not play-acted, he rasped, 'You've *what*, sir?'

'I have negotiated – hear me out – what seems to me to be the best solution to a difficulty that has now become unacceptable. I feel that I have been rewarded with a generous response from the rest, the majority, of the team, and they have given me categoric assurances on how the curtain can be brought down on this piece of silliness. It is silliness, Banksy, and I will not tolerate anything as daft as this affecting the work of the team, now or ever. I have their agreement.'

That experience, death brought close to a child, had left him with a legacy of remoteness. He had nurtured, as a uniformed constable in west London and then as a detective constable in the south-west of the capital, the ability not to share his inner thoughts. The investigation of burglaries and domestic violence was not adequate to hold his attention: he had applied for and been transferred into SO19, the firearms unit. His heritage from his father was the ability to handle a gun: from the age of six he had walked the fields with a single-barrel .410 shotgun and his spaniel. He had thought to find in the unit something challenging, exciting, dramatic and worthwhile, and still sought the Grail.

'I'm pleased to hear that, sir.' He had narrowed his eyes, and respect for rank was lost in the night. There was a hitch of insolence in his voice.

'It's not going to take much. In private, to the members of Delta only, you will put this matter behind you with a straightforward general apology. Then, to the colleague you struck in an unlikely moment of temper, you will make a specific apology – and that's the end of it. You should do that in the morning and turn a new leaf. Not bad, eh? An end to it.'

His studied gesture of contradiction was a slow shake of the head. 'If I have nothing to apologize for then I cannot, with any sincerity, apologize.'

'That's not what I'm looking to hear, Banksy.' The palms were clapped together, better to make the point.

'It's me that's owed the apology.'

It was his habit, guarding the privacy of his thoughts, to remain on the fringe of any group, and it could not be hidden from those he worked with that he did not share their enthusiasm for the fellowship of belonging. If he socialized he seldom drank. If there were off-duty recreations – sea-angling, a trip in a cabin on the London Eye, a theatre visit with tickets courtesy of the show's management – he would decline. If he had no conversation to contribute, he did not speak . . . But David Banks was as good at his job as any in the team. That could not be gainsaid.

'Right, right . . . I won't have it said that I didn't try. I've busted my bollocks on this one. I told you that you were looking at the edge of a precipice, and I'm saying that the step back for you is an apology – actually two, one general and one specific.' The desk's papers were abruptly shuffled together, then dumped in a drawer: meeting concluded, evening wasted. Bitter . . . 'So, for the record, are you going over that cliff face? Are you refusing to apologize?'

'When it's not my call – just to keep the waters calm – I do not apologize.'

The chair was pushed back. A snarl tinged the voice. 'Your head, Banksy, not mine. You that's going into free-fall, not me. I've tried very hard to be reasonable and adult. It was just some damn notebook, wasn't it? A bit of larking around, what's the damage in that? But you're on your high horse because somebody picked up your notebook in fun, harmless fun. What's so special?'

It was in his pocket, the right-hand pocket of his suit jacket. The notebook gave extra weight to the pocket and with it were coins and a couple of quartz pebbles he had picked out from the shingle on Brighton beach at last year's political conference. The weight of the money and the pebbles, augmented by the notebook, would make it easier to throw back the jacket's material if he had to reach for the

Glock in its pancake holster. The notebook, the testament of Cecil Darke, was more a part of him than the pistol in its holster.

'You weren't there, sir.'

He stood and glowered across the cleared surface of his desk. 'I'll tell you what you have – and it's about as damaging to a copper's career as anything gets. You have, Banksy, an attitude problem.'

'If you say so, sir.'

A cupboard was opened, an overcoat retrieved, and a briefcase picked up. 'Just like that, have to have the last word. It's a bad, *bad*, attitude problem – and don't come running to me when you feel the consequences of it.'

'Good night, sir, and thank you for your time.' He turned and walked to the door.

A final volley, a fusillade of bullets, as if they were on automatic, was aimed at his back. 'I gather you gave a defence, a strident one, to the cult of a foreign suicide-bomber. A suicide-bomber, if you didn't know it, is our top-of-the-tower enemy. I hear you defended them: "brave and principled", yes? They are scum, and if they come where we can hit them, we bloody well will. You're out of line and out of kilter, Banksy. There might be just a half-second to decide whether to shoot, but not a half-second to have a bloody seminar on "brave and principled". I didn't want to say that but it's what the rest of Delta team thinks. You may not be up for it, dropping the scum in his tracks. Get out.'

Banks closed the door silently after him. In the movement his jacket flapped on his hip where the holster was, and he felt the added weight in his pocket of the notebook. He thought that he had stood the corner of his great-uncle, and had had no option but to do so.

'I've only one question, Joe, and I'll listen to your answer, whether it takes two minutes or two hours. Is this hard information or gut instinct? Convince me it's hard and you can be guaranteed that I'll push it to the desks of serious customers with all the influence I have. Tell me.'

The intelligence officer, based at the British embassy in Riyadh, had been in-country only four months. Joe Hegner had not met him, but then, Joe forswore the fruit-cocktail circuit of diplomatic receptions. And the tone of the man, Simon Dunkley, suggested a polite indulgence towards a 'cousin' from a sister service – as if the Bureau agent's reputation was not known to him. It happened often enough. In Iraq, one week in four, or in Riyadh for three weeks in four, he was familiar with the sensation of being unknown and unproven. The Briton drove, rare for an expatriate and probably unwise, but it was at Joe's suggestion that he should be picked up at his embassy's outer gates, and he thought they headed in the darkness for the desert sands: he had asked for the air-conditioning to be switched off, and had felt for the window button. Now the wind raked his cheeks, which gave him pleasure.

'I deal with the world of the young men and women who seek to attack our civilization by the sacrifice of their lives. The suicide-bomber is, believe me, the most efficient weapon you can dream of. More valuable than a bomb from an aircraft, which can be affected if darkness or low cloud covers the target, more accurate than an artillery shell, where the strength of the wind or the density of the humidity can alter its trajectory path while in flight. He or she can go right to the core of the target. The accuracy in the delivery of the explosion by a suicide-bomber cannot be bettered.

'If I talk to you of the devastation made by suicide-bombers against the state of Israel in the last several years, it is to remind you of the equivalent death toll – *per capita* of population – that your country would have suffered and mine. Imagine it, ten thousand of your citizens dead, and forty thousand Americans. In Iraq it is many times worse. The bombings are not a strategic use of weapons, but in the tactical field they have massive impact. Maybe you were in London twenty months ago, maybe you know a little of the chaos. They are not a danger to the stability and survival of the state, yours or mine, but their effect on the national psyche and economy are incalculable – and we don't know of any protection against this threat other than the vigilance of law enforcement and gathered intelligence.

'The experience you have had in Britain came from inside. That, oddly enough, can be dealt with more easily. The probability is that links will be found with those providing safe-houses and supplying the explosives, and that the network's cell will be dismantled. I can accept the argument. Intelligence will flow from the investigation and the gate-keepers in local mosques will be identified on the back of the discovery of the bombers' backgrounds. It's slow and painstaking, but evidential routes are uncovered that will lead inevitably, I promise it, to the destruction of the cells. That is what you have had, and I consider you fortunate because then you have the possibility to cut with scalpel knives into the mind of your attacker.

'What is worse? Far worse? It is when there is no mind to saw into. If the bomber is foreign you cannot so easily explore the nucleus of the cell structure that facilitates his act. He materializes from that familiar "clear blue sky" and, with detonation, he returns there – and nobody knows a thing. Understand me. He has never been in your gaols, where his recruitment can be identified; he has never been in your mosques or cultural centres, again where traces will have been left; he has never been, younger, in street protests where he might have been photographed and where group leaders have been seen. He comes from nowhere – all right, that is *somewhere*, but beyond your reach. If you knew him you could raise the walls around him – but you don't so you can't.

'Already, in your country, the trauma of Seven-Seven has passed and I'll bet your security services' guard has slipped. You're vulnerable again, because memories are short. Of course you have paid agents – informers – scattered in the mosques, and all meetings of the firebrands are monitored, but they will not deliver you the foreigner. He uses links that are beyond your sight. If, in Iraq, the suicide-bombers were home-grown the problem would have been cauterized by now. They aren't. They come across the international frontiers.

'The route used most frequently into Iraq is from Syria and their nexus point is Damascus, but plenty come over the Saudi frontier. My own injury was caused by a boy, barely over twenty-one, from a good and respectable Saudi family. Now the Saudi chain, and my work is to monitor it, is controlled by one man. I don't know his name or his face, but it's like he's a street trader and the melons, apricots, peaches and dates arrive on his stall . . . What I have, right now, is the scent on him. I call him, because it fits, the Twentyman.

'So, here we stand. I caught the scent of the Twentyman. I have a boy whose family thought he was in the Yemen visiting family, but was in reality boarding a European flight out of King Khalid International. Ibrahim Hussein is twenty-one years old and a promising student of medicine. He is not with his relatives but is heading for Europe where he has no friends, no contacts, no family. What he's got is sibling guilt – two brothers dead in Afghanistan – one killed by the Soviet forces, and one by our boys. I have his picture for you.

'If I were a betting man, I'd bet the ranch that Ibrahim Hussein, only surviving son of an electrical-goods retailer in Asir Province, has journeyed to Europe with the sole intention of killing himself in a public place. Southern Europe – Spain, Portugal, Italy, Greece – isn't a target for a flight into Amsterdam. In the north of the continent, on the mainland, there is most likely a "covenant of protection" – France, Belgium, Holland and Germany have, in differing degrees, opposed the coalition intervention in Iraq, which leaves only the conveniently placed United Kingdom where neither "covenant" nor "protection" exists. I hope you're following me.

'I've got a gnawing feeling in my gut. The Twentyman operates out of Saudi and concerns himself only with attacks of the greatest ferocity. A boy has left the Kingdom and is now within spitting distance of your country. My gut tells me there is a mix of *hard fact* and *hunch*. I can't divide 'em, or weigh their different parts. To me, they run together. But the "hard fact" is that the boy has travelled. "Hunch" is that he will die in your country and take as many as he can with him, himself to Paradise and them to wherever unbelievers end up. In the opinion of Joe Hegner, your society is threatened. Now, you are perfectly entitled to pull the vehicle over, turn it around, drive back, drop me at the embassy gate and do nothing.'

The car bumped on to the hard shoulder, turned, then sped back towards the city.

Late into that Friday night, as the end of the holy day approached, the officer of the Secret Intelligence Service sat in his protected office, behind steel-plated doors and blast-proof windows, and fashioned the signal he would send to London . . . and he reflected on the prematurely aged, small, dumpy man, with the drawled red-neck accent, who peddled his theory of catastrophe. Travelling at night, glorying in the blast of sand-laden air on his face, his eyes hidden by tinted glasses, the stick always in his hand and slotted against his

knee, the man had offered Simon Dunkley what was only a hunch –
but so believable.

He was going far out on a limb. He imagined the reaction to his
signal: chaos. Then the enquiries: new on station, wasn't he? Had he
the experience to assess the supposed intelligence? No bloody option
but to send what was another agent's, another national's, *hunch* . . . It
went to code, was transmitted. For a long time he stared into the
night and could not lose sight of his source. Then the call-backs
started.

To each of them, Simon Dunkley had the same answer: 'I have sent
what I have been told but, personally, I'd rest my life in Joe Hegner's
hands. It's the man he is.'

Chapter 7: Saturday, Day 10

The phone rang. Spread across the kitchen table, among the coffee mugs, toast crumbs and the plate on which he had been served scrambled egg and grilled tomatoes, were the brochures. With his breakfast, Anne had been feeding her husband on holidays and the choice was Dickie's. He could plump for an early-season Mediterranean cruise, last-minute booking and therefore at a cut-rate price, or a railway journey to the Swiss Alps, or a boat trip up the Rhône with excursions to vineyards. But the phone yelled to be answered and he saw irritation on his wife's forehead. Under duress, he was looking at the train trip to the mountains. She beat him to it and Naylor was only half out of his chair by the time she was at the door and heading for the hall table. She'd said that as soon as he had erected the flat-pack greenhouse, and put in the tomato plants – she had already arranged for Mrs Sandham next door to water them – they should be off to the Mediterranean, Switzerland or France.

The ringing had stopped.

Did he care which it was? Not a great deal. He wasn't good on holidays. Whether it was Bournemouth, Bruges or Bordeaux, he would do the tramping, the galleries and museums, then buy a newspaper and, back in the hotel room or cabin, he'd flick for the running news channel on the television, and the books he'd brought stayed unread. She told him each time they went that he only lightened up when they were travelling with home as the destination, and work the next Monday morning.

She was at the door. 'It's Penny, doing night duty. She wants to speak. I said she'd caught us just before we went out – she said she needs to talk to you.'

She stood aside, arms akimbo, hands on hips, her familiar gesture of annoyance.

He smiled as if helpless. 'On a Saturday morning – funny, that.'

Naylor went to the phone, paused and looked down at the receiver. It lay off the cradle and on the *Yellow Pages*. He hesitated, then lifted it. 'Dickie here – good morning, Penny.'

From Riverside Villas, it was not a secure line to 47 Kennedy Avenue in Worcester Park. Guardedly, he was told of a signal that had come across the river from the 'Sister' crowd, and that it had created 'something of a flap'.

'Who's in?' he asked.

'All the minor bosses, and the major boss is on stand-by and might be in by mid-morning. From what I can see, Dickie, it's a big, big flap.'

'And is it ours?'

'Yes. It's what we do.'

'Is Mary in?'

'Been here an hour. She said it wasn't necessary to spoil your weekend, it being the last. Now she's in a meeting, and I thought it right to call you. I wouldn't have bothered you but nobody's walking, everybody's running.'

'I'll be straight there,' he said.

Back at the kitchen door he offered a curt apology to Anne. What was she supposed to do? Go to the travel agent on her own? She should. And book? Whichever option she preferred. He was on the stairs when he heard her angry hiss: 'Daddy never went in at weekends. What do they want you for when you're virtually out of the door? Daddy would have told them to go jump.' He thought, reaching the landing, that only if he were blessed would he never again hear of her father. In their bedroom, he dragged a suit out of the wardrobe, a work shirt and tie from a drawer. His black London shoes were under a chair. He stripped off his Saturday clothes and dressed again.

Back in the hall, unhooking his coat from the stand, he called, to the kitchen, 'I don't know when I'll be back.'

'How much do I spend?'

He grinned cheerfully, 'As much as you can lay your hands on. Splash out, why don't you?'

Naylor was gone. A brisk stride down Kennedy Avenue, as much of a shambling run along the main road's pavement as his sixty-five years permitted, then a scramble up the steps at the station.

On the train, he sat sandwiched in a football team of teenagers with their bags restricting his leg room. Of course he would never be free of her father. Naylor had been a junior inspector in the colonial police and serving in the Trucial States in the early 1960s, transferred to Aden when internal security had collapsed and been seconded to the RAF's police investigation branch. She had been a secretary at Government House. They'd met at a drinks party. Rather unpleasant, but he'd done the right thing – she'd told him, two and a half months after a late-night swim session on Gold Mohur beach, that she was pregnant, and they'd married in the main salon of the Residence. A month later she'd said that she'd got her dates wrong and that no sprog was on the way. No sprog had been on the way since.

Aden had ended and Government House had been abandoned to the apparatchiks of the National Liberation Front; the RAF and he had flown home. The dust had not gathered under his feet. Daddy, once of the Palestine Police, was now a senior MI5 officer with an empire at Leconfield House and had slipped the word that his son-in-law was a 'good sort and reliable', which had been more than enough for his recruitment into the Security Service. He was not privy to whether he had been a disappointment to Daddy or not but the introduction had ensured his employment for thirty-nine years, and he was grudgingly grateful for it. It gave him, and had done since he joined, a thrill to work for an organization charged with the Defence of the Realm, to see the innocent and ignorant around him and know that he – anonymous and unnoticed – was charged with their safety. God, he would miss it.

It had taken Dickie Naylor an hour and three minutes to make the seamless transition from domesticity to his professional workplace.

If he had been under oath and cross-examined, he would have sworn that the face of Mary Reakes fell as he swept into the outer office – she would have known that treason was abroad, and he'd been telephoned. Penny, the guilty one, had her face close to her screen and seemed to hide behind it – she'd earned, at the very least, a box of chocolates. He would make his point and give not a damn if he verged on rudeness.

'So that everybody understands, from this coming Friday evening I will not be called in if the heavens open. Up to this coming Friday evening, while I am charged with the running of this section, I have responsibilities and will exercise them. So, please, Mary, would you bring me up to speed?'

It was done with reluctance, but he was handed the digest of the signal that had come across the Thames from the sisters at Vauxhall Bridge Cross. He read it. He thought that *at last* something meaningful was before his eyes. He read the name of Ibrahim Hussein, medical student and citizen of Saudi Arabia, then his movements. Suddenly the final days had purpose, and he was not ashamed of his excitement. As he held the signal his hands trembled. He studied the photograph of an open, pleasant face. Then a winnow of fear: would the matter run beyond the stretch of the coming week at the end of which his swipe card would be taken from him? There was a reference to the Twentyman, then the signal's two bottom lines: 'The information given is a *hunch*, no more than guesswork, but the source (Josiah Hegner, FBI agent/Riyadh) has unique and personal experience in his field.'

He said, 'Right, let's go to work.'

In his office he pushed the buttons and his screen lit; the box engine ground to life. He looked up. She was gazing into the cubicle, embedded in thought.

'What has carried you away, Mary, and where to?' he called to her ... The positioning of her new desk, the placing of the new filing safes, whether to go with magnolia, peach or ochre on the walls.

'Just, Dickie, that it's such a strange code name for an enemy, and I haven't an idea what it means – the one Hegner calls the Twentyman.'

He walked briskly. There was no rain and a pleasant, cool sunshine played on his face. It was because of a British boy from the city of

Leicester, to the north, that Ajaq had gone early that morning to the coach station close to the Victoria terminus, had bought the ticket and boarded the bus to the town of Bedford. That boy had been with him for a night and a half-day, four weeks back, after being collected at the market point along the frontier with the Kingdom. A few hours earlier, the courier had come back from the mountains of the Tribal Areas and had delivered the detail of instructions as to how he should travel from Iraq to the place from which he should launch this attack of importance. He had stripped that boy's mind and memories of anything that might be of use, the siting of cameras and the levels of surveillance, and had decided then that the closest observation was on trains and on the capital's underground railway. Because of what he had learned from the boy he had used the bus network, first for a long-distance coach, then for the connection – painfully slow – to the village. After that night and half-day, when he had leached what he thought significant from the boy, Ajaq had sent him on his way, towards a Shi'a district of Baghdad, with four kilos of military explosive under his loose robe.

He had talked of the matter with his friend, and the Engineer had scowled drily at what was asked of him, and the device was remotely controlled. The boy might have frozen at the moment of detonating the device against his chest, or panicked at the sight of the security men round the recruits' queue outside the police station, might have remembered a girlfriend or a mother, might have sweated too much; it was not possible, after what he had asked the boy with his incessant questions, that a bomber should fail, be captured, then interrogated. The Engineer had killed him, from a vantage-point two hundred metres away, by sending a dialled electronic signal to the mobile phone encased in the bomb against the boy's chest. Twenty-two dead in the queue and, more importantly, the knowledge of travel inside the enemy's territory gained.

From the village bus shelter, with his bag hitched on his shoulder, he had followed directions and gone past shops and small businesses, a house used by a dentist, another by accountants, and fine homes. Then he had hit open road. A small pink-painted cottage, with rose briars clambering on the walls but not yet in flower, was the final building in the village, and a man shuffled on the grass on hospital sticks but did not see him. There were flat fields on his left and a hill with bare-branched trees to his right. Cars sped past and did not slow because he was unremarkable ... as unremarkable when he walked away from the village as Muhammad Ajaq, the Scorpion, when he moved in the crowds of the Triangle's towns. How many times had he been through the roadblocks of the Americans, his face disguised and his papers doctored? So many times. Then his demeanour was humble and filled with respect for the soldiers.

He saw grazing cattle. He saw a tractor far away in a field and thought it planted seed or scattered fertilizer. He saw peace that was total and without danger. And in the middle of that peace he saw the small, low, white-painted building, and turned down the lane. There was a sign: Oakdene Cottage.

Mud was splashed on his trouser ankles and puddles soaked his shoes. He approached the cottage, then saw movement at a window. He came to a wooden gate, straightened his shoulders and lengthened his stride so that, from the beginning, he assumed an image of authority. Where he fought, Ajaq would have had a weapon. His authority, there, would have been backed by a loaded rifle or pistol, or by a knife sharpened on a stone, and by the reputation of his name – the Scorpion. Here, in a cottage in the English countryside, that authority would rest on his bearing and in his eyes, and from the respect his voice demanded.

The door opened in front of him. The Engineer greeted him.

They hugged as if it had been weeks, not hours, that they had been separated.

He was not led inside, where shadows hovered, but was walked into the garden, the Engineer's arm in his. They went to a corner where the hedge was high and they were hidden from the farmhouse across the fields.

His head flicked towards the window. He knew that, there, they would be watching. 'How do you rate them?'

'They are both shit and satisfactory.'

'How are they satisfactory?'

'What they were asked to provide was provided. I can build it and I have started on it.'

'How are they shit?'

'So soft, with no hardness, and they talk. All the time they talk ...

I tell you, I trust none of them. The girl cooks well but she and all of them are inquisitive. They believe themselves to be important. You should whip them.'

'What else?'

'I feel this place is a trap. It is like, in my mind, a trap we would place on the banks of the Euphrates, if we had chickens or ducks, to take a fox. If we trap a fox, we bludgeon it. I am not comfortable here, or with them.'

'You prefer home where there are many traps.'

'I think only of home and – God willing – my return.'

He punched the bulk of the Engineer's arm. He went inside, stooped under low beams and checked the rooms – his, the Engineer's, the girl's, and the room that was still empty. He saw the air-beds spread across the floor of the largest bedroom. Then he called them together, using the staccato voice of command. One, who seemed the youngest, with great thick spectacles on his nose and a clear-skinned face, said that it was time for his second prayer of the day, and could they wait until he had knelt and faced the Holy City?

Ajaq said, 'The war does not wait, and I do not wait. You want the opportunity to pray, then fuck off away from here and go back to your mother. Suckle her milk and pray. You pray when I give you the opportunity. First, you must learn obedience. Nothing that I say to you is for debate. I am to be obeyed. Where I come from, if a man or a woman fails me I kill them. I may kill them with my hand and break their neck. I may kill them with a knife so that their blood runs in the sand. I may kill them with a shot that disintegrates their skull. For disobedience, for the ignoring of my instructions, I kill. You may believe yourselves to be of importance, to be persons of significance. Then you are wrong. You do not have the importance of a single bullet. The desert sand I scoop up with my hand and use to wipe my arse, each grain of it has more importance than any of you. If you show vanity, I will beat you, and if I beat you, you will live in pain for many days. Remember it, you obey me. Do you have questions?'

There were none. The silence clung round him in the room. He looked into each of their faces, but none dared meet his gaze. He thought that the girl in the T-shirt and jeans had a good body but the scar spoiled her.

He went to a comfortable chair, sat and rested, and he waited for the last of them to come – the escort and the Threatened Swan. Muhammad Ajaq slept. He dreamed of blood and wire, the whine of a ricochet and the clatter of a machine-gun, the vivid pure light of the exploding belt and the charcoal grey cloud that followed it. He slept deeply.

It was beyond the limits of her experience and she did not know how to respond.

They had been in the kitchen and Faria was at the sink, washing plates and bowls, when the sound of the car came labouring towards the cottage. None of them – Khalid the driver, Syed the watcher or Jamal the recce man – had helped her, or offered to dry what she rinsed. The washing-machine had been churning with their clothes when the first murmur of the car had been heard. She had put her own underwear and tight T-shirts in with their jeans, socks, sweat-shirts and boxers. Later she would carry the damp load into the garden and hang it out. The strength of the sun and the breeze would dry it, and she did not care whether the men were offended by the sight of her flimsy white garments against theirs.

He seemed so small and vulnerable.

They had been in the kitchen, the quiet settled on them, since the lashing they had been given in the living room – and through the shut door came the gentle snore of a man at peace. The man who had built the bomb was in his room and there had been the sound of the door locking from the inside. What had made the lashing more terrifying was that the voice had never been raised. The intimidation, threats, had been spoken calmly and each of them, while they were battered, had cringed forward to hear him better. Faria understood it: they were in his control, doll figures held in the rough palm of his hand, and all could be crushed if he closed his fist.

He seemed to look round him, and across their faces, to measure their mood, then gave a smile of deep, genuine warmth.

On hearing the car, they had spilled out of the kitchen. The noise from the opening and shutting of doors, the slamming of the car's, had woken the man in the chair and he had started up with violence in his movement. His hand had snatched at the air above his lap – as if a weapon should have been there while he slept. Faria had seen, then, a flicker of annoyance on the man's features – as if he had

142

betrayed himself. It was gone and the calm of authority bathed him.

Ramzi, the thug, was behind the boy. All of them, from the kitchen, had formed a crescent in front of him, but the boy looked past them to the chair, and the face there had softened and was unrecognizable from that of the beast an hour before. The face lit and the smile spread.

She heard a key turn in a lock and a draught hit the back of her neck. She smelt the breath of the man and heard the wheeze in his throat, then the door was locked again, but she could remember what she had seen: wires, sticks and the slim little detonators, the batteries, the soldering iron she had bought in the late-night hardware shop, the needle and thread and the waistcoat . . . and all for this young man. He seemed so frail. She fidgeted, as did the others in the crescent. She was not alone. Khalid, Syed and Jamal all shifted their weight and did not know whether to go forward to welcome him or hang back. The smile spread brighter, wider. When he half turned and faced the chair, his coat was thrown open and she saw clearly the motif of the bird on his chest and thought it tried to make a show of protecting itself – but she knew that if a wing was broken it was helpless and would die. In her mind, she seemed to see the images from the videos, from Chechnya, Afghanistan and Iraq, of explosions and mutilations. Faria shivered. He had no fear. She saw none. He went to the chair, bent, kissed the cheeks offered to him.

She heard, 'I rejoice, my leader, that I have found you.'

'I welcome you, Ibrahim. You have my respect and you are honoured.'

What was she? What were Khalid and Syed, Jamal and Ramzi? They, she, were of lesser importance than grains of sand used to wipe a bottom after defecation, but he – Ibrahim, so slight and so threatened, walking with death – was respected. Love, she thought, shone in him. He went from the chair, from the sheikh, to the end of the crescent's line. As if he performed a ritual, Ibrahim took the hand of Khalid, held it and kissed the driver's cheeks. Khalid was rooted and could not respond. Then Syed, whose eyes blinked with uncertainty. Then Jamal . . .

He was condemned. He had come to them, and his love for them was blazoned, and he smiled into their eyes, and their work was to help him successfully to destroy his body. When he was a pace from her, she closed her eyes and vomit rose in her throat. He bobbed his head at her, and edged past. She sensed it. The hand was taken, the fingers linked. The hand, the fingers, had come from the table where the bomb had been constructed. They handled the sticks and the detonators, they might have had on them the stains of the soldered fluids, now dry, that fastened the wires to the terminals. She heard, too, the gentleness of the kiss on the face of the man whose eyes pored over the intricacies of the device. The vomit climbed from her throat to her mouth.

Faria ran.

She went down the corridor, flung open the bathroom door and knelt over the bowl. It came from her stomach and her body shook. Which of them, if asked, would have done it? Would Khalid or Syed, Ramzi or Jamal – would she – have worn the waistcoat that was being made, with its load, in the locked room behind her? She was in the bathroom until her gut had emptied.

She – and Faria swore it as she retched – would not return the love that was given. Not ever.

He was stood down as were the others, divided from him, of the Delta team.

Time to kill. David Banks was on the far side of the canteen from them. Weekends in the police station had the character and life of a morgue, an empty, soulless place and so quiet. The mass of civilian staff was absent and a wedge of polished, cleaned tables separated him from his team. All would have known that he had been offered a route back to acceptance – a fulsome apology – and that he had thrown it back in the inspector's face. He sat in a distant corner, beyond the fruit machines, the chocolate and soft-drink dispensers, and was in shadow.

He was on overtime rates, double time. They should have been doing the escort of a Principal – a former home secretary, responsible for contentious legislation in the earlier days of the War on Terror – but at the last minute the man had pleaded a bout of influenza and cancelled his speech. The team was booked for the day, the overtime sheets had been issued, and the monies would be paid whether they were inside a draughty hall in Bethnal Green or idling in the canteen. In the rest of the Delta team, they were as decent men as was Banks;

as tolerant as was Banks; as bloody-mindedly stubborn as was Banks. He did not move towards them, they did not move towards him. If the team had been on the road, or in the hall and listening to the Principal's speech, there would have been professional linkage between him and them; the job would have been done. But they were in the canteen and there the relationship had collapsed. Of course Banks had thought about it . . . Push his chair back, get to his feet, cross the chasm of the canteen and spout the necessary. A place at the table would have been found for him, a magazine would have been heaved at him and he would have been told, 'Good shout, Banksy. It never happened. What do you reckon on those long-johns? They say your bollocks'll never freeze in them, but they're forty-eight quid a pair and . . .' But he didn't, couldn't, was never even close to pushing back the chair and starting the walk. For Christ's sake, one of them could have done the trot over the canteen floor, and none had.

He had read late into the night after getting back to his bedsit, had had to read slowly because the handwriting was steady in its deterioration, and what was to come – he sensed it – would be agony.

If he had not been on double time, weekend duty, he would have been tramping the streets, not reading the diary of Cecil Darke but getting himself over to Wandsworth and a little cul-de-sac where a developer had squeezed in a block of modern terraces. He would have been heading for Mandy's home. Pathetic, but still she dominated him. The divorce had gone through years back, but Mandy obsessed him, her and the money. If he had reached there, had turned into the cul-de-sac, he might have stood on the corner and looked along the street to where she lived, or he might have hit the door with his fist and started the futile inquest again; the source of the acrimony was always the money – the worth of the wedding presents, his maintenance payments, the sale of the old house, his cut and hers. The escape from it was overtime and maybe, now, the leather-covered notebook in his jacket pocket.

The other guys, the rest of the Delta team, talked marriages, relationships and girlfriends, and would have included him if he'd wanted it. He had never talked of Mandy with them – it wasn't any of their damn business.

They'd ship him out. He'd heard there was a WDC on the Golf team who was off on maternity leave and had heard also that a DC

145

on the Kilo lot was transferring to the Anti-Terrorist crowd. He would be parcelled off, and it would not be the end of his world, just a different set of magazines and different chat. On Golf or Kilo, life would go on – fresh start – and he would have the same status . . . What he thought, sitting in the shadows of the canteen and as far from the big window as he could be, he had stayed true to Cecil Darke, his great-uncle. Precious little else in his life was as important as staying true to that man. He reached down.

There was no bloody purpose in his own life. None, and it hurt.

Too right, that man was a hero. He'd had principles, guts, but no bloody thermal socks and long-johns and no training days in the Alley to sharpen him. He hadn't had the best weapons all oiled and loved in the Armoury, but he'd had hope. Banks had not intended to produce the notebook, but he did. He lifted it from the pocket. He turned aged pages that told of the great journey. In the emptiness of his own life there was only, as a goal, a transfer to Golf or Kilo . . . and the cold, and the brotherhood of friends. He found the place where he would walk again with a hero.

He read.

13 February 1937
These have been the worst forty-eight hours of my life. I have little ability to describe them, but can only try. I did not know that the world could be so savage, but now I think I have learned the depths of despair.

I should start with our advance. We were moved forward after the Moors crossed the Jarama river on the night of the ninth. It is said they came to the French volunteers' position making no sound to alert our comrades, and that they cut the throats of the defenders, having taken their trenches without warning. I have not slept at all since then. I do not think it possible to sleep in the first-line trenches, or the second or the third, if there is the thought that the Moors can come into our positions and kill us while we sleep.

The British battalion is now under the command of the XVth International Brigade. We are called the 1st Battalion, and also called the Saklatvala Battalion – Saklatvala was an Indian Communist who called for the independence of the colony, but I had not heard of him. I write this because what will come later, and must be written, is so awful. I put off what I have to write.

Our brigade commander is Colonel 'Gal', and he is Russian. The British battalion has a new commanding officer, Tom Wintringham, who is a good man but we do not think he has military experience. He has led us since Wilfred Macartney was shot in the leg by the political officer, Peter Kerrigan, who was cleaning his pistol. Under Captain Wintringham we went forward to hold the line and block the Moors, and we were sent to a hill and ordered to defend it to the last. We call it Suicide Hill. It is where I am now.

We were supposed to dig in. It is not possible. The ground is frozen solid and we have no spades and no pickaxes. We make holes with bayonets if we have them or with our hands. The staff officers say we should not give a yard, but they are not with us. All through today we have been under the fire of machine-guns from the Germans, the Condor Legion, and from heavy artillery, and from the bombing attacks of the German pilots. This is a hell place, and we cannot burrow away from it. We are not rabbits and we are not rats. The machine-guns are above us, on a higher hill in the village of Pingarron – the name should be known because from there hell comes and falls on us. In the afternoon, because we had taken so many casualties, volunteers were called for to advance off our Suicide Hill and to attempt to reach the machine-guns. I did but was not chosen. Ralph did, but he too was not chosen. Daniel was chosen.

We could see him. He ran with those others off our hill and down a slope and started to climb towards those murderous guns. All of their attention was now on this raiding party and we could lift our heads from whatever cover we had and watch. He was hit.

I saw it. He seemed to be spun round and to fall, but then he stood again, and he followed those who were unhurt, and then was hit again. I saw Daniel go on to the bare ground a second time, and I saw also the spurts of earth of more machine-gun fire. Just once he screamed. It was as if, at that moment, the battle had stopped – no bombs, no shells, no bullets, and I heard Daniel's scream, then nothing. Then that moment of quiet was over.

I asked Captain Wintringham if I could look through his binoculars. Daniel did not move. It was finished.

A brave, good life was gone. Because darkness has come, the Moors now will be out in the no man's land between our hill and their machine-guns, and we know what they do. They mutilate the bodies, slash the private parts of their enemy, and they steal anything of value from the dead . . . It is what they will do, or have already done, to Daniel.

He and Ralph are the best friends I ever had.

147

We cannot get to him to bring him back and bury him. Ralph and I said a prayer for him. Ralph said it clearly and I mumbled it. I could not control my tears. I thanked God for the darkness that hid my weeping. The prayer, Ralph said, was from Psalm 137, and he has a beautiful voice. It was clear and bold against the guns.

> *By the rivers of Babylon we sat down and wept*
> *When we remembered Zion . . .*
> *How can we sing the songs of the Lord*
> *While in a foreign land?*

I hope I never forget Ralph's prayer – as I will never forget my friend and brother, Daniel.

The political officer came an hour ago. He said that we had held the line. He told us that the front was stabilized. We will be pulled back before dawn.

So, we shall have left Suicide Hill when first light comes, and I do not believe I shall ever again see where Daniel lies – and so many others, us and the Moors, who have charged our position, and there are many who are not dead and who moan and cry out.

If I had known what it would be, I cannot say I would have come.

I do not know now why I am here. I do not know now for what I fight.

I feel despair, and I dread the next day that comes 'in a foreign land'.

It is so cold – for Daniel it is worse. Ralph and I, when the candle is finished and I can no longer write, will be together, body against body, for warmth, but we cannot warm our brother, our friend.

They had gone. Probably, Banks thought, they were now in the stand-by room and had taken over the bar-billiards table. He had hardly noted their going and doubted that anyone had glanced at him. He put his marker in the notebook, an Underground train ticket, and dropped it back into his pocket. He was haunted by what he had read, and sapped . . . but would have felt shame if he had not stood shoulder to shoulder with Cecil Darke, and had not refused to make the negotiated apology that was asked of him.

He felt the wet in his eyes.

It was the Nobbler's moment. He had sat in the car for three hours and his eyeline had given him a decent enough view of the white-painted front door, and the wheelie-bin; the little wicket gate was askew on its hinges. The house reeked neglect, financial hardship and lack of pride, which was as Benny Edwards wanted. He had read a newspaper from cover to cover and eaten a sandwich; the last dregs in the coffee Thermos were cold. He shifted in his seat to look through the sunlight blazing on to the windscreen and knew that the wait was over.

The buzz ran in him – excitement, adrenaline, expectation. It was always the same when it was his moment. The day was long past when he had worked for money and what money bought him. Today or yesterday he could have gone to an agent – he could go tomorrow – and bought the airline tickets for Faro or Málaga, have done the electronic cash transfers and bugged out to the southern sunshine, could have found the place – with a wide patio, a pool and a view – where he would spend the rest of his days, but he would be without the buzz. He craved it, could not exist without it.

They came out of the door. The Tango first, then a girl who had a holdall in her hand. The wife followed her daughter to the step, kissed and hugged her, but had nothing for her husband. The Nobbler had allocated the whole of that day, and Sunday, to searching out the optimum moment for the approach. It was never an exact science, needed the flexible thinking on which he prided himself. The only place that an approach, first time up, never worked was at the home when the juror's partner was there, and the doorstep was the poorest option. He wanted the Tango alone and off his beaten track. In his car, on the back seat, a canvas satchel held the carrot, and in his pocket was the photograph that would be the stick. For some Tango subjects the carrot or the stick was quick, for others slow, but the Nobbler had the two days of the weekend to make his approach with carrot or stick.

They were off down the pavement. He couldn't know where the Tango would lead him.

He liked what he saw of the scrote, his Tango. The girl was ahead of her father, as if she couldn't wait to be shot of him. He had those daft sandals on and bright socks that the sunlight caught, old trousers and the windcheater from court. He read the shabbiness that was the same as the front door, and the gate on to the pavement that was half off its hinges. He did not believe that the Tango would need the stick on his back, just a bite at the carrot – but he'd show the stick. It was his way and well practised, and he rehearsed the opening words: told his own boy, who would take over the trade when he was past it – not bloody yet – that the first words of the approach either sold or sank a deal. He nudged his car after them.

They went out of the road on to the main drag and were on the far side of it from the Nobbler.

They went to the station, crossed the forecourt and stopped where there was a rank for buses to pull in. He understood. The dutiful dad was doing his family bit, escorting his girl, maybe aged fourteen, to the bus and was going to stay with her till it came. He would see her off and would say, doubtless, 'Have a good time at your friend's, don't drink tonight and *don't* get shagged.' The Nobbler parked on a double yellow, nowhere else, took the Disabled card from the glove box, displayed it and waited some more.

The bus came.

As if it was a chore, the girl pecked the Tango's cheek and was away up the step and inside.

The bus left. The Nobbler noted that the Tango watched it go across the forecourt, raised his arm and waved, and was still waving when it was round the corner and gone, as if he didn't want to let it go.

The car door closed quietly after the Nobbler. He straightened, his hands flicked over his clothes, smart casual with a decent jacket, as if to smooth creases from them. Important to look good – a grin swept his face – and respectable.

He came behind him.

He said pleasantly, 'Excuse me, isn't it Mr Julian Wright? It is, isn't it?'

He spun awkwardly. 'Yes, that's me. I'm Jools Wright.'

'I was hoping to meet up with you. Actually, I was trying to.'

He had been far away in a cloud of thoughts. His daughter and Hannah. Bad thoughts and good thoughts. The little cow, cheekier by the day, sided with her mother . . . Hannah, whom he'd be with that night. He squeezed his eyes shut for a moment, as if it would rid him of the cloud.

'Do I know you?'

'I don't think so, but . . .'

'Are you a parent of one of my students? I have to tell you – sorry and all that – I cannot discuss school affairs here.' A new cloud had formed: suspicion.

'Steady on, Mr Wright. Nothing about school.'

'About what, then?'

'About something that might be of advantage to you, Mr Wright.'

'I'm in rather a hurry. I have to get home – I have to—'

'Considerable advantage, Mr Wright.'

'Well, some other time. If you'll, please, excuse me.'

He wanted to run but felt caged – as if he were fettered. A hand was on his arm. The grip tightened. He knew it then: he would have to fight to be free . . . but Jools had never fought in his life. Had never struggled, never kicked, never eye-gouged. He felt panic rising.

'Nothing for you to worry about, Mr Wright. What I said, something of considerable advantage, and that's going to be worth a few minutes of your valuable time – yes?'

'I don't know, I really don't.'

'Let's go and sit in my car for those few minutes. Where's the harm in that?'

His arm was held vice tight. Jools said limply, 'I can't be late home. I've got to go out again.'

'So I'll drop you. Now, let's go to my car. No problems, are there?'

He was walked to the car, his liberty gone. Only when a passenger door had been opened was the grip on his arm loosened. He sagged down into the seat, the door was closed on him and the man walked round the front, then sat behind the wheel. Jools realized that this was the first time he had registered the man's appearance: middle age, average height, average build, average hair, a jacket of a neutral grey, and a shirt with a light check in it, slacks that were a darker grey. But the eyes burned with authority and the grip had been fierce on his sleeve. Under that veneer of reasonableness, almost charm, there had been the implication of violence. Jools sat hunched and taut; his teeth bit into his lower lip. The radio was turned on and there was a low babble of voices from the speakers.

'Now then, Mr Wright, I hope you'll listen very carefully to me. You will?'

'Yes.'

'And you'll hear me right through till I've finished?'

'I'll hear what you have to say.'

The man leaned back and edged himself more comfortably into his seat.

'You, Mr Wright, are currently sitting as a juror in court eighteen at Snaresbrook, right?' His voice was quiet.

Oh, God . . . He understood. Jools sighed. What chance of getting clear of the car and running? None. His head dropped and he whispered his answer: 'Yes, I am.'

'I represent some friends of friends, Mr Wright. The friends of my friends are the Curtis brothers, and you are hearing their case. Now, my friends say that you look to be a reasonable, fair man, one with an open mind and not prejudiced. You see, Mr Wright, the Curtis boys have been stitched up by the Crime Directorate. They have been subject to lies and untruths. They are good family men and they are honest, straight businessmen, but you wouldn't know that from the perjured evidence of the police. They are also, Mr Wright, men of exceptional generosity, most of which is directed towards local charities – a child with leukaemia near where they live was sent to the States for treatment, a Boys' Club needed premises, which were funded – but a substantial example of their generosity would be directed towards anyone who stood up for them against all that untruthful police evidence. It's why I said, Mr Wright, that meeting me could be to your advantage. No, don't say anything, just listen, please. To be rewarded with that generosity, you would have to guarantee that your vote would go to a not-guilty verdict, and that you would give your best effort to persuading others on the jury to follow you. Your advantage, their generosity, adds up to twenty-five thousand pounds, Mr Wright, cash in hand. I think you'll agree it's an attractive offer . . . and I am aware that your financial circumstances are not healthy. It would be a new start, a fresh page. It's on the table.'

His breath came in little gasps. Under his windcheater, his shirt was soaked in sweat. The man's hand dropped into his jacket pocket.

A photograph was lifted out. Jools saw the face of his daughter Kathy, her grin and wink to a friend. It was held in front of him, his eyes lingered on it, and then it was back in the pocket.

'Very pretty girl, Mr Wright, and long may she stay that way. Good complexion, unblemished skin, not a mark on it . . . I wouldn't, and neither would my friends, want the generosity of the Curtis brothers abused. It would be very sad, with consequences, if a considerable trust were broken.'

Jools sat very still. Kathy wanted to train as a hairdresser, but no one would want to employ a salon girl whose face had been slashed.

'You might think it's possible to sit on a fence and play in both sides of the field – that is, to take advantage of the offer *and* go to the police. Don't consider it. We know where you live, we know where your daughter goes to school. There's an old saying about running but not being able to hide, and I think it comes from American boxing. There would be nowhere to hide. My friends have long arms and longer memories . . . Now, so that we understand each other, you have two choices, Mr Wright. You can straighten out your finances and pay off your debts and forget about it, *or* you can spend every minute of your day looking over your shoulder, wondering whether there's a petrol bomb coming through the front window, concerned if your daughter's face is going to stay unmarked, whether what's done to your legs will let you walk again . . . But I don't think you're an unco-operative man. I reckon you'd realize when generosity was shown you.'

Could he have stood up to them? He couldn't even meet the gaze, from the dock or the witness box, of Ozzie Curtis. Just looking at the man, with half an army of security and court staff for protection, terrified the wits out of him. And Jools thought of the new credit-card statements and the bank's overdraft letters and the builder's invoice that would be landing on the mat behind his front door. The voice dripped on, and he thought himself shafted. Why not bloody moaning Peter, or that toff Corenza? But it wasn't them who was trapped in the car: it was Jools bloody Wright. The blood surged to his face . . . Yes, damn right, they'd chosen well.

'It's half down now, and the other twelve and a half thousand will be in your bin the night the verdict's given, you've voted against conviction and the jury's hung . . . I almost forgot. If you turn out to be the Great Persuader and talk the others round to an acquittal, it's another twenty-five. Nice money, if you can get it . . . and, Mr Wright, you can. So, what's it to be?'

He hesitated. 'How do I know that . . .?'

'That the secret stays . . . ? Of course it does. My friends have made an art form of discretion. You'll never hear from us again, believe it.'

'I do have some financial worries.' Jools grimaced.

'All in the past, Mr Wright. My advice, use the money in small amounts, nothing big and nothing flash. Pay off the debts in hundreds, not thousands. Don't draw attention to yourself.'

'I don't know your name.'

There was a sweet smile. The man drew surgical gloves from his pocket, put them on, reached behind him and took a package from his canvas bag. It was wrapped in brown paper, sealed with tape, and it was dropped on to Jools's lap.

The car brought him back to the end of his road, and the package was lodged inside his windcheater. He had already thought where to hide it, and he hadn't reached the half-fallen gate to his handkerchief front garden before the car had accelerated away and was round the corner . . . He didn't have a name and didn't have the car's number.

Then the shock took him. His hands trembled and his legs shook.

Chapter 8: Sunday, Day 11

Through the window, Ibrahim saw her in the garden. She hung washing on the line. He was not yet dressed and he kept himself half hidden behind the curtains but there was a sufficient gap between them for him to watch her. He ignored the voices and the sounds of the day starting and watched her, waiting for the repetition of her movements. She was bent over the basket and the jeans were tight against her buttocks and hips. She lifted out a shirt, a pair of under-pants, or something flimsy that was her own, then stretched up to reach the plastic line that was suspended between two trees. When she reached up her T-shirt rode higher, leaving him a clear view of the skin at the small of her back, and sometimes the flatness of her stomach, the little indentation of her navel. At the moment that she fastened whichever garment it was to the line with pegs, she would arch her back, when the swell of her breasts was most pronounced, and then she would start again.

He felt breathless. He could not comprehend that she was one of his own Faith. She contradicted everything he had been brought up to value in a woman, above all modesty. It was when she turned and lifted the basket, had her back to the line of clothing that swayed in the wind and the sun caught the intricacies of the items that were hers, that she looked – and he thought there was almost sadness on her face – at the windows, but she would not have seen him because he had ducked away. Those who had been his friends in Jizan would have sniggered at the long scar on her face, as if it made her worthless, but Ibrahim did not think it a blemish on her prettiness. When he was back, his nose and mouth close to the glass, she was gone, but he lingered to see the movement on the line of what was hers, what was worn under the jeans and beneath the T-shirt, and there was a tremor in his breathing, and . . . more movement, on the far edge of the grass behind the cottage.

The man had no name that Ibrahim knew. He was the heavily built man, the sole member of the group to whom the Leader paid attention. Ibrahim understood what the man did, and the proof of it was in the hours the man spent shut away in his room. There had been the smell from under that door, and then under Ibrahim's, of the heated soldering iron. The man had not spoken to him, not a word, but when they were in the main room together the man seemed to watch him . . . and Ibrahim thought it was with the care that a customer in his father's shop behind the Corniche gave when he evaluated the most expensive, most prized wide-screen television.

The man crossed the grass and went to the gap in the hedge that divided the garden from the field. In his hand he carried a plastic bag and a short-handled spade. There were no beasts in the field, but the man lifted his leg over the barbed wire and went into it, then started a slow, methodical search of the ground. Every few yards he stopped and set down the plastic bag, then used his spade to scrape up old cattle dung from the grass, which he tipped into the bag. When the bag was more than half filled he returned the way he had come. Ibrahim understood why the man who made the bomb went into the field and collected the waste of the beasts. It had been on the television and radio at home, on the Al Jazeera satellite channel, that the shit from animals was mixed with screws, nails or ball-bearings, and the shit would be against his washed body when he walked.

He had begun to dress when he heard the light rap at the door.

He wore his trousers and socks, but had not yet pulled on his undervest and T-shirt and the cold shimmered on his chest.

He called out.

She filled the doorway and he flinched back towards the window. His sisters would never have come into his room at home before he was dressed, and the maidservant would not have entered while he was there. He saw the scar on her face and its anger, as if the sides of the wound would never knit sufficiently close for it to be anything but obvious. If he had gone on with his training as a medical student at the university, if he had graduated, qualified, it would have been his responsibility to suture such an injury, but that was behind him and gone. He stared at it, the livid line, and her hand went up to it – he had seen the day before how frequently she touched it – and he thought that running a finger down the indentation was like a tic in her, as if she could not leave it alone. Because he stared, ice covered her eyes.

'I should have asked you earlier. Have you any washing?'

He had not thought whether he would put on the T-shirt with the swan printed on it again, but it was grimy with perspiration. There were three pairs of underpants in the bottom of his bag – he had put on the last clean pair he had brought – and four pairs of socks.

'Don't know. I'm sorry.'

'It's not anything to apologize for. If you have clothing that needs washing, I'll run it through the machine,' she said brusquely.

'Well, I do . . .'

'OK, so give it to me.'

He would wear laundered clothing when he went on the walk. He must be clean in his soul, his mind, his body and his clothing when he made the journey to God's table . . . but he did not know, because he had not been told, when that day would be. So, Ibrahim did not know how many washed T-shirts, pairs of underpants or socks he must wear before his walk. The clothing in his bag, on the carpet of the room had been against his skin, his private places. In his presence, should she handle them? He felt the same breathlessness as he had when he had watched her through the window.

He hesitated. 'I think I have some things.'

'Of course you do. Just give them to me,' she said curtly.

'But I don't know what I will need.'

She was remote from him, as if nothing should bond them. 'You'll be told. I don't know. I'll take everything that needs washing.'

'I am not told anything,' Ibrahim blurted.

'Nor me, nor any of us. Please, your washing.' She shrugged, dismissive.

'But I have faith that will sustain me, and I know I am going to God. I am dedicated to what I shall do . . .' He lifted the underpants and socks from his bag, the T-shirt off the floor, and gave them to her. 'I hope to be worthy of the trust placed in me. Yes, I think I am dedicated enough to carry out my duty . . . Will you be close to me when I walk?'

'I don't know.'

'I think I have been chosen because I am dedicated.'

She said quickly, seemed to spit it, 'We are all dedicated, not only you.'

The door closed on her. Ibrahim sat on his unmade bed and held his head in his hands. He would have liked to know that she would be close to him, to feel the comfort not of a brother but of a sister.

That Sunday morning, at the bottom of the steps to the town's Arndale Shopping Centre, the posters were stuck up in the windows of the closed Burger King restaurant. More were fastened in the doorway at the top of the steps. Workmen with paste and brushes plastered them on to the glass.

Wherever there was available space, the posters went up.

The next Saturday morning, it was advertised, a 'Super Sale' would start in Luton, with special offers discounted down to fifty per cent of the usual amount. There would be 'Give-away Prices', everything 'slashed' in the chainstores that filled the retail outlets inside the cavern of the shopping centre. And on that morning a celebrity from the local radio station would open the Super Sale.

The manager of a chemist's in the centre spoke to a councillor who sat on the Trade and Commerce Committee in the town hall as they watched the slapping on of the posters from a vantage-point among the trees of St George's Square.

'I hope this bloody works,' the manager said. 'Rents are up, takings are through the floor. If this doesn't pull the punters in, we're well and truly shafted.'

'They'll be fighting to get in, just you wait and see, when the doors open.' The councillor slapped the manager's back. 'Could be a special day for the Arndale next Saturday. They'll be shoulder to shoulder and lined up right round the corner. It's the sort of initiative this town needs and that shoppers respond to. They'll come with filled purses and wallets. It'll be like the Saturday before Christmas.'

It was Jools's routine on a Sunday morning. Out of bed, Hannah's, out of her flat and down the alleyway into Inkerman Road. Up Manchester Street and past the town hall where that damn great clock was striking, along the pavement past St George's Square, the wine bar, Travelcare, the Oxfam shop and Tasty Fried Chicken. Then the closed doors of three building societies and the Age Concern unlit windows on his right, and the dive into the newsagent that sold fags. Every Sunday morning was the same: Hannah would be making breakfast and he would be on the quarter-mile tramp for a carton of cigarettes and a scandal sheet.

And, as it always did, his mobile rang.

His father: 'Just to tell you, son, that Babs rang and I said you were out, and would you call her?'

His father and mother, fifteen miles north of the town, were an active ingredient in the deception Jools practised. The familiar bleat from him to Babs was that they were elderly, getting frail, and that it was important he visited as often as possible, both to show them his support and to do jobs round their house because they could no longer afford, as pensioners, to have a man in. They hated telling the lies for their son's adulterous relationship but, as he told them when it was fraught and he was challenged, the alternative was a split with Babs and their granddaughter without a father at home. Babs would ring on a Sunday morning, and Jools's father would swallow his truth culture and say that Jools had just popped out, then telephone his son. Jools would call home on his mobile and would concoct anecdotes of what he'd done at his parents' house for them. Did he care? Not much . . . He bought his cigarettes and the paper, and as he walked back he spoke to his wife, and forgot her as soon as the mobile was back in his pocket.

That Sunday morning Jools Wright had much to reflect on.

And he was not sure – in a welter of confusion – where his priorities lay.

Could have been his performance in bed with Hannah, bloody abject and useless. Could have been the package in the bottom of the wardrobe at home with his shoes and spare sandals covering it.

What to do? If the Inkerman Arms had been open, he might have headed into the public bar and ordered up a double Johnnie Walker, no ice, but it was not.

He had seen the posters going up outside the shopping centre. When Babs and he went out to buy things, it usually ended up in a whispered bickering about what they could afford, what they couldn't, and which credit card or cheque book might still be functioning. Different times. There was twelve and a half thousand pounds, presumably in fifties, in his wardrobe and he could go down to the shopping centre next week and buy half of any of the damned outlets bloody near empty.

He passed the Inkerman Arms and heard a vacuum-cleaner inside. He was within sight of Hannah's door. The trouble with Hannah was that she had an appetite, and women with an appetite needed regular feeding, and if she didn't get satisfaction at one outlet, she'd go looking for another. It was the way she was: if Jools wasn't the flavour she'd be heading off elsewhere, and he'd be getting the phone call to say he needn't bother to come again. If he had that call, it would push him down into the gutter.

He didn't blame himself. Never had done and wasn't about to start. *Every* man had a price. Damn certain, if enough noughts were racked up, Mr Justice Herbert who was God Almighty in court eighteen, had a price. He grinned at the thought of the big brown-paper parcel being slipped into the judge's grip. It didn't enter his mind that he should fight, kick and scratch against corruption. Christ, he needed the money. Pretty damn lucky that the offer had been to him, Jools Wright, who was deputy head of geography in a sink school filled to the gunwales with yobs and who had the original debt mountain, than to Rob, Baz or Vicky. It would be hard to keep a straight face when Mr Justice Herbert sent them out and Jools stated to the rest of them, 'I hear what you say, but on the basis of the evidence put before us, and disregarding the prejudice against the accused that the police evidence has tried to manufacture, I really cannot – in all honesty and sincerity – find the Curtis brothers guilty. No, I'm listening but I'm not about to change my viewpoint when the liberty of two citizens is involved. You can call me what you like but my vote is for an acquittal.' They'd be raging at him – but in his wardrobe there was a parcel of money . . .

When he opened the door to Hannah's flat, he smelt the cooked breakfast.

She wore only the long sports shirt he'd given her and an apron. In the routine, they'd have breakfast in bed, then the trays would go on the floor and it was back to what Heaven sent.

He told her he thought he had a cold coming on, wasn't himself, but that he'd have thrown it off by next weekend. They had breakfast in the kitchen. An hour later he rang his father and told him, it was necessary to be consistent in his deceit, that he was on his way home to Babs. He didn't talk while he ate, as if his silence was a symptom of his cold, but he could see Hannah's annoyance, which seemed to say she thought she'd been short-changed. He was far away, thinking of the brothers and whether on Monday morning, tomorrow, he'd have the bravado to look them in the eyes because he'd taken their money.

They walked round the exercise yard.

'Nothing to do but wait,' Ollie Curtis said. 'I hate waiting.'

It was a banal remark, but true. It was the third time that the younger brother had made it, and they were only on the fourth circuit of the small area used by Category A remand prisoners, and they would get in another twelve circuits before the prison officers called them in and locked them up.

His voice spattered on: 'Can only wait for the morning. I suppose then we'll hear fast enough what Benny's done for us, get it from the brief. I'm with you, Ozzie, it's the only bloody chance. I reckon you're right. The witness won't stand up to another year of hanging about. The mis-trial's all we've to look to, then going after that witness, but the waiting's a bastard.'

Beside him, Ozzie had his hands deep in his pockets, his head down, and he trudged the circuit at pace.

'What you reckon, Ozzie, are you feeling good or what?'

The elder brother shrugged, his mind elsewhere. Young Ollie was always a dripping tap and talked when there was nothing to say. The 'only bloody chance' was with the Nobbler. Why? Because they were in Belmarsh where the security was tighter than it was at any other gaol in the country. There was a joke question among the 'ordinary' remand men: 'Where is the biggest and most flourishing Al Qaeda cell in the country?' And a joke answer: 'In Belmarsh.' The hate guys, the bomb-plotters, had damn near half a landing to themselves. They had their own cook and their own religion man and the officers stayed off their backs. But them being there meant more wire on top of the outer walls, and more supervision, and guns outside in the locked-up boots of the armed-response vehicles. Where the brothers walked now, in the piss-poor little yard, there was a heavy tangle of reinforced wire above them. And it would be no better when they went to court because there were more guns in the escort vehicles, and guns at the Snaresbrook holding cells and round the courtroom. The Nobbler was the 'only bloody chance' because the option of a break-out did not exist. In a year and a month on remand, Ozzie Curtis had searched for a chink of light peeping through the security, and had yet to see it.

'By now Benny'll have done his approach,' Ollie Curtis said. 'You think this jerk would double-cross us, take the money and not do the business? It's a hell of an amount of money, and there's no guarantee. Would he dare?'

There was a grimace from Ozzie. He would have preferred to walk alone, but could not. If young Ollie told his mother, when the cousin brought her up on the first Saturday of every month, that Ozzie wouldn't walk with her darling baby, aged forty-four, there would be tears and bloody shrieks. He walked with his younger brother . . . Let the jerk try. He'd get the full treatment. Given the spade out in a wood and told to dig the pit, then get down in it, and he'd look up at the barrel facing him. When half his bloody head was shot to hell the hole would be filled in on him. The life of Ozzie Curtis was one of 'service industries': a service to supply the wheels, another to fence, a third to provide a slaughter-house where cash and diamonds were stashed and safe, a fourth to hire out firearms. There was also an industry, expensive but worth it, for a man who double-crossed on a deal. But it wouldn't come to that because the Nobbler would have spelled out the consequences of a double-cross, and only a bloody idiot would have ignored him.

'What's getting to me, Ozzie – while we're waiting, and it's going on like a clock ticking – is this. If we get put away big-time, how long's the respect we're getting now going to last? Does respect last if we're down for fifteen or more?'

God, why couldn't his kid brother shut his damn mouth? Respect mattered to Ozzie Curtis. He was a blagger, not a druggie importer. He did not fraternize with Crime Squad detectives, did not have any cosy little relationship that meant informing on rivals. The druggie importers were crap and he didn't mix with them on the landing but he reckoned that any of them, if they learned something confidential about him that they could squeal on to their advantage, would shop him. Inside Belmarsh, Ozzie Curtis had status, but he would lose it if the sentence was heavy. He would just be another shuffling wreck, getting old, a target for any arrogant kid on the block, and he'd have his bloody brother whimpering in his ear. He depended on the Nobbler.

'If we go down, Ozzie, there'll be all of those Asset Recovery guys crawling all over us. They'll bloody strip us bare. You thought of that, Ozzie?'

Targets for Asset Recovery, and he didn't need to be told so, included his house down in Kent, which was worth, minimum, one point two five million, his Lexus four-wheel drive, the wife's top-of-the-range Audi, and the villa on the hills above Fuengirola – a place in Spain of that size was another three-quarters of a million – and there were the Cayman accounts, the Gibraltar money, the investments in the Black Sea apartments and . . . His status in Belmarsh would seep away once he was down and the Asset Recovery team were digging at him. He'd be a bloody pauper, and there was no respect on the landing for one of *them*.

'Nothing to do but wait,' Ollie said. 'I hate waiting.'

'He must have courage,' Faria whispered. Then the pitch of her voice was bolder: 'Which of us would do it?'

She had cooked chicken breasts and served them with rice and a curried sauce. It was what she would have given her parents if she had been at home, and her two brothers, if they had not been doing religious instruction in Pakistan. She had looked up before she put that question. The doors to the dining area were still closed. Before she had brought the food from the kitchen, she had called through the doors that their lunch was ready.

'Would you? Would you do what he is going to do?'

'I have not been asked,' Khalid answered, but looked away. 'It is immaterial what I say. It is not expected of me. You want honesty among ourselves and between ourselves? No.'

Her finger jabbed at Syed. 'Would you? Do you have that bravery?'

'If it were necessary, perhaps. But another has been chosen. I do not have to answer because the question is on a false premise. I do more for our struggle by staying alive, by continuing as the servant of the Organization. I was never a volunteer, and I am thankful I was not asked.'

Leaning across the table and her food, her eye and finger moved on to Ramzi. 'Is the Faith in you to do what he will?'

'I would have, if I had been selected.' His chest swelled. 'Already I told people that I was prepared for martyrdom. It is a disappointment to me that I was not chosen . . . Yes.'

Her gaze crossed three empty places and came to rest on Jamal. 'Would you walk with the vest against your body?'

'I don't know. I can't say. Many heroes have, in Chechnya, Palestine and Iraq, so many that we no longer know their names.' He giggled, childlike. 'Do I believe what many of those heroes were told? Do they go, in Paradise, to the virgins? Are the virgins waiting for them? There are *imams* who say the virgins are there . . . Perhaps I would do it if I believed in the virgins.'

There was a chorus of the same question. 'Would you, Faria? What about you?'

But doors opened. She seemed to see what she had read: heads spiralling into the air, severed at the neck, flying high, across the room and out through the open window. They fell to the grass and rolled there, like the footballs boys played with in the side-streets off the Dallow Road. She saw the heads of Khalid and Syed, Ramzi and Jamal . . . then her own. She did not have to answer. The places at the table were taken. She ducked her head and ate. She did not look up until her plate was clean. Then, nervously, she glanced around her. She was the first to finish. Her eyes met his.

Ibrahim smiled, then said with gentleness, 'That was wonderful and I compliment you. I am grateful.'

She gulped. None of the others had thanked her. Was he captured by the thought of virgins? She had never slept with a man, of course, and never would. Did he dream of the virgins in the gardens of

164

Paradise, search and lust for them? She would not sleep with a man because she was scarred and would never find a husband, she knew it.

'It is not the same food as we eat at home but it was good, or better. It was excellent,' he said softly.

She flushed. A few days ago, before he had arrived, she would have thought that the final days of the countdown to the walk would have been spent in earnest collective prayer and political lecturing, with hectored statements of commitment. Her recruiter had told her, in the back room of a mosque tucked behind the main Dunstable road, that at the moment a Black Widow pressed the button as she stood on a bus filled with Russian paratroops and heading for Grozny she attained the height of bliss and would feel herself floating to another life. She would know for certain that she was not dead, but living and close to God. She stood up. Only he seemed prepared to stack plates to make it easier for her, but she shook her head briskly. She took the plates off the table, carried them through to the kitchen and brought back a bowl of fruit – oranges, apples and pears. She thought herself honoured to help him make his journey to Paradise. She put it on to the centre of the table.

There was a rasped question. 'Do we have bleach here?'

'I don't know,' she stammered. 'I have not looked.'

She saw the cold, glinting eyes of the one they all called their leader now as he reached for an apple. Again the voice whipped her: 'I have. I have looked under the kitchen's sink. There is disinfectant but not bleach. I want bleach and you should buy it tomorrow.'

She felt anger and hurt. 'Is the house dirty? I clean each day.'

'A big bottle of bleach. Buy it tomorrow.' The teeth crunched into the apple.

Faria went into the kitchen, ran the hot tap and started to rinse the saucepans. The water scalded her hands and . . . The thought was a thunderclap in her mind. The boy, so gentle and genuine, so dedicated to killing, pressed the button but his head did not fly, climb, soar – pressed the button and heard silence. A plate fell from her hand and cracked as it hit the draining-board. She was not criticized: there was no rebuke from the dining room. She could not believe anything would be more humiliating than to fail.

*

He stood alone. The rifles covered him. The shouts battered in his ears. 'See there, the mother-fucker's got a wire showing. It's done a fucking malfunction! Don't let the fucker run! He's mine, the mother-fucker's mine, Sergeant.'

They came from behind the roadblock's sandbag walls. They stormed out from the cover where they had crouched as he came closer to them. Traffic had backed off on the airport road, out north-west from Baghdad's centre. He was overwhelmed and was crushed down on to the Tarmacadam. A big black fist tore the switch from his hand. Tape went over his eyes and darkness surrounded him. Boots kicked him. He was lifted. He was thrown heavily on to a metal surface and heard an engine roar. A boot was at his throat. He was driven away.

He did not know then that three hours after his inability to achieve martyrdom, bright lights would be shone piercingly into his face. If he closed his eyes he would be slapped, and questions would rain down on him.

'Did you get food, Mr Hegner?'

''Fraid not, was in the air. I'll tell you, I'm mighty pleased you called me, and it was pure luck there was a flight coming over.'

'I can get you anything you want,' the intelligence officer said. 'A burger, sandwiches, fries?'

'Just a coffee. I want to say that those grunts did a real good job. To get one of them suckers alive is a rare bonus. I wasn't thinking about lunch, just getting here. Now, is he doing it the Irish way?'

'I don't follow you, Mr Hegner.'

'The Irish have got the line on counter-interrogation resistance: "The best thing to say is to say nothing." Would you put him in that category?'

'No, Mr Hegner, he's singing. That'll be the shock. We did what you suggested last time you were over when you drew this scenario, put a woman interrogator with a kind motherly voice alongside him. He's from the Saudi town of Dammam, a university-grade economics student, and he was brought across the border about – we reckon from what he says – half-way between Hafr Al-Bain and Arar. That was thirty-six hours ago. You want to go face to face with him?'

'Not for me to break the lady's stride. But there's some questions I'd like to get answered.'

'Not a problem, Mr Hegner.'

He was driven to the holding cages. Cindy had done well. Within fifteen minutes of the first flash reaching Hegner's territory – a suicide fouled up – she'd tracked down an air-force executive jet that was lifting two senators from Riyadh to Baghdad on the next leg of their inspection tour, and the limousine had taken him from the embassy with no qualms about speed and stop lights. He was led, a loose hand on his arm, from the jeep to the outer gate, then keys clanked and he could smell the stench of the interrogation cage – same as it was anywhere – body odour and urine and pungent disinfectant. But she wore scent.

The intelligence officer had been brought to him. 'It's a pleasure to meet you, Mr Hegner. I feel privileged.'

'What I want to know, Captain, is whether he has met with two individuals. I hear whispers of them, murmurs on the wind. You see, the Saudi route he was brought through is one used by these two. The facilitator is known to me as The Scorpion, what the whisper calls him. The Engineer – more whispers and murmurs – makes the devices, and it's unlike his to fail. What I need to know, did he pass through their hands? If he did, where and when?'

'I'll do my best.'

Another coffee was brought him, and a chair into which he sank heavily. He heard the sounds of the cage around him. Men moaned, and there was the clatter of the guards' boots, the rattle of keys. His mind drifted. A young man, probably identical in background, dedication and motivation to the one now being interrogated, had walked into the garrison camp mess hall in Mosul. Joe Hegner, fresh from a speech to the division's officers on combating the newly flourishing weapon of suicide-bombing, had been queuing with intelligence analysts and had just asked for tuna hash, baked beans and grape juice, when the flash had come, the pain and the darkness ... Everything afterwards had been – was – personal.

He heard the soft footfall of a woman.

'It was a good question, Mr Hegner. He met neither the facilitator nor the bomb-maker. He says he heard men talking last night. They were fearful, both about the target reconnaissance and the makeup of the device. What he heard, was not supposed to but did, the Scorpion and the Engineer would have returned next week or the week after . . . I suppose that means they're out of the country. Does that help you, Mr Hegner? Is it enough to justify your trip?'

'Thank you, Captain, you done good.'

On the drive out to the runway where the small jet was parked, he phoned Cindy in Riyadh and told her what he wanted. He apologized to the senators and their staffers, already strapped in their seats, for having caused the delay in their schedule, and nestled down to doze.

They chewed it, dogs with a dry, meatless bone.

In Riverside Villas, Dickie Naylor shuffled between meetings. The building's lights now blazed down on the Embankment and spread far enough to glimmer on the river. All day, he had stood his ground firmly enough to dictate that it was he who ran the section, not Mary Reakes, and would run it for one further week.

He hustled along a gloomy upper-floor corridor and she was in his wake.

He rapped on the door of the assistant director, Tristram, to whom he reported. It would be the last meeting of the day, and his age wearied him. He had been up since six, out of his front door by seven and in his office by eight. Tiredness seeped through him. He had met with the surveillance people, the immigration teams who watched over ferry and airports, the duty liaison man from Special Branch, the Anti-Terrorist unit and, last, the security official from the Dutch embassy. The assistant director had driven back from a family christening in the north-west.

Naylor was called inside. He gave a résumé of what he knew, precious little.

Maybe he'd stumbled over his words too many times.

Mary would have done it better, more crisply, but he had the determination. He finished and pushed across the table the three photographs of a boy from a distant land: one showed a shadowed figure, black and white, caught on a CCTV camera at Riyadh's King Khalid International Airport; another, similarly grainy, revealed the same boy coming into Arrivals at Schiphol, Amsterdam's airport, same T-shirt, easily recognizable. The third was a colour portrait of the boy, Ibrahim Hussein, who wore on his head and shoulders a loosely wound *khaffiyeh* cloth. In none of the pictures was there an indication of threat, danger. He had a pleasant face with a wisp of shyness in his eyes and modesty at his mouth. Naylor was reflecting that it was impossible, from the boy's features and expression and from the calm of his gait at King Khalid and at Schiphol, to believe that the threat and the danger were real. A pencil tapped the table in front of him and his head started up. Beside him he glimpsed Mary Reakes's eyebrows roll upwards.

'You all right, Dickie?' Tristram asked.

'Yes, yes.'

'Don't mind me saying it, but you look knackered.'

'I'm fine, thank you.'

'Well, that's that . . . So, where do we go? Let's throw it around.'

He had his hand over his mouth as if that would hide his yawn but it engulfed him. 'Sorry about that. We go with the intelligence. If it's necessary for a lock-down in London, so be it. We jack up the threat status. I don't see the alternative.'

There was the hiss of Mary's breath. Then she chipped, 'It's hardly "intelligence", more like a bucket of supposition. What we have is a deception about a visit to family in Yemen and a flight to Holland. The rest is all theatrical. I suggest we wait until the Dutch have brought us more, picked him up or provided proof of his leaving their territory. Simply put, we don't have enough.'

Sensing the opportunity, Naylor hit out, 'It will not be me, I assure you, who will ever lay himself open to the accusation that I was the man who ignored the intelligence, or supposition, indicating the risk of an imminent atrocity.'

The assistant director kept his silence but twisted the pencil faster.

She said, 'That's a cheap shot, Dickie. I'm saying we don't have enough to ratchet the threat status. The intelligence isn't there. We cannot do lock-down – with all that it costs, and the manpower – until we know more. We should watch, listen and learn, then decide. In my experience, the American community are paranoid and hysterical. Bluntly, they cry, "Wolf."'

Her experience, Naylor knew, was substantial and growing. She had been fast-tracked after a degree in Islamic Studies, first-class honours, was fluent in Arabic, had worked in Northern Ireland with distinction, then run a desk in D Branch and had been integral in the team that had put seven young Muslims from the home counties into the cells at Belmarsh. If Mary Reakes hadn't been snapping at his heels, hadn't had the paint chart ready, he would have admired her. But he could feel her breath on his ankles and he loathed her. 'I doubt we have time to dither,' he said.

How many times had he sat in meetings since Nine-Eleven, more particularly since Seven-Seven, where scraps of intelligence had been thrown into the ring? Endless hours spent digesting little morsels of information. Mornings, afternoons and evenings exhausted with staring at fuzzy or focused photographs of the supposed enemy, and all the little bastards smiled at whatever camera had caught them.

'Emotive language, Dickie,' she said. 'Only trouble is that you don't have enough for lock-down.'

There was a knock at the door.

Tristram called, 'Please, come in.'

It was Penny. She tiptoed across the carpet, dropped an envelope on to the table, and was gone.

Naylor opened it. A photograph spilled clear and a three-line note. He read, then passed the note to Mary. No satisfaction showed on his face. He stared down at the grey images. He saw her jolted, and she pushed the note across the polished surface.

In a flat voice, Tristram intoned, 'Well, Immigration's cameras at Waterloo's terminal would seem to me to suspend the argument. Rather fortunate that our friend is wearing that ludicrously recognizable T-shirt. What is it – a swan? Peculiar, bizarre, but it's him and he's here.'

Mary said, 'Actually, it's *The Threatened Swan*, by Jan Asselyn, early seventeenth century, housed in the Rijksmuseum, Amsterdam. Last year, on a trip with my art-appreciation group, I saw it. It's impressive and—'

'I think, Mary, that it is not the moment for an assessment of Asselyn's work. I'll brief the director in the morning, but you can take it as read. It's lock-down and bugger the budget. Thank you, Mary. Dickie, would you, please, stay on for a moment?'

She swept up the photograph and the note and left them.

He was waved back to his seat and offered a drink. Didn't usually accept alcohol at work, but said he'd have a Scotch with ice and liberal water. It was given him and the assistant director perched on his desk, let his feet swing.

'She's a bright girl, has a brain on a computer's scale, just needs a bit of polishing round the edges – please, Dickie, don't huff and puff, because you're not good at it. You're right, of course. You saw it coming before that wretched photograph surfaced and that's because you're an old-school warrior. Suspicion, like malaria, gets into the veins and stays there. You've got it, a bad dose . . . Anyway, cheers and good health.'

Glasses were raised, clinked.

'I'm going to miss you, Dickie. Very sincerely, I will. Two reasons . . . First, my being something of a *protégé* of your father-in-law but, second, for your common sense and good reasoning. I'd keep you on if I could. Human Resources wouldn't hear of it. I can't. On Friday night, Dickie, you finish. Now to the point. You wouldn't disagree with me if I suggested that we wriggled through by the skin of our teeth after the Underground and bus bombs – what the Iron Duke said after Waterloo is appropriate: "The nearest run thing that you ever saw." The knives were out for us but we were only nicked, and that won't be repeated. Another major catastrophe in London and there'll be a wholesale cull of the veterans, and those bloody little people in Anti-Terrorism will be crawling all over us and taking primacy. Lifetimes of endeavour, Dickie, yours, mine and many others', will be reduced to dust and ashes. You're following me?'

Naylor nodded. The decanter was eased closer to him and his glass was refilled.

'I called you an old-school warrior. You're from former times. Their benefit was that we concentrated on prevention, not the gathering of evidence to set before a court. Kept the Soviets at bay, the realm intact, and the dock at the Old Bailey hardly mattered. We won't have time on this one for evidence, only – if we're very lucky – for action and that's the "action", Dickie, of an old-school warrior. We may – and you have to believe that Fortune will look kindly on us – find, or have offered to us, a small window of opportunity in the hours before the inevitable detonation of the bomb that will, I have no doubt, be carried by this ghastly young man to a point of maximum impact. Only a small window – are you following me, Dickie?'

He lifted his glass as acknowledgement. He was.

'I take no pride in saying it, but the new broom – the Mary Reakeses of our Service – are so damned *moral*. They care for the fine print of legality. You don't, Dickie, and probably I'd follow in your lane. The attack will be this week, that's a certainty, and it will be on your watch, Dickie. If that window were to open I'd like to think you'd know how to scramble through it with vigour, and without the constraints of a more conventional morality. It's in your past, am I correct? It's a different war and we may have to dirty our hands. I'm sure you know what's necessary . . . Thanks for staying on, and my best regards to Anne.'

Naylor took the stairs down.

Mary looked up from her screen. She said briskly, 'Well, you were right and I was wrong. We're going into lock-down. Oh, the source of it all will be here in the morning, Mr Josiah Hegner.'

'By whose invitation?'

'Not mine. He invited himself.'

He felt a net tightening round him, like the noose on the neck of a prisoner when, long ago, they were taken to interrogation. He seemed to see mud and filth encrusted on his hands.

'Hello. Surprise, surprise. Is that meeting over already, Banksy?'

'No, still in full swing.'

The armoury used by the Delta and Golf and Kilo teams was in the police station's basement. It was the territory of Daff, a predictable Welshman in blue overalls, who clung with adhesive commitment to his Caerphilly accent. Behind the counter, stacked on racks, was weaponry sufficient to start a small war. It was where Banks came any time there were demons in his mind, and he found comfort there – never failed to. Late on that Sunday evening, he needed it bad.

'Beg pardon, I'm not understanding you, Banksy. Big flap, everybody in, pagers bleeping. Why aren't you sitting in?'

'Not wanted,' Banks said grimly. 'Had the door shut on me.'

'That's ridiculous, a man like you and with your experience, daft . . . I have to say, Banksy, I had heard there was friction in the Delta lot.'

'A bit of friction, but I didn't think it would come to this. I was told there was a query about me, about my commitment. I was put out of the briefing before it started.'

The shock was still with him. The inspector had said, 'Sorry and all that, Banksy, but your pager going was a mistake. You won't be involved in the security up-grade. You shouldn't have been called in. My regrets that we screwed your evening. Drop by tomorrow and I'll set the picture out for you, if I've time.' He had stood and walked up the aisle in the briefing room, had known that every eye was on him but he had looked straight ahead. Outside the room he had heard the door shut behind him and a key had turned. He'd leaned against a corridor wall, shaking, then headed for the only place he knew where he could find comfort: Daff's basement.

'I suppose it's the little woman,' the armourer said, confidential, dropping his voice. 'Three years, isn't it? The world moves on and you have to forget her. Have I told you that FBI recruiting story about women?'

He could have said that the friction inside Delta had nothing to do with any of the scratchiness in his relationship with the others, the old tensions his divorce had created. Mandy did not figure, but if he had disabused Daff he wouldn't hear the story: the armourer's reputation for stories was gold-medal standard.

'You haven't,' Banks said drily, 'but I expect you will.'

The lilted tale began. 'It's like this . . . The FBI had an opening for an assassin, a dedicated killer. After all the security checks and interviews they were down to a short-list of three: two men and a woman. For the final test, the FBI's Human Resources took the first man to a big metal door and handed him a Smith & Wesson, and said, "We must know that you will obey orders to the letter, no matter what. Inside the room your wife is sitting in a chair. Kill her." The first man said he could never shoot his wife, and he was told, "You're not the right man for us. Take her and go home." The second man was given the same order and he took the pistol and went into the room. There were five minutes of quiet. Then he came out with tears on his face and said he had tried but finally realized he could not kill his wife. He was told, "You don't have what it takes, go on home with her." It was the woman's turn. Her husband was in the room, sitting in the chair, and she was to shoot him. She took the gun and went inside. Shots were heard, one after another, the whole magazine. Outside, they heard screams, crashes and bangs, then everything went quiet. Would have been at least three minutes more, then the door opened slowly and the woman stood there. She wiped sweat off her forehead and said, "This gun was loaded with blanks. I had to use the chair to kill him." Women for you, Banksy.'

He laughed. He laughed till it hurt. He realized it was the first time he had laughed, from deep in his belly, in the eleven days since the funeral – since he had been handed the diary kept by Cecil Darke. 'I like it.'

'Is it women? You got women aching in your gut?'

'No . . . Daff, it's a bit worse than women.'

The armourer's face contorted in mock horror. 'God, that bad? Then you have my sympathy, Banksy. Well, go on, chuck it up.'

He had come to the basement, to his friend – perhaps the only one he had – to get himself up against a shoulder that would take the burden of his problem. He spoke, haltingly at first, of words written seventy years before 'in a foreign land' and he quoted the verse of Psalm 137, and Daff knew it from chapel in childhood, and he said what had happened in the canteen, kids' play ending in spilt blood, and that he was damned if he would apologize when he had no guilt.

Blinking, Banks said, 'What it's come down to is that there is now a doubt as to my dedication to the job. Would I, because of what I said of my great-uncle, have the ruthlessness to shoot a suicide-bomber who might just be a "brave and principled" young man? Would I hesitate at that moment, going into double tap, and not think of him as a scumbag, a rabid animal, who should be killed – like it was in the Underground train? In their minds, the doubt exists.'

'No one knows, Banksy, how they'd be.'

'There's enough who talk up the macho stuff.' Banks's bitterness flowed. 'Plenty who say they're sure. I'm no longer trusted.'

The face across the counter brightened. 'Did you read that one about the suicide-bomber in Baghdad the other day? You didn't? It's real, it happened, went like this. A suicide-bomber drives his bomb-primed car right under an American M1A1 main battle tank and lodges beneath it and between the tracks and it weighs more than sixty tons. The crew hop out, think it's a road traffic accident and find this guy pinned in his crushed car. He tells them he's a martyr but the way the car's squashed he can't reach the switch to detonate himself. But he still dies, because they do a controlled explosion that kills him, but the tank isn't damaged. What do you think God told him when he got there? "Dear me, you look miserable, have a bad day at work?" You're not laughing now, Banksy.'

'No, I'm not. It's a new war and a new enemy, and maybe they *are* brave and principled. I don't have the answers – others do, but not me. Daff, I feel like I'm flawed.'

'What do you want me to say?'

'Don't know.'

'Well, I'll offer this. If you're in shit, get clear of it. If you're in a quagmire, crawl out of it. Hack on in there, Banksy, don't let the bastards destroy you. Always believe it, something'll turn up.'

'If only it were that easy. I'll see you, Daff.'

At the top of the stairs to the basement he met the crowd of Delta, Golf and Kilo guys and was ignored. Without him, with their briefing finished, they went to draw their weapons.

She sat on the bed and her silent sobbing shook her. From the next room, she could hear the beat of Kathy's music. Beside her, on the duvet, was the brown-paper package with one end torn open and the banknotes exposed.

She had found it an hour earlier when she had brought the ironing upstairs and two pairs of his socks had fallen as she had stacked his clothes on the wardrobe's shelves. The socks had dropped among the shoes at the bottom. It was so obviously hidden and not intended that she should discover it. She had, and she had ripped back the paper. It was more money than she had ever seen. She knew of no reason, other than a criminal one, for so many banknotes to be in her house.

The door clicked downstairs. His voice called, 'Hi, love, you up there? Everything fine? Mum and Dad send their love.'

She heard his footsteps on the stairs and pushed the package further away from her, so that he would see it better when he came into the room.

She wiped her eyes and twisted to face him, contempt coursing through her. She saw his face go ashen.

Chapter 9: Monday, Day 12

He handed the envelope to the jury bailiff. The man studied it, a frown knitting his forehead. He seemed to hold it with suspicion, but he read what was written: *By Hand – for the personal attention of Mr Justice Herbert, Court 18.* There was hesitation. 'Is this something I can deal with?'

Jools said tartly, 'No. If it were I would not have addressed it to Mr Justice Herbert.'

'Actually, in the hour before his court sits, he's rather busy.'

'I'd like it delivered to him now.'

'And when he's busy he has a short temper. Are you telling me this is urgent?'

Jools looked sharply around and behind him, but the remainder of the jury seemed not to have noticed his conversation with the bailiff. 'Look, it's not some bloody complaint about the food or the chairs we sit on. It's urgent and should get on to his desk soonest – like now.'

'Right, then. Be it on your head.'

All the way to the door, the bailiff examined the envelope as if still doubtful of its importance, then was gone. Could not be called back. Jools thought he had cast the die. He was sure that nothing in his life would be the same again.

He felt sick. Vomit had risen from his stomach and was lodged in his throat. He swayed. His eyes, bleary and bloodshot, ached . . . as well they might. He had been up half the night as Babs had scalpelled the truth from him. In the bedroom, her voice stiletto sharp and quiet, his murmuring early evasions and late honesties, she had cut the story out of him. When she had finished, he had been tossed aside. He had spent what was left of the night on the living-room settee, and when he was about to leave she had hurled the package, now retaped, into his midriff. He had clutched it against his chest, under his anorak, all the way to Snaresbrook Crown Court. It was now in his locker, hidden under his coat.

He swayed and felt weakness in his knees. Through the night, as truths were dragged out of him, she had belted him: 'You disgust me, you make me cringe with shame . . . Don't give me the craven excuse that there was a threat to Kathy, me, you. Policemen exist to protect us from such threats . . . It's not too late. You took the money and now you will hand it in to the court's authorities and come clean . . . If you have not done that by the time you come home this evening I will be straight down to the nearest police station and you will be looking at a charge, from your vantage-point in the cells, of conspiracy to pervert the course of justice, or whatever they call it . . . Why didn't you just throw it back in that awful little man's face? Isn't there an iota of decency, pride, self-esteem, in you? . . . And you're a person responsible for overseeing the way children are brought up, your own and at school – God, what a damn Pharisee you've turned out to be, and unfit to have children in your care . . . There is, if you didn't know it, a clear division between what is *right* and what is *wrong*, but since you don't seem to understand that, it falls to me to kick you down the right road . . . Do you think I could ever look myself in the face, stand in front of a mirror, if I knew that our debts were paid off with that money? Do you? Well, think again. I'd prefer to starve in the street, destitute, and Kathy with me, than spend a penny of it . . . Get out of my sight because I don't want you in my room and most certainly not in my bed . . . So, there will be consequences – well, the police will look after us, and my trust lies in them, not in the word of criminals . . .' Always had had a way with words, his Babs.

'Hey, Jools, you been on the juice last night?' Baz had sidled close to him, and grinned.

'More like a right junket.' Fanny giggled. 'What did you have? A gallon or two?'

He reeled away from them and slumped on to a chair.

Fanny came to him and crouched beside him. She said softly, 'Don't mind them, Jools, they're just silly and spiteful. Is it that you're ill or is it *Angst* in the mind? You can tell me – I only share secrets with my cat.'

He thought her a dear and chaotic woman, with rather an admirable chest that was a usual attention point for him in post-lunch court sessions, but was damned if he would confide. 'There was no alcohol involved. I merely happen to have slept poorly,' he said sharply.

The hands of the clock on the wall advanced. The time came and went when the bailiff would normally have urged those who needed it to make a last visit to the toilets. The others had now retreated to the hard chairs round the walls and were buried in newspaper word teasers and crossword puzzles, except Fanny, who knitted from a pattern. Their bailiff had come back into the room, had hovered with an expression of crisis on his face, then had been called out, had returned again, then gone once more. By now they should have been gathering up their notepads and filing into court. Jools felt the earlier tiredness and sickness ebb out of him, replaced with a sensation near to exhilaration. None of them except him knew the cause of the delay. It was as if, and none of them had seen him do it, he had pulled the pin from a pineapple-shaped grenade, rolled it studiously across the floor, and it had wobbled to a stop in the centre of the room. The bailiff was back with them and coughed heavily, not to clear his throat but to attract attention – Jools was counting down the seconds till the explosion.

'I regret, ladies and gentlemen, that we have a delay this morning and I cannot say for how long it will be. Our judge asks for your patience. A matter has come to his notice that he has to deal with. As soon as he has an answer to a difficulty that has arisen, he will call you in. I am afraid I am not at liberty to discuss the matter, the difficulty, with you.'

Jools motioned to the bailiff to come to him, then reached into his trouser pocket for his locker key. 'In my locker there's a package that'll be corroboration for what's in the letter I wrote to old Herbert,' he whispered. 'Please retrieve it, without a song and dance, and get it to him.'

He saw it done with discretion. He threw his sandalled feet forward, leaned back, yawned, and yawned again. They'd think of him as a bloody hero, wouldn't they? They would never know he was merely the spineless bloody coward who had crumpled under the weight of his wife's morality.

'You'll put it in place, Chief Inspector. I will rely on you to do that.'

'The cost, sir, of such a procedure is prohibitive.'

'I am not in an area of discussion and argument. It will happen. I will not countenance the losing of the case at such a late stage. I would estimate that the Crown has already invested more than two million pounds in this prosecution and if we go for a mis-trial – and a subsequent rehearing – we will be looking for another million, at least, in expenditure. There is the further consideration, and it is a weighty one, that the abandonment of the trial in its last hours would be a victory for the forces of corruption. No, if the jury needs protection, I am charging you with providing it.'

If Mr Justice Wilbur Herbert was flustered by what he had learned that morning, he gave no indication of it. He anticipated that preliminary estimates of cost and expenditure were now scrambling at speed in the chief inspector's mind. But justice was his concern, not the spilling of further sums from the public purse. He had played the card of the expense of a retrial, and had loftily dismissed the prospect of such an action, yet he was economic with his motivation. Regina v. Curtis and Curtis was a high-profile matter, one that would attract the attention of the Lord Chancellor: a successful conclusion would enhance his prospects of a legal peerage and, ultimately, a seat on the benches of the Court of Appeal. He had no doubt that his diminished jury would bring in 'guilty' verdicts on all counts, and had already framed a wording of the statement he would make to the accused when he sent them away to serve most, if not all, of the remainder of their lives as Category A prisoners. Well hidden under a veneer of polite calm he felt a fierce desire to purge, whenever it was within his power, the culture of organized and serious criminality. If he had lived half a century before, Mr Justice Herbert would have had a clerk slip a freshly ironed and uncreased square of black cloth carefully on to his wig, then pronounced the death sentence on murderers. Not appropriate here, but breaking stones in a quarry would have been – in his opinion – proper retribution by society on such men as Ozzie and Ollie Curtis. Preferably granite.

The chief inspector, the senior investigating officer on the case, seemed to squirm. 'The cost, sir, is but one side of the problem.'

'I'm not in the mood for having problems deflect us.'

'The reverse face is manpower, sir.'

'I doubt that is insoluble. An officer of your experience and ability can and will, I'm sure, find a route round such difficulties.'

The objections were shoved aside with the ruthlessness that was the hallmark of Mr Justice Herbert's successful climb on his career ladder. But when he spoke it was with his old-world courtesy, with which all who appeared in his courts were familiar. There was a thoroughness about him that scuppered the mention of appeals being won on the basis of his guidance to juries and his dealings with defence lawyers. His exterior was one of moderation and patience. His listed hobbies of reading Victorian melodrama, poetry, and sailing an eighteen-foot yacht off a mooring at Southwold, along with his regular Sunday attendance at morning worship in the cathedral of his home city, St Albans, all proffered an image of caring reasonableness, and truth was disguised. He believed that the chief inspector would soon weaken, but he tolerated a trifle of the man's obstinacy and allowed him his moment.

'The cost, sir, of protection is awesome. We have a jury of ten persons and although we have had one jury member come clean about an offer—'

'And not only "come clean", but also hand over a most considerable sum of money, thereby giving two significant markers of honesty and courage.'

'Of course, sir . . . but I cannot assume that this one individual is the only one who has been approached. You are asking me—'

'I am *instructing* you, Chief Inspector.'

'Yes, sir. Your instruction means that I have to rustle up the manpower to protect the jury members, ten of them, *and* look after their families. I would have to move the jury for the rest of the trial into secure accommodation, while at the same time ensuring that their families are guarded in their homes. We are talking about upwards

180

of a hundred officers, and the requirement that a percentage of them would be armed. That's a big call, sir.'

'Then your job is to make the call.'

'Over and above that, we would have to acknowledge Duty of Care for the future, both to the jurors and their families. It won't all grind to a halt, sir, when the case concludes, could go on for months. Frankly, I hear a cash register going out of control here, and we could be looking at relocation.'

'The price of justice, Chief Inspector, is not cheap. What'll you do? Put the jurors into a hotel for the duration?'

'I don't think so. Hotels are about as insecure as things get – people wandering in and out, unvetted staff, back-of-the-building fire escapes and trade entrances . . . I'll look elsewhere. Then there's the business of keeping the jurors calm: "Who's going to be looking after my wife, my mother, all the rest?" They could panic and want out.'

'That is my responsibility and I will field it. I'm very grateful for your positive response, Chief Inspector, and I guarantee that your co-operation will be reflected in the personal letter I will write to your commissioner. Confidently, I leave these matters in your capable hands . . . and let us not forget the public-spirited action of this most courageous man, Julian Wright. Thank you.'

Signifying the termination of the meeting, Mr Justice Herbert returned to the hillocks of paper notes on his desk, but he saw from his eye's corner that the chief inspector had slipped on plastic gloves before he picked up the package that was ripped open at one end to show the wads of banknotes. He was alone in his room. Did he care about the costs? He did not. Did he care about the disruption of the jurors' domestic lives? He did not. Did he care about a mis-trial and the prospect, then, of losing the opportunity to make a crafted speech on the threat of organized crime to society at large? Most certainly. Modern intruder alarms were wired throughout his home: he himself lived under a permanent threat of attack from the associates of those he had sent down for long terms of imprisonment. Because of the obligations of justice, he wore a hair-shirt, as had the ascetics and penitents of history, and others could ape him.

He buzzed his clerk. He told her that he needed the presence in his room of the QCs heading the prosecution and defence. He saw them, heard their comments. When they had finished, he thanked them effusively and announced that he would resume in ten minutes.

He wrote a note of what he would say, pondered on each sentence and checked a reference to a case a year before that had gone to appeal. He rewrote a line, then slipped into his robes. In front of the mirror he adjusted his wig and tightened his sash. He put the envelope and the letter into the floor safe, swung the combination dials, locked his room's door behind him, walked the corridor and heard the shout ahead of him: 'All rise.'

Mr Justice Herbert, with the full majesty of his office, swept into court eighteen, took his seat and read out what he had written.

Every eye was on him. Not a cough, a shuffle or fidget disturbed him.

He concluded, 'Ladies and gentlemen of the jury, you have listened to me with due attention, but I will take the liberty of going again over the chief points I have made. These are matters of great importance and there should be no misunderstandings . . . It has been brought to my notice that a conspiracy exists to bribe one or some of you to bring in a verdict of not guilty for the accused, and that a reward of money has been offered. This is police intelligence. Because of that intelligence, it will be necessary for you to face restrictions on your movements and freedoms, which I greatly regret . . . We have been together a long time now and I urge you with due emphasis not to consider providing a spurious excuse and abandoning the trial in its final hours. You have shown such dedication that I am confident I can depend on you and, in anticipation of your co-operation, I am sincerely grateful to you all . . . Now, I am repeating myself because this is at the heart of the matter, you should draw no conclusions regarding this case from what I have just told you. There is no evidence that either Mr Oswald Curtis or Mr Oliver Curtis is in any way implicated in any plot to suborn you. As far as I am concerned, they are completely innocent of any such involvement. I cannot emphasize that more strongly. Ahead of us now are the closing speeches of the prosecution and the defence. Then I will offer you my guidance, and you will retire – either at the end of this week or the start of next – to deliberate on your verdict but you will *not* infer, from certain precautions put in place round you, that any of these allegations of bribery or intimidation reflect on the accused. They do not, and are not a part of this case, which you will decide only on the sworn evidence that has been put before you. You have to dismiss these allegations – which is all they are – from your minds. Right, ladies and gentlemen of the jury, we will now adjourn but I have to ask you for your patience. Please, you will wait in the jury room until certain arrangements are in place, and we will resume our hearing in the morning – but do not forget what I have said. You will judge this case only on the testimony you have heard in the courtroom – nothing, absolutely *nothing* else . . .'

'The bastard, the fucking little bastard, I'll—'

'Please, Mr Curtis, refrain from that sort of language and from shouting.'

'He's took my money. I'll fucking have him.'

'You're in danger, Mr Curtis, of being heard throughout the entire building.'

'He's got my money, and the fucking Nobbler has! We're fucking screwed.'

The barrister, Ozzie Curtis's 'brief', took the force of it and Nathaniel Wilson was thankful for a minimal mercy. He stood with his back pressed to the cell door. As if he was in a trance of disbelief, Ollie Curtis sat on the bed's vinyl-coated mattress, stared up at the barred window and had nothing to contribute, unlike his elder brother. The rant had started at the moment that the barrister and Wilson had been admitted by a poker-faced prison guard. That bastard would have been pissing himself once the door was shut and the bolt pushed across. Wilson wondered if it was the wasted money that hurt his client most or the knowledge that the jury – if it held together and stayed firm – would now, inevitably, convict.

The barrister said wistfully, 'The problem is, Mr Curtis – and it's his skill – that our judge was at pains to exonerate you from any blame. He could not have said more. Of course, when I was in with him, I did all the stuff about a jury inevitably being prejudiced and went for a mis-trial, but I was turned down and he's covered that ground. Areas of appeal, should this trial go against you, are considerably reduced . . . Our judge knows his stuff.'

'And it will fucking go against us.'

'I fear so, Mr Curtis.'

'And that bastard took our money. What you going to fucking do, Nat?'

'Well, what I'm not going to do, Ozzie, is rush upstairs, use my mobile and have that traced. It's a difficult situation, Ozzie, needs thinking about.'

'I want that fucking man having good fucking grief, and you're going to fix it.'

Nathaniel Wilson did not answer. The barrister rapped on the door for it to be opened. He was not involved. Wilson was in the quagmire up to his damn neck. He thought of the man who sat in the back row of the jury box, with the stubble on his face and the sandals on his feet, and wondered how he could have been so stupid as to cross his client, take Ozzie Curtis's money, then play-act at being a hero. And his mind turned, with rare longing, to a life outside the little flat that he shared with his wife over the office. Ozzie, thank the good Lord, had retreated and now leaned his forehead against a wall of the cell, spent. Later, when he had the security of fire breaks to mask his communications, he would contact Benny Edwards. He reckoned the man who had turned in the money to be as great an idiot as any he had known, with 'good fucking grief' ahead of him.

The bolt was drawn back. The same impassive officer let him and the barrister out.

The door had opened and there had been the pad of footsteps in the corridor. Now Ibrahim Hussein heard the toilet flush.

The sounds broke the quiet of the cottage. Hours earlier, he had seen his leader leave by car and head away slowly up the track. Khalid had driven and the girl had been with them and Jamal. Later, Syed had wandered off along the track and would now have settled himself in the clump of trees half-way up it from where he would have a view of the cottage, and its approach, and be able to see across the fields round it. The guard, Ramzi, was slumped in an easy chair, reading a magazine featuring colour photographs of body-builders with grotesque muscles. The clock in the hallway, by the front door, ticked noisily. Time passed in the life of Ibrahim Hussein, from the town of Jizan in Asir Province, and he did not know how much would pass before he walked. He reached out for his Book and thought his hours were best occupied in learning better the printed pages. His door opened and he started. The Book fell to the carpet.

'Please, would you come with me?' The heavy-built body of the man filled the doorway. 'Would you, please, bring that jacket – the leather one – with you?'

He lifted it from the back of the chair and followed. He was led into the room at the far end of the passageway and had to duck his head under a blackened beam. The table was in front of him.

On the newspaper that covered it was a waistcoat. Pouches had been sewn over its pockets, and the sticks lay in them. Flies swarmed incessantly over plastic bags tied to the pouches with fine string and their buzzing overwhelmed the clock's ticking. In the bags he could see, among filth, heaps of close-packed nails, screws and ball-bearings. Wires ran from the sticks to two batteries, and another wire came from the batteries and was linked to a button switch. He gazed at the waistcoat, in awe of it.

He was told briskly: 'Please, I want your arms out.'

The waistcoat was carefully threaded over them. The weight settled on his shoulders, was a burden, and Ibrahim had to flex his upper-body muscles. Fingers were tugging at the material, straightening, raising, loosening it. He was in the tailor's shop on the Corniche; his father sat and watched with smiling pride because a sole surviving son had come of age; a tailor who was a distant cousin of his father fussed over the fall of a robe that was held together with pins and had yet to be finished to perfection, new clothing for the start of a student's first term at the medical school. Cased in plastic gloves, fingers probed and poked, then more tape was bound tight over the most protruding joins with the shiny silver detonators.

'Is it comfortable?' The question was asked with less respect than the tailor, the distant cousin of his father, would have given, but it was the same question. Then, in the flush of youth, the excitement of going away and beginning his studies, he had pirouetted and the robe had swung free at his hips and knees; his father had clapped. He did not know what he should answer, and the flies rose from the bags and flew into his eyes, nose and ears. He was told, 'It has to be comfortable. If it is not comfortable, you will walk with discomfort and bad walking is recognized. A man who walks well is not noticed, but he must be comfortable – or he betrays himself.'

'I am comfortable,' Ibrahim said hoarsely. 'But the flies are—'

He was interrupted, as if his query was unimportant. 'No matter, there is a spray in the kitchen that will kill them. What concerns me – is it too tight, is it awkward? I can take out a vent at the back if you need it looser.'

'It is not awkward.'

The jacket was lifted off the back of the chair and passed to him.

'You will wear this? It is a good length. It is heavy enough not to show a bulge on your chest. Try with the jacket, but gently because the connections are not yet finally fastened. Do it.'

He smelt the leather, felt its strength, put his arms into the sleeves and let it settle on him.

'Button it, but not roughly.'

He did as he was told. The fingers were back at his chest and pulled at the jacket's front. He saw a flitting, coarse smile of satisfaction.

'Much room, enough, not too tight . . . You can take them off, but carefully.'

He dropped the jacket on to the floor, then worked the waistcoat off his shoulders, and felt freedom when he had shed its weight. It was taken from him and laid again on the table, but the flies were still in his face.

'What do I do now?'

'If you have a complaint about the waistcoat, you tell me. If you have no complaint, you go back to your room. Do not misunderstand me, young man. I am not a coffee-house talker. I am not a recruiter who persuades young men to rush towards Heaven. Others talk and others persuade, but I am an expert in ordnance. I am a fighter and I use what weapons are available to me. It was your choice to volunteer and your motivation is not my concern. Do you have a complaint?'

'No.'

'Then go back to your room.'

Ibrahim turned, bent and picked up the jacket that was his prized possession. He told himself, harsh words in silence, that he was not afraid, that he did not need to be comforted. He let himself out of the room and did not look back at the table and the waistcoat.

*

'If it is a problem, drop your trousers and piss on it.'

Tariq, now the Engineer, had learned the value of the suicide attack, of martyrs to God, as a junior lieutenant aged eighteen, serving in the front line of the Fao peninsula.

The problem was the overheated barrel of a PKMB 7.62mm Russian-built light machine-gun.

What the platoon sergeant had told him, Tariq had done. He had exposed himself, his head and shoulders above the parapet of sandbags. He had crouched over the barrel, loosened his belt, lowered his trousers and urinated on the barrel; steam in a vapour cloud had hissed off the metal. Then he had loaded another belt of ammunition, fired again – and they had kept coming.

The machine-gun position nearest him, thirty paces to his right, was abandoned. In the one to his left, fifty paces from him, the gunner had collapsed over the stock of his weapon and the corporal shook with convulsive sobbing. It was hard to kill kids. One man had run from the children's advance and another had collapsed, but Tariq had continued to shoot with bursts of six to nine bullets each time his finger locked on the trigger.

He knew that their ayatollah had said: 'The more people die for our cause, the stronger we become.'

The assault across open ground, beyond the swamp reeds, towards the machine-gun nests was codenamed Karbala 3 by the enemy. As they ran, the kids shouted in shrill wailing cries, 'Ya Karballah, ya Hussein, ya Khomeini.' They came in dense swarms. Tariq knew, because the Ba'ath officials had dinned it into every soldier on the forward positions, that children were used in the van of an attack so that their drumming feet would detonate the anti-personnel mines laid in front of the wire that protected the sandbag nests. By using children, the regular troops of the enemy and the Revolutionary Guard would not have to advance through minefields. In the opening year of the war, his sergeant had told him that the enemy's commanders had tried to use donkeys to clear the mines but when one had lost its legs in an explosion the rest had proved too obstinate to go on, even when gunfire was put down behind them; and in Iran there were more children than donkeys. He could barely see over the wall of the children's bodies in front of the wire. He fired, changed the belt, fired again. The gunner to his right had fled because his replacement barrel was now worn smooth and useless, as was the first. The gunner to his right had collapsed, traumatized at the killing of so many children.

Above the wall of bodies he saw myriad little heads, on which were bright scarlet bandannas, and faces that were smooth and young but contorted with hatred. He swept his sights over them. At fifty paces' range, the PKMB machine-gun – in the hands of a good, calm gunner – was said in the manual to have a 97 per cent chance of hitting a man-sized target. Harder to achieve that strike rate now because they were so small, but they compensated by bunching into groups, like kids running in a school playground. Some were caught on the wire and blood drenched their T-shirts, on which was printed the message 'Imam Khomeini has given me Permission to enter Heaven'. They screamed then for their mothers, not for their ayatollah, and he could see, over the V sight and the needle sight, the little plastic trinkets hanging on string from their necks.

He knew what the lightweight trinkets were because the Ba'athist official had lectured them on the matter. The children wore plastic keys looped into the string. The keys would unlock the gates of Heaven for them. The official had told his unit that, earlier in the war and during the Karbala 1 campaign, they had been made of metal but there was a shortage of that now in Iran and plastic was more available and cheaper to manufacture.

That day Tariq, who was a teenage lieutenant, had fired in excess of 5,500 rounds of 7.62mm ball ammunition at children. When dusk had come, and the wire in front of him was unbroken, he had ceased firing and the screams had died. In the silence there was only the whimpering murmur of the wounded. He had learned the value of the willing martyr when he had had to piss on a machine-gun barrel, and had not forgotten it. For days afterwards, the crows came to feast and the stench grew. Then the armour had pushed forward, driving back the Iranian enemy, and bulldozers had been deployed to excavate pits and push the children's bodies into them.

A medal had been pinned on his chest by the President, and he had received a kiss on his cheeks, and the lesson of the martyr's awesome power had stayed with him.

Working at the stitching of the waistcoat, he could not recall how many martyrs he had helped on their journey to Paradise. Taping more securely the batteries' terminals to the wire, the Engineer knew with certainty that he created terror in the minds of his new enemy: the Americans and their allies.

The martyrs were merely weapons of war. They had no more significance to him than a shell, a bomb, a mortar round or a bullet. The martyrs performed the task he made for them and in return were given, perhaps, fifteen minutes of fame. Then the satellite television channel that had transmitted the video of them would move to another item.

It was irrelevant to him whether he liked the boy or not. What mattered to the Engineer was that the boy walked without revealing himself, and that the leather jacket hid the bulges of the sticks of explosives, the bundles of contaminated nails, screws and ball-bearings.

He did not hurry. The gloves would have made his finger movements clumsy if he had rushed his work. His devices were manufactured to a foolproof standard . . . but he yearned to be away from this place. He hated it, feared it. He would be long gone before the boy walked with the waistcoat secreted under the leather jacket.

The farmer asked his wife, 'What do they do down there, all day every day?'

'Don't know and don't particularly care.' She was wrestling at the kitchen table with accounts.

He sipped his coffee. 'I'm not complaining. Their money was useful . . . It's just, well, what do they do?'

'Does it matter?'

'Don't suppose it does . . . The car went out this morning, I saw that. Half the bedroom curtains were still drawn, but there was washing on the line. A bit after that I was crossing the Home Field on the tractor and one of them was sat on his backside among the trees in the Old Copse, looking a right zombie, just staring at me. You reckon they're on drugs?'

'I doubt it. The girl didn't seem the type – if I know what the type is . . . That's it, celebrations are called for. Thanks to them, their contribution, we're all right for this month.' She bundled the paperwork together, buried it in a file, then dumped it in the table's drawer.

He chuckled. 'Could be magic mushrooms . . . What I'm thinking, maybe one of us . . .'

'You mean me?'

'. . . maybe you should pop down there, some time this week, just make sure they haven't . . .'

'Wrecked the place? You didn't meet her and I did. She's very pleasant . . . It's a family gathering – none of our business what they do all day . . . But I will. Not today, because I've got to do the ironing, and finish that embroidery if it's to be in time for the Show . . . but I will. Don't expect they'll bite me. I'll call in tomorrow or the day after. Satisfied?'

He grinned, stood, then bent and pecked her cheek. 'Just to be on the safe side, tomorrow or the day after.'

He went out, stepped into his wellingtons and walked, in his rolling gait, to his tractor. He would resume harrowing the Twenty-Five-acre field, which was beyond the Home Field. He wondered whether the zombie was still parked on his backside in the Old Copse, and couldn't imagine what an Asian family was doing at Oakdene Cottage and why, mid-morning, half the curtains were still drawn . . . but she'd find out. She had a nose as good as any vixen's for probing and prying.

It was about trust, and the Scorpion was short of it. He trailed the girl across the square, and at his shoulder was the youngest of them, Jamal. Her hips swung in front of him but he cut his glance from them and stared around him as he walked. His eyes raked over the signs for the sale that would start at nine in the morning on the next Saturday in the shopping centre. But he did not trust enough to show his interest. She walked to the steps and turned.

She said softly, 'On Saturday morning, before nine o'clock, there will be a queue here. There will be many people.'

At his grandfather's side he had learned not to trust the father who had abandoned his pregnant mother. Walking in orange groves with his grandmother he had learned not to trust the mother who had discarded him to find escape in death. Sitting in a classroom at school he had learned not to trust fellow students who sneered that he was a bastard and without parents. As a paratroop recruit he had learned not to trust the 'chutes' packers because a man in front of him had fallen to his death when the canopy hadn't opened. As a qualified paratrooper in the Jordanian army, trained in warfare against the Zionist enemy, he had learned not to trust when the frontier was opened to Jewish diplomats and a craven deal was done. After he had disappeared from the barracks in Amman and travelled to Baghdad to volunteer for the fledgling guerrilla militia, he had learned not to trust when, two months later, the Republican Guard units had disintegrated when attacked. In the ranks of the *mujahidin*, operating from the supposed safe haven of the Triangle, he had learned not to trust when captured colleagues informed.

He did not fully trust any of the cell that had been assembled for him. His trust for the girl who stood on the steps was at best incomplete, but he could live with that.

He spun on his heel and walked away through the square. He saw the confusion on the youth's face and heard the clatter of the girl's shoes as she ran to catch him. He walked briskly to the car park.

At the car, she asked, blurted, 'Is the place not right?'

His survival was based on a culture of mistrust.

He said to Khalid, in a firm voice, decisive, 'I want to go to the city of Birmingham. It is the second city, yes? This is a shit place, too small and not worth his sacrifice. I am going to Birmingham to do a reconnaissance for a target of importance.'

The faces of the girl and the youth fell, as he had intended. He told them they should take a bus back to the village, that only he would go, with Khalid to drive him. He thought the youth was near tears, and that the girl's mouth – below the scar – quivered in anger at the slight. He said he would be in Birmingham for the rest of that day, the night, and that he would return to the cottage on the following day.

Deceit, lies, evasions fashioned a protective web behind which the Scorpion, Muhammad Ajaq, existed.

Through the gates, past the dense rhododendrons, the grounds opened out, and beyond the flat grasslands – big enough for half a dozen soccer pitches – was the old edifice of the building. David Banks, detective constable, barely noticed the brick and stone façade, or the folly towers high over the main entrance. He hadn't seen the lake, the ducks and geese on the water. He was in no mood for sightseeing, no mood for a bloody tourist expedition to Snaresbrook Crown Court. He parked in a bay that was supposedly restricted to the disabled.

'Don't blame me, Banksy. You've made a rod for your own back . . . Yes, I did approach both Golf and Kilo, but a bad word is like a bad smell. It spreads, got me? Neither of them wanted you. I'm sorry, but I've done what I can for you. Maybe in the next few days you should reflect on where you've put yourself, then sort yourself out . . . In the situation we have in London right now, I don't have any more time to devote to your personal situation, Banksy. My final word on all this is that the guys you should be working with have lost confidence in you. As Protection Officers, at a time of maximum threat, they have the right to expect total loyalty from all members of their teams. Sadly, they've got it in their heads that if push comes to shove you'll blink and won't pull the trigger. Don't worry, you won't be sitting around twiddling your thumbs, your feet up, while the guys are doing their stuff. No, in answer to a request for manpower, you're going to leafy Snaresbrook to do valuable work in the field of jury protection. You made your own bed, Banksy, so go and lie on it.'

He'd left his inspector's door open behind him, had heard the REMF's shout for him to close it. Had ignored him and kept on walking.

Down in the basement armoury, he had drawn his Glock, ammunition, a ballistic blanket, a sack of gas canisters and stun grenades, and a first-aid box. For once, Daff had not helped. The armourer had told him cheerfully that every man and woman authorized to carry a firearm was out on the streets of London, that his shelves were stripped 'damn near bare' . . . but had added, with a widening grin, that 'Protecting a jury is pretty important work, don't you know?' He'd rammed the pistol into the belt holster, heaved the rest of the kit into his bag and the final rejoinder from Daff had been, 'And don't shoot the bloody judge, Banksy . . .' He'd gone to his car, slammed it into gear and driven east of the city where lock-down had settled.

He went into the building, used the main door at the side of the bloody useless and decrepit façade, showed his warrant card and asked for court eighteen. It was years since he had been in a Crown Court. One of the precious few advantages of being a Protection

Officer and fawning over Principals was that the days of hanging around court corridors waiting to give evidence were finished. God, and it came back to him fast, the smell of those places. Banks saw the sign and stamped towards it.

Three uniformed men were by the double doors. He did not acknowledge them, strode past them and heaved on the doors' handles. They were locked and he couldn't shift them. He heard a titter – like it was good to see a pompous sod, without the time of day for colleagues, put down.

Banks barked first the statement, then his question. 'I'm with the protection outfit. Where are they?'

An usher was called. He was told he would be taken to the room where the rest of his people were gathered.

The usher, disabled and dragging his foot, led him, and chattered: 'Grand place, isn't it? I suppose it's your first time down here, you not knowing where to go . . . Biggest Crown Court in the country, does more than two thousand five hundred cases a year in twenty court rooms, a proper mass-production line. Wonderful building. Started off as an orphanage and was completed – money no object – in 1843. The main supply of stone was from Yorkshire, but the facings were from Bath and France. Fell into disrepair and was turned into a court in the middle 1970s, but they had a heck of a problem with the foundations and had to put three thousand tons of concrete under the main building so it didn't collapse. We see it all here . . . What's going on in court eighteen, anyway?'

'Haven't any idea,' Banks said. 'As you reckoned, it's my first time here.'

He hesitated at the door, listened for a moment to the rumble of voices inside. The rest of Delta, and the guys from Golf and Kilo, would be preening themselves as they made concentric circles of protection round the best and the brightest on the high ladders of achievement. Each last one would be imagining the plaudits – coming in wheelbarrow loads – if they managed a double tap on a suicide-bomber, a *foreign* suicide-bomber, a foreign *fighter*. His career was on the floor. Banks was assigned to a sodding jury out in the back end of nowhere. He opened the door and went inside. The talk stopped. Eyes were on him. He saw that a coffee mug, lifted towards a mouth, was held in mid-air. The hush closed on him.

Then, a voice boomed cheerily, 'Is that David Banks? Yes? Brilliant. You're the last bit of our jigsaw. You're very welcome.'

A hand was thrust towards his. He took it and his fingers were crushed with enthusiasm. 'Thank you,' he said limply.

'Hey, let's have a smile. I'm DCI Brian Walton, Wally to you. The way I run a ship we don't stand on ceremony. I'm the case officer, but also the threat-assessment bloke. I tell you, we've all fallen on our feet. This is a real fridge-freezer job, and could get even better – could get to be a conservatory job, know what I mean?'

He did, and a smile slipped on to his face. It was an overtime payer: unsocial hours at time and a half, and extra days at double time. Big overtime paid for fridges, freezers and cookers in the kitchen, new carpets in the living room and hall, concert-standard sound on home-cinema systems – and the biggest overtime dollops could mean funding for a conservatory at the back of the house. He hadn't expected to be welcomed, greeted as a new friend.

Almost shyly, 'Good to meet you all. I'm Banksy.'

The voice progressed, boom to bellow: 'You treat this man with respect, hear me, guys? He's the proper thing, not one of you yokels rounded up in the backwoods of Thames Valley, Essex and Norfolk. He does the Prime Minister, royalty, all the toffs, but he's been given to us, and he'll show us how to do the job. When Banksy speaks, you lot listen – me too.'

Banks had to grin, then grimace, and probably he blushed, but he felt the warmth of those around him. Perhaps his jacket, weighted by the notebook, the pebbles and coins, had ridden back, but all eyes were now on his waist, his belt. He looked down and saw the smear of gun oil on his shirt, the edge of the dark leather holster. He understood. It was a team, perhaps twenty in all, put together in a spasm of panic. Not specialists, not high-flyers, but the men and women whose absence from their normal day-in and day-out duties would go unnoticed. They were what was available. He moved fast among them, took each hand and shook it, then cursed himself for not initially giving them what they offered him, warmth.

Wally clapped his hands. 'Right, your attention, please. This is my case and I'm not willingly going to lose it. I've bitched to the judge, Mr Justice Herbert, about the cost of it all and been given a flea in my ear, but at the end of the day I'm not arguing with him. To do this job properly would have taken three times as many of you as I've been given, but you're what I have and we'll cut our cloth accordingly. We're down to the essentials and we'll make it work. The case before our judge is the Queen versus Ozzie and Ollie Curtis and they are two old, unreconstructed blaggers. They do armed robbery successfully – that is, up to the time they knocked over a jewellery shop in the south-east. We found a witness, put her under the protection scheme, and she was a star in the firmament when she came to court. They're going down, the Curtis brothers are, and it's about as far down as fifteen years minimum. For them it's desperate, so they pushed for a nobble. A juror was approached and given big money. This jury, with another week or so to do, is reduced to ten, so if one more had pulled out or voted not guilty, then we have a mis-trial. With a mis-trial, we get another hearing in – if I'm lucky – a year's time, and I don't reckon I'll hold my witness for all those months. I need a guilty verdict next week . . . One juror had the guts to report the approach and the cash payment to the court. A very brave man, as courageous as it gets where the Curtis thugs are concerned. He deserves our protection and full support, and I aim to give them to him. Have other jurors been approached and caught in the web? I don't know. Are other jurors more vulnerable to corruption? Don't know. But I'm going to throw a net round them that puts them in a bubble: no mobiles, no contact with the outside. The court is adjourned for the day. You're going home with them. You'll watch them like bloody hawks. They'll each pack a bag and make what arrangements they have to, and you will escort them here in the morning. Tomorrow evening they'll be bussed to secure accommodation. That's where we are, and I'll take questions at the end. By the by, this is going to be a good little earner, and it won't end with the verdict. Health and Safety legislation requires duty of care, and that can run for a fair few weeks. Finally, I emphasize to you all, these jurors are not going to become your long-lost friends. You treat them with politeness and firmness. Their safety must be ensured, and the chance of a nobbler getting near them is removed, but my priority is the conviction of those low-life brothers. That's it.'

Banks thought he'd done well, couldn't fault it. Wally had a list, names and addresses, moved among them and allocated them.

Banks thought, passing, that he might have been blessed, that – at last – he was drummed into some police work that was valuable, worthwhile.

He went to pour himself a coffee from the dispenser, sipped it and watched the detective chief inspector meander across the room. He realized that he had been kept for last.

He wondered, if time was available, where he would next find Cecil Darke, and what misery he would meet.

'You gone somewhere else, Banksy? I'm relying on you for the big one.'

'That's not a problem.'

'You're going to do the prime target – that OK? The juror who coughed up and did the decent, he's for you.'

'When we do threat assessment, we have a scale. E5 is the bottom level, and A1 is at the top. Where on the scale are you putting him?'

'His name is Julian Wright. What I've seen of him, he's a dreamy blighter, beard and sandals, a teacher. Last nine weeks I've watched him in court, and I never rated him as being anything other than a guy who'll go with the flow. But I was wrong . . . Now he's shoved a stick into a wasps' nest and twisted it. It's the Curtis brothers' nest and they'll be powerfully angry. Not only has he taken their money but he's also grassed on them. Given the chance, they'll kill him and all those dear to him. It's why I'm grateful to have a man of your pedigree alongside him. On the threat-assessment scale, Julian Wright is at A1. Is that enough?'

Banks said simply, 'I'll do the best I can.'

Wally said he was going now to talk to the jurors, fill in their picture books, that he'd be back in a half-hour. Banks found a chair in a corner, and even in a crowded room he was alone with his notebook.

5 March 1937

I feel it tonight, so strongly that it is hard to describe – I have not shared it with Ralph but I do not doubt he has the same emotions as me – but I will try to express it.

There is around us an atmosphere of _evil_. It is suspicion and fear. The commissars tell us that treachery is all around us. We are _infiltrated_ by Fascist spies and Trotskyist agents. Ralph has heard that some of the brigadiers speak of this obsession with betrayal as 'Russian Syphilis'.

I am hesitant of writing where I could be seen. Only Ralph knows that I have my diary. There are many English lads in our unit but I would not let them know that I have the notebook and my thoughts.

It has rained very heavily in the Jarama valley and our trenches are flooded. We have three inches of water in our bunker. We try to bail the water out each night before we sleep but it is useless because the water comes in faster than we can clear it. It is a place of misery.

The British company is now attached to the French battalion, and alongside us were the Americans from the Lincoln brigade . . . I think they started the Jarama campaign with a force of 500 men. Ralph says that they have lost 120 dead and 175 wounded. They have a song that they sing, and the commissars permit it because they are Russians and do not understand the words: 'There's a valley in Spain called Jarama, It's a place that we all know too well, For 'tis there that we wasted our manhood, And most of our old age as well.' It is two days now since the Americans – they are younger than us, mostly students and very naïve, but honest – were pulled out of the line. They had <u>mutinied</u>.

They had refused to go forward.

Their officers said they would not advance because they had poor kit and were only given impossible targets to capture.

They refused the order from the staff. We could not see this, but word of it had spread by the evening. They formed up, their backs to the enemy, and set off for the rear, marching in step. Within a mile they were blocked. Machine-guns and an armoured car were across their road. They were told that if they took another step forward they would all be killed. They retreated: they had no choice.

What sort of war is this? Machine-guns at your front and at your back.

Commissars at the rear order us forward for offensives and tell us not to retreat, 'not a metre', when we are attacked by aircraft and tanks and the Moors. But they always stay safe and are distant from the battles. Their skins are not risked.

What sort of war is this?

Last week the commanding officer of the French battalion – they call it the 'Marseillaise' – was arrested and accused of incompetence and cowardice, <u>and</u> of being a Fascist spy. He was put before a court martial and found guilty. On the same day as his arrest and trial, he was <u>executed</u>. He knelt, and showed no fear, and was shot in the back of the head.

It is that sort of war.

I do not know whether it is better to die facing the enemy, or facing those who are supposed to be colleagues, comrades in arms.

Tomorrow we are told that the film star, Errol Flynn, will visit us. Maybe he will come far enough forward to get mud on his shoes, and then he will be able to return to his hotel in Madrid and tell people that he has shared our hardships.

There is no retreat. A volunteer in the German battalion shot himself in the foot and thought it would be sufficient to have him sent to the rear. A self-inflicted wound is an offence and he was shot by a firing squad. There is no way out of this hell.

I thank God each day that Ralph is beside me.

It is raining again, heavier, and I must bale some more.

The call was answered. Dickie Naylor held the telephone close to his ear and mouth. Mary Reakes was at her desk in the outer office and he thought she strained to learn who he called, why, and with what message. He whispered, 'Is that Xavier Boniface or Donald Clydesdale? It's so long, I can't remember your voices – what, five years? ... Ah, Xavier. It's Mr Naylor ... Yes, I'm well, I'm fine. Xavier, there might be work to be done, for both of you ... Not certain, but if you were willing I'd like to put you both on stand-by. Can't say more, not on this phone ... It'll be this week if it happens ... So grateful. Regards to you both.'

The wail of seagulls was in his ear, the rumble of the sea and the wind's whine.

He returned the telephone to its cradle.

Probably in response to a message on her screen, Mary stood, then used her handbag mirror to check her hair or her lipstick, and was gone.

The photograph of the young man, the son of an electrical-goods salesman, stared smilingly back at him. He had fastened it, with Sellotape, to the glass panelling at the side of his office door. The smile seemed to mock him because it had the power to corrupt. He was a defender of the realm, and the proof of it was on the head of every sheet of notepaper he used, with its Latin words. As a defender he was able, if he twisted morality to a degree that Mary Reakes would not, to justify corruption. The Service, to an old-school warrior with a week's work ahead of him – then forgotten oblivion –

was *above* morality and legal processes . . . and he had orders. *It's a different war and we may have to dirty our hands.* A man such as Dickie Naylor needed an order and required leadership, was always happy when given a little nudge forward. *I'm sure you know what's necessary.* He was a functionary. Men such as Naylor – in uniform and in civilian dress, in democracies and in dictatorships – had always sat behind desks and received orders, had believed that the threat to the state outweighed moral and legal niceties. He was not a Gestapo man, God, no. And not an NKVD official . . . He heard tapping. It had a regular rhythm and was far down the corridor and came closer . . . Perhaps he was a man who could justify to himself the bending of due processes.

He had not lost sleep over it in the Aden Protectorate, or in the holding cells of Castlereagh or the barracks at Portadown. Men screamed, blood dripped, bruises coloured – and the likes of Mary Reakes would have wet their knickers – but information had been gained. Information saved the lives of innocents. He did not need a tumbler of whisky or a pill to help him sleep. So he had telephoned a distant island and put two men from his past, proven as reliable, on stand-by to come south . . . The tapping intruded into his thoughts, was loud, the beat of a stick on the corridor's walls.

Mary Reakes came into the outer office.

A man used one hand to hold her arm, and in the other was a white-painted stick. He used Mary and the stick as his guides, and swung the stick forcefully in front of his legs and hers. It rapped the door jambs, desk legs, the backs of chairs. The man was weathered from sunshine, stooped, and had thinning grey hair; he wore tinted glasses.

At Naylor's door, Mary said, 'I've brought up Mr Hegner. I told you he was coming. Mr Josiah Hegner of the Federal Bureau of Investigation, their Riyadh station.'

'I'm Joe,' the voice growled. 'How d'you do?'

Naylor was on his feet. He saw the creases in the clothes, and thought the agent must have come straight from the airport, not cared to take the time to change from what he'd slept in. He was starting forward to move a chair to a more accessible place, but backed off in the face of the swinging stick. A chair leg was whacked. The hand that had been on Mary's arm was loosed and found the chair's back, and the man dropped down into its seat. This was the expert, and he was blind.

'Thank you, Miss Reakes – that's kind of you.'

'Again, I'm going to apologize about the front entrance.'

'Water under the bridge, Miss Reakes, and no offence taken.'

'I was totally ashamed,' she babbled to Naylor. 'They wouldn't let Mr Hegner inside the security barrier until he'd gone through the metal-detector arch. Had his coins from his pocket, his glasses and his watch, his stick because it has a metal tip, and still wouldn't pass him through. It was a disgrace.'

Below the spectacles a grin of mischief formed. 'I still got an ounce, that's an estimate, of a bomber's shrapnel in me. So I said, "You want to see the scars?" He didn't answer so I dropped my pants and lifted my shirt. That seemed to satisfy him. I don't take it badly when a man's got to do his job, but I doubt I look like a goddamn wannabe Islamic martyr.'

'It was quite uncalled-for,' she said. 'I'll make some coffee, proper stuff.'

They were alone.

Naylor stumbled, 'I thought you'd have done the embassy and a hotel first, had a bit of sleep after a night flight.'

'Nice thought, but I reckon there ain't enough time for luxuries. Mr Naylor, you're in the eye of the storm.'

'I'm Dickie, please.'

'You're in the eye of the storm because I think you got the Twentyman here, and—'

'I don't understand – who or what is the Twentyman?'

'An Iraq-based insurgent commander. Uses suicide-bombers to effect. Has many names but that's mine for him. His attacks never fail to kill at least twenty, usually many more but that's a minimum. I'm here because I think the Twentyman is too and, if I'm right, that makes a real bad picture for you.'

Chapter 10: Tuesday, Day 13

'Ah, up with the lark, I see . . .' Dickie Naylor shrugged out of his coat. It was not yet eight o'clock, but his visitor was already in place, sitting comfortably in the easy chair, cradling a steaming coffee mug in his hands. '. . . and no problems, I trust, at the front entrance?'

'No problems. That feisty Miss Reakes smoothed the way. I didn't have to strip down this time. So as we don't lose time on mini-malities, I'll cut to the chase. I want to share my knowledge with you, Dickie.'

'I'm going to have a rather busy day. I don't know how much time I'll have for—'

The American's voice had a lacerating whip in it. 'Now, I think you're going to have to fit me in, Dickie, where your "busy day" permits. Make phone calls and I'll stop, but play with your computer and I'll talk – you ought to get used to the idea that I'm with you and am staying . . . What I heard, when you guys were hit the first time, you concentrated investigations on the bombers and their identities, but you failed to get at the kernel of it.'

'We think we did tolerably well, and "fail" is not a word we care to bandy about.' He did not care if his irritation showed. Mary bloody

Reakes had not brought him coffee. An interloper had intruded into his workspace. He felt himself, already, treated as an imbecile. 'And I have a meeting in ten minutes.'

He might as well have kept silent: he was not heard.

The voice drawled and rasped at him. 'I'm going to say it. There was, Dickie, a *failure* in that you have circulated no information on the facilitator, or on the bomb-maker. Your efforts were aimed at the foot-soldiers. You boys should get it into your heads that foot-soldiers are in plentiful supply. Facilitators and bomb-makers are where you hit pay-dirt. Cut down the foot-soldiers and another crop will seed and spring up. Locate and eliminate the facilitator and the bomb-maker and you hit the Organization where it hurts most. The facilitator is known to me as the Scorpion, but the Twentyman is my pet name, and I know the bomb-maker by the title of the Engineer. In the unlikely event that you could walk more than a couple of hundred yards outside the fence wire and the blast walls of any military encampment in Iraq, that's the Sunni part, or beyond the Green Zone in Baghdad, and not have your throat cut, then settle down in a coffee-shop, interrupt the guys reading their newspapers or watching Al Jazeera on the screen and ask a question, it would be "Who is most successfully carrying the war to the Coalition?" The answer you will get – assuming you don't have a company of marines round you, which you'd need if you wanted to keep your head on your shoulders – is that the Scorpion is the top guy, and alongside him is the Engineer. Kill them and you got yourself a real victory. Those men don't grow on trees. Look, Dickie, in Afghanistan and Palestine, Chechnya and Bosnia, there has always been one son-of-a-bitch who gives himself the Scorpion moniker. It ain't me, it's them. A wriggling, burrowing little shit with a sting. He has made a mistake, and that mistake may well prove to be of dramatic proportions. He has come off familiar ground, he is no longer – if I am correct – in the heartland of Ar Ramadi or al-Fallujah or Baquba or any of those murderous little enclaves of the Triangle. Whether from vanity, obedience or his understanding of duty, he has come on to your soil. I believe that making the journey was his mistake. Now the son-of-a-bitch is vulnerable.'

Naylor looked down at his watch. 'Sorry, but I've to go to that meeting.'

'No problem. I ain't going anywhere. I'll be here when you get back, and we'll talk some more.'

'Has he returned yet?'

It was the third time that morning that Ibrahim had left the loneliness of his room, come into the living area and asked the question. He interrupted the first snarls of the argument, watched from a low chair by Ramzi. The heap of dirty clothing was in the centre of the carpet.

Syed said, waspish, 'If he was back you would see him. If you cannot see him he is not back.'

Faria said, 'You will hear him when he comes. I told you yesterday and I told you today, he has gone to Birmingham. When he has finished, he will return.'

'Where is Birmingham? What is in Birmingham? Why has he gone to Birmingham?'

Looking away, not meeting his eye, Syed muttered, 'You don't need to know.'

Staring at the ceiling, Faria blustered, 'It is better you stay in your room. You should be in your room.'

He retreated and shut his door on them. Nothing was as he had believed it would be. Again, and it was the same each day and each evening, they isolated him. From the moment he had been chosen in the desert and had sat close to the Leader, he had believed that he would be asked to express his desire as to the sort of target he would walk towards, and also asked what he wished to achieve by the sacrifice of his life . . . but he was shut away. His desires, wishes, were insignificant.

He could hear the movements in the room next to his, where the waistcoat was prepared, and he remembered the feel of its weight on his shoulders. Then, beyond his door, the argument broke again.

Syed's voice: 'I am telling you, do my washing.'

Faria's voice: 'Do your own washing, I have the meal to make.'

'You did *his* washing. You will do mine.'

'I will not.'

'My mother or my sister does my washing.'

'Then take it back to them and they can slave for you.'

'You take *his* washing, so why is mine different from *his*?'

Faria's voice, rising: 'Because – because *he* is different. Are you an idiot? Can you not see that? Different—'

Syed's voice, yelled anger: 'Women should do washing. You should do my—'

A door opened. The shout of the man who had so calmly, like a tailor, checked the fall of the waistcoat over his chest and stomach: 'Can you not be quiet? Do I fucking care who washes, who does not? I do my own washing. I have work to do, intricate work, and you disturb me. Where I am, I wash my own clothes – maybe in the river, maybe at a well, maybe under a standpipe, maybe in a ditch. I wash my own because my wife is dead, killed by my enemy, and where I fight I do not have a servant. Get that fucking washing off the floor. I tell you, where I have come from you would not, any of you, survive a single day as a fighter. Your only use to me would be with a belt round your waist, and then I would not care whether there was filth on your clothing, whether you smelt like a fox's arse. And a fucking minute after the explosion of the belt I would have forgotten your name, your face.'

He heard the front door slam.

A minute later, through the crack in his curtains, he saw the man who had made the waistcoat pace in fury on the grass.

She had done *his* washing because *he* was different.

Would he be forgotten? Would she forget him?

He sank down on the bed and his head dropped into his hands.

'You're back. Let me pick up where I left off. I was talking vulnerability.'

Dickie Naylor grimaced. 'Sorry, et cetera. I've only a few minutes, Joe, then another meeting.'

'So, the Saudi boy who lodged the shrapnel inside me was a student of economics, probably with an intelligence quotient higher than mine, and he killed twenty-two men. Some of them were queuing for lunch and some had just sat themselves down at a table. He wounded a whole lot more, and I was one of them. Embedded in his bomb were ball-bearings, two-inch nails and one-inch screws, and it was one of those that robbed me of my sight. That was at the Marez garrison camp in Mosul – it's the forward operating base at the airport. The boy is unimportant, might as well have been a parcel in the post. The man who brought him out of Saudi, who collected the intelligence required to get him into our mess hall, who oversaw the documentation he needed, and the transport and the safe-house for the night before, is a master of his trade. He is the Scorpion . . .

'Of course you risk failure against a man like that. You, Dickie, you have the assistance of gadgets and staff alongside each step you take. You have computers, you have telephones with land-line connections and analogue and digital systems, you have assistants, you have a line manager who guides you, you have a building that is secure and protected. What does he have? He lives like a fugitive, sleeps rough, cannot use any form of telephone and is constantly aware, around him, of the sophistication of his enemy's arsenal . . . But he has the charisma of leadership, and will enforce it with ruthlessness.

'He had a prisoner, an American boy from Utah and from the 1st Infantry Division. There was a charade of negotiation but the boy was doomed to have his throat sawn through. The boy, clever and brave, escaped his hell-hole – but was recaptured and murdered. The Scorpion would have thought one of the guards helped the boy to that short moment of freedom. His reaction: he personally killed fifteen, *fifteen*, of the men charged with the boy's imprisonment, which made certain he had the right one, the traitor . . . He is that ruthless. But, and I live in hope, by coming here he may have made a mistake. In his game, mistakes have fatal consequences. How are we doing?'

'I have to be gone,' Dickie said.

It was the chance that Ramzi had waited for.

In the kitchen, Syed – pathetic and unworthy of a place in the cell – was sourly studying the washing-machine manual. He had measured out the soap powder and spilled enough of it on the floor. Beside Syed, not acknowledging him, Faria – arrogant, full of herself, too ready to argue – was cutting vegetables on a board. Jamal was up the drive and out in the trees . . . and the car had not come back . . . and *he* was in his room . . . and he could see the shape of the man's back, hunched in anger, as he strode on the grass like the caged animals he had watched on school trips to zoos.

He slipped from the chair. He did not think Syed or the girl had seen him move. He padded, tiptoe, across the carpet and into the corridor. He counted his way past the doors, then his fingers dropped to a handle. He turned it and the door, unlocked, opened. When the man had surged out of the room to demand an end to the dispute, he had come in explosive fury and Ramzi had not heard him turn the key . . . and that had created the chance.

What was it like? His home was swamped by women, his mother and sisters, and they watched the satellite channels from the Middle East, and they cooed together in a sort of keening wail of excitement when the last video message of a martyr was played. What was the feel of it? His sisters idolized the young men whose faces flickered over the satellite, and each time the message of sacrifice to the Faith was complete they would look across the room at him. It was never said, but was implicit: he, too, could gain their especial love and esteem. What did it weigh? He thought his sisters would have flushed with pride, not wept, if it had been their brother whose face was on the television and whose words were played on the speakers . . . but the opportunity had not been given him. What was the size of it? His elder sister had downloaded a document – *The Virtues of Martyrdom* – from the Internet, and his younger sister had read to him: 'There is no doubt that the sacrificing of one's soul for the sake of Allah in order to defeat His enemies and support Islam is the very highest level of sacrifice.'

What was the shape of it?

It lay on the table. It was inches from his hands.

He skirted the table and the bed, went to the window and gently held back the curtain. He saw the man striding, relentless, as if he tried to lose devils that trailed him. The face was knotted with fear or anxiety – but the man had not lost them and would walk more.

He was back at the table. There was an envelope and on it were two tickets. On opening out their leaves, he saw the printout for ferry sailings, noted the port of departure, the dates and times – different – and names he did not recognize. He closed the tickets because they did not seem of importance to him, and his eyes roved on across the table.

It seemed so simple, so ordinary. Ramzi thought it something that children could have put together, like a school's project. He had read in the newspaper of a school in Palestine, in Gaza City, where teenage boys were taught the virtuous lessons of the bomb on their bodies, the journey to Paradise and the welcome of the virgins . . . a school for martyrs. The quiet clung round him. He reached out. He had the right to touch, to learn. He was treated with contempt. He did not particularly admire any of the others, but the same level of contempt was shown to them all. A bomber, a martyr, should be revered, not forgotten – it was what the maker of the waistcoat had said – after *one* minute. His sisters did not forget and could recite names from Grozny, Jenin and Baghdad. In secrecy, he would tell them of what he had seen, would whisper in their ears how it had felt, the weight, the size and the shape of it.

He touched the material and the coarse stitching was against his fingertips. They ran on over the wires and the taping, and flies buzzed round him. He could see, inside the plastic bags, the clusters of nails and screws, the small ball-bearings. He touched the batteries, then moved to the switch. He lifted it and dared to allow a finger to brush, so softly, against the button. In Palestine there were posters in schools and on the walls of public buildings of the smiling young men who were martyrs. He eased a stick from its cloth socket. He was careful not to tighten the wire, to break the taped connection. He held the stick in his hand and it was smooth, moulded, with a tackiness on its surface. He let it lie in the palm of his hand. The weight of the stick rested there. He bent, put his nose close to it and tightened his grip on it, suddenly fearful that it might drop and wrench clear the web of wires, but it had no odour. He replaced the stick.

He lifted the waistcoat.

He held it by the collar and raised it so that its hem cleared the table. He saw himself, side view, in the mirror. It was against his body; his sweatshirt was hidden by it. The mirror was on a chest of drawers, old, stained and flawed, and the image of the sticks was thickened and the wires seemed to Ramzi to cascade into a tangle, and hanging loose, below the mirror's field, was the button switch . . . Perhaps a mosque would have been named after him or a cultural centre. He would go to God with the love of his sisters. But the waist-coat was too small for his muscled shoulders, was meant for another and would not have fitted him. He panted, almost an exhalation of relief. He could not have worn it. A shadow crossed behind him.

A hand was at his throat and he froze. He felt the fingers tighten and the breath was squeezed out of him.

He choked and he could not turn. Past the opening in the curtains he saw grass, then the hedge and an empty field. His strength from gymnasium weight-lifting did not help him. He could not break the hand's grip.

He was freed. Ramzi staggered back. The waistcoat was laid neatly on the table, but his hand, which went up to his throat, where the pressure had been, still had the tackiness on it.

He ran from the room, and in the corridor he heard the sound of a car's approach.

'I've less than five minutes, Joe, then I must rush. It's our A Branch, the surveillance people – not that I have anything to offer them for tracking but it's a matter of keeping them in the picture.'

'We were talking mistakes, Dickie. The Scorpion is the equivalent of a corporation's chief executive officer, except that he's not all warm and comfortable on the thirty-ninth floor, and he doesn't have Research and Development below him, or a finance section, or half a hundred from Media Relations or Human Resources. He has to do it all with couriers, use cut-outs, flit between houses, byres and holes in the ground under the stars for sleep. Yet, without a CEO's back-up, this guy is running us ragged. But, and this is important, when the business big-shot makes a mistake, he has minions to clear up the mess. Not my guy. He is alone, and more alone on your territory than if he had stayed in Iraq. What does he think of the people he has to work with here? A British Asian is from a different culture, has not been toughened by combat, is used to having sheets on the bed. He will think little of them. His mistake was ever to have travelled. I tell you, Iraq is a safe environment for him, but this is not. To make him pay, and dearly, for that mistake, we need one thing. That's the price-less commodity of luck . . . Now, off you go, Dickie, if you're not to keep those good folks waiting.'

'He could have damaged it.' The anger, cold and controlled, sparked in the Engineer's eyes.

'But was it imbecility or sabotage?'

He had come into the cottage, followed by Khalid. The driver had carried the box and the big plastic bottle, and before he had set them down on a chair, the Engineer had burst into the living area and made the accusation. For a moment, briefly, Ajaq had floundered. Now he had heard the story. His glance, withering, fell on Syed and Faria and they had turned away as if they believed the guilt of Ramzi was their responsibility too.

'Probably stupid, without thought, but handling it under no supervision could have damaged it, and I would not have known. What do I do? Do I check every fastening, unpeel every taping join? He could have broken it.'

'But it was not sabotage?'

'I don't think so.'

'If there is, in your mind, a whiff of the scent of that, then . . .'

The sentence was left unfinished. He did not need to speak it. If his friend, the Engineer, had harboured that suspicion the consequences were clear. A knife from the drawer in the kitchen. Himself and his friend taking the creature away into the fields in the evening, when darkness had come, and one of them bringing a spade. A walk across the ploughed fields to the trees.

'He is stupid, vain, but a child.' The Engineer's voice dropped to a murmur and its pitch would not have reached Khalid, Syed and the girl. 'It is a shit place and they are shit people. They should not have been given to us. We should be out, gone.'

'Friend, when we are ready. Not here, later, we will talk . . . Where is he?'

'In his room. Probably he whimpers for his mother.'

'I will speak with him.'

He told Khalid to open the box, take out the contents and learn to work the camera. They scuttled with it to the kitchen. He slapped the arm of the Engineer in affection. They were colleagues, brothers, but far from home. He went out of the room, ducked his head under the beams and came to the door.

As he entered, the boy lay on the bed, but started back and cringed against the headboard. He saw the terror bright in the eyes and the heavy shoulder muscles quivered. But the world of Muhammad Ajaq, the Scorpion in the files of his enemy, was both the creation of fear and the breeding of loyalty. He smiled. He allowed the warmth of his smile to run on his lips and he saw confusion spread over the idiot's face ... But he could not mask the contempt in his eyes, because they carried truth and the smile was a lie.

He said, 'Your life, Ramzi, was in the palm of the hand of my friend. If there had been with my friend a suspicion of betrayal then you were dead. Not a martyr's death but a traitor's. My friend says to me – and he held your life in his hand – that you were stupid ... So, you live.'

The voice was hoarse, as if a fist was at the boy's throat. 'Thank you ... I meant no ...'

'You meant no harm. I understand. You were inquisitive. You were given to us, Ramzi, put into this cell because it was thought you could be relied on, depended on. Where I fight, a cell must be secure or it will fail, and failure comes when respect inside the cell is lost. Trust was placed in you. Should I doubt that trust?'

'No ... no,' the boy stammered.

'It will not happen again ... will not.' He stood over the boy, above him. He saw again the squirming movement against the pillows. He did not realize then the mistake he made, the scale of it, or the consequences. His hand rested loosely on the boy's shoulders – as it had on Ibrahim Hussein, who would die when he walked – and he felt the tension in the muscles there.

The mistake was made and he had no knowledge of it.

He left the room.

'Let's pick up where we left off, Dickie. *Mistakes.*'

'Would you like more coffee, Joe? I can get it made.'

'No more coffee. I'll need to relieve myself. No, thanks ... How long we got this time?'

'We have a desk officer, downstairs, assigned to this. He's pulling together what strings we have – supposed to be with him ten minutes ago. Anyway ...'

Joe Hegner said, 'I was at mistakes ... But there is pressure on the Twentyman, the Scorpion. If we take a wider picture, over the last few months there have been in excess of sixty suicide-bombs, walking and driven, in Iraq. They are pumping them through and there is no sign that the belt is emptying. Each bomb has a diminished impact – the same happened on a lesser scale in Israel. Life has to go on, because for the living there is no alternative. Children go to school because they must have education. Families shop because they must eat to survive. Men stand in queues outside police recruiting offices because they have no other alternative of employment. Many die, atrocities are frequent, but the social fabric continues to exist, even if at Stone Age levels. I said "diminished impact". That is crucial to the mistake. The war against the Coalition demands *impact*. Can't find impact in that God-forsaken place. Impact requires *momentum*. Momentum gains headlines in newspapers and leads on the satellite channels. Bali, Madrid and your experiences a year and a half ago gain newspaper inches and television time.

'You Brits, your society is flabby and has an unprotected underbelly. You could not sustain what is the daily chore of life in Iraq. So, the son-of-a-bitch is sent here where the hazards to his safety are so much greater. In the wake of his arrival there are the growing – perhaps inevitable – chances of more minor mistakes, which, if you boys are lucky, will kill him. Why is there the probability of "minor mistakes" to add to the big one? In Iraq, on his own ground, he is among everything that is familiar, and he surrounds himself with proven men. Here, he cannot. Here, it's about who he has now to work with and—'

'It'll have to keep, Joe. I'm sure you understand.'

Through the wall of the room, Ibrahim heard the sounds of a man's weeping.

It should have been a time of joy as the day approached. He should have been able to share joy with brothers and a sister, but there had been dispute and argument, and now he heard desolate weeping.

He recited to himself from the Book, 3–169: 'You must not think that those who are slain in the cause of Allah are dead. They are alive and well provided for by their Lord.' He had thought the words would comfort him, but they did not. Despair was hooked in his mind. There was no celebration of what he would do when he walked, when he held the switch in his hand, only raised voices – and now hopeless tears were offered him through the wall. Why? Why was there no joy?

Ibrahim left his room, went down the corridor and away from the crying. He came to the living room and the curtains were drawn there. He stood in the shadows at the door. He was not seen.

From the centre of the room, a beam of light sliced the darkness and fell on the face of Jamal. The source of the light was a small video-camera – what his father would have sold in his shop – and its beam was on Khalid's face and his eyes, which blinked. Syed was behind the camera, and at his side was Faria. None of them saw him. He was not noticed. He held his breath and listened.

Khalid held a sheet of paper in his hand, and complained: 'It's so difficult – it's hard to read with the light in my face.'

'Doesn't matter,' Syed said. 'He will have had time to learn it.'

Faria said, head angled and her hands on her hips, accentuating her curves, 'I'm not sure it sounds right, do it again.'

Syed took on the accent of an American – he was crouched over the camera, eye pressed to the view-finder, as if it was Hollywood. 'Ready? OK. Action. Go in five.'

Beside him, her hand out, Faria dropped each finger as she counted down five seconds, then pointed to Khalid.

Khalid gazed at the lens, and his eyes seemed to water. 'Here we go . . . "I would like to say to you that I have come to Britain in order to strive in the path of God and to fight the enemy of Muslims. I am the living martyr. God, be He exalted . . ." It's so difficult to read this. Do I keep going? Right . . . "At this time we say to the whole world, and declare it as a mighty shout, that the will of Muslims will not weaken and that the retaliatory fire will blaze until the crusaders and oppressors have departed from the Muslim homeland . . ." Do I have to read it all, or can I go to the end?'

'Just do the end,' Faria said.

'The last sentence, his sign-off,' Syed said.

'Going in five . . . "To Blair and Bush, I say that the curse is on your faces. I will await you all, my brothers, in Paradise. Do not forget me in your prayers . . ." That's it. Can he learn that, no stumbles, straight to the camera?'

'Yes, he can,' Faria said. 'At the moment it sounds like the written word, not the spoken word. It needs to be drafted again.'

Syed mimicked the studio director: 'Cut. Break the set.'

'It is impossible to read it with meaning and make it a sincere testament because it is not me that is going to walk,' Jamal said.

Ibrahim turned away, went quietly into the corridor. Then lights flooded on and he heard the curtains dragged open.

'He will say it well,' she said, her voice faint to him. 'Just as he will walk well because he has the dedication – we do not – and the strength.'

Dickie Naylor said, 'We're moving fast, little pieces beginning to slot together. It's all about *The Threatened Swan*. I apologize, is that a riddle to you?'

'Miss Reakes briefed me on the work of Jan Asselyn in the Rijksmuseum, but out in Montana we're not big on art,' Hegner said, drily.

'I don't know how many hotels, accommodation addresses we've checked but it'll be hundreds . . . It's the swan on the T-shirt that did the business. Ibrahim Hussein was in a hotel in north London until Saturday. They remembered him checking in. Never left his room all the time he was there. So, he's somewhere in London and we have the city in lock-down. There were others in the hotel, probably linked, and it's being worked on. For the first time, Joe, I feel a faint justification of optimism.'

'Not warranted, Dickie.'

'Christ, you ape a kill-joy well. Why not?'

'Where I come from, Dickie, all the bombs are not at the airport or up against the Green Zone of Baghdad. A few, but not the majority. They hit round the country, not where the security is tightest . . . Here, it won't be London. You call for a lock-down and you've every gun-carrying policeman you can muster on the streets, off days in lieu and furlough breaks, and every one of them who would be doing thieving, mugging, fraud, rape and administration. Your capital is stiff with policemen standing shoulder to shoulder. So, the Twentyman, the Scorpion, leaves it well alone. Go look where you're soft and unprotected, where your citizens gather in numbers, because that is where the threat will be. Look where there are no guns, no barricades. Look where ordinary people go about their daily business, where your citizens think they're safe.'

'But that could be anywhere.'

'I'm telling you it won't be London but somewhere that thinks it's safe and out of the terror frame. Somewhere there is still innocence, and ignorance.'

A wraith figure, Lee Donkin followed the woman. The light ebbed on the Dunstable road. The woman was perfect and soon she would come to the underpass tunnel. She was on her mobile as she walked and the handbag on her arm wasn't even zipped. And it all went bloody pear-shaped. This gang spilled out of the food shop, saw her and recognized her, and it was all kisses, and she was in the middle of them – in a knot of men and women – and she'd been perfect. Wasn't perfect any longer. He crossed the road, drifted on and never looked back. Twenty minutes he'd been following her. Twenty minutes wasted. He cursed, kicked a can off the pavement into the traffic, and went through the tunnel. After twenty minutes of it, psyched and steeled for the snatch, then let down like the fix was finished, he hadn't the will – or the energy – to go looking for another target. He went on into the town centre, head down and hood up, but his savage mood was short-lived. He was in the square. Through the trees, past the vagrants and the dossers on the benches, Lee Donkin saw the posters on the Arndale's walls . . . Bloody good, bloody *ace*. Sales, bargains and giveaways on offer this coming weekend. Starting up Saturday, nine a.m. Bloody brilliant. Punters would be coming into town, women would have their purses bulging, and they'd be half asleep, hurrying down the Dunstable road. Bloody first-class pickings.

Naylor scribbled reminders on the sheets of his Post-it pad and stuck them on his desk surface, where clear spaces could be found. Joe Hegner was far back in his chair and talked on. So much was now crammed, squashed, into Dickie Naylor's mind. Everything that day, the meetings and the briefing, had been of critical importance but his ability to absorb was failing – his thoughts were far away, where he had heard the gulls, the waves and the wind.

'Dickie, his problems are with the quality of the cell he has been given. They're not people of his choice. The Twentyman, or the Scorpion, has not interviewed them, has not had the chance to run vetting over them, or to check references – as a CEO would have. The only one alongside him whom he's certain of is the bomb-maker, the Engineer. The rest he has to take on trust, and that's a big step for him, but he cannot do without them. He will be in safe accommodation, probably a short-term rental. With him will be a driver, a guy who has done the necessary reconnaissance of a target, another who will provide immediate security where the cell is gathered, and another who is there to watch over the perimeter of those premises and is staked out at the end of the street or wherever, and he will need some sort of logistics individual. Can he rely on any of them? He will not be happy to depend on individuals whose recruitment was not in his own hands. Then, introduced into this little coven, there is the boy who will do the walk or will drive the car. They are all, believe me, boxed up together, and there will be tensions – have to be tensions – and it is then that mistakes are made, and you have the chance to get lucky. But the stakes for him are high and he must live with the stresses that might be fracturing the cell. If there's an opportunity, you have to be able to exploit it. Will you? Can you?'

Outside his cubicle office, Mary stood at her desk, gestured to Naylor, tapped the face of her watch and pulled a droll face. She seemed to have looked after the self-invited guest well, because each time he returned there was a new sandwich wrapper beside his chair, or a fresh glass, and most recently there had been a finished soup bowl.

'Sorry and all that, time's up. My answer is, most definitely, I will and I can react to Lady Luck or a mistake.'

The gulls wheeled and shrieked over the disintegrating carcass of a cod that had been discarded from a fishing-boat. The sea beat in a fury against the headlands of rock fingers at the extremities of the bay, known in the old language as Port Uisken. The wind, with rain in it, came from the south-west at a strength of force eight, blistered spray over the rocks and whined in the telephone wires . . . On those telephone wires, the message had come that had put them on stand-by status.

Two men trudged into the teeth of the elements and returned to their home. They came over a hill, too slight in elevation to have been given a Gaelic name but it had provided them with a minimum of protection while they were in its lee. Now they were exposed: the wind whipped them and the rain thrashed them, but they struggled on with the determination that was their hallmark. The taller of them carried a new-born heifer calf under his waterproof jerkin and the shorter steadied his friend when they came down off the hill and over weather-smoothed stones where the lichen was soap-slippery. Trailing them was a Highland cow and, behind them, the afterbirth mess that by the following morning would have been taken by the carrion crows or the ravens if the pair of big eagles that nested on the cliff, the Cnoc nan Gabhar, had not ventured up and found it. The calf, still wet and with slime on it, was under the jerkin of Xavier Boniface. The steadying hand was that of Donald Clydesdale.

It had been dark still when they were woken, in their separate rooms but at the same moment, by the distant bellow of the cow, perhaps a mile away. They had dressed, gulped a mug of tea and gone out with the wind on their backs propelling them forward. They had found the cow in a difficult labour under the shelter of the millennia-aged stones on the slope of Cnoc Mor. Neither man would have considered turning away from the cry of anguish.

On a better day, as they had tramped to Cnoc Mor, as they had assisted at the birth, as they had turned for home, they might have seen the slow, languid turns of the great white-tailed eagles, the flying barn doors with a wing span in excess of seven feet, and that would have given them rare pleasure. They had not seen the majesty on the wing of the birds, or the hobby hawk, but they had heard the coughed shout of the ravens that had a nest on Aird a Chrainn.

Xavier Boniface and Donald Clydesdale, in the tiny community – twenty-six souls when the summer tourists were away from Ardchiavaig – that was their home, had no past, only a present, and their future was unknown. The two men, lankily tall and muscularly short, had arrived fifteen years before at this remote corner of an Inner Hebridean island, had taken over a ruined croft's shell, built a roof for it, dug out a damp course and plastered the interior walls. They had used rough carpentry skills to construct a staircase, had laid a sewage pipe to a cesspit, and excavated the ditch that brought them water from an historic well. Electricity and the telephone links came on the wires that the wind bent and were held up on posts that the wind had angled. It was a place well suited to two men whose expertise and past were best hidden.

The head of the heifer calf, born with a red-brown coat, peeped from between the opened buttons of the taller man's waterproof jerkin; he held it tight against him as if with love. The shorter man held his arm as they came off the last stones of the hill, then sank down into a reedy bog; the grip showed the extent of their friendship. The cow followed them. Unsaid between them was the extent of their guilt that she had been left out and had dropped the calf in foul weather, but the birth had been a full ten days before the scheduled time and a week before they had expected to lead her down to the stone byre behind the croft. They owned, the two of them, the one Highland cow and now one Highland heifer calf, fifteen ewes and a ram, half a dozen goats, eight chickens and a cockerel, and two geese. All were loved.

But they were now on stand-by status: the call had come from London, from Mr Naylor, and if a second phone call was received, they would be gone because that was their past, and the McDonald family, who had the nearest farm to them would see to their beasts and birds. It was five years since they had last been called away, and they had travelled then from the Inner Hebrides to the mountain towns of Bosnia; seven years and ten years before, they had gone to the wild border country of the province of Northern Ireland. Whenever the past demanded their presence, they responded. And the McDonald family would not have queried where they went and why, or the McDougalls, and not the McPhersons, or Hamish who brought the post each day in mid-afternoon, or the Sutherland widow whose husband had been lost from an upturned crabbing boat. When they had returned they had not been quizzed on their business away from the island.

When they journeyed away it was because of their knowledge of thresholds.

A warm smile crossed the face of the taller man. 'Look at it, Donald, it's breaking. It's the last of the rain and the gale's taking it. See the sunlight coming?'

With reverence, the shorter man said, 'And there'll be a rainbow to follow it, and then good skies, Xavier. It's a sign she'll be a fine beast. We did it. We saw her into this world.'

'Makes you feel well.'

'Makes you feel the best, Xavier.'

'If her mother's Marigold, she should be Daisy.'

'Marigold and Daisy, good names. I'm not arguing with that, Xavier.'

They cleared the bog and reached the field of cropped grass. Their sheep and goats stampeded towards them. In Ardchiavaig, where the winter of the last months had been brutal in the intensity of the storms – as it was every year – Xavier Boniface and Donald Clydesdale, both with their sixtieth birthdays behind them, would have been thought of as somewhere on a scale between lunacy and eccentricity. But none of the community they lived among would have cared. They were accepted for what they were – for what they were thought to be. They brought home the heifer calf, Daisy, and Boniface laid out fresh straw on the byre's floor of stone slabs while Clydesdale went to the store shed for a precious bale of hay for the cow, Marigold. It was the best straw they had and the best hay. When it was done, when the cow suckled her calf – only then – when the wind blew the sunlight against the stout walls of the croft, when the incoming tide thrust the whitecaps on to the beach, when the rough beauty of the place had settled on Ardchiavaig, they went inside to check the answerphone recording. The second call had not come.

The knowledge of Xavier Boniface and Donald Clydesdale concerned the thresholds of pain, carefully regulated as an arm of interrogation. The inflicting of pain, enough to make a prisoner spit out truths but not enough to win a babble of lies, was the prized expertise of these two elderly men and it came from their distant past, when they had first worked with Mr Naylor. They drank tea and made toast, the sunlight lit their room, and they gloried in what they had achieved that morning. They were usually called to action, where the thresholds they knew of were involved, when a target made a *mistake*, then paid for it in pain.

The handler, with seventeen years' experience behind him, knew well enough the value of *luck*, but it came sparsely.

He worked with spaniels that were trained to sniff and find, then to address the target, sitting on their haunches and barking, till he came to investigate. His last dog had been a drugs sniffer, and life had been exciting and busy. That little treasure had had a score of convictions to her name, and a dozen commendations for finding heroin, cocaine and amphetamines. But Smack had been retired now for three years: she lived at home, with a basket in the kitchen, and was the ageing playmate of his children.

The new dog was Midge, a pedigree bred from Welsh stock; as a working dog she had a kennel and pen out at the back. She was faster to boredom but had energy and intelligence. Boredom afflicted her because she was explosives-trained, and explosives were rare in the East Midlands. With her handler she did preparatory search work whenever royalty or a prominent politician was visiting the county, and was called out when a resident reported a 'suspicious' object at the railway or bus station; she had never found a 'live' cache of dynamite – not even a hidden sack of Second World War ammunition underneath an allotment shed. Razor sharp on exercises, Midge seemed to her handler to recognize that the 'real thing' had eluded her.

Another day done. They had been out on loan to the airport at Castle Donington, where he'd taken her through Baggage Reclaim and let her scramble over the trolleys before the bags and cases went on to the carousel – showing the flag, really. After that, he'd had her alongside the check-in queues and she'd sniffed at the bags and cases stacked with holidaywear. The handler and his dog were as much a part of the reassurance-to-the-public policy as the officers who patrolled with machine pistols hooked on to their chests. But his duty day was completed . . . Every late afternoon, when they were finished, he'd leave the van in the driveway, shed his uniform, and walk the spaniel up on to Rose Hill, on the edge of the Normanton district of the cathedral city of Derby, and let her run free. There, kids played with her and she was everybody's friend.

It did not matter to the handler whether it rained, sleeted, or if the sun baked him. He would be on Rose Hill at the finish of his shift – and tomorrow, because he had a nine o'clock start, before his shift began – and Midge would be charging and careering among the other walkers, the mums with their prams and the vagrants on the benches. Twice, Smack had identified kids with heroin wraps on Rose Hill, and that was luck, and the handler had made arrests. Never, of course, had Midge identified an ounce, not even five grams' worth of military or commercial explosive in the park, but the little beggar wasn't one to stop trying: she sniffed at everything and everyone – just never had the opportunity to bark raucously and have a 'real thing' moment.

He whistled; she came.

He gave her a reward, a half-biscuit, tousled the hair on her collar, fastened the leash and started out for home.

'I spoke, Dickie, of the kid who's been brought in to do the business. I'd like to focus on him and—'

'I don't want to seem rude, Joe, but the assistant director's waiting upstairs for me – I hope Mary's looking after you.'

'She's doing a fine job. Another day of this and I'll be fatter than a Thanksgiving turkey. Keep your man on hold a couple minutes. Imagine the kid. A Saudi Arabian boy, from the limited background of an upbringing in Asir Province, is in circumstances way out of his depth. He's far from home and has only his Faith to cling to. Where he is, in the safe-house, he has no friend. He is alone. I could almost feel sorry for him, Dickie – except that it was a kid like him who walked into the mess hall at Mosul. Those with him, except for the big man, are of an alien culture. They're not Arabs but Muslim Brits. They won't know how to talk to him, won't understand his feelings, and cannot offer him succour. His isolation is total. Some of those British will be jealous of him because he's going to be martyred and have that quarter of an hour of fame. Others' fear of death, eternity, will have been heightened by his presence, proximity. Strains and stresses will create an atmosphere you could cut with a blunt-edged knife . . . and around them, bickering and complaining and wishing he was someplace else, is the big man. You following me? OK, so you have to go. Enjoy your meeting, Dickie.'

The trial lurched on.

After the lunch adjournment, the prosecution's barrister had started on his closing address to the jury; Mr Justice Herbert made a play at normality and busily wrote his longhand notes; the Curtis brothers glowered from the dock and the security round them had been reinforced by the presence of two more prison officers; the solicitor, Nathaniel Wilson, kept his head down as if that way he would not be noticed; the police guard in the public gallery had been doubled. The normality the judge had aimed for could not be achieved.

Some of the jury seemed to listen to the barrister's droning repetition of the evidence laid before them; others scarcely made the effort.

But in the morning when the jury had gathered in their room, and again during the adjournment, there had been lively anger, confusion, and an almost excited meld of gossip and anecdote between them. Confidentiality was gone, and something of a brotherhood in adversity had been shaped. They all – bar one – had difficulties with the new situation confronting them.

Rob, a mouthpiece for the general anger, had said, 'No one seems to have given us a thought. My darts team's on the board tonight, and I'm the fixture secretary. I'm expected to turn out – but I'm told I can't. Where am I going to be? Nobody's told me.'

While the bickering complaints had played in his ears, Jools Wright had said *nothing*. Could have. Could have spoken of the dour detective who had driven him home, who had introduced himself curtly to Babs and nodded with bare politeness to Kathy, who had checked all the windows and door locks, paced round the back garden, then drawn a plan of his home, who had asked for each of the family's blood groups, then been on the phone for an age with a map on his knee. There had been a red pen circle round the nearest Accident and Emergency hospital . . . Who had called him *sir* and his wife *ma'am*, who had said he was either *Mr Banks* or *Detective Constable Banks*. Could have told them all that the detective had bridled sharply when referred to as a 'bodyguard': 'That's what film stars have. I am a Protection Officer. You are not some minor celebrity, you are a Principal – and in case you have the wrong idea about all this, you have been assigned this level of security after a threat assessment recognized the danger you and your family now face. We are not friends, don't forget that. A final thing, we use a jargon phrase, "dislocated expectations". It means we can plan for what we think will happen but when the opposite turns up we have to be prepared for that. So, to cover it, I require you all to obey my instructions immediately I give them. I will not entertain discussion.' Could have said that a holdall bag had been brought into the hall and unzipped. The stubby shape of a machine-gun with a magazine attached was displayed, and a big fire extinguisher – like those in his school's corridors – was laid beside the holdall. Could have said that an hour of discussion, ignoring Jools, had centred on where *Mrs* Wright and her daughter would stay after they abandoned their home, and that this, too, was telephoned through to his control. Could have said that after he had gone upstairs to the spare room, he had not slept and had heard the regular checks made by the detective of the ground-floor windows, and low-pitched conversations with the police-car people outside. He'd come down for a coffee after three: the detective had been reading from a weathered old notebook and had not acknowledged him. Could have said that *Mr* Banks had been yawning and taciturn as he had driven Jools to Snaresbrook through the rush-hour traffic, and his eyes had spent more time snapping up at the mirror than on the roads ahead.

But Jools Wright had said nothing.

In the last hour of the afternoon, Banks still had a mountain to conquer, with an apparently endless list of tasks to be completed. He reckoned that the detective inspector, Wally, regarded him as capable and the rest as second rate – maybe third.

Twenty minutes on a phone trying to find a coach that had privacy windows. Failing . . . Getting a coach that had done a school run and was littered with crisps packets, supervising its cleaning, and himself Sellotaping newspaper pages over the passenger windows. Working through the drills with the motorcycle escorts, where the traffic would be blocked to allow the coach to get clear of the court without risk of it being followed. Waiting on a security check and vetting to come through on the coach driver. Finalizing the route to the destination with the driver and the escorts. Calling the destination to demand catering facilities for the jury members, the escorts and the security detail. So much to be done and the clock ticking against him. And the thought kept scratching in his mind that he was on jury protection while the Delta, Golf and Kilo teams were strutting their stuff in the capital's streets where a suicide-bomber was thought to be on the loose, where the security status had been ratcheted up to the highest level. Not David Banks's bloody concern but his mind couldn't escape it. He was out of it because he was rated inadequate – big pill to swallow with a bitter taste. Told himself he didn't care, and tried to believe it. It was time to move.

Carrying suitcases and grips, they filed from a back door into the closed yard used to load prisoners into the vans. He thought some looked curiously at the coach, and others glowered in resentment.

Banks was the last to climb the steps, carrying the holdall. He did the head count. All present, all correct. He gave the thumbs-up to Wally, who would follow in a chase car, and the driver swung the door shut. His hand, in an automatic gesture, slipped to the holster, felt the Glock's butt and the hard edges at the end of the magazine. The high yard gates opened. The coach drove through; the motor-cycles gunned their engines and slipped into their stations. He went down the aisle, took the empty seat behind the key man and sat.

The school teacher, Banks thought, had not the marks on him of a hero. Funny that. Looked rather ordinary, hadn't the appearance of a man brimming with public spirit. Seemed pretty damn average. And there had been only a pretend kiss on the doorstep that morning, the hero and his wife, with daylight between their cheeks.

The coach accelerated. Banks thought he could handle whatever might be thrown in his face – even 'dislocated expectations' – with ease.

'Don't mind me saying this, Dickie, but something seems off. Did your meeting not go well?'

'It went fine, thank you.'

'Something's off. Deny a man his sight and his instincts compen-sate. Why don't you get Mary to take on some of your load?'

'Your concern, Joe, is admirable, but I'm able to cope with my job.'

'Where was I? Yes, the big man, he's the target worth having. I—'

'Very interesting, Joe, but from my perspective the target worth having is the little scum-bag who has the intention of killing and mutilating as many people as he can gather round him. Am I wrong? How is your perspective so different?'

'Not only are you bent out of shape, but you're also getting irritable and that, Dickie, is exhaustion. You're not a law-enforcement officer. You are, Dickie, a counter-intelligence officer: a whole world of differences, a canyon between them. Getting the bomber saves a few lives, short term, but in the scheme of things is peanuts. The elimination of the Facilitator – my Twentyman, my Scorpion – is a battle of importance won and—'

'Because, I suppose, he's responsible for blinding you.'

'That's below the belt, Dickie. I'd started to think better of you.'

'I apologize . . . Christ, I'm tired.'

'Water under the bridge . . . *He*, by now, is as tired as you are, but more stressed. He does not have limitless reserves of self-control and will be looking towards the preservation of the skin on his back – the way out. He will not be here when the bomb is detonated, will be long gone. The detonation is for the son-of-a-bitch who carries the device and the lowlifes who are with him at the end. I did not come here, Dickie, to attempt to use my experience in the prevention of one bomb exploding. I came to get up close to the Facilitator of many bombs. He will have no feelings for the lowlifes or the kid, because his own survival is paramount for him. As soon as he believes that the operation is in place, that creases have been ironed out, he will ditch them and run. However fast you respond in aftermath time, you will be too late, and all you can hope to net will be the foot-soldiers. It's all about mistakes and luck, the ability to exploit. Who's waiting for you now?'

'Just the desk man. I'll be half an hour, Joe, perhaps a bit more.'

The bus slowed, then stopped. By craning his neck, looking over the heads in front of him and past the screen behind the driver, Jools could make out wire fences, a lowered barricade, arc-lights, a guard-house and sentries. The soldiers were in battledress and had rifles against their chests. Jools grinned to himself. He understood why they had not been told where they were headed, or what was their destination: it was a bloody army camp.

The detective, a morose blighter and without conversation through their hour's journey, had gone up front, had spoken through the open door to a sergeant, then turned to them. 'Thank you indeed, ladies and gentlemen, for your patience. You will be shown to your sleeping quarters, then given a meal. You are all, I guarantee it, quite safe here, and–'

'It's not my safety I'm concerned with, it's my cat's,' Fanny piped.

'– every effort will be made to ensure your comfort.'

Safer than a vault of the Bank of bloody England, Jools reflected. But for how long? The little toad man had told him: *There would be nowhere to hide. My friends have long arms and longer memories.* He felt the cold through the open door of the coach, and shivered.

'I don't want to say this but, Dickie, you don't seem so well.'

'Just tired . . . I suppose I ought to invite you for a bite to eat.'

'Wouldn't hear of it. What you need is bed, and maybe a Jack Daniel's for company. Don't have a conscience about playing host to me. I have a date, and I'm told it will be Italian so I'm going to go out there and make a fool of myself with a spaghetti bowl. I'll be dropped back at my hotel.'

'See you in the morning, Joe. Hope you don't feel your day's been wasted.'

'Been a good day, Dickie. We're only short of one thing. Luck.'

The cottage slept, but in one room the curtains flapped and an open window whined on its hinges.

Chapter 11: Wednesday, Day 14

Fine rain fell on Ramzi. He was sitting on a bench. Before him, while he buried his head in his hands, was the city that was his home, laid out below him, the lights of its streets blazing through the mist. Far to the east, above the lights and beyond them, was the first smear of a softer grey. Soon the day would come.

When the others had slept, he had made his preparations for flight. He had disguised his bed. He had opened the window with great care because the hinges creaked from the rust on them. He had dressed and pulled on his trainers. After each movement he had paused to allow the quiet of the night to settle around him again. Once, Syed had called out, but had not woken. He had stood on the bed and lifted his left leg out through the window. He had been astride the sill, half in, half out, his knee close to a little china bowl that was a decoration there, when Jamal's cough had exploded, but none of the sleepers had been roused. He had worked his right leg through the gap, settled for a moment on the outer sill, then lowered himself into the flower-bed below and had felt the earth clog on his trainers. He had tried to close the window, fasten it, but that had not been possible so he had abandoned it. Ramzi had run and heard the flap of the curtains behind him, the swing of the window.

The strengthening wind had been on his face. He had run as if his life had depended on it, had charged across the lawn, because he had believed himself to be condemned.

He had gone through the hedge, missing the gap where the thorn was sparsest and the wire was down to knee height. He had struggled to free himself from the wire's barbs, the thorns, tearing his trousers and lacerating his hands. When he had slipped in the field, mud had smeared his face, hands and clothing. He had blundered to an open gate and there had gasped for breath, looked back and seen the dark outline of the building – but no lights were snapping on and no shouts carried on the wind, only the rain. He had skirted the far side of the wood that was near to the track leading to the building. The muscles he had built in the gym, with rings of weights, were in his shoulders and in his arms – they could be seen and gave him the stature he craved – not in his stomach and thighs. At a shambling trot, he had staggered towards the village.

He had come into it past the closed and blacked-out pub, past the shop, which had only a dim security light, and had crossed the street. For Ramzi, the countryside, its quiet and isolation, was an alien, unfamiliar place: he was used to concrete, paving, noise and the dense terraces of closely packed homes. He no longer had the will to run but he stumbled forward, going north, along the pavement. When he came under a high light, he had seen the mud from the ploughed field on his top and trousers round the tears. When he had cleared the village, gone past the last set-back houses, a car had swept past and he had waved – too late – at the driver. When the village was far behind him, and there was no pavement, and he meandered in exhaustion on the road, there was the scream of a horn as a van swerved by. His waved arms – frantic – were ignored. An hour later, when Ramzi could run no more, barely trot, only walk – and he was two or three miles from the village – he had heard the grinding approach of a heavy lorry. He had turned and stood with his arms spread, at the side of the road, and had heard the brakes wail. It had come to a stop fifty yards ahead. He had summoned his strength and run to the high cab door that had been opened.

He would have called the lorry driver a Crusader. He would have thought of him as an enemy. He had planned to kill, and the Crusader, the enemy – or his family – might have been close to the explosion, near enough not to have been able to duck away from the flying shrapnel of ball-bearings, nails and screws: it was what he had hoped to achieve. An arm had reached down, caught his fist and heaved him up into the warmth of the cab, where music played. 'Christ, you look a proper mess. What you done? Not my business, eh? Well, I like a bit of company – where you trying to get to?' He had named the city that was his home. 'Can't do that. Tamworth's the best I can manage, but you'll get a train out of Tamworth for Derby – yeah, I like a bit of company on a night run.' He had seen the driver when the cab light was on: he wore a sleeveless shirt and his arm was tattooed with a picture of a naked girl.

They had driven at speed through the night along deserted roads. 'Just so as we understand each other, if you're in trouble with the law – trouble with anything – I don't want to know. It's just good to have someone up here. Pity you're not a pretty bird . . .'

Ramzi had never before been so close, shoulder to shoulder, with a Crusader, an enemy. The family had no friends outside their own community. At his schools, the kids had all been Muslim and dominated by lessons on the Faith. At college, before he had dropped out of the computer-studies course – eight months into a two-year curriculum – the other students' families had originated from Pakistan and Bangladesh. The benefit office he used was staffed from the ghetto. The shops he, his mother and his sisters went to were inside the ghetto. Where he worshipped, where he had been recruited, the evils of the morally corrupt society of the Crusaders had been drilled into his mind. The television he watched came on the satellite, and the websites he visited trumpeted the successes of martyrs in the fight against the enemy.

It was a soft voice, a Birmingham accent. 'You want a sandwich? Sorry, sorry . . . I'm a daft bugger, they're ham. But there's rock cakes my missus made, and the flask's coffee.' He had wolfed three cakes, and drunk from the mug on top of the Thermos, and he had learned of the life of the driver, and his family's life, and their home in the Smethwick suburb of Birmingham, and the holiday he was looking forward to – 'Can't come bloody fast enough, know what I mean?' – in a caravan park on the Yorkshire coast, and the job he did delivering shelf supplies to supermarkets. He had been driven into Tamworth, and a sign for the rail station had been pointed out.

'You'll be all right now, but better when you've had a wash and brush-up. Been good knowing you.'

He had stepped down from the cab. He had seen the smile above him, and the little wave. Should he have said it? Should he have told the kind Crusader, the generous enemy, not to go with his family next Saturday morning into the centre of Birmingham? It had been in his mind, deep in his throat . . . But the lorry had pulled away, and the warning was left unspoken.

The first train of the morning service out of Tamworth had brought Ramzi home. He had fled because he was condemned. Not in words . . . *Where I fight, a cell must be secure or it will fail, and failure comes when respect inside the cell is lost. Trust was placed in you. Should I doubt that trust?* The hand had been gentle on his shoulder, and a smile had been at the mouth. The words had been honeyed, not the eyes. The eyes had told him he was condemned – perhaps not that day, perhaps the day after, because Ramzi had lost respect, and trust in him was doubted, and the eyes had pierced him and had spelt out their contempt. He was dead if he stayed so he had run. If he walked slowly, he would reach his home within fifteen minutes, and he would hit the door with his fist and a sister or his mother would unlock it, and the story of his failure would be prised from him. They would learn of his disgrace, his shame, his humiliation. His old boasts replaced by a stuttered confession. Their old pride in him gone.

He sat on the bench and the cold sank into his body.

The handler was always the first in his home to rise, shower, shave and dress. A biscuit for the grand old lady, retired, in her basket. Then the kettle on, a pot of tea made, a mug taken up to his wife, a bang on the doors of his kids' rooms and protest groans as a reward. It was still dark. He heard the six o'clock news on the radio every morning unless he was on early turn and already at work. He ate toast and listened to the news, then climbed into his waterproofs. On his pager, he read a bald text of an increased security alert down south in the capital, but the spin-off was that he was tasked to show the flag and let his spaniel sniff round the city's railway station and the bus terminus. It had been a regular routine since Seven-Seven, since the bombers had taken an early train into the heart of

London with explosives in rucksacks on their backs. The radio told him that the Dow was down overnight, that big redundancies were forecast in the north-west, there had been a homophobic attack in the south-west, a junior minister was entangled in scandal, two suicide bombs in Iraq . . . The handler barely took in the litany of gloom. He savoured the tea, the toast and the quiet. By being dressed in time for the six o'clock news he was able to enjoy the peace of the house, and he would have said, if asked, that it was the time of day he enjoyed most, particularly in autumn, winter and spring when it was still dark outside, and he could think and reflect.

What he thought of most often, reflected on most frequently, was that he fitted no stereotype as a police officer in the city of Derby. Wouldn't have been in the force if he hadn't been a dog-handler. He had few ambitions and had never shown an interest in sitting the sergeants' examination; there were plenty who did and were fast-tracked towards it. In fact, nothing that was memorable or worth a commendation had ever intruded on his career. Most certainly, if he had not been a dog-handler, he would have resigned rather than face the bloody binge-drunk rioters in the city centre every weekend . . . but he had been spared that since he had taken on Smack and now Midge. Wasn't in a hurry that morning, and after the news and the weather forecast, bloody awful, he caught up with last night's *Evening Telegraph* and the Ram's predicted line-up for the coming Saturday's match. Then he poured some more well-stewed tea.

Few slept well in the cells at HMP Belmarsh. Most woke early, at the clangs of unlocking doors, the rattle of chains and the stamp of boots. Some did not sleep at all and gazed at the ceiling bulb behind its cover or the glow through the barred window of the perimeter walls' arc-lights.

Ozzie Curtis had not slept.

He burned, and hatred was a fire in him.

Didn't reckon that Ollie had missed out on sleep. The dozy bastard relied on him, leaned on him and left the worrying – and hatred – to his elder brother.

He checked his watch, did so every five minutes, and thought it was about the time it would happen.

If it wasn't for the work and the planning – the hating and burning

– that Ozzie put in, Ollie would have been running a stall most likely on the Columbia Road flower market; Ozzie had always split down the middle line, fifty-fifty, but had done the worrying. To show for Ozzie's worry, Ollie had a pad in Kent of the same value as his own, the same bloody investment income and the adjacent Spanish villa.

They were going down, both of them; with the jury in protection and the judge bloody poisoned against them, they were looking at long bird. They would be bloody old and bloody decrepit when – if – they emerged from a prison's gates, and they would be without authority.

The fire burned in him because the man with a beard, and his feet in bloody sandals, had *taken* their money, then grassed them up.

In his mind, flames burned.

Bright flames flickered, flared, then spread.

He looked again at his watch.

At that hour, in a distant suburb of east London, most households slept. Only a minimal few had been roused by alarm clocks and the automatic switching on of radios.

The few were those who had furthest to travel, those on the earliest shifts, those who were key-holders and had to open up factories, businesses and offices . . . and among the few who were about their trade before dawn were the three men in an old saloon car, with substituted number-plates, who had cursed at the stench of petrol and had not dared to light the chain of cigarettes on which they would normally have survived.

The car was parked beyond the end of the road, and the driver was left with it. He did not have to be told that he should keep the engine running. First out was the Nobbler, and in a gloved fist he carried a plastic supermarket bag tightly wrapped round a half-brick. The second man held the source of the petrol stench: a fuel-filled milk bottle with a wad of old shirt rammed into its neck. He had in his pocket a snap-open Zippo lighter.

In the world of Benny Edwards, two options of persuasion existed. They were the choice of the carrot or the less welcome alternative of the stick. The choice was gone, and with it had disappeared his client's cash and a segment of his own reputation of success: the alternative of the stick, however, remained. It was now of great

231

importance to him – his hard-won reputation relied on his ability to deliver hung juries or acquittals. For the stick, given the chance, he would have gone along the route of a child's face slashed and disfigured with a razor-sharp blade, or a woman's legs hit by a car's bumper as she walked along a pavement. But Wright's daughter was not there, nor his wife, and the opportunity to send a message from either of them while they lingered in Accident and Emergency was not available. Early the previous afternoon the driver of the car, ducked down in his seat had watched as the child and the woman were hustled with their bags through the front door and the gate by uniformed and plain-clothes filth, and dumped without ceremony in the back of a police wagon. When they had sped out into the traffic stream their road had been blocked by a car with a blue lamp flashing on the roof and the chance of pursuit had not been there. But a message needed sending and could still be sent. A message was the least of Ozzie Curtis's demands on Benny Edwards. *He who pays the piper calls the tune*: that was obvious to the Nobbler. A message would reach the bastard Wright, and he had been told of long arms and longer memories. There was a good chance that the stick, on fire, would dictate the bastard's decision in the jury room.

It was raining. The pavement shimmered under the street-lights. The two men, walking briskly, carrying the half-brick and the milk bottle, had hoods over their heads and scarves on the lower half of their faces. The Nobbler presumed that a junior filth would have been left inside the house – there was an unmarked car by the front gate, empty – and that a camera lens would have been mounted above the front door. Better to presume everything . . . They went past a closed van, with the logo of a window-cleaner on its side and ladders on the roof, and the house, the target, was now less than fifty paces ahead. The Nobbler quickened his stride, and the man behind him.

Benny Edwards was familiar with success. He would not have admitted to complacency, but success – and the enhancement of his reputation – came often enough. He backed his nous, his instinct, and it had been wrong, which had confused him. The money had been taken; the deal had been done; end of bloody story. What had gone wrong? When news had reached him – second-hand, via that callow shit-face of a solicitor – of the new security ring thrown round the jurors, he had gulped in astonishment, but his own people had seen the coach pull away from Snaresbrook and the windows had been covered with newspaper. Four days earlier, at home in his corner jacuzzi, soaking and relaxed, he would never have thought – not for a bloody moment – that Julian Wright, the bastard, would be the one to play the goddamn hero, take the money and piss all over a deal. The thought of it was beyond his comprehension. He had seen nothing in the man, or in the bloody demands, bank statements and credit-card sheets, that had rung warning bells. The bastard had been as pliable as a bloody wet turd. More important, he had left the Nobbler looking like an idiot and an incompetent, and that hurt.

'You ready for it?' Benny Edwards spoke from the side of his mouth.

He heard a grunt of acknowledgement behind.

He stopped. First, his eyes flitted over the darkened road. He saw nothing that aroused his suspicion. Then he twisted his head, raised the scarf higher on his face and looked at the terraced house. His glance went over the gate that hung from one hinge, across the little flower-bed to the door where the paint had peeled. There was no glimmer of light from behind the glass pane at the top, but he fancied – was not sure – that he had identified a lens from a pinhead camera, but he was prepared for that and his face was well covered. He checked the bay window beside the door: curtains drawn. He sucked in breath, held it in his lungs and listened . . . He heard nothing.

'We'll go for it.'

There was the click of the lighter behind him. The Nobbler swung back his arm, the plastic bag with the half-brick in his hand, and heaved it at the bay window. The crash of the glass – enough to wake the bloody dead – pealed in his ears. Then he was roughly pushed aside. A small flame had caught on the material in the bottle's neck. There was the slosh of liquid. He watched his man hurl, short arm, the missile through the splintered hole the brick had made and break as it landed. There was a flash, then a growing roar as the fire caught. A light upstairs, across the street, snapped on.

'Come on, leg it.'

His face, behind and above the scarf, felt the heat of the spreading blaze, and he started to run. Well, he wasn't a kid, was he? Couldn't run fast, could he? Do the best he was capable of, wouldn't he? Hadn't gone fifty paces and his stride was already shorter and he could hear his man behind him, panting like a bloody pig, and he heard the shouts and the cackle of the radios, then the pounding of bloody boots. Benny Edwards, the Nobbler with the reputation, thought his world was caving in on him.

It did, sooner than he'd reckoned possible.

He was a couple of strides from the back wheel, breath sobbing in his throat, when the door of that bloody van – the window-cleaner's – heaved open, swung on the hinge and was right out, blocking him. He tried to swerve but hadn't the control of his legs and fell. In the fraction of time before his face hit the road, he saw the big fuckers spill out of it. He was down. Two of them were on him. Hands searched his clothing, probed into his pockets, and his arms were wrenched into the small of his back. He felt the cold of the handcuffs on his wrists. He'd always thought, if it went sour on him, that there'd be a ring at the door around five in the morning, detectives in the hall with the courtesy to let him dress decently and give the missus's cheek a peck, and a solicitor – not that fucking Nat Wilson, no way – at the police station by the time he reached there. But he was on his face with the grit of the road in his eyes and he felt suspended in the depths of humiliation . . . and was.

13 July 1937

It is called the battle of Brunete, and within four days our offensive has failed.

Brunete is a village, but it is worthless. Every building in it has been destroyed by our artillery, by their artillery and bombing. We advanced to within two miles of it and were halted. I do not understand how our commanders could have ordered its capture and been prepared to sacrifice so many lives in the attack.

I have asked Ralph how it was justified, but he will not answer me. Each time I question him he turns away. I have relied on Ralph so often to lift me – he is so strong in dedication and purpose – but here he will not.

Our battalion was ordered to capture a long ridge of ground that was completely bare of cover. We reached it. We have called the ridge Mosquito Hill. We gave it this name because the bullets buzz round us like the swarms of those damned insects, but the bite is worse and so many have been bitten, for nothing.

Huge forces have been used by our side, but we have not made the break-through that the commissars assured us was inevitable . . . and this evening we buried our gallant Major George Nathan. He was a wonderful man and we have followed him through every hell that the commissars have sent us into. (The commissars are never with us in the heat of the fighting.) He always carried a gold-tipped baton, and none of us ever saw him flinch or show fear. He was hit by splinters from a bomb. At the time he was wounded, grievously, we were under attack from the new German Messerschmitt 109s and also a formation of the Heinkel 111s. I have never been so frightened. Our own aircraft, Russian, abandoned us.

Major Nathan's last order to us was that we sing to him. As he moved towards death, in a shell-hole, we crouched round him and he had the final company of our voices. I could hear Ralph's above all others. After our major had gone, slipped away, we knocked together a crude coffin from planks, gouged out a shallow pit in the ground at the bottom of the hole, and there were olive trees – broken by the enemy's shell-fire but still standing – and we left him where there was a view, at some different time, of the dried course of the Guadarrama river. We never had a better officer, nor ever will.

This afternoon we were ordered to dig trenches, which is always the sign that the offensive is finished. It is impossible to dig. Not even with pickaxes can we break the ground. (We covered the earth on the Major's coffin with stones, so that foxes and rats would not get inside it.) There is no water here. Even if we could get to the river, which is under the enemy's guns, we would find no running water in it. The Americans to our right have taken so many casualties that their two battalions are now joined as one, and that is under strength; they have no water for their wounded.

It is as hot, now, on Mosquito Hill as at any time since I came to Spain. The bodies out in front of us are already swollen, their skin is black and the flies swarm on them. Our mouths cry out for water – not cry, my error, but croak. When we sang for Major Nathan it was a supreme effort, and my throat is now as sore as if I had rubbed it with a carpenter's rough paper. It is rumoured that we have captured only twenty square miles, but at a cost of more than twenty thousand casualties. If God exists, He has not come near to Mosquito Hill.

Is it the heat, the thirst or the suffering around me, but I wonder now if I will ever leave this country? If I am ever permitted to go home to you, dear

Enid, I believe – accept my promise that the force of the sun breeds delirium in us – that I would take the trolley-bus into the City and go to the office where Mr Rammage is and I would beg him, on my knees, to accept me back. But I think the sun and the death that is everywhere have affected my mind.

It hurts so much that Ralph will not talk to me.

But as I write by the moonlight – and at last the guns are quiet, as if the mosquitoes have been swatted away – I think he watches me, and I sense that he believes me a fool to have committed my thoughts to these pages.

We are so isolated from all past experiences. We wait for death to choose us. Death is an end that may be preferable to living. Is a man who is dead in pain from a parched throat? Does he yell, a crow's call, in the night for water? Is he at peace? Does he lie in the arms of his girl? Maybe I should try to write a poem – like Sassoon or Rosenberg, Owen or Graves – and hope that it will be read, one day, when the Poetry Group meets, if any there remember me. No, it is a delusion.

I think I ramble. I am, I realize it, gripped with arrogance. I am no Owen, but a wretch with a dried-out throat and a shattered mind. I am of the Doomed Youth that was the 'Anthem' of Owen. I say his words, but soundlessly: 'What passing-bells for those who die as cattle?/Only the monstrous anger of the guns./Only the stuttering rifles' rapid rattle/Can patter out their hasty orisons.' I am wrong . . . Cattle in a slaughter-house die better than we do.

Soon it will be dawn.

We are lost souls, and the dream has forsaken us.

Dear Enid, I have to try to sleep. The 'Anthem for Doomed Youth' was written for me, and I am walking towards hell and am alone, and I have forgotten what cause it was that brought me to die 'while in a foreign land', here or somewhere else.

The dawn comes quickly, too fast.

Propped up on his bed, Banks's eyes lingered on the page of the notebook, and he reread again the last line. *The dawn comes quickly, too fast.* There were distant shouts as the garrison camp woke, as there would have been on Mosquito Hill when the officers roused their men. He had been awake for an hour and, against all better judgements, had started on the entry written by faint candlelight so long ago . . . He never skipped, and he resisted the temptation to find the last page, the last words written by his great-uncle. There was not the scream

236

of the day's first artillery shell fired from a 155mm howitzer by German gunners or the nationalists, or the first howling low-level flight over the ridge of a Messerschmitt fighter, but a high-pitched jingle of tinny music.

He reached on to the bedside table in the barely furnished room of the camp's visitors' quarters, lifted his mobile and clicked 'receive'. Sharply he gave his name, then listened.

'But they're not there. They were moved out . . . What's the damage?'

He was told, and some more.

'But that's brilliant, Wally, picking up the lowlife . . . What should I do, and when?'

He shaved fast, dressed, then slipped on his suit jacket so that the pocket hung down over the pancake holster on his belt. He locked his door and went down the bright-lit corridor, heading for his Principal's room. By the staircase, half-way down the corridor where a uniformed constable lounged on a plastic chair, there were windows and he saw that darkness still cloaked the parade-ground. He knocked, said his name, heard an answering grumble, went inside and switched on the ceiling light. Wright was in bed and blinked up at him. Like any other policeman, he was familiar with the work of delivering bad, sad news, and had learned it should be done briskly, without emotion. His Principal might be a hero but he was not a friend.

He said, matter-of-fact, 'Sorry and all that, but I have to tell you your home was attacked an hour ago. Of course your wife and daughter were not there and are quite safe. A window was broken and a petrol bomb was thrown into your living room. The street was staked out, across the road and down it. The guys were in there pretty fast with extinguishers and most of the damage is smoke and scorching, not structural.'

Some would have wept, others would have let free a volley of oaths, obscenities. His Principal merely grimaced.

'Because we had the stake-out and were able to move so sharp, your neighbours won't have been affected other than by the drama. The homes on either side of yours are fine. Yours is now boarded up. I suppose, when you went to the judge and told him of the approach made to you and turned in the money, that you realized there could be retaliation. People on high are singing your praises.'

The Protection Officer expected a platitude response. Something about 'duty' and something about 'ethics'. The Principal only shrugged . . . Peculiar.

He bored on: 'Actually, we've had a rather good result, and my boss is well chuffed with it. We have three arrests – a driver, the jerk who threw the petrol bottle, and the one who chucked the brick and broke your window for the petrol to go through. He's Benny Edwards and it's the first time, and not without trying, that he's been nicked *in flagrante*. He's a specialist in nobbling, but that's as far as I can go on him.'

No reaction, nothing. Banks had anticipated something . . . Bizarre.

'I'm not permitted to discuss it further because of any possible conclusions you might draw in relation to the case you're sitting on, Mr Wright. What's paramount is that nothing I have said to you prejudices your opinion on the trial. That is why you have not yet been asked for a statement on the approach made to you, why you have not been sat down with a book of photographs so's you can identify the people you met, and the circumstances under which you were given that sum of cash. It's all being kept till after the verdict you and the rest will reach. Does that make sense?'

His Principal could have said bloody something. He saw the roll of his eyes.

The man seemed so calm. It was like, Banks reflected, his Principal was indifferent to having had petrol splashed into his living room and lit. Banks would have been mental with fury at such violation of his territory. He realized that he understood so little about the man. He had not managed to dig his way into the school teacher's trust – that was why he had won no normal, predictable reactions. But they called him a hero. There, perhaps, he fitted a pattern. A *hero*, in David Banks's world, was not a special forces' trooper – up a mountain in Afghanistan with all the high-tech gear hooked on his webbing – but the little man, ordinary as sin, who was confronted, from nowhere, with acute danger to himself and others. His *hero* was a man who made a bridge of his body for many to crawl over when a ferry-boat turned turtle, in darkness with panic around him. His *hero*, man or woman, young or old, had gone back into the smoke and toxic hell of a bombed Underground train, deep in a tunnel, to help those so badly injured they could not make their own escape. His *hero* was Cecil Darke, without water and with the smell of the dead round him, on the ridge of Mosquito Hill. They came in all shapes, all sizes and fitted no stereotype, and what made them so special was their lack of preparation for what they would endure. He felt, rare for him, a keen admiration. Whatever his emotions, Wright had them successfully bottled and corked. What did they say? They said, 'Don't make a drama out of a crisis.' The man was now identified by twin echelons of organized crime, had acquired the enmity of two brutal clans, would live with that weight on his shoulders – and his family's – for years to come. He had stood up and been counted against the forces of corruption and intimidation. Not bad for a bloody school teacher, but the mark of a nobody who was found to be a *hero*, too true. Maybe the man was in shock.

Banks said kindly, 'I can rustle up a cup of tea if you'd like one.'

His Principal rolled over in the bed, away from him. 'I'd prefer it if you got lost and let me go back to sleep – switch the light off on your way out.'

He did, and shut the door quietly behind him.

Another day was starting, and Banks did not know what it would bring – if anything.

In a Belgravia hotel room, where the street below the window reverberated with a road-cleansing lorry, a couple made love. They had barely slept.

He thought the younger woman was clumsy through inexperience but relished her passion.

She thought the older man was now almost drained of his strength and doing it from long unused memory cards but was childishly eager.

An opened champagne bottle, its contents going flat, was tilted in a silver bucket. She'd said she was teetotal and didn't need the stimulation of alcohol, and he'd followed suit but the wasted bottle would be on his bill.

She was astride him and he was on his back, and the sheets were rucked off the bed and on the carpet with their scattered clothes. He was in her, and his hands reached up for her breasts. He talked and she listened. Then, when he was flaccid, limp – between times – she talked and he listened, but mostly it was him who talked and while he did she helped him to get ready for it again. A wife, Gertrud, who had been a childhood sweetheart, and a divorce of twenty years ago that had come through, final papers, on a fax machine in a foreign city. A boyfriend at university who had only shagged her on Saturday nights when the hall of residence was heaving in unison. A secretary where he worked who cared for him but as a younger sister and didn't share a bed with him. A young man, a staffer at the Home Office, whom she'd ended up with after a Christmas party.

For too long he hadn't done it; not often enough she hadn't.

He bounced his buttocks on the bed and heaved into her.

She thought him a cob horse who'd remembered what it was about.

He didn't know whether it was spontaneous.

She didn't know whether he'd planned it.

He felt privileged; and she felt damn, *damn* good.

There was no relationship for the future. They were ships that passed.

She felt him shrink and wriggled off him. She lay beside him and heard his breathing, harsh but regular, and he had nothing to say . . . Silence, and the road-cleansing lorry had moved on. Quiet . . . No one who knew her where she worked would have believed she had copulated three times in a night with a man nearly old enough to be her father and gloried in it. No one who knew him would have reckoned him capable of giving and taking acute pleasure. She was off the bed and walked naked to the side-table, her feet kicking aside a drift of sheets and clothing. She switched on the electric kettle and tore open coffee sachets. It was the first time, afterwards, that he had not spoken about his wife, his secretary, his life or work.

'You all right?'

'Just thinking.'

'What were you thinking about?' she asked.

'Oh, mistakes and good luck.'

'I don't regard this, what's happened, as a mistake, and . . .'

He said, distracted now, 'No, no . . . I was thinking that this might be the day when the mistake is made, and when we've gotten lucky.'

*

'For what you paid, Miss, what did you expect? A high-performance Alfa?'

The nurse from Accident and Emergency tossed and twisted in her bed as the first light of the day seeped through her curtains. She had not slept and would be a rag doll at work that morning. As it had through the night hours, irritation swarmed in her mind, with frustration over the reception she had faced at the car-dealer's yard at the end of her shift yesterday afternoon. Knackered after another difficult day, Avril Harris had explained the problem: backfiring on deceleration, particularly on the approach to stop lights, sometimes once, sometimes twice, with a gunshot's report. Wasn't it under warranty? She had been told, slyly, that she'd never asked about warranties but if she had she would have been told that they did not apply to a car priced at under a thousand. The problem could be handled but the work would have to be paid for; the dealer had denied obligation. 'Sorry and all that, but it was bought as seen.'

What he was prepared to do, without cost to her, was explain the fault that she had described with a mounting anger. It was about the timing, about the exhaust valve opening as the piston exploded; she knew how to operate a complicated defibrillator, or any of the maze of equipment that surrounded a patient in trouble immediately after admission – but had no comprehension of the workings of the internal combustion engine under the bonnet of an old Fiesta. She was told about the crankshaft, the timing belt, the camshaft and the valves, and she was tired, flushed, and had lost him. He'd shrugged – and she'd hoped the unthinkable: that one day the bastard would be wheeled on a trolley into her care, parked in a corridor and left to sweat – and smiled showing bad teeth. 'It was tried and tested by you, Miss, and you didn't have a complaint then.'

It was like, Avril Harris had thought, the dealer had never seen the damn car before. Until they had a look under the bonnet, he didn't know whether it would be a fifty-pound job or a hundred – work and parts, but for cash there'd be no need for VAT added on top – and she could drop it off any time she wanted and they'd take that look, then tell her what the damage would cost her. She had decided that – whether it made a noise like the gun battle at the Alamo each time she came to red traffic lights – she was damned if he'd get her trade.

Not ever. She'd strode away. He'd called after her: 'You want to go somewhere else and get another quote, well, Miss, that's your privilege.'

She would get it fixed 'somewhere else' in Luton, but not that week. Hadn't the money until the end of the month. Would have to ask round the A and E staff for a recommendation. It had done a double backfire at the lights at the bottom end of the Dunstable road. So damned unfair, and it had kept her awake, irritated and frustrated, but until the money was in the bank she must cut her cloth and live with it.

The window slammed, and Khalid woke. He heard the water that dripped from the sill. The wind whistled through the gap and the curtain flapped.

Which fool had left the window open? Not himself. Not Syed and not Jamal, because they had both been asleep before him. Ramzi? Ramzi had been reading from the Book, with a side-light when Khalid had faced the wall, sought sleep and found it, dreamless . . . No, the window had been shut, fastened, when they had gone to the room, undressed, climbed on to their mattresses.

Again, the wind caught the window, seemed to seize it and pull it open, wider, and the curtain was lifted and the spatter of water was louder. Khalid did not understand how Syed, Jamal and Ramzi could sleep unaware of the open window. Could any of them have risen in the night and unlocked it because it was too warm in the room? Impossible, and the cold was against his skin. Syed and Jamal were nearest the door, but Ramzi's mattress was under the window; the noise was beside him and the water from the driving rain would be falling on him. He knew it was the day that the video would be made.

Khalid crawled off his mattress. He hoped – had prayed for it – that after the recording of the video he would be permitted to return to his home and the mini-cab office. He had not been treated with respect. He had driven to Birmingham, had endured a night in a flea-ridden hostel, had driven back and not been thanked. Not a word of gratitude. Silence in the car. No leadership, no exhortation, no inspiration . . . as if he had no value. He wanted to be gone, to be at home . . . In the gloom of the room he stretched, and his knees cracked, but none of them woke.

242

Syed was on his stomach, breathing noisily, and Khalid padded past him. He skirted the next mattress where Jamal lay, hugging his pillow, and he thought the kid pathetic. He was beside Ramzi's mattress, the one who was all talk and who had been tongue-lashed in front of them, and there was the dark shape of his body: the muscle man seemed to have buried his head under the blankets, to be sleeping and not moving; the covering over his head masked his breathing. The window swung again. He could make out, in the darkness of the room over which the shadows of the curtains bounced, the rainwater's brightness on those blankets. He reached forward, above the mattress and Ramzi, to catch the window.

The curtain billowed into Khalid's face and covered his eyes, blinded him. The window cannoned into his fingers. Pain arced up from them. His feet snagged on the cable of the side-light, which went taut and toppled him. He fell on to the mattress and the sleeper. He expected a convulsion of movement and to be thrown off by thrashing arms and legs, but he sank down softly.

Under the blankets, and lined up in the shape of a body, his hand – bleeding – found two pillows, a tight bundle of clothing and a closely rolled blanket.

The curtain was pushed back by the wind, and the rain ran on his face and settled on his hair. He realized the enormity of what he had found.

He pushed himself up and looked through the window. He did not feel the rain or the wind's force on his skin.

Khalid shouted, a spirit that wailed at the approach of death. He screamed. Around him, they woke.

The older men, in pants and T-shirts, were at the open door – and Faria in pyjamas. The ceiling light was snapped on.

Khalid pointed first to the open window and the sodden curtain, then to the mattress, the pillows, the bundle and the rolled blanket. He tried to hide his shiver, but it was not from cold. Fear tugged at him.

The voice snapped behind him: 'That fucking imbecile with the big mouth, how long since he was seen?'

Who would answer? Who would dare to face the fury? Khalid steeled himself, hesitated, then looked down at his wrist-watch and stammered, 'Other than him, I was the last to go to sleep. He could have been gone for seven hours. What do we do?'

'Behave, if you are capable of it, like soldiers – not brats still crying for their mother's breasts.'

The door slammed. All of them – Khalid, Syed and Jamal – trembled as they dressed in silence, and none went near the open window. Would it be aborted? Would they be sent home? By association, were they disgraced? The questions seared the mind of Khalid, but he dared not ask them.

Chapter 12: Wednesday, Day 14

As he lay on his bed, the tumult beat round Ibrahim. He could hear but not see. His door stayed closed. Whatever crisis raged in the cottage, he was not part of it. No one came to his room. Breakfast had not been brought to him, nor had he been called to the kitchen. Before retreating to his bed, after the shouting and door slamming had started, he had faced the wall, knelt and prayed with intensity. Then he had lain on the rucked-up sheets. What he could hear told him little.

He remembered moments of confidence, some extreme, but they were now behind him. They played in his mind: walking from the mosque where the *imam* had spelled out the rewards available to the virtuous, the brave, the dedicated; cleaning his room personally, not leaving it to the servant, tidying his affairs secretively, and polishing the glass in the frames holding the photographs of his brothers, the martyrs; telling the untruths to his father and sisters, and justifying them because of the pride and glory his family would know when his name and face were on the television screen; being called forward by the Leader, the man of war, chosen above the other eleven, walking for him and being praised. Then confidence had surged in him, and it had been with him when he had stepped towards the departure gates at Riyadh's King Khalid airport – the calling of his name had not deflected it – and as he had walked past the checks and the armed police at the train terminus, his leather jacket thrown open to show the swan, and as he had arrived in the car at the cottage, knowing he would be carrying the bomb when he left it ... But now the confidence was gone, had ebbed with each hour of the days and nights that he had been left in the room.

Should he have thrown open the door, stalked out and demanded to be told what was the cause of the crisis?

He wished the girl would come ... Alone among them, she was the one he wished had come to his room.

It was because she was flawed, her face crossed with the scar, that he valued her.

Until now, beyond his door there had been a babble of shouting. He was forgotten. The voices had been indistinct. He recognized then that Jamal and the girl were in the corridor outside his room. Did they realize that he was on his bed, abandoned but straining to hear?

Jamal said, a hoarse whisper, 'I don't think we can go on now.'

She said, softer, 'Then the work of so many is wasted, was for nothing.'

'I am intelligent, yes? I have a place at the university in London, yes? I am not a fool, yes? I see it, do you not? We are all in danger now.'

'I had thought it would be easier ...'

'A big man was sent, a commander and a fighter, but he does not lead us. He has brought down chaos on us. We did not need him ... and we did not need the Saudi kid,' Jamal murmured, but the boy heard him. 'I would have done it, if I had been asked.'

'You boast as Ramzi boasted. You do not give *him* what he is owed – respect.'

Savagely hissed by Jamal: 'The respect I have, now, this moment, is for the scale of the catastrophe falling on us. Do you not understand? You do not need education from a university to comprehend what we face – imprisonment all our lives.'

'What does *he* face? *He* faces two situations. *He* may be sent home, back where he came from, his martyrdom attempt a failure, and that failure with him for the rest of his life because he will never be chosen again. Or *he* faces a worthless martyrdom – not at the place

246

and time of maximum advantage, rushed to a street where the casualties are scaled down, where *his* death is wasted. Not only, Jamal, do you boast but you display a selfishness that disgraces you. You do not think of *him*, only yourself.'

The boy heard a bitter, whinnying laugh. '*He* might be free, and–'

The boy heard the hiss of her response: 'Or kneeling in a square at home while an executioner raises a sword and prepares to behead him.'

'– and might be walking forward, thinking of virgins awaiting *him*, and not caring whether *he* kills ten or one, wounds ten or one. *He* has virgins in *his* mind.'

'You are obsessed. You disgust me. *His* Faith is to be admired, not sniggered at.'

'What obsesses me – with Ramzi gone – is the thought of a prison cell with the key thrown away.' The shouted answer. 'And it should obsess you, too, and—'

There was a yell from deep in the cottage, as if they were called, and the boy heard their feet patter away. He gripped his raised knees. He had learned the cause of the crisis, the reason for the catastrophe, and what was thought of him. To all of them but her, he was as worthless as an animal sent for slaughter. To her he had importance . . . but she had not come to his room.

More voices. He came off the bed.

Voices beyond the window. He edged back the curtain but kept his body hidden.

The older men searched the garden. 'He has the whole night's start on us.' They started at a bare dug bed under the window along the outer wall from his. 'I should have cut his fucking throat when I could have.' They crouched there and made a close examination of the ground. 'Will he go to the police and talk with them? Will he have gone home to his fucking family? I don't know . . . If he has gone home, then is arrested, will he be able to endure interrogation?' They stood and gazed across the grass, and the rain fell on them. Neither had a coat or seemed to notice it. 'At least here, in a *democracy*,' the boy heard rough, braying laughter, 'it will not be as severe inter-rogation as in Abu Ghraib. It will be *decent* and *polite* – but would he break?' Then they tracked away over the grass, like hounds scenting a quarry, and came to the break in the hedge beyond which was the expanse of the ploughed field . . . and Ibrahim no longer heard them.

What he did hear, faintly, was the sound of a vehicle approaching, an engine's grind.

Ajaq listened.

The Engineer, close to the hedge, said, 'My decision is made. My work is finished. I will not stay another hour.'

Ajaq thought his friend had been too long and too often near to the source of explosions that the damage to his hearing was irreparable. The noise of the vehicle was growing, and he imagined it heaving between the rutted lines in the track and the potholes. 'You, my dear one, should be with me. Tell me you will be.'

He heard the voice of his friend, urgent, and he thought of the men in mountain caves, or in the compound of a tribal chief in the foothills, who had sent him and who now listened to their radios to learn that the faith placed in him was justified. He heard the engine of the vehicle, racing in low gear, and he thought of the myriad skeins of the web that had been put together. He heard a shrill call for him to come back to the cottage, and he thought of how many had risked so much to place him where he now stood and how they would crumple if the mission failed or was ineffective.

'You cannot delay. You cannot remain here. You were given rubbish to work with. You would not be fairly blamed if you quit. At home, where you belong, where you are a leader of fighting men, you would have finished with this, moved on and found another target.'

He heard the howl of the vehicle's engine. He looked over the neat chopped top of the hedge, across the ploughed field, beyond the wood of dense tree-trunks, and into the distance where a cloud bank settled on a shortened horizon. He saw the wheel of the birds' flight and sensed the innocence of the place. There would have been the same innocence to be seen if he had gazed out from a derelict hut, once used to shelter livestock, at groves of trees that bore dates, or irrigated fields of maize. Innocence reigned in the moments before the Apache gunships materialized above a horizon of gently swaying branches. On his fighting ground in Iraq, if a new cell member had fled in the night, he would have abandoned the place he slept and his current plan, would have started again from point zero on the laborious preparation for a new attack site. Too many now depended on him, and he knew that he would ignore the entreaties of his friend.

'If it is ready, you should go,' Ajaq said.

He walked away from his friend, across the wet grass. Inside the Triangle, on the banks of the Euphrates and Tigris rivers, innocence was unknown to him. Once, he had been captured. Once, the army of the enemy had had him defenceless and within their power, his freedom gone. Once, for an hour less than half a day, he had sat hunched down in the blister of the sun, with his arms held in the small of his back by plastic restrainers, his eyes taped over. But his papers had held up to examination, and the interrogation in the field had been rough – a few kicks, some belts with a rifle's butt – yet bored and cursory. He had been freed. With the wide, staring eyes of an idiot and the limp of a man disabled by polio – as listed on his documentation – he had shambled away from the Americans. And that night Muhammad Ajaq, who was the Scorpion, had started an inquest inquiry as to whether he had been betrayed or merely fallen into the enemy's arms by misfortune, but men had died because he *might* have been betrayed. There, innocence did not exist. Here, his ability to recognize a mistake wavered.

He heard a vehicle's door slam at the front of the cottage.

He left his friend, the Engineer, behind him. The curtain flicked at a window, the boy's room.

He should have killed the bastard . . . but he had not.

He came round the side of the cottage, where the climbing rose was thickest.

He heard the woman's piping voice. 'I just wanted to see that you were all well, all enjoying your holiday together.'

And heard the girl's stammered reply: 'Very well, very much enjoying being together.'

At a front window, pressed close to each other and up against the glass panes, were the faces of the rest, staring like fools and frightened. With his hand by his thigh he snapped his fingers at them and saw their retreat. The girl, Faria, had come out through the front door and intercepted the intruder by the porch. The woman was middle-aged, jowled at her throat, and had crow's feet at her eyes; she wore an old waxed coat and a tweed skirt. He thought her strong. He thought she would fight, and saw the nails on her fingers and the heavy boots on her feet – would fight hard for her life. She stood square in front of a mud-spattered Land Rover, parked beside their own car.

She had not yet seen him. 'It seemed only polite that I should call round – you know – to be satisfied that everything was working, that you had everything you needed.'

Neither had the girl seen him. 'Everything's good, fine, no problems, wonderful.'

If he needed to, he would kill her. The woman would condemn herself if she gained entry and meandered through the bedrooms, if she saw the boy, if she entered the room where the waistcoat was laid out, if her questions were persistent, prying.

'There has been a problem with the shower unit – I forgot to tell you about it – and sometimes it needs a bit of a tweak. With so many of you here it might need that . . . I said to my husband that I really should call by and check the shower flow . . .' She was moving forward, about to skirt the girl.

He saw the girl's hand reach out, as if in panic. 'There's nothing wrong with the shower.'

'Best to be sure.'

'There's a mess inside – I wouldn't want you to see—'

'Too early, am I? Only take a moment – it's awful when a shower hasn't got the flow.'

The woman was past the girl, on the step, and the door was wide open. The girl's hand snaked out, caught the arm of the waxed jacket, and the woman stared into her face, surprised by her grip. By his orders and planning, Ajaq had killed many, perhaps high hundreds. With his own hand, by shooting, with a knife or by strangulation, he had killed tens. Man or woman, he had never lost sleep for those he had killed. He saw the woman's thickened throat, below the jowl, and buried in it would be the windpipe, where the pressure of his thumbs would be if she entered the cottage. He did not believe there was malice in her, only curiosity, but it would be sufficient to condemn her to death – by strangulation.

He stepped forward briskly. 'Can I help you, madam?' He smiled at her.

'Oh, didn't see you . . . I just popped over to see that all was well with you all. You understand?'

'Madam, I think you embarrass my niece.'

'So sorry, didn't mean to. I just thought . . .'

He charmed. 'And will embarrass my nephews. Madam, we are late up this morning, and have not yet tidied the cottage. Some are still using the bathroom. Another time, another day would be more suitable. You know, madam, what young people are. Please, madam.'

He took her arm and turned her gently. It was the courtesy that his grandfather would have shown, an old and near-forgotten skill. As a commander in war, he rarely used courtesy, charm, the richness of his smile and the soft persuasion of words, but now he scratched in his memory for them.

'Are you sure – nothing I can do?'

'Nothing, madam. Everything is perfect. And you have our gratitude for the use of a home, at this time that is so special to us, where the comfort and facilities you have provided will be long remembered. We thank you, madam.'

Would she live or die? He could smell soft scent on her. She hesitated, as if she were not often balked, and he saw disappointment slide on to her face. But she turned and, in doing so, safeguarded her life.

She said, 'Well, we all know what young people are, and the mess they leave around . . . Anyway, if the shower is working . . .'

'Thank you, madam, for your concern.'

'Right. I'll be on my way. I do Meals on Wheels for the elderly as a volunteer on Wednesdays . . . So nice to meet you.'

'The pleasure, madam, is for me.'

He opened the Land Rover's door for her, then closed it quietly. She reversed, did a three-pointer, and he waved as she drove off up the track. He did not tremble, or pant, but the fingers that waved her off were those that would have strangled the breath from her lungs.

The girl understood.

Ajaq said, watching the Land Rover labouring on the track, 'Stupid fucking interfering bitch – one step more and she was dead, but she did not take the step.'

He left the waistcoat on the table, surrounded by the carcasses of dead flies, and checked the room a last time. Satisfied, he closed the door after him, locked it, and carried his bag down the corridor. He did not pause, or glance at the room where the boy was but went past it.

The Engineer walked through the living room and into the hall. Two of the kids, and the girl, were in the living room but he ignored them. They were no longer of importance to him.

His friend was at the front door. The Engineer had a choke in his voice – he told his friend that the button switch was taped over, that the device was live. From his pocket, he took one of the two ferry tickets in the envelope and passed it. They hugged, and he heard the car start up. He said, 'I am an old fool, the worst of them. I have done what I came to do, with ill grace but done it. You should be with me . . .' His cheeks were kissed. '. . . trust none of them.'

They broke apart. He looked into the face of his friend. 'Trust no one. Move. Set it in place, and run. There's no shame in running. Come back to me. Hurt them some more in our place, not here.' He felt his eyes watering. 'Is it that important?'

His shoulder was cuffed. He strode to the car and did not look back.

He was driven away. He did not think of the boy who would wear the waistcoat. He had lost count of the number of young men for whom he had made waistcoats and belts, for whom he had rigged the firing switches in cars and lorries. The building of the waistcoat, with the sticks, the debris and the wiring, was so basic to an artist such as himself that he could have fashioned it in his sleep. The car turned on to the main road and they drove by low hedges that had been cut savagely. Once there was a flash of the cottage. Already he thought of the battlefield that was his home.

He settled back in the seat.

He yearned to be beside his friend, lying in a ditch, hunkered down in a grove of palms, or in the upper window of a house, with a wide straight road in view, and the distant rumble of a lorry convoy or a Humvee patrol approaching. With his friend beside him, he would have in his hand a mobile phone whose signal could detonate a device built round a 120mm artillery shell with ten kilos of rocket propellant to give it the kick to break through the strongest armour plate reinforcing the sides of any enemy transport vehicle. He thought of the great flash, the crimson and orange flames rising, then the soaring columns of blackened smoke and falling debris. He did not see other traffic, or the homes beside the dual-carriageway, or the kids who kicked footballs, women who pushed buggies and men with small, straining dogs. His thoughts played on sacks of refuse dumped at the side of another dual-carriageway – and in one, under a mass of garbage, and holed by scavenging rats, ten or fifteen kilos of explosive were buried.

The boy who drove him had switched on the car radio, and music blared round him, but he did not care or complain. His thoughts had moved on: a narrow, shallow trench was dug in a dirt road used by patrols at night, used by Humvees with their lights off and with night-vision goggles on the drivers' faces – local men in the villages along the dirt road had been ordered not to drive a tractor or a car on it. A soft rubber pipe was laid in the trench, filled with water and sealed at one end. At the other were the fuse wires that connected when the pipe's water, under pressure from the weight of a Humvee, forced them together – they led to the bomb – and the trench was filled in, dust swept over it.

They hit the motorway. The biggest roads had construction work to reinforce the bridges for the enemy's main battle tanks: a factory turned out the concrete blocks that would strengthen them. Already hollowed out, blocks were brought to him from the factory and he packed the cavity spaces with high-grade explosive putty, then wired in the detonators. Labourers loyal to the struggle cemented in the blocks and routed the wires from them, and the remote firing triggers. He was starting his journey back to the world he knew. Would his friend, ever again, be beside him when the fire, the thunder and the smoke erupted?

The mood, melancholy, ached in him.

He was driven south and the rain slashed against the windscreen, cascading from the wipers. He imagined the reunion, him sweating from the heat, and his friend. A soft footfall, the creak of a door, the shadow coming into a room, the growl of the voice ... and he thought that when, *if*, they met again he would weep, not contain his tears as he had done before getting into the car – and he cursed.

He and his friend, they should never have come ... and he did not know where a trap was set and how it would be sprung.

*

The handler and his dog quartered the Rose Hill park.

He didn't do the discipline bit on these early-morning or late-afternoon exercise sessions. He let Midge run. The discipline would come in the day's work. Then he'd be obliged to have her on a short or long leash and under firm control. She was biddable when they were on duty and would not pull. For now, she ran and covered the grassland at pace. The rain mattered not a damn to her, but there was a heavy towel in the van and he would rub her down before he drove into the city.

She'd done business, and he'd used a plastic bag to clear up after her. The handler's mind was far away. He saw her, careering off to his left, but did not bother to call her back to him. She, and he, had another ten minutes of freedom before he turned his back on Rose Hill . . . He was thinking of how much he would have to spend on a reliable mountain bike for his daughter on her twelfth birthday, and how long it would be before she grew too tall for it to be of further use.

Abstracted, he followed the line his dog took. He saw the boy on the bench . . . Pink was his daughter's favourite colour . . . An Asian boy, his head hidden in his hands . . . Who'd ever heard of a kid having a pink bicycle? . . . There was an Asian community in the Normanton district's warren of terraced homes, a century and more old, but he seldom saw their kids here . . . If she couldn't have a pink bicycle, perhaps green or blue would be more suitable . . . His dog ran to the boy . . . More suitable and more easily bought, but was colour important? His dog sniffed at the boy's legs, and the handler focused on him. He thought the boy looked half drowned, as if he'd been hours out in the rain, maybe half the night, and the shoulders of his clothing clung to his big torso . . . Damn right, colour was important to a girl on her twelfth birthday . . . and his spaniel had stretched up on her hind legs, had her front paws on the boy's knees, and her nose was at the hands that held the drooped head . . . Colour was critical to . . . The tail wagged with increasing energy, and the nostrils were in the hands.

He forgot the bicycle, and watched.

The dog should not have climbed half over a boy sitting and minding his own business on a bench, and probably the boy had pawmarks over the thighs of his jeans now. He tugged at the string round his neck that held the high-pitched whistle, but the dog was now off the boy, sitting in front of him and barking furiously. Extraordinary that a little creature, his spaniel, could make that cacophony of noise.

For a moment, the handler had the whistle at his lips but he did not blow. The dog's barking would have raised the dead in a cemetery. The rain had come on harder, and he would need the few extra minutes left to him to towel down her coat. The handler thought the spaniel was behaving as if she was out on a training exercise.

On exercise, under supervision that required about half a telephone directory of completed forms, live explosives were brought to the site by the army's people and little caches were hidden under stones, or in plastic bags, which were buried under rubble in the corner of a derelict building, or wrapped with tinfoil and pocketed by a stooge suspect. Then the dog, on the long leash or running free, was urged to locate the caches. She always did, and she'd sniff, find, rock back on to her haunches lift her head and bloody bark for his attention . . . as she had been taught, as she was doing right now in front of the Asian boy on the bench.

But this was not an exercise and his time, and hers, was up.

He whistled hard.

The dog, Midge, did not respond.

He cursed, then strode forward.

'Come to heel, Midge. Come. To heel.' He yelled it, full voice.

On exercise, when she located the ounce or so of TNT, Semtex – whatever had been hidden for her to find – the reward was a biscuit and loving words. The bag of biscuits was in the van . . . The spaniel came half of the way back to him, but looking behind her every two, three yards. He was about to grab her.

He called to the boy on the bench. 'Sorry about that. She's a young'un, but not normally daft. Hope she hasn't mucked your clothes . . .' He bent to take the loose chain collar and had the leash catch in his hands . . . What struck him, there was no response from the boy: not a wave of acceptance for the apology, not a protest at the mud smeared on his jeans by the dog's paws, and the head stayed down . . . His dog was as agile, at that age, as a bloody rabbit, and it was gone again. The dog raced over the grass and back to the bench, but did not sniff the hands again. The dog, a yard in front of the Asian boy, barked with ever-increasing intensity.

So, the handler had a problem. Had those long months of training been wasted? The barking rang in his ears.

The handler was a proud man, and his pride rested securely in his belief that he had the best dog in the force. Because of his own efforts, Midge always found the minute caches of explosives on exercises, and he had never known her – at the East Midlands airport, or at Derby's main railway terminus – settle herself in front of a passenger and make that bloody noise. He was also an obstinate man and he did not care to believe that all of that training time was wasted.

He caught his breath.

Then, pride and obstinacy ruled him.

The handler had few doubts, but those he harboured were sufficient for him not to call out an armed-response vehicle. He would do it himself.

Walking with a good step, but with his heart pounding, he went to the bench. The Asian boy never looked up, didn't seem to see his approach, didn't kick the dog away. It fitted no pattern that he had learned on exercises.

Beside him, the spaniel's tail thrashed in excitement.

He said softly, 'I am a police officer. Please, sir, would you stand up? That's right, sir, now turn away from me and put your hands together at your back.'

The handler was obeyed. The boy stood, huge and muscled but without an iota of fight in him, and the handler could not tell whether it was rain that ran down his cheeks or tears. He snapped on the handcuffs, then patted down the body and found nothing. His breathing eased. He told the boy why he had arrested him, quoted from a host of anti-terrorism legislation, and cautioned him.

Then he murmured, 'I hope to God you're bloody right on this one, Midge. We're for the high jump if you're not, and it'll be a bloody high one.'

The dog's eyes were on the cuffed hands, and still she barked.

He called in on his radio. Gave his name and call-sign, his location point on Rose Hill as nearest to Grove Street, requested the cavalry get here and soonest – Special Branch and Forensics – and said, 'He's clean, not wearing any form of improvised explosive device. I'm just going on what my dog tells me, and the dog's telling me his hands are contaminated. Over, out.'

The handler knew that, by lunchtime, he and his dog would either be the laughing stock of the force or front-line celebrities.

'Won't be long, sir, then we'll have you in the warm and dry.'

He left the taxi in the forecourt with the meter running and hurried into the hotel foyer. After trying three times to ring the room number, Dickie Naylor had diverted the taxi into Belgravia. Should have been a short run from his club – actually, not a club in the grand sense of the West End, more of a dingy hostelry for retired military officers – to Riverside Villas, but he'd embarked on this course of action and was now down fifteen pounds. It would be twenty when he was dropped, with Hegner, at the side door beside the Thames. He'd slept in central London, just too damn tired to face a night journey back to the suburbs, and he'd been on the pavement, the rain cascading off his umbrella, searching for a vacant taxi when his pager had gone.

Nothing proven, of course. A lad picked up by an off-duty dog-handler in an East Midlands park, and the initial report was of explosives traces *believed* to be on the lad's hands. Naylor had reacted. Three working days left to him, and in his mind he had wiped away the hesitations and lack of confirmation as yet. Wanted to *believe* it. So desperately chasing the Grail, willing it to be truth and linked to this last investigation of his career. So, pompously, he had telephoned Anne, had told her that 'Events are moving, my dear, cannot say more, moving at pace, also may not be back this evening, seems we're at the vortex of the storm . . .' The curtain was coming down on his career, and that career had been utterly unmemorable; three working days remained to right the wrong. He prayed that a dog-handler – one hundred and twenty miles from the capital – had turned up a diamond, not a cut-glass bauble.

He was at the hotel because the American's theme, the previous day, gave logic where there was as yet no proof. He went to the desk, and the lobby oozed understated comfort where his own club had none. When he had telephoned before he had been told that the room's occupant had ordered the switchboard to put no calls through. Face to face with the receptionist, his steely aggression won the day. The connection was made, he was handed the phone.

'Joe? Dickie here. What you said last evening about mistakes and luck, and an ability to exploit – well, with some confidence I think we might be getting there. I'm downstairs with a taxi. Quick as you can, please.' He was about to ring off, then thought. The man was blind, might take an age to dress, could need help. 'Do you need a hand? Shall I come up?'

He was told, and thought he heard a giggle, that a hand was not required. 'I'll be right down.'

Naylor checked his pager, then his mobile – no messages, no texts. He picked up a complimentary newspaper. He sat deep in an armchair and started on the crossword, then that bloody numbers puzzle – and gasped. He had not achieved more than half a dozen of the clues, or more than two lines of numbers . . . The breath whistled through his teeth. 'Damn me, the old goat,' he muttered.

Hegner came out of the lift and did not need his stick swaying in front of him to find obstacles. Mary Reakes had his arm and guided him. Hegner was dressed smartly: he had on a fresh laundered shirt and his tie nestled flush in the collar. Mary Reakes had on the same suit as the day before and the same blouse. He looked like a cat that had found a carton of cream; she looked as if she had been well and satisfactorily shagged. Naylor's jaw dropped. He would not have thought it possible . . . Those hands, badly blotched from little shrapnel shards and with the veins prominent, had been over the prim, preserved body of Mary Reakes – he knew they had; her eyes blazed defiance at him – always that way the morning after an office untouchable from Riverside Villas had been bedded overnight. Could recognize it a damn mile off. She seemed to challenge Naylor as she led the American close to him . . . He couldn't help himself, was wondering whether she kept spare smalls in her desk drawer, and spare— She fixed him, dared him. He crumpled. In all the years she had worked in the outer office beyond his cubicle door, he had never had a remotely personal conversation with her. He did not know what to say, so said nothing.

Hegner, without sight but with that increased intuitive understanding of atmosphere, grinned. 'Hope I haven't abused your hospitality, Dickie. I don't think so . . . Overpaid, over-sexed, and

258

over here. Guess I scored two out of three ... Shame the Bureau's salary levels don't match those of the private sector.' The grin settled to a laugh.

They went through the swing doors and out into the rain. Naylor saw the care she employed to get him down the steps, across the forecourt and into the taxi.

'So, what's this about? A mistake and luck?'

Naylor saw the American's hand rest on Mary Reakes's thigh as the taxi crawled away in the early traffic. He thought himself churlishly abrupt, to the point of surliness, as he briefed quietly, a short paraphrase of what he knew.

And Mary bloody Reakes did not remove the gnarled hand with the surgery scars on it and stared straight ahead at the back of the driver's neck.

The American said, 'I think that was worth getting out of my pit to hear ... It figures, it's what I told you. Now, I have just two observations to make. First, you do not allow anyone, that is *anyone*, to shut me out, because I'll tell you, I've forgotten more than you'll ever know on these matters, and you'll learn damn quick that you depend on my instincts. Second, if you allow the law-enforcement process to crawl over this son-of-a-bitch, you will have made an error of seismic proportions, like pissing into the wind ain't too clever. Got me?'

She said, and didn't shift the hand, 'Our aim is to defend the realm, and that is by the maintenance of civilized standards, and civilized standards involve the gathering of evidence to set before a court. We don't go down into a gutter.'

Naylor said, 'I believe the points you've made, Joe, are understood.'

He thought that age seemed then to catch him, not as the waft of a breeze on his face but as the surge of a gale into his midriff, as if it could have felled him ... and he seemed to hear the call of those gulls from far away, and the rumble of the Atlantic's waves on rocks and the whine of wind in overhead wires ... and she'd moved the hand, had dumped it back in Hegner's lap. On a grey London morning, with the rain spitting on the road, Naylor appreciated his dependence on the American, and where it would take him – and he had three more working days of service. And the words clamoured in his mind: *Look where ordinary people go about their daily business, where your citizens think they're safe.*

The group trailed after him. The town's self-appointed historian, Steve Vickers, had one inalienable rule: he never cancelled for inclement weather. He was in good voice as he led the Townswomen's Guild party through High Town; a little forest of dripping umbrellas followed him.

'More than anywhere else in Britain, indeed in the empire, Luton was the greatest centre of hat- and bonnet-making. In the 1851 census, eighty-eight per cent of High Town's females were involved in making headwear to be worn by women in Great Britain and exported – even girls as young as six were described in the returns as "sewers". Any woman in London's Mayfair or Edinburgh's Princes Street or in Dublin, Sydney, New Delhi or Toronto, when dressed at her best would most likely be wearing a hat or bonnet made in these humble streets.'

On a better day, he might have held the attention of the ladies from the Townswomen's Guild.

'Obviously, the annual boom in the trade was from December to May. The customers wanted new models for the summer, and then thousands more women came to High Town from the surrounding villages to boost the numbers of sewers and stitchers, and most popular of all were the straw hats – not that they would have been in great demand on a day such as this.'

He laughed, smiled, and was rewarded with a sullen response. He knew that a coach where they would be warm was parked by the station and would take them on to Woburn Abbey, the next leg of their outing. The ladies were drenched and only ingrained politeness kept them from abandoning him. He had done the pre-history bit, and the Roman bit. It irked him that his tour of what he called 'The Hat Trail' could be so poorly received.

'The manufacturing lasted through the thirties up to the outbreak of the Second World War. Then habits changed. Women no longer regarded it as essential to wear headgear when they were out and—'

A voice piped up, 'Fascinating, Mr Vickers, and we're very grateful to you. But, as the Guild secretary and speaking for all of us, I really think we've had enough. Please would you be so kind as to lead us back to our coach before we drown?'

He did. If he had ignored the plea and continued with the Trail, his audience would have gone. But Steve Vickers was seldom deflated. His next booking was for Saturday morning, again an early start, and the tour of the town centre – the clock that chimed like Parliament's, the story of the Peace Riot, and he'd heard on the radio that the forecast for the weekend was good. He would not show disappointment at the curtailment: to have done so would reduce the volume of tips as they scrambled on to the coach.

'Yes, I think we have to acknowledge defeat, but you have been wonderful and it has been my privilege to share a little of the town's rich heritage with you. Thank you so much for your interest.'

There was a desultory clapping from under the umbrellas. He led them away. He took some comfort from Saturday's forecast, when he would be in St George's Square, under the town hall's clock, across the open space from the shopping centre; he hoped then for a good attendance and a better purse of tips.

He realized he hated the man.

David Banks sat in the public gallery. His Glock was on his hip and gouged awkwardly into it; it was with Wally's agreement that he had been allowed to wear it into court eighteen – too much palaver to check it into the police booth at the main door, then get it back when he followed the jurors to their sealed room and stood outside at an adjournment, and he'd sensed that the chief inspector had a distaste for firearms but he'd promised – and smiled drily – that the safety catch would be firmly on. He wore the loaded pistol at his belt and had given his guarantee that the weapon could not accidentally discharge a bullet. If the holster, and the Glock's handle, had not pushed into him, Banks might have dozed: nothing to hold his attention as the prosecution's barrister droned through the minutiae of the evidence that the court had heard, that would convict the lowlife brothers. Banks did not close his eyes, let his head sag.

The public gallery was divided into two sections by an aisle. The case detectives, men and women from the Crime Directorate, were in the other section, and among them were uniformed constables of the beefed-up security detail. On the row in front of Banks, two women had gold at their throats, real fur on the collars of their coats and highlights in their hair; he thought them cousins of the lowlife or mistresses. Beyond the court door were more uniforms and some of them had Heckler & Kochs slung from black webbing straps, but Banks's was the only firearms officer inside – and the damn thing hurt him.

Nothing of the Victorian history of the building seeped into court eighteen. It was, he thought bitterly, 'customer friendly', designed to put men and women at their ease, to make them lose sight – with the soft pastel paint on the walls, and the beechwood furnishings – of the real world of crude violence, that of the Curtis brothers. The judge, didn't seem a bad sort, was on a shallow raised dais to his right, and the brothers were at the far end to his left; there were only low panels hiding their legs, no armoured glass screen or a cage's bars to keep them in place. Between the judge and the prisoners there were layers of lawyers, then the court staff, and the prosecution's man ploughed his way through his prepared notes. About the only damn action was from the stenographer who rattled away at her keyboard. Opposite Banks was the jury.

His Principal was in the second row. The guy lounged easily in his seat and was one of the few who took no notes of the barrister's address. Didn't have on a clean shirt, as the other men did. Hadn't combed his hair, and the other men's was tidily brushed. Banks knew the first names of the jury, and his Principal was close, too close, to the woman on his right, Vicky. She wore a cheesecloth-type blouse and a loose-fitting cotton skirt of bright print colours, both of which showed off her body's contours, and his Principal was too bloody close to her. The chests, shoulders and heads of the front rank of jurors cut off his view of the hips and knees of the one called Vicky and his Principal, but he fancied they would be touching, which was too damn close.

The hatred gnawed in him. He could have stood up then, pushed himself to his feet, interrupted the calm and quiet of the barrister's words – could have yelled, full volume, from the depths of his throat, a torrent of obscenities.

David Banks loathed Cecil Darke, the man whose notebook was in his jacket pocket with the pebbles and coins, resting on the Glock's holster.

He had no photograph of Cecil Darke, his great-uncle, only imagined images. Probably small, probably slight, probably anonymous in a crowd, probably had a squeaky voice, probably had no distinguishing marks . . . His ignorance consumed Banks . . . Probably had courage, determination . . . The man overwhelmed him, had destroyed already the delicate equilibrium of his life. Cecil Darke had pitchforked his way, uninvited, into the life of his great-nephew. Each hour of the day, and most of those at night when he slept and dreamed, Banks now walked alongside the volunteer in the British battalion – and had been with him when the vitality of hope was lost on the sodden, frozen or parched fields of battle. Had learned to love and admire Cecil Darke. Had learned of his own life's destruction by association. Had learned to curse. Had learned to hate, loathe, detest. The words from a canteen lark played in his mind, and a senior man's, and the caution of an armourer: his defence of Cecil Darke had imploded on him. David Banks was, and could recognize it – as a price for that defence – rejected by his team and cast out, alone . . . He was with a bloody jury, was reckoned unreliable by the Delta crowd, unable to hack the big-time. They wanted, in Delta, 'steady' men, 'team' men, and they thought his defence of his great-uncle left him short of the qualities they demanded. He had no one to confide in – felt naked, vulnerable, a failure.

He would read, in the lunch adjournment, another page and another entry of lost hope and growing misery. He could not help himself . . . The hatred surged in him for what the diary had made him.

His teeth scraped together. Then he bit savagely at his tongue – because that was what loathing did to him . . . And his bloody Principal – a hero of the hour – sat too damned close to the woman in the blouse and the full skirt.

He was gone again, had returned as a witness to the wire and the foxholes, and he seemed to hear the thunder of exploding shells and to lie on the dusty earth as aircraft circled above him, searching for targets. He could not free himself from it.

They were like those twins, joined at the hip . . . and unlike those twins featured on TV, joined also at the knee.

If she didn't like it, she was free to have shifted in her seat.

Perhaps she had not wriggled clear of him because she hadn't noticed that his hip and his knee were against hers, perhaps she didn't give a toss whether his hip and knee were pressured against her, perhaps ... God, the prosecution's wind-up speech was crushingly dull. Why bother? Guilty on all counts – and chuck away the bloody key.

What mattered now to Jools Wright was the afterwards, and the afterwards was getting damnably complicated. They'd all been given the lecture on Duty of Care ... but not given an answer to the question of how long Duty of Care ran for. A week, a month, a year after the finish of the trial? Didn't know. How long would he have a sour-faced policeman travelling with him, sitting with him, not speaking to him? Didn't know. Where were they going to be living, him, Babs and Kathy? Didn't know. When was he going to be able to go back to work once the jury-service cash finished? Didn't know ... What was lovely was the soft, giving feel of the pelvic bone against his hip, and her knee against his. Nice lady, Vicky, and to be respected because there weren't many who could make their own shoes – and there was a quite lovely beddable scent to her, as if she hadn't washed well that morning in the stampede to get breakfast down, be on the charabanc and out of that dismal camp – and there weren't many who would have tolerated his hip and knee against hers. Had he ever spoken to her? Anything more than 'Excuse me, could you please pass the salt?' 'Excuse me, the brown sauce, please.' 'Excuse me, do you have it verbatim what that Forensics woman said?' No, he didn't think so. It was almost cheeky of Vicky, but half the buttons on her blouse were undone, and the ones that were fastened bulged fit to bust. A very nice lady was Vicky ... No, the *afterwards* concerned him.

He looked up. God, the man looked miserable. Furrows on the forehead that came together in a knotted mess. He stared across the court and felt the slight motion of Vicky's body as she wrote busily on one of the sheets of paper pulled from her chaotic tapestry bag. He had heard not a word the barrister said. What had that bloody detective on his mind that pulled a face so damn abject? What was his 'afterwards'? Mr Banks, because he only responded if given a title, had allowed – with bloody awful grace – one phone call to Babs,

264

from the breakfast room. He'd said quietly, 'Just thought you'd like to know, my love, where your spirit of Trafalgar Day bravery – and your ethical certainties – have left us. We had a Molotov cocktail through the front window this morning. Not to worry, minimal damage to furniture and fittings, and the Criminal Compensation crowd will meet the cost. Hope you're both well, and my regards to your parents . . . Oh, I've stolen your gladrags. To the police, I'm an alpha-grade hero for doing my duty, a shining example to a law-abiding society . . . Lots of love, have to dash, off for a spot more heroism. 'Bye.' None of the others knew it was him who'd coughed the load, under duress. His little secret. Jools could have said, 'I am not what I am' – *Othello*, good old Shakespeare – but would not: the deception gave him pleasure. He stared across the well of the court. His glance was met coldly . . . bloody miserable sod. The detective – Jools reckoned – looked like the burden of life crushed him . . . Finally, the prosecution had sat down, and that smug look played at the lawyer's mouth, must have given a peroration at the end, and he couldn't recall a word of it. Three cheers, caps in the air, and the defence was on his feet. They were getting there, nearer to the *afterwards*.

His imagination? Was the pressure of Vicky's hip harder against his? Just so damn lovely to dream.

Jools thought he sleep-walked – trouble was, he didn't know the destination.

A convoy had come, with no regard for the legal speed limit, south down the M1.

A motorcycle, lights flashing, had cleared the fast lane in front of the two performance cars that rushed towards the capital.

A prisoner, huddled in the back of the lead car, sat sandwiched between two Branch men and wore white-paper overalls.

A uniformed officer held the traffic on the Edgware Road and the cars slewed right and into the basement yard of Paddington Green police station.

A blanket was draped over the prisoner's head as he was hustled inside the cell block.

A news blackout lay over the arrest.

A spaniel sniffer dog, far to the north, wolfed biscuits happily and was the celebrity of the hour.

Chapter 13: Wednesday, Day 14

He heard Naylor give his name, then say, 'And with me is Mr Josiah Hegner, of the Bureau and out of Riyadh, who has made a study of these matters and, in an advisory capacity, is fully welcomed by my superiors . . .'

His world was darkness, but his senses were acute.

'. . . and this is Mary Reakes, from the Service. Where are we?'

Where? Well, Hegner had been told – on the walk between the car and the building – that Paddington Green was the high-security place where all high-flier terrorists arrested in the United Kingdom were brought for questioning; and had been told it was bombproof, stormproof, and escape-proof. Seemed simple enough to know where they were. A place like this was available to the Bureau in a score of American cities, and there was the cordoned-off holding area at the Baghdad airport military wing, the Mabatha interrogation centre out south from the Saudi capital . . . Should have been 'Where are we *getting*?'

Mary had his arm, and he kind of liked that, but she didn't do leading him as well as his Cindy did.

A voice said, laconic and like his presence – and Naylor's and Mary's – was an intrusion, 'Early days as yet. Because he was picked up at dawn, then brought down here, we've let him stew in his cell – as we're obliged to – and he's been offered a meal, declined it, and a chance to pray, used it. It's been done by the book, and we've had him in here for a couple of hours . . . Like I say, early days.'

His nostrils picked up the recycled, regurgitated airflow of the block. The same air, damp and stale, circulated in these buildings everywhere Hegner had been. And there was always a television screen cabled through to a ceiling camera in the room where the jerk was. He heard the low voice, the question, but there was silence for an answer. He swung his stick in front of him, hit a table leg and moved forward skirting it, swung the stick again and heard a yelp of pain, then, 'Hey, steady with that thing, if you don't mind.' Hegner went to a speaker, stood under it. He reached out with his hand, touched the covering material, then eased his ear against it.

A second voice, irritated, 'Excuse me, but you're half in my lap.'

He heard again the question, then the silence. He said, 'Mary, get me a chair here.'

There was a snort of annoyance. He didn't care. The chair was brought and he settled on it, but his ear stayed against the speaker. He heard the crackle of the connection, the rustle of papers, the clink of a bottle's neck on a glass and the silence . . . and he knew what he would say but was not ready to say it. He heard Mary's breathing near to him, and Naylor's cough.

'Do you want a coffee, Joe?' Mary asked.

He gazed into the blackness, and strained to hear better from the speaker. Hegner said, 'A coffee'll make me need a leak. What I want is you to describe him to me. I want to know him.'

He sensed around him the resentment his presence created, and it did not concern him. Little sounds, not from the speaker, told him of the three men and one woman in the room, and they would have thought themselves the experts, and he was the intruder. As an intruder, he was familiar with resentment. Sometimes he used folksy charm to dismantle it and sometimes he didn't bother, as now. If it had been his territory that was invaded he would have bawled them out, slammed the goddamn door on them.

She said briskly, 'It's a monochrome screen and the lighting's poor. He's in a paper jumpsuit. He's Asian, maybe middle twenties . . .

He's a big man, powerful, heavily muscled, but his shoulders are down. The tongue's out, flicks his lips. He's frightened.'

Not frightened bad enough, like he would have been – Hegner thought – in the Mabatha interrogation centre or at Baghdad's airport, or if the cold, bad guys of the Bureau had him in a 'black site' military camp.

The question came over the speaker, conversational: 'It's confirmed, Ramzi, that there are traces of explosives on your hands, and I'm giving you the opportunity to explain them. How did they get there?' No reply.

'What's his eyeline?'

'Seems, Joe, that he's looking at the ceiling, not at the officer across the table. On the ceiling and staying there.'

The patient rephrasing of the question: 'Look, Ramzi, there may be a perfectly innocent explanation for these traces on your hands, and I'm giving you the chance to tell me how they came to be there.' He listened to the silence.

Mary said, 'The eyeline has changed. It's gone to the wall, the bottom of it, to his left. He's sweating, hands clenched and fingers locked. I'd say frightened but fighting.'

No exasperation, no bluster and hurry: 'It would, of course, be best for you, Ramzi, to be utterly truthful with us. You've been in a cell with comrades, but you're now alone. Help us, and you help yourself. You realize, don't you, the advantages of co-operation?' The silence echoed in his ear.

Mary said, 'I wouldn't swear to it, but I think he is, if anything, more comfortable now than when we came in. Still frightened, but it's like he believes he can survive . . . The eyeline is still on the wall by the floor. He doesn't risk contact.'

Nor would he. Didn't have to. Hegner asked if anything had been said by the prisoner. 'Nothing,' was the laconic voice's response, 'not a single word.' What had he said in the car coming south to London? Hadn't opened his mouth. They had a name – had they now an address? Officers were still at the house, with his mother and his two sisters; his room was clean, bare, and his lap-top computer had the hard drive removed. There were no posters of Islamic *jihad*ists and no books and no pamphlets in his room that were relevant, and all that had been learned was that the man had been absent from home

– on an IT course, his mother said, but had not known where – for thirteen days.

He did the arithmetic in his mind. Ibrahim Hussein, wearing the T-shirt of *The Threatened Swan* had gone through King Khalid airport, had flown out of Riyadh, seven days before. Ibrahim Hussein, still in that damn shirt, had come off the Eurostar five days before. Hegner leaned back, groped, found Mary's arm. 'That boy was met at that train station.'

'But we didn't have a face for the greeter, only the boy.'

'Describe the build of the greeter.'

He heard the snap of the lock on her shoulder-bag. He had already decided on the body shape. He sought only to confirm his status. She was rifling among papers. Another question was put, was met by the same silence.

Mary said, 'Big, heavy and filling an anorak, over six feet in height, and two thirty – could be two forty – pounds was the estimate.'

Hegner stood; in doing so he kneed the groin of the officer beside him, did not apologize. He swung his stick ahead of him, hit the leg of another officer and the table's. 'I find the air kind of suffocating in here,' he said.

He shook Mary's hand off his arm. From the door he called, 'Thank you for your welcome,' and he murmured, too softly to be heard, 'Keep going the way you are and you might break him by Christmas.'

He set off down the corridor at pace, and Mary Reakes was skipping to keep up with him. He remembered exactly each step he had taken into the building, and the route to get clear of it.

Hegner stopped, stood in the yard, and the rain lashed him.

He said, 'They're going nowhere, and fast. That was a joke.'

He heard Naylor: 'Quite predictable, they never talk – all of them have had the training on resistance to interrogation.'

'That was no interrogation, that was like a PTA conversation.'

He heard Mary Reakes: 'In the gathering of evidence to go before a court it is not permitted to suggest that co-operation will be rewarded with a reduced sentence. It would be what we call "offering an inducement". It's not admissible – would most likely lead to acquittal.'

'Mary, you're a great lay but this is old men's work and you'd do well to go sit in your tower, dream moralities and stay clean.'

There was a gasp, a choke, then a clatter of her heels, and he heard their car door open, then slam.

Naylor said, hoarse, 'Spit it, Joe, get it out.'

'Do you want to crack this guy or not? Do you want to listen for the bang, then scrape up the bits on the pavement and up the buildings' walls to stay clean? Who's going to go the extra mile? Where I work, we do that mile, get the mud on our boots, then they talk. You got hang-ups, Dickie? Are you in the lady's camp, waiting for the explosion? Think I got you wrong, Dickie. Maybe you're a man to go slack on me. Do you have people who'll do the business, do what's necessary?'

'I'm not her cheer-leader but what you said to her was out of order. She's in the car now, sobbing. Please, make your peace . . . Yes, I do have such men and I've put them on stand-by.'

'Get them here – talking is wasting time. Trust me, Dickie, you ain't got time.'

Hegner went to the car.

Naylor stood in the centre of the yard, the rain coursing down his face. He dialled.

He thought it was about duty. About, of course, the carrying-out of a verbal instruction – no minutes taken, nothing on paper . . . no. He covered himself in those two frail cloaks. It was the right thing to do, and it was an order given him.

His call was answered.

Dickie Naylor understood the effect of a bomb blast: the hammering detonation, the sound coming faster and louder than an express train from a tunnel, the orange- and yellow-tinted flash that almost blinded, the leaping column of acrid smoke and the slower climb of the debris, then the pressure wave of heated, dirtied air. He understood also the injuries of a bomb blast that killed and mutilated . . . men and women and children thrown down with their bladders and sphincters loosened, pieces of concrete, glass, stonework and roofing tearing into their chests and stomachs, heads and limbs and shredding them. For many only tiny fragments of their humanity remained – the fingers on a severed fist or a shoe still worn on a foot; the spinal column often survived intact but lungs collapsed fatally from compression and so did spleens and livers; entrails were exposed and heads cast off . . . and if it was a cold day, or a chilly night, when a bomb exploded, steam exuded from the cut-open bodies of the dead and the living . . . And then there was quiet. Dickie Naylor, the nearly man, could justify his call to an island of the Inner Hebrides.

He spoke briefly, concisely, said what would happen and what should be done – and heard the gulls, the sea, the bloody gale's whine, and rang off.

Still it rained; still he stood in the centre of the Paddington Green yard. He dialled again. He could not see into the car, did not know whether the old goat comforted Mary, or whether she, too, now received a lecture on martyr cells and motivation – maybe on the virtues of the legitimate weapon of torture . . . His call, into a personal line, was answered.

'Tristram, it's Dickie . . . Yes, I'm fine, yes . . . I'm at the Green. Our boy is sitting in an interview room and looking at the floor or the wall or the ceiling, saying nothing. Tristram, we need to move on a stage, on to areas we discussed . . . Yes, they're coming, but I need transport for them. I can't authorize, at my level, RAF flights. That has to come from you. I suppose we need a helicopter and a lift to a fast jet, an executive, for the leg down here . . . No, Tristram, I haven't a clue where the helicopter should pick them up, but there must be somewhere that isn't bog. When you've done the necessary, get the boys in blue to call me and I'll have the phone number they can liaise with . . . Tristram, I doubt I have to stiffen your resolve, but the clock's ticking. There is no alternative . . . I'm grateful, Tristram, for your appreciation of what needs doing. I'm on my way in and we have a mountain to clear, know what I mean? . . . Yes, "obfuscation" is an apt word for it. Be with you in an hour.'

He felt a burden was now shared and was relieved for that.

He strode to the car, brushed the rain off his coat.

Mary Reakes sat bolt upright in the seat beside the driver.

Hegner was saying, '. . . I accept there are no stereotypes for activists, but what is a common factor is the sense of brotherhood, family, tribe that exists inside the cell. It has taken over the role of parent and sibling. He might, after a few days of gentle probing persuasion, betray his father, mother, brother and sister, his cousins.

He will not, unless under extreme pressure, betray the cell . . . Dickie, you look like hell. You gotten things moving?'

He nodded bleakly, and slipped into the car. He could not get out of his head the quiet voice on the line, the birds' cries, the waves' roar and the gale's song.

They walked together, bent against the surge of the wind, to the McDonald farm.

At the door, declining politely an invitation to come inside for a pot of tea, Xavier Boniface told the farmer that they had business on the mainland, and would be away three days, or four.

Donald Clydesdale, and he knew there would be no hesitation from the farmer, asked if care could be taken of the cow, Marigold, and the heifer calf, Daisy, born in the lee of the hill that was close to the cliff of Cnoc nan Gabhar.

They would be attended to, and their sheep, goats, fowls and geese.

Boniface asked the farmer if he had seen the sea eagles up over the cliff and hunting in bad weather, and the farmer said they must hunt because the young in the eyrie had hatched. And he wished them well and did not ask what was their business off the island.

They trudged back to their house to pack their bags and make ready the gear they would take south. The light was failing and the weather worsening. It would be a rough flight for the helicopter's pilot, and there would only be the bright lights of their flashlamps to guide him in, but neither Xavier Boniface nor Donald Clydesdale had considered refusing the summons to come south.

His voice torn away by the wind, Clydesdale said, 'It'll be a hard nut to crack if Mr Naylor's called us.'

'Hard or soft, it'll be an important nut and needing to be cracked quick,' Boniface said. 'Nuts – hard or soft – with the right treatment, they all crack.'

The camera lens, like a fierce eye, caught him. He had the sheet of paper on his knee. Ibrahim Hussein, the drop-out first-year medical student, thought that at last he had memorized the text given him. He sucked in air, waited for the dropped finger to tell him to begin and felt a tightness through his body . . . He was told the bulb was blinking, that a new battery was needed, and the tension subsided, the text vanished from his mind. He heard the hiss of annoyance from the darkness behind the light that beamed on to him.

He knew now that Ramzi, the muscle, had run. Knew, too, that crisis engulfed the cell. Knew, also, that time was precious. It was to be his fourth attempt to speak the words written for him, and on three attempts he had stumbled and the thread had been lost. The filming of the video had first been held up by an argument between Faria, who had written it, and Jamal, who operated the camera: what language should be spoken? The Arabic, with the dialect of Asir Province, that was easiest for him and most suitable for the Al Jazeera satellite audience? The English that she had composed and that was aimed at the Crusaders' society? But Ibrahim Hussein did not have the depth of vocabulary to translate from English to the Saudi tongue, and Faria and Jamal had the taught Arabic of the Book, which was insufficient . . . The argument had been resolved by the Leader's cutting response to the delay: 'It is not important. He will speak what is given him.' Then more bickered problems.

Should he, or should he not, wear the waistcoat?

The martyrs in Lebanon, Palestine and occupied Iraq wore robes when their video statements were recorded, carried weapons and had slogans in praise of God painted on to the wide bandannas tied across their foreheads. There were no robes in Oakdene Cottage, and no Kalashnikov assault rifles. She denied it had been her responsibility to provide robes that fitted him. Jamal criticized the lack of a weapon, even a replica. The Leader had said, 'Again, it is of no importance. He does not want to wear the waistcoat, he does not – he does and he wears the waistcoat. Ask him.' They did. Ibrahim had said he would wear the waistcoat and, taking great care not to dislodge the wires between the sticks, the batteries and the button switch, the girl had eased his arms into it, then settled it on his shoulders.

The waistcoat's weight was on him. The girl sidled close to him, took the sheet of paper and he saw, momentarily, her smile – as if she encouraged him. He tried, in desperation, to remember what he would say – and why.

The finger dropped.

Ibrahim gulped.

The light bored into his face and the lens was bright.

He recited what he had learned. 'I would like to say to you that I have come to Britain to strive in the path of God and to fight the enemies of the Muslim faith. I am the living martyr. God, be He exalted. At this time when the oppression of the Crusaders and infidels destroys our people in all of the world where we live, I look for martyrdom as a sign that we – believers of the true Faith – can never be defeated. I . . .'

The voice from the darkness was guttural, cold. 'You sound like a parrot. A parrot is taught words that have no meaning – they are just spouted. Do it with feeling, or forget it.'

He cringed. The waistcoat constricted his breathing and lay heavy on him; in his nose was the stale smell of the filth in the bags. She came from the side, slipped into his vision. Her hand was on his neck and her fingers massaged the tightness of the muscle – where the pressure from the waistcoat's weight was.

She said, 'We love you and we admire you. Nothing can stop you, no one. We are privileged to walk in your shadow. The sun shines on you and God's hand is on you and will guide you. In this country, in little streets and in homes and in all holy places – wherever Muslims live and gather – your name will be spoken and God's greatness will be glorified. You give us an example of dedication that we will strive to follow. Believe it, and say it.'

He believed it. Her hand loosed his shoulder. Where there had been a listless struggle to remember, there was passion. She slipped back and was beyond his vision. He said it: 'I give my life readily because the British authority attacks Muslims where they are weak and cannot defend themselves. I avenge the wrongs done by the British, and many more will follow me. I go, God willing, to Paradise. Pray for me.'

The voice from the darkness growled, 'It is satisfactory. Save it and box it.'

He slumped. Light flooded the room and the curtains were pulled back.

The girl helped him out of the waistcoat. He thought there was tenderness in the motion of her fingers. *We love you and we admire you.* It was as if, Ibrahim Hussein believed, she alone had time for him . . . Then a stark truth hit him. There was now no retreat. He must walk.

His testament was recorded. He had said: *'I go, God willing, to Paradise.'* His own words condemned him.

He carried his tray away from the counter. He skirted the tables and made a target of the one furthest away from them. Into Banks's ears came the bleat of the one called Peter: 'This stuff might be all right for strapping young soldiers needing their strength built up – not for us. Sausages and chips. A pork chop that is more fat than meat and chips. Fish that drips with batter and chips ... Someone might have told these people about cholesterol levels. What's this going to be doing to our hearts? Frankly, it's a disgrace.'

Food did not matter to him. At work and at home in his bedsit, he ate what was fast and convenient. He would have reckoned his fitness levels compensated for the rubbish he swallowed, snatched when he had time.

A plate loaded with sausage, bacon, beans, fried bread and chips was on his tray, with a can of soft drink. He sat at the table, distanced from them. He ripped back the ring-pull, swilled the drink and started to eat.

He had not dented the plate's heap when he heard the shuffle of feet, loose sandals, behind him. 'Mind if I do? Is it permitted?'

He emptied his mouth. 'Please yourself.'

It was hardly a welcoming invitation, but enough for his Principal. On Wright's plate there was a chop in a pond of gravy, peas, but no chips.

'Not much to write home about, is it? The food ...'

'It's what's on offer,' Banks said curtly. It had been his intention to sit quietly, alone, at the table, clear his plate and then submit to the addiction – open that bloody notebook, take his fix if he could find a vein to lance the needle into.

He kept his eyes on his food, listened to his Principal eat.

Banks had meant it, what he had thought in the courtroom, the *hatred*. But the guy was in his pocket, in his mind, and the bloody place where the guy was ... There should have been a photograph. Maybe an outing from work, before he'd travelled, down to the coast; a group of young men in suits and shirts with collars, ties knotted below the stud. Without a photograph, he could hate but could not ignore the damn man. He was thinking of Cecil Darke's food: no meat, no fat, no fried chips served up in the forward positions on Mosquito Hill.

'Well, Mr Banks, what sort of day have you had?'

'Just a day, a day's work.'

'Me, I've had a good day.'

'Pleased to hear that, Mr Wright.' He mouthed it, hoped that his lack of interest would register and be rewarded with quiet. No bloody chance.

'See that Vicky, sat behind you?'

He didn't turn.

'I reckon anyone, and wouldn't take too much patience, is in there with a chance, a damn good one. Shoving her curves out for everyone to see. She's rather lovely, don't you think?'

He lied: 'I hadn't noticed her.'

There was a grin opposite him. 'Don't you do women, Mr Banks? Don't you have time for them? God, I'm telling you, it's an empty world without women – specially women like that Vicky. You married, Mr Banks? That why you don't do women?'

'Divorced, actually.'

He didn't have to – could have put his head down and gone on clearing the plate – but Banks broke the rules of his trade: he told his Principal about Mandy, about Mandy's adultery, about the dispute on the money share-out, about the collapse of any reasonable post-marriage, post-divorce relationship. It was no business of his Principal's but he was given it, chapter and verse, as if that was a way to lose a load that had festered. Couldn't have justified it, but he spilled out confidences on Mandy.

'Sorry to hear that, Mr Banks . . . Never mind. Look on the bright side. You're free, can play the field.'

'Things seem to get in the way,' Banks said. He felt inadequate and squirmed deep in his gut.

He looked up into Wright's face, and took the full-impact force of a smile.

Wright said, 'I don't suppose we're exactly a roller-coaster of thrills. Are you usually with people like us, life's flotsam?'

'The people I'm usually with would not appreciate the description "flotsam",' Banks said, and warmed to it as if the smile chipped at his natural reserve. 'What's normal for me, as a Protection Officer, is minding royals, diplomats and politicians. You see, Mr Wright, we're a finite resource, and by the time the big cats have been looked after there's not many of us left to look after – I'm uncomfortable with the word – "ordinary" people. Don't you see us on TV? We're jumping out of cars, opening doors, heaving back the great unwashed so they don't get too close. We're part of the scene of pomp and circumstance. Those people, they judge their importance by the number of Protection Officers assigned to them. There's a pecking order. The actual threat, well, that's a whole different argument. Take Churchill in the war, see him walking through the East End after a bad blitzing, and look for how many men there are around him with Sten guns – none. How many men in long raincoats with a Smith & Wesson in a shoulder holster? Two, maximum three. Now a junior minister in Northern Ireland, where there's supposed to be a ceasefire, has a whole busload of them. We open the doors and close them, we book restaurants, we do the shopping. They're the élite, and we're an integral part of the panoply. Odd thing, but they need us to massage their vanity, and we need them to show how important we are . . . A crowd of jurors, you and them, or a Protected Witness is damn lucky to get us for more than the bare minimum of days.'

He was interrupted: 'We were told about a duty of care . . . and I was told by the man who approached me of "long arms" and "long memories". Don't we get looked after?'

Banks grinned, sardonic, and was finally enjoying himself – couldn't remember when he had last talked freely outside the corral of the Delta team. 'Don't hold your breath, Mr Wright. It'll all be about the budget that's been allocated. When the coffers are dry you'll be dumped. You'll be given an in-house alarm and a few telephone numbers. You'll be up the creek and no paddle. Of course, if you were a politician the coffers don't go dry.'

'Is that the party line, Mr Banks?' The smile spread.

'Think about it. We rely on people like you to pedal the justice system forward, but don't expect thanks for your efforts.'

'But you – you as well, Mr Banks – you're a man of substance.'

'Am I? Haven't heard anybody say so.'

'Stands to reason, you have to be.'

'I doubt it.'

'Wrong . . . Wrong because of what's on your belt. Wrong because of that oil smear on your shirt. That's trust, isn't it? Is it loaded?'

Banks hesitated. He sensed they were off territory. The way he sat, the tip of the holster dug into the flesh of his upper thigh. He saw mischief dance in the eyes in front of him. Could have retreated, should have backed off . . . He shrugged. 'Not much point in having the thing if it goes to Condition Black, but you have to hold up your hand. "Can we please have a break while I go to the car and load up?" It's loaded, and I carry replacement magazines. Each morning, though, I clear the bullets out and reload them. If you don't, if you leave them there for a few days, a week, you can get a jam. Condition Black is an imminent and real threat, and I just have to flick the safety. That's all.'

'When would you do it – shoot?' More of the mischief, more of the sparkle, and Wright had pushed away his plate and was hunched forward, as if the talk was their conspiracy and not to be shared.

'If my life was in danger.'

'That's good – *your* life. Brilliant, I'm so reassured.'

Banks said, 'I don't remember if I said it to you – if I didn't I should have. We aren't bullet-catchers. We don't stand in front of Principals and make heroic sacrifices and end up a bloody paraplegic with a thirty-eight-calibre slug lodged in the spine. We do realistic assessments of threat and we evaluate our resources, and we have as our Bible the theory that the bad guy cannot get close enough. It's about as far as it goes.'

Maybe he was mocked. 'You're telling me that it's not John Wayne, life ebbing, in the dirt of Dodge City, the lady's arms cushioning his head, violins going on full scrape, and the smallholders saved from the wicked rancher – not that?'

He grimaced. They were areas he had never discussed before with a Principal. Should have closed his mouth, should have stood up and walked away.

'I've never fired for real. No one I've worked with has ever fired for real. You have a micro-second to decide what to do, that's the training . . . but it's only training. If you shoot, your life will be destroyed, and I don't mean if you've taken the wrong option. I met an officer on an exercise, and he'd done it, had fired and slotted a gangster, and that gangster had a firearm in his hand and had already used it. Double tap and the gangster's down, dead, but it took two years for the process of investigation formally to clear the officer so he could go armed again. Two bloody years of his life and he was entirely justified in what he'd done. And if he hadn't been justified he would have faced a charge of murder. There's a post-shooting incident procedure, the inquest into what's happened, and the officer will get no sympathy, no support, from his seniors, and every moment of the confrontation leading up to the weapon discharge will be picked over, vultures at carrion, by Complaints and Discipline. Does that answer you?'

'Tells me what to expect.' Wright chuckled. 'Tells me to stay in bed tomorrow morning.'

'You'll be all right.' He pulled the wry look. 'It *never* happens. We pretend it's going to, and simulate it, but it doesn't.'

'Could you? It's not to disable, is it, it's to kill? Mr Banks, could you shoot?'

'When it happens I'll answer you – hasn't this gone far enough?'

'Am I keeping you? Come on. It can't just be training, it has to be in the mind. Wouldn't be in mine. Look into a man's face, over the sights, might be a pleasant face, or a scared face, even if he's a threat, then do judge and executioner. Not me. Don't have the certainty or the guts.'

'You're being trumpeted as the hero, Mr Wright.'

'Probably you didn't do Shakespeare's *Othello* at school. A very bizarre line, "I am not what I am," whatever it means. My question was, could you earn your corn, could *you* shoot to kill?'

'I don't know.'

'That's not a very good answer.'

'Try this one. There are some who say I couldn't,' Banks blurted. 'It's what was said. A team said it.'

No more mischief, and the sparkle was gone. A frown cut Wright's forehead. 'Is that the truth? Your own people said it? Said you couldn't shoot to kill? But that's your bloody job ... means they think you're useless.'

'Why I'm here, why I drew this fucking straw, the short one.'

He stood up. Should have done so a quarter-hour before, and could have.

Banks said, 'My apologies if I've destroyed your confidence in me, Mr Wright. It's about someone I never met, never knew ... about somewhere I've never been ... It is why I am categorized as *useless*,

and about why I could be spared from a state of alert in London –
reckoned not able to do it – and be here with you. Goodnight.'

The notebook flapped in his pocket. He walked briskly – having
made an idiot of epic proportions of himself – across the room. He
passed a rubbish bin as he threw open the door. Should have, could
have, dumped the notebook.

12 November 1937
We are in the second line, not the forward line. A blizzard is blowing again,
<u>*again*</u>. *The 'bunker' I am in, dear Enid, is an old shell-hole over which there
are two wood doors that we liberated from a farmhouse. It was a big decision,
last week, whether we could spare the two doors and use them as roofing, or
whether we should burn them. Anything we can burn, other than the two
doors, has now been used for warmth. The cold is awful. A local man told us
two days ago that this was the worst winter in his memory, and he was an
old man. The snow is thick over the forward line and our line, and we have
not been brought food from the rear today or yesterday. The cold is so bitter
and there is no more wood to heat us . . . In this cold we cannot fight – nor
can the enemy. Their artillery guns are quiet and their aircraft cannot fly.
The new enemy is the cold, the snow and the ice.*

It is not only nature that is cold, but also God's <u>heart</u>.

*Ten days ago my friend, my best friend, Ralph, was taken out of the line
on a litter: dire sickness had weakened him. He could not stand. Even the
commissar accepted he was no longer fit enough to stand sentry.*

Today I heard from a medical orderly that Ralph had died.

*It was told me so casually. Ralph had died in a field hospital. The cause of
death was pleurisy. By now he will have been buried, but the orderly did not
know where and could not tell me what service, if any, was held at his grave.*

I feel an emptiness. Ralph has abandoned me, God has deserted me.

I do not believe I will ever have another friend.

*I am alone. It is not possible to leave. If I could I would. All our papers
are taken from us, and without documentation, a man, a foreign volunteer,
cannot pass through the checkpoints of the SIM – that is, dear Enid, the
Servicio de Investigación Militar – because I would be arrested and shot: I
will die here properly, with any dignity I can find, not as a trussed chicken
at a post and blindfolded . . . and I cannot leave, with the fight not done, my
friends behind in unmarked graves. I stay close to Daniel and Ralph.*

The candle I write by is near finished.

I have only the darkness, the cold and the despair.

All that is left me is my pride – and the memory of my folly. But I cling to that pride because nothing else is left for me but the Psalm's words:

> *By the rivers of Babylon we sat down and wept*
> *When we remembered Zion . . .*
> *How can we sing the songs of the Lord*
> *While in a foreign land?*

Goodnight, dear Enid.

'Of course, it's different when you're operating abroad, far away, on foreign territory. No Queensberry rules there. No monitors watching over you, and no human-rights pinkos. You do your job . . . You go in after your target, fair means or foul, and all that matters is that the target is captured and handed over, or it's his hand or head that gets brought back . . . Has to be something, or you won't get the bounty payment. Did I ever tell you what the rates were for bounty on a Taliban guy in Ghazni Province?'

He was perched on his stool at the left end of the bar, and his surgical sticks were propped between his legs. George Marriot's audience migrated between the bar and the dartboard. The golf team was back after victory on a sodden course, and the darts team were throwing. The crush at the bar suited him well.

'Didn't I? Well, for an Ali Baba – that's a thief, operating on the road, turning over aid convoys – there might only be a thousand dollars in it. Hardly worth the effort. I'd a team of more than a dozen to keep sniffing and interested after the Tora Bora. Did I tell you about the Tora Bora? Don't remember. Well, another time . . . I've this team to keep happy, damn good trackers and the best fighters any-where, and the way to keep them happiest was to go up into the foothills of Ghazni Province, maybe up into the mountains, and go after the Taliban. Hard bastards, but I respected them – they'd have had my head off my shoulders soon as spit at me, if they'd had the chance. Yes, I respected them as quality opposition. For a big Taliban man, one of the old regime who'd been close to Mullah Omar, I was looking at a bounty – alive or for a head, ears and fingers for taking the prints off – at twenty-five thousand minimum. The Yanks, fair play to them, weren't cheapskates and they paid on the nail. They weren't easy to get, the big Taliban men, took days of tracking, weeks of hunting through the caves, and when they were cornered they fought like rats in a sack . . . Did I ever tell you how I got that grenade stuff in my leg, Russian made HE-42 with a hundred and eighteen grams of high explosive, did I?'

How many times had the story been told? One day – God, it would not be a pretty sight – the landlord swore he'd tell GG to drop his trousers, right there in the bar, and show the damn scars. One day . . . No, no, it would be cruel – no scars there to show. They listened politely and tolerantly, carried their pints away from the bar counter, left the story for the next customers, and talked their golf and darts, their business and families.

'Myself, I'd never ask a man under my command to do something, go somewhere that I wasn't prepared to do or go. I led into this cave. Knew it was used because the earth at the front was all scuffed. Went in with my torch, and the beam caught his eyes, like a damn cat's, and my finger was off the guard and on to the trigger bar but the grenade came bouncing at me. I stayed those seconds too long, gave him the whole magazine, thirty rounds of ball, then chucked myself down, but not fast enough and not far enough away. My boys, they carried me back down but not before they'd taken off his head, his ears and his fingers. The man I'd killed was a big man, a proper Taliban field commander. He was a man like me, a true fighter, not one of those who'd get some daft kid – a suicide-bomber – to do the work for him, hide behind a kid. He'd have heard me and the boys come to the cave, and wouldn't have thought of surrender, knew he was going to die but tried damn hard to take me with him. Have to respect that sort of man . . . The Yanks did, gave me thirty-two thousand five hundred dollars for his head and his bits. But I was finished, too bloody wrecked to go back up the mountains after the hospital.'

He was asked, a snigger from an accountant who queued for service, whether he'd worn the same shirt when he was in Afghanistan. Frayed cuffs and collar, the colour gone from it. He heard the laughter ripple round him. He was told that the shirt, it might be clean on that evening, looked worn enough to have done time on his back in Ghazni Province. Did he know that a sale – with bargains at giveaway prices – was staged that weekend in the town down the road? Another piped up, said he should have left the shirt up the mountain. The ripple of laughter was a gale. Had his sister sewn up the shrapnel holes in the shirt and washed out the blood-stains? He should treat himself to a new shirt, not leave thirty-two thousand five hundred dollars untouched in a biscuit tin under his bed.

George Marriot sensed, and it was new to him, that gentle mocking had gone nasty, was ridicule. His hand came off his glass and his fingers touched his collar, felt the loose, worn cotton, and he saw the threads that hung apart at his cuffs. He let his sticks take his weight, left his unfinished drink on the counter, dropped his head and pushed forward towards the door. He heard a protest: it was only a joke.

He elbowed the door open.

'Safe home, GG, see you next week,' the landlord called to his back . . . then, quieter, 'Shouldn't take the piss, just because he's soft in the head.'

The door swung shut behind him.

The two men ran heavily towards the helicopter's open side hatch, their heads ducked below the thrash of the rotor blades. Each carried small cheap bags of clothing, but between them they shared the weight of the Bergen rucksack in which their work kit was stowed.

The hand of the loadmaster reached down and helped up Xavier Boniface, then Donald Clydesdale.

Old thrills surged in each of them, and old habits came naturally. The loadmaster was waved away. They dropped into the bucket seats, slotted the shoulder harnesses across their bodies, fastened the clamps.

'You all right, Xavier?'

'Fine, Donald.'

'It'll be good to see Mr Naylor.'

'A gentleman. It'll be fine to see him.'

The helicopter lifted and yawed in the face of the wind. The engine pitch strove for power and suffocated their voices, then each closed his eyes and they were oblivious to the tossed and thudding flight as they climbed.

They were veterans of campaigns from the end of empire. As young lads in the marines, 45 Commando, they had been assigned in the Protectorate of Aden – forty years before – to guard the life of an officer in the RAF's Special Investigation Branch. They had taken him, Sterling submachine-guns loaded and cocked, most days from his Khormaksar billet across the causeway to Sheikh Othman, then past the roundabout where the concrete block and sandbagged Mansoura picket tower stood, and they had huddled with him between them in a Saracen armoured personnel carrier for the run to the fort where prisoners were held. At first, the initial couple of weeks, they had lounged around the fort's yard, and the officer had been inside the interrogation cells with captured men from the National Liberation Front. Each evening he had emerged in a state of growing frustration: he couldn't get the time of day from his prisoners, and most certainly no intelligence.

Now, inside the helicopter, bucking in the wind and leaving the island's coast behind them, neither could have said which had made the suggestion to the officer, but made it had been: 'With respect, sir, why are you pussyfooting around? There's lives at stake, right? Don't you think, sir, it's time to take the gloves off?' Perhaps it was both of them who had made the offer. They had gone with their officer into the cells the next morning. At first it had been fists and boots, then they had learned a little more of the trade, and water buckets, lights and noise had been employed. Intelligence had been extracted from choking throats, from mouths without teeth. Only the intelligence produced by pain had been written down by the officer – where a safe-house was, where an ambush site was planned, where an 81mm mortar was hidden or a blindicide rocket, where an arms cache was buried. They'd left on the same evacuation flight, one of the last from Khormaksar, as their officer. After touchdown – and he'd kept his new wife waiting a half-hour beyond the arrival doors – he'd taken them to the bar and bought them two doubles each, might have been three, and had promised to be in touch if the need for their skills arose again. The officer, of course, had been Mr Naylor. That had been the start.

When the helicopter's nose dipped and it lost height, both woke.

Awaiting them at Glasgow airport was an executive jet, in RAF colours, fuelled and ready to fly them south.

They lived in dangerous times, and such times, they knew, demanded 'taking the gloves off'. Neither Xavier Boniface nor Donald Clydesdale would have said that this call from Mr Naylor would be the last.

He lay beside her, the scent of the ageing hay bales in his nose. The cottage was only five hundred paces away, but fifteen minutes' walk with the load they had brought across two fields.

The boy slept, breathing heavily, on a bed of fodder they had made for him on the far side of a low wall of bales.

Only the three of them remained. When the house had been cleaned, and the bedding bagged, he had sent away the lightweights – the driver to his mini-cab company in west London, the watcher to his family's fast-food outlet in the north of the capital. The recce man would still be travelling to reach his father's cloth shop in the West Midlands. They all believed his target was Birmingham – as did the kid who had fled. It had been a precaution of Muhammad Ajaq, the Scorpion of a faraway war where the strength of his sting was a legend, to deceive them with a lie, but his survival had always depended on precautions. The barn where he lay beside the girl, on damp, musty hay, was set back from the lane into the village. In an hour, before dawn came, he would make a fire at the back of the barn and burn their bags of bedding.

He manipulated her mind. His hand was under the coat she wore, the sweater and the T-shirt. His fingers played on the skin of her stomach. His nails made gentle patterns on the smoothness, softness of her navel. He did not work his hand up towards her breasts or down to her groin. She had not moved his hand.

He was not aroused by the touch of her against his fingers: what he did was a tactic of war. He made little sensual movements and could hear the growing pant of her breath. The experience of his mother, and the scars left in him by the learning of it, had left deeper wounds on him than the pitted line across the forehead and cheek of the girl. He had no trust in emotion, believed it weakness. To have had sex with her would have disgusted him . . . perhaps frightened him. He heard the rustle and knew that her legs opened for him, but his fingers, nails, stayed on her stomach. Above the scent of the straw he smelt her wetness. He teased her, but it was only as a tactic of manipulation to achieve what he thought was necessary.

She was a virgin. If she had not been she would have pulled down his hand, buried it in her hair, and she had not.

He heard the breathing of the boy, steady but heavy with catarrh, beyond the wall of bales. It asked so much of him, the simpleton who was in love with God, that he must endure the delay, and he had thought hard as to how he could hold the resolve of the boy for more hours, more days.

The nail of his forefinger penetrated her navel cavity, and he heard the small gasps. He moved his hand away, rolled on to his side with his back to her, left her.

There was silence, long, and her breathing slackened.

He had angered her, knew it and intended it.

She was the pick of the cell, the only one among them that he valued.

Her anger burst. She spat out her whispered anger: 'Is it arrogance that drives you, or cowardice that rules you? Which? Are you, in your mind, too *important* to die, or too *frightened*? Which? It is never the leaders who make the sacrifice. The leaders choose targets, they make the vests, they recruit, and they tell young men of the rewards of Heaven and of the praise that will be heaped on them when they have gone to Paradise, but at the last they stand aside. Are you too valuable? Is the fear too great? Everything you have done since you came is to ensure your own safety and ability to run, to be clear. I have not seen, ever, from you one moment of compassion for *him*, nothing. And I have read that in Palestine it is not the young boys of the leaders who wear the vests, because they are sent away – abroad – for education and it would never be permitted for them to wear one. I tell you, I think that *he* is the one with true courage, but you treat him as if he were a package, disposable, to be thrown away. I despise you.'

The anger stilled. She would not have known it, in the darkness and with his back to her, but he smiled and was well satisfied.

Chapter 14: Thursday, Day 15

The ceiling light had been on, dull behind its mesh, since they had brought him back from the last session of questioning, but it was the cell door opening that woke Ramzi.

He jolted up on the mattress. For moments he did not know where he was, then the clarity came. A uniformed man stood in the doorway, eyed him with withering distaste, then tossed a bundle of clothing and a pair of trainers on to the end of the bed. He blinked, wiped his eyes. He realized his home had been raided, searched, and the clothing had been brought from there. For a few seconds he thought of his mother and sisters, of the violation of their home by men with cameras and plastic bags, and their sifting through his family's territory. Confusion wafted in him . . . Why? Why had he been brought clothing and shoes from home? He looked for an answer from the man, but there was none, only a grim, sour face staring back at him. He pushed up off the mattress and felt the stiffness in his muscles.

Under the man's eye, Ramzi peeled the paper suit off his shoulders. Slowly, he dressed in the new gear given him, and he did not understand. When he was dressed, the man's finger beckoned for him to follow. He was led out of the cell, and the paper suit was left behind.

He did not know of the bitter row in the small hours, between a superintendent of the Anti-Terrorist Unit and an assistant director of the Security Service, that had raged in a corridor of New Scotland Yard's tower building. He did not know that an assistant director had won the hour. Or how.

In the corridor outside his cell's door, a clutch of men formed up round him, and none had a word for him. The echo of metal-tipped toecaps and heels played in his ears, but his arms were not held as they had been on each of the times he had been taken from his cell to the interviews ... He had said nothing. He had followed every instruction given him when he had been recruited those many months before. He felt pride in that silence. Truth was, if lost hours could have been regained, if actions could have been undone, he would never have left the cottage – would have stayed in his bed and not disguised it. But Ramzi could not retrace those steps and all he could offer to the family – Syed, Khalid, Jamal and Faria, the Leader and the bomb-maker – was his silence, was the places at which he had focused on the floor, walls and ceiling. He had a small stirring, but growing, pride in his silence. And he walked, in the corridor, then through barred gates and up the steps, the better for his pride. Another door, steel-sheeted, was opened when numbers were punched by the head of his escort into a sunken panel. He was led left, and there was more uncertain chaos in his mind ... They had used two interview rooms to question him – and to listen to his silence – but they were off, through a set of swing doors, to his right. He was brought to a counter on which were laid two plastic bags, and he hesitated.

He did not know that the two teams of detectives who had posed those questions were now stood down, asleep in their beds. He did not know that the assistant director had produced a single sheet of paper, headed with the printed address of a Home Office-sponsored forensics laboratory. He did not know that the superintendent had sworn out loud as he had read, 'I confirm that an initial examination of the swabs taken from the hands of the suspect R/01/18.04.07 was flawed. Further and more detailed tests have shown conclusively that no, repeat no, traces of banned explosive materials were present on the samples given to us. No indications exist that the suspect handled or was in direct proximity to such materials. My department apologizes for the earlier false analysis provided to you, and trusts you have not suffered inconvenience. Faithfully . . .' There had been a scribbled set of initials over the typed name of a professor of Forensic Studies. He did not know anything.

Around him he felt a wall of hostility. Nothing was said, but it radiated. The plastic packets were pushed towards him and he reclaimed his watch from one, his wallet from the other. He stood to his full height, heaved back his shoulders and believed he had destroyed their best efforts – and the disgust and shame that had swamped his mind when on the bench bed were gone. A form was handed to him – which listed his watch and his wallet – with a biro, and he made an unrecognizable scrawl to acknowledge receipt.

He did not know that a whole chain of uniformed policemen, those close to him in the prisoner-reception area and those who wore suits to question him and were in their beds, had been kept in absolute ignorance of what was planned for him.

The pride veered towards conceit. His silence had beaten them. He said, 'It is always the same. You persecute us. To be Asian, a Muslim, is sufficient for us to be persecuted. Innocent people, as I am, are abused, imprisoned without cause . . . I am free now?'

He had thought he faced fifteen years or longer. There was so much that Ramzi did not understand. In a moment of idiocy he had handled the sticks that were in the waistcoat pouches, and the dog had found the traces that the rain had not washed off. Then he blanched, and his shoulders fell. Why was he released, freed?

But a voice, behind him, wiped the confusion. Quietly snarled, 'That's right, chummy, *free* to piss off out of here.'

He spun, did not know which of them had said it.

He looked down at his watch. 'What am I supposed to do at this time in the morning, five o'clock?'

Another voice, again behind him: 'Don't bloody complain, you don't have to walk. There's a car waiting for you – will take you where you want to go. Goodbye, friend, and goodnight.'

He smelt the staleness of their breath, and the whiff of whatever fast-food they had swallowed in the night hours. They made a little aisle for him, and he walked through it to the door gaping ahead. He did not look back.

When the cold was on his face and the rain cascaded in front of him, a hand snaked past his body and pointed down the street to his left. He saw the rear lights of a car parked against the pavement.

He imagined the faces beading at his back.

He went fast down the steps, past a drenched policeman who stood guard with a weapon slung against his chest, hit the pavement at speed. He ducked his head to keep the rain from his eyes, the car's tail-lights ahead. He ran, did not slow to see the car's make or its registration. As he charged towards it, the rear door on the pavement side was opened – but the rain sluiced on the rear window and he could not see inside it. He fell into the car, sagged down on to the back seat, and an arm came across him and pulled the door shut. At the same moment the driver raced the engine and they screamed out into the empty, glistening road. He wiped the water from his face and heaved a sigh of relief, and the sigh hung on his lips . . . Pain flooded him, then darkness.

It was done so expertly and so fast. The pain was when his arms were wrenched behind his back, then pinioned. The darkness was from the hood, with the smell of cold sacking, that covered his head. He lashed out with his feet but caught only the back of the front passenger seat, and there was more pain from a blow across his face, and more darkness as he screwed his eyes shut in response. Then tears came through his closed eyes, and the fight fled him. He subsided.

From the front, a voice asked calmly, 'Everything all right back there, Donald?'

From beside him, a voice replied softly, 'Everything's fine here, Xavier, and I'm confident the gentleman's going to be sensible.'

Then, quite gently, as the car sped into the night, he felt a force he could not struggle against, pushing him down on to the floor, wedging him between the seats; boots lay across his spine and the back of his head.

'Does it ever stop raining in this country? Describe this place to me, Dickie. I feel the emptiness, but paint me a picture.'

They stood under the umbrella that Naylor held. He favoured Hegner with it but could not protect the American's legs. Unnecessary, really, to have left the car hidden in the only one of the wide Nissen huts that had survived. They were on old Tarmacadam, beside a single-storey building's open doorway; its iron window-frames had long lost every pane of glass. In the dawn light, a red flag flew limp on its pole. The approach road, a taxiing run for the aircraft, had become obsolete sixty years back.

Naylor said, 'There's one runway left, the others were dug up by the landowner for urban hardcore. One Nissen remains, probably would have been a workshop for damaged aircraft, and the rest were dismantled after the war and sold off. About all that's left is the Tarmacadam, the Nissen, and a single building that was once the station's armoury, too solidly built for easy demolition. This part of England was thick with bomber stations, and most are in this condition – desolate and forgotten. As far as the horizon there are flat, ploughed fields and it looks to me as though the crop will be peas, for the supermarkets, and there's a red flag flying. It's used a couple of times a year for live firing by the local police, and the flag's hoisted so that the locals know to stay clear . . . So, I had it run up last night. They're very good, the locals, not at all inquisitive. We use it every two or three months for A Branch, open country, surveillance exercises – and it is, I promise you, damn difficult to get a mile from here and not be seen. So peaceful now. Sixty years ago it would have been a base for a heavy-bomber squadron, twenty-two Lancasters if they were at full strength, some limping home with flak holes, and others belly-flopping down with their casualties. So quiet now . . . I'd say it's a place of ghosts.'

'I have that picture. You chose well, Dickie,' Hegner said, and Naylor saw a slow, sardonic grin cross the American's lips and he thought the man had not the slightest sprinkle of charity in his soul. 'It seems to be a real good place for a new ghost – know what I mean?'

Naylor did. At Riverside Villas there were enough, mostly from the recent intakes and young, who derided the Agency's tactic of shipping detainees, known as ghosts, off to the remote military bases of the willing Polish, Romanian or Albanian allies, or to Uzbekistan and North Africa. No information was given on them. They disappeared without a trail of paper. They were exposed to brutality, to the extremities of agony, and an American from the Agency would sit in an outer room and wait to be passed tapes of the interrogations. Naylor felt the damp that had gone into his shoes. He, too, dealt in *ghosts* and had done so since service in Aden, during time in Northern Ireland and in the worst days of the bloody Balkans affair. Naylor valued them, and had less than two working days to exploit the latest ghost to cross his path . . . But it was war, wasn't it? It was as much a time of war as when the heavy-laden bombers had trundled on the triangle of runways and lifted off, had flown to targets where civilians cowered in shelters, where firestorms had raged – wasn't it?

'Dickie, you've gone quiet.'

'Just thinking of ghosts.'

'I reckin this ghost's on his way.'

Naylor hadn't heard it. He peered into the mist and low cloud above the runway that had run west to north, saw nothing and heard nothing. A full minute after the American had alerted him, he caught a first glimpse of the grey shadow that was a car, and it was not for a half-minute more that he heard its engine.

'I think I'd like to sit in, Dickie.'

'I'd expected that you'd want to,' Naylor said drily.

'See that the right questions are asked.'

'They know what's required of them. I won't be there.' He followed with what he hoped was irony. 'I wouldn't want to be in the way.'

'My experience, Dickie, is that in these circumstances it's easier to give orders and not get dirty – easier on the conscience.'

He thought a dart speared him. The car had stopped. He recognized the two of them. They reached inside a rear door and dragged out their ghost. Both were heavier in the body and thinner in the face than they had been when he had last seen them. The ghost tried to shamble between them, but then his feet were kicked out from under him and they dragged him as if that would augment the wretch's fear and humiliation, his helplessness. The taller one, his hair greyer than Naylor remembered from the Bosnia-Herzegovina assignment, had the rucksack hooked on one shoulder. The shorter one was balder, his head shinier than when a Serb warlord had been the ghost – and the answer required had been the location of a kidnapped aid-worker, being held by Arab fighters, whose life was in extreme jeopardy. He was seen; the shorter man – Clydesdale – tapped his chest, as if to indicate that the envelope delivered to RAF

Northolt was secreted there. He was noticed; the taller man – Boniface – raised his spare fist and gave him a thumbs-up. They were as unconcerned as the pair of jobbing gardeners, father and son, who came to his home every month and always had pleasant small-talk for Anne.

Holding the umbrella, he guided the American towards the door of the building. He reached the entrance, saw a torch beam roving and heard their surprised pleasure.

'Oh, that's good, Donald, there's a new power point. Oh, gets better! There's a tap and all.'

'Excellent, Xavier – water and electricity, couldn't be better.'

The hooded figure cowered against a wall. For a moment Naylor was a voyeur and could not take his eyes from him. On an A Branch night exercise, a generator was run off the power point – the cable laid at the Service's expense – and the water supply had never been cut off after the war; then and now it was used for brewing tea.

Naylor said brusquely, to assert his authority, 'Excellent to have you both on board. Time is of the essence, and we don't have much of it. My colleague will be with you, and he has my full confidence. Myself, I've calls to make.'

He stumbled away, the lie ringing in his ears, back out into the rain. His age caught him, and shame, and he shook, could not control the trembling. He left them with the American and the ghost, and thought himself damned.

She was alone. Groping her way through the house, Faria was guided only by slivers of light that came through the boarded-up windows. Around her was the smell of old, dried filth, but it was *old* . . . The yobs who had wrecked the interior had not been inside for months, no vagrants had slept there for weeks. It would do for them.

She checked the dismantled kitchen, the back room, the front room and the hallway, but not the stairs. She heard the scurry of the mice as they fled ahead of her and her face brushed against thick spiders' webs. She was alone but trusted. After their flight from the cottage and after being told the schedule they now worked to, she had said that she knew of a house out to the west of the town centre, behind Overstone Road, that was owned by the cousin of a friend of her father, that was derelict, that would not be put up for sale until there was improvement in the property market. Faria lived in the ghetto fashioned by the ethnic minority to which she belonged. Inside it, she was isolated. It shaped her. Within it, her feelings of revulsion for the society around her, beyond self-created fencing, spawned spores . . . Meandering through the grey darkness of the house's ground-floor, she could recall each insult that had been offered her. She believed she had the strength to earn the trust. His fingers had been on her stomach, in the crevice of her navel, and she would do what was required of her – that strength had been given her.

She used her arms, extended, to warn herself of obstructions – the toppled, legless settee, broken chairs, torn-up carpeting – went back into the kitchen, and stepped over the fallen cooker. She went down on her knees and pushed back the bottom plank that had been nailed against the outside of the door and that she had prised away with a half-brick. She lay on her stomach, in the dried filth, wriggled through the gap and emerged into the light. She gasped down the cleanness of the air, then crouched in the rain and replaced the plank.

She crossed the garden area, overgrown with grass and weeds, ignoring the rubbish scattered there, and went through the broken fence on to the wasteground. Faria retraced the way she had come from where she had left them, went to tell them that she had found a safe-house, that the trust in her was well justified.

'The prosecution's case, members of the jury, is a concoction of innuendoes, half-truths and – believe me, I get no pleasure from stating this, but it must be said – slanders against the good names of my clients. I am asking you, most earnestly, in the name of justice to reject that concoction.'

Banks listened from the public gallery, and thought he despised the barrister.

'Much has been made by the prosecution of the supposed identification of my clients by that conveniently produced eye-witness. I urge you to reflect on how much weight you can place on the word of a young woman, scarcely out of her teens, who has lived for months cheek by jowl with police officers, who, of course, are anxious to obtain a conviction. I am not saying she lied . . . I am saying that she was influenced – I am prepared to believe in her innocence – by those officers. I put it to you that this simple young woman, without education, has sought to please. Can you say, in all honesty, that her evidence was not doctored, was not rehearsed under the supervision of the officers? I doubt it.'

He had not, of course, seen the witness give her evidence, but he had Wally's description of her. The inspector was beside him, his body tilted back and his face impassive. What David Banks thought, as the barrister droned, was that the previous evening – for a mature adult, who'd been given responsibility, had been issued with a killing weapon – he had made a complete and utter *idiot* of himself. It had gone on too long.

'You find yourself, members of the jury, asked to convict two businessmen whose sole interest in life – other than caring for their sick mother – is trading, buying and selling. I cannot tell you that their dealings with the Revenue are totally transparent. Nor can I say that their returns on VAT demands are wholly satisfactory . . . You are not, and I emphasize this, judging my clients on matters of taxation. You are hearing a case that involves a quite desperate and reckless attack on a jewellery shop, and the prosecution's efforts to vilify my clients – in respect of it – have failed.'

The barrister's voice had an oiled sincerity. Never could tell with a jury, Wally had said. Unpredictable, they were. Could be swallowing what was served up to them – not one of them, his Principal. His Principal, for what it was worth, had played hero. What happened to him, weeks and months ahead, was not Banks's concern. What was his concern, it had gone on too long. He squirmed in his seat.

'I will say what I can on an area of extreme delicacy – and you will receive further guidance on this from our judge. There are now restrictions on your movements and freedoms, and I regret them. You should, however, understand, that no connection exists – I repeat, no connection – between my clients and such restrictions. You will, and I rely on you, as do my clients, ignore the circumstances under which you are hearing this case.'

He thought of them in London, in the capital under lockdown, the men of Delta, Golf and Kilo, doing what he should have been doing. Sitting in court eighteen, he realized he did not care a damn whether Ozzie and Ollie Curtis went down, whether they had an arm long enough to reach from a gaol cell and hit Julian Wright, his Principal. He had short-changed himself . . . It had gone on too long, and he would grovel, whatever it took. He imagined the racks behind Daff's counter – emptied, the ammunition issued – and heard the Welsh lilt of the armourer: *If you're in shit, get clear of it. If you're in a quagmire, crawl out of it. Banksy, don't let the bastards destroy you. Always believe it, something'll turn up.* He seemed to hear the gallows humour around him, and rough camaraderie, and his isolation from his team ate at him . . . and he craved it. He stood up, bobbed his head at the judge.

He walked out of court eighteen.

He crossed the forecourt and strode towards the centre of a great expanse of grass. Ahead of him were the lake and the geese. The rain was in his face.

He took his mobile from his pocket, and dialled.

He didn't call him the Rear Echelon Mother Fucker, but said, 'I'm hoping, sir, that you've got a moment. It's Banksy, sir.'

The reply was dismissive. 'Only a moment.'

'What I wanted to say, sir, was . . . well . . . it's . . .' His voice died and he stumbled for words.

'If you didn't know it, Banksy, I have better things to do than listen to your breathing.'

'It's just that I've been thinking . . . what I should be . . .' Again he was caught out and could not find them.

'Christ, Banksy, you sound like a teenager asking her mother if she can go on the pill. Don't you know things are *quite* busy back here? I've another phone going, do I pick it up?'

'Thinking what I should be doing and where I should be.'

'Think a bit harder about your orders: *what*, is looking after jurors – *where*, is Snaresbrook Crown Court. All right? Is there anything else?'

He heard that second phone answered, and a second caller was asked if he could wait a minute, no longer. Banks let the hesitation go fly. 'I realize now, sir, that my attitude to colleagues was out of order. I am prepared, absolutely, to make a fulsome personal apology to the rest of Delta for my behaviour.'

'Wouldn't that be *nice*? Quite touching.'

Banks swallowed hard. 'I want back in. I need, sir, to belong again.'

'Am I hearing you right?'

'I want to come off this crap job and rejoin Delta. I will, sir, apologize with no strings. I admit that my behaviour to colleagues was unacceptable. Do I, sir, have your support? Please, sir.' The rain mixed with the sweat on his forehead and the damp seemed to shrink the collar round his throat, and his jacket clung tightly to him. 'That's what I'm asking, sir, for a chance to get back to Delta. It's where I should be.'

'You're a bag of laughs today, Banksy.'

'I know that Delta's doing a proper job of work, and I reckon I should be with them. Sir, I've learned a lesson and will not speak again out of turn. I don't see that I can do, say, more . . .' A hand was over a phone, but he heard the muffled request for the second caller to continue waiting, and the quip: 'It's just a little administrative fuck-up to sort out, but I'm about there – give me thirty seconds.' Banks knew now what he was: an administrative fuck-up . . . and knew his value. He listened.

'You want to come back in, want everything forgotten . . . I'm not enjoying this, Banksy. I have every man and woman capable of carrying a firearm out on the streets, and some who are so ropey and stale on their training I wouldn't want to be within a half-mile of them. They're all doing double shifts, sixteen hours a day, while you're joy-riding round the Home Counties in your jury bus. God knows how many of them are popping pills to stay awake. Why? Because this city is under threat, real threat. They are looking for a suicide-bomber – not possible, not probable but actual – and if they see him, and I pray to God they do, they'll slot him. They're the front line in the defence of London. Oh, wait a minute, good old Banksy – superior bastard but we'll forget that – wants to rejoin the team. But it's not as easy as that, Banksy, not any more. You see, the doubt exists as to whether you're just a square peg that won't slot down into the round hole, whether you're up to the standards demanded of the job. That's the feeling, and whining about apologies won't change it. Sorry and all that . . . My advice, go back to jury nursing and leave the real work to those who've the bottle to handle it. In the pleasantest possible way, Banksy, get fucking lost.'

He switched off. His jacket, heavy and sodden, with the notebook in the pocket, slapped against his hip.

He walked through the smokers on the building's outer steps –

they skipped aside to let him pass – and flashed his card at Security. In his wake the corridor floor was sheened with the wet off his shoes and the mud. He went into court eighteen and took his old seat. He looked across the court at the brothers, at the barrister who was on wind-down, at his Principal.

Wally leaned close. 'You all right?'

'Never been better, ' Banks said.

'Sure?'

He heaved a sigh, and murmured, 'I did something I shouldn't have, and from it I learned some truths. Not to worry now, because I've unravelled that problem and it's behind me. I'm fine.'

He was a traitor to two men, one in his mind and the other across the width of the court. He caught the eye, saw the wink directed at him, and stared back at the juror.

'Did you see that?' Ozzie Curtis rasped the question to his brother.

'See what?'

'God, you're so dumb – don't you see nothing?'

'Seen nothing.'

Ozzie Curtis's mouth was against his brother's ear. 'The bastard's doing eye contact, winks and all, with that 'tec in the gallery.'

'Which one?'

'The one that's come back like a drowned rat.'

'How'd you know he's a 'tec, Ozzie?'

'Because he has a shooter on his hip – haven't you seen it?'

'Haven't.'

'Well, start looking at the bastard. See him, he's all smug and comfortable, and the bastard thinks he's safe, with his shadow . . . We're going down, Ollie, and –'

'You reckon it, definite, we're going down?'

'– and, I promise you, we're taking bodies with us,' Ozzie Curtis growled, savage and feral. His face twisted as his tongue rolled on the words. 'Plenty of bodies – Nat bloody Wilson's body, and the Nobbler's, and that bloody bastard's. He's going first, and that's my promise.'

'Yes, Ozzie, if you say so.'

'I say so.'

Ozzie Curtis gazed over the shoulders of Nat bloody Wilson, past the robed back of the bloody barrister, to focus hard on the bloody bastard . . . but the eyes didn't meet his. He had that gaze, cold and threatening, that would empty a bloody bar in bloody Bermondsey when he used it, but the bastard never looked at him. Looked instead at the drowned rat in the public gallery. He vowed it then – didn't matter how much of what he had was taken by the Assets Recovery crowd – he would use his last penny to take that bastard, above all others, down with him . . . his last penny. What made his anger more acute, the bastard seemed so calm, and kept eye contact with his shadow.

A wan smile was returned to him. He listened to the barrister and wondered how much longer the peroration could last, scratched hard in his beard and tried to think of Hannah. Tried, but not with success, and tried again.

Jools did not have Vicky, close up and pressuring his hip and knees, to fall back on for thinking of. He'd been late into court, the back-marker as they'd filed into their seats with their escort pressed round them. Vicky had Corenza on one side of her and Fanny on the other – he didn't know whether purposely or by accident. As the last one in, he'd had the choice of sitting between Rob and Peter, or between Baz and Dwayne . . . Some damn choice. He had ended up with Baz and Dwayne.

He missed the press of Vicky against him. A silent chuckle rumbled in his throat. Babs and his daughter, they were never there. The weekend and Hannah, Jools decided, was about building bricks: like they did in a nursery. Bricks were put together. Bottom of the pile was the protection officer, Mr Banks, the starting point. Hannah and his weekend would be built on the leverage he had on the armed detective, and confidences given. Big enough confidences. With such confidences having been turfed out at him, he couldn't see that a weekend liaison with Hannah would be too difficult to achieve . . . Jools felt good.

The brothers' barrister was obliterated from his mind – and why his protection officer had been out in the rain for a half-hour, had had a soaking and looked so damn mournful, and useless – and he was between Hannah's thighs and she squeezed on him, and . . . He was there.

The cottage lay empty, abandoned. So clean. The beds were stripped of sheets and blankets, and had been loaded into black bin bags. Every surface was wiped down, had been scrubbed, and the smell of bleach, toxic and sweet, permeated each room. Carpets and rugs had been vacuum-cleaned three times, and the mess of dirt and hairs had been extracted and dumped in the bags with the bedding. Piping-hot water had been run from the kitchen and bathroom taps, and from the shower, to flush down the pipes leading to the cesspit. Gone from Oakdene Cottage were all traces of a 'family' gathering. Not just their fingerprints, but also the body hairs and body fluids that carried traces of the cell's individual deoxyribonucleic acids – the DNA samples that could have identified them. It had been done painstakingly and with rigour. Windows had been left open, not to allow rain to spatter inside the rooms but to let out the trapped air contaminated with explosives molecules. Quiet hung in the cottage, and its new-found cleanness.

Across two fields, an upstairs window opened.

On any morning, when it was not raining, the farmer's wife would have shaken her sheets from it, as her mother had.

The window was opened because the old mullioned glass, set in leaded diamond shapes, distorted decent vision.

The farmer's wife had at her eyes the binoculars most often used for following the flight of birds over their land.

She called down, stentorian, 'Just my imagination, I'm sure, but it's not right at Oakdene. The car's gone, the lights are off, but the windows are all open. Am I being silly?'

'Probably gone out for the day,' was the answering bellow. 'You fuss too much, love.'

'Maybe – but there are too many of them for one car.' She frowned, then lifted the binoculars again. 'There's a fire burning by the Wilsons' barn – you know, the one past our Twenty-Five-Acre.'

'Can't be, they're away. Aren't they on a cruise? Where is it, Madeira, Tenerife?'

'Come and see for yourself.'

She heard his grumble, then the tramp of his feet up the stairs. He stood beside her, took the binoculars from her.

'Haven't they hay in the barn?'

'I'll take a look at it,' he said. 'And I'll take a look at Oakdene as well – when I've had my lunch.'

The screams were past, long gone.

The prisoner whimpered without sound.

'I don't like it when they're so quiet.'

'Means we're not getting through to them.'

They'd made a hole for a hook in the concrete of the ceiling. The hook was big, heavy, and had been given to them by McDonald in their second year at Ardchiavaig, because he was no longer permitted by regulations to slaughter his own stock and then to hang carcasses. It was Xavier Boniface who'd recognized that the hook might – one day – be of use, and it had done service for them in County Armagh and in Bosnia-Herzegovina. Donald Clydesdale had packed it in the Bergen with the galvanized bucket, the truncheons, the wires and all the other kit they carried when they went to work. Their prisoner was bound at the wrists, the binding looped over the hook, and suspended high enough for his toes just to touch the floor, but not his heels or soles. They'd started – as they always did – by allowing the prisoner to view the kit, and they'd explained graphically how they used it. Then Boniface had asked the first question on their sheet of paper. Their gentleman's head had tossed back, the loose hood had ridden up, his mouth had been exposed and he'd spat into Clydesdale's face. Not a good start, Boniface had said. Not being sensible, Clydesdale had said. Had hit him with the truncheons – in the small of the back, in the kidneys, and had let him scream. Had had his trainers off, and belted him on the soft soles of his feet. It was good when he screamed because their experience was that a screaming man was close to breaking. Then he'd gone all quiet, which was not so good. They'd done the beating. He'd coughed up blood – they'd seen it in the sputum dribbling down under the hood's hem. Then they had returned to that first question, and had not yet been answered.

'What about a brew-up first, before the bucket?'

'Good shout, Donald, my mouth's proper dry ... Mr Hegner, would you like a mug of tea?'

They'd brought everything in the Bergen: the collapsible chair on which the American sat, a tiny camping stove that ran off a small gas canister, four plastic mugs and plates and, of course, the canvas bucket that was used most days for the grain they scattered for their fowls.

Hegner nodded, would appreciate a mug of tea. The American had a miniature tape-recorder on his knee, what a company executive might use for dictation, and his thumb had hovered on the depress switch when the prisoner had screamed, ready to hear him. But his thumb was off the switch now, as if he sensed they were still far away from breaking their man. They were both hot from the efforts put into the beating, maybe showing their age, sweating more than they ever had in the stinking, fly-blown heat at the gaol in Aden. The camping stove was lit, water was poured from a plastic bottle into an old and dented mess-tin that was then laid on the ring.

Clydesdale crouched beside the stove to watch the water rise and begin to bubble, then made ready the tea-bags, the mugs and the little carton of milk. Boniface stood behind the man and hit him some more in the kidneys but did not get a scream as a reward.

Clydesdale said, 'Won't be long, Mr Hegner.'

'Would that be answers to questions, my friend, or that cup of tea?'

Boniface said, 'You're very droll, Mr Hegner . . . A sense of humour always helps with this work.'

They didn't take a mug outside to Mr Naylor, thought he'd probably have his own Thermos in the car.

'You got a moment, Banksy?'

'I was just about to bring them through from their room and on to the coach. Can it keep?'

'Don't think so, just a moment will be enough.'

Banks turned, faced the inspector. There had been nothing in the voice behind him that offered warning. He was led away from the jury-room door out into the corridor and was manoeuvred so that his back was to the wall. The inspector closed on him and the smile was gone.

'Just hear me out. I'm surprised that an officer of your experience is unaware that codes of honour, *omertà*, silence, are not strictly the preserve of the criminal class. You've been snitched on, Banksy, grassed up. I had a call this afternoon from your former guv'nor, who was anxious to put the knife in and twist it. To say that I'm disappointed in you is my personal understatement of the year. You may think that what we're doing is second-rate, beneath your bloody dignity. You may wish you were poncing about in London in a fat cat's detail. You may hope that you can be shot of us soonest. Well, Banksy, think and wish and hope again. You're staying with me . . . I understand from your man that, back where you came from, they don't reckon you're up for it, that you're short of the necessary dedication, haven't the bottle for it. So, get it into your head that you're not wanted. It may have escaped you, but *ordinary* people worry a damn sight more about coming face to face, which is terrifying, with organized-crime barons waving guns – they will use guns – than about the remote possibility of being alongside a kid with a rucksack on his back. Ordinary people, sometimes, have the guts to stand up and be counted. Like my witness. Like Mr Julian Wright in there. Especially like Mr Julian Wright. So, come down from the clouds, get fucking stuck in and walk alongside those people. Forget about your own bloody importance. Got me?'

Winded, as if he'd been punched in the solar plexus, Banks nodded. Humiliated, he went to do the escort bit to the coach.

Chapter 15: Thursday, Day 15

He heard the screams, the shrieks, then the quiet.

They came from inside the Nissen hut, into the car, and Naylor flinched. Silence rang around him.

A dog-walker, a woman with two yellow labradors, had come to within a half-mile of the hut, and the brick building. He had seen her through the steamed-up windscreen. She had paused by the pole that flew the red flag. Probably she walked there, wrapped in her waterproofs, shod in wellingtons, every day. He had thought the raised flag blocked a regular route, and she would have looked for the parked vehicles that proved live firing was expected. None of the usual Transits that brought police marksmen to the old airfield were there, but the flag had been flying and she had obeyed the disciplines it imposed.

The screams and shrieks were gone. He heard the rumble of his stomach, hunger. Darkness was coming. He grimaced, remembered what Xavier Boniface had told him when, years before – before the first pangs of rheumatism had settled into his hip – they had lain with Donald Clydesdale in a bandit-country hedge in County Armagh and had waited for a farm-boy to come out of a barn, to lift him and interrogate him ... remembered: 'Mr Naylor, dogs are always a right nightmare when you're lying up. So bloody inquisitive. Best thing for them is a pepper spray up the nose.'

The screams and shrieks had cut at him. Now the silence did.

He reflected: What would the woman have thought? What would have been her response if she had walked past the flag, had approached the building, and he had intercepted her? 'Of course you understand, madam, that those screams, shrieks, are from a prisoner currently undergoing procedures of extreme *torture*. In the interests of the greater good, to learn where a bomb will explode, we have torn up all that human-rights jargon and are inflicting extreme *pain*. If you'd like to, madam, you're very welcome to go in there and have a look at the wretch because – you see – it's all in your name . . . Your name, madam.' Would she have gone white, blanched at the gills, or fainted? Would she have shrugged, as if it was none of her concern? Would she have cared about the torture and pain suffered by a fellow citizen, or would she not? It was done in her name. And he reflected further, with the hunger pinching at his gut: it was easy enough to do torture and pain abroad, but not against an obesely muscled boy from an East Midlands comprehensive, 'home grown'. Before, there had always been a plane to get on to, and the debris left behind. But this was close, new.

He left his car, went to see what was done in the name of a woman who walked a pair of yellow labradors. He strode through the rain, oblivious to it, and came to the building.

'That you, Dickie?'

'It's me, Joe.'

Hegner was sitting easily in a collapsible chair, picnicking. Boniface and Clydesdale were hunched on the floor, eating, but were not on their backsides because water lay in splashed puddles across its whole width and length. The prisoner was prone, still hooded and bound, with most of his weight against the back wall. Above him was a quite ghastly meat hook, and a canvas bucket was beside him. His body was soaked and his shivering was convulsive. Naylor understood the use of the bucket, had seen it often enough and knew its proven value. A man's head was forced down into a filled bucket. Water was swallowed and ran through the nostrils, and he was held down for perhaps ten seconds. Then he was dragged up, coughed, spluttered and choked, and was asked a question. No answer was given. The head went back into the bucket, perhaps fifteen seconds: no answer. The bucket was refilled, and the head was inserted again, for perhaps twenty seconds – and the coughs, splutters and chokes were worse, and it was ever harder to get the water up out of the lungs. On and on, through thirty seconds and thirty-five. That was torture and pain – and it was expressly forbidden in the police interview rooms at Paddington Green.

Boniface looked up at him. 'Just having a break, Mr Naylor, and something to eat. It's only MREs, but you're very welcome to what we have.'

Clydesdale said, 'Meals Ready to Eat, Mr Naylor. I can do you a beef curry.'

He saw the small tins in their hands, and the little plastic utensils. In Ireland or Bosnia-Herzegovina there had always been a garrison barracks to return to. He had never eaten from a Meals Ready to Eat tin, and the sight diminished his hunger. 'Don't think I will, but kind of you to offer.'

He saw that the prisoner had not been given food.

Hegner leered at him. 'We're getting there, Dickie, slowly but surely. Before we stopped for lunch, we'd gotten far enough down the line to have a location and an approximation of the time. The target, he says, is Birmingham and the timing is the coming Saturday morning. That's what he heard but was not told it directly. He does not know where in Birmingham or at what hour. He was not in Birmingham, himself, on the reconnaissance.'

A sharpness in Naylor's voice. 'Do you believe him?'

'I think I do, haven't found a reason not to.'

It had to be said. Naylor would not have admitted to being expert on the arts – bloody dark ones – of torture, but papers crossed his desk that raised the question. Psychiatrists – and God only knew where they'd been dug out from – wrote that men or women, under the extremities of agony, would blurt out *anything*, any damn thing, to halt the pain. He saw the twitch in the prisoner's body and could smell that the sphincter had broken. It must be asked.

'After what's been done to him . . . You know, after . . . Well, is that information to be relied upon? There are heavy consequences if it cannot be.'

There was a little chorus of mild complaint.

306

'Not like you to doubt us, Mr Naylor.'

'No, not after all these years.'

Hegner said, 'I'm sure you won't want to rubber-neck, Dickie, and I'm sure you will want to communicate what's been told you. I'm watching your back, but these are fine men and don't seem to need an oversight . . . It's best, Dickie, that you get on out and not clutter up the floor space.'

He was flustered. Their calm detachment from their work bit into him, but his eyes were on the hooded body and the tremors running through it. 'It's only a start that you've given me. I need so much more – the size of the bomb, what the bomber is likely to wear, targets that have been talked about, the safe-house, the numbers in the cell and the identities, the recruitment, the—'

'Get on out, Dickie. I'm very clear on what you need to know.'

The tins had been dropped into a plastic bag, mouths were wiped with handkerchiefs and fingers sucked clean. Hegner settled back in his chair, and the two men – not unkindly – hoisted up the prisoner and linked his hands back over the ceiling hook. And he screamed. Naylor fled into the dusk, and ghosts scrambled round him.

From his car, he made the call to Riverside Villas, and told what he had learned.

The row erupted on the coach. As with anything volcanic, it had simmered and rumbled for an hour. When they were within a half-hour of the barracks, it fractured the membrane that had hidden it. It spewed, and the catalyst was Peter. He articulated what they all knew.

'I can see it, and you can see it, what old Herbert's schedule is . . . All right for him. Damn certain he didn't stop to think of us. Defence grinds on all day, and could have done it, said it, before lunch. Summing up from Herbert should have been this afternoon, but he's doing it tomorrow. So, instead of us going out in the morning and getting the whole thing wrapped up by midday and going *home*, we're stuck in that God-forsaken place for the weekend.'

Peter was acquiring the mantle of spokesman. Now he was out of his seat and had advanced in the aisle as far as Rob, the foreman . . . and Rob, Jools realized, was canny enough to see the strength of the wind blowing Peter's sails, and stayed quiet; probably felt the same.

'The legal crowd, they're all finished for the week. The judge is finished, has a nice couple of days at home. The brothers are banged up and aren't going anywhere. It's only us. What a time we're looking at. It'll be a weekend to remember. We're going to be locked inside a damn barracks from Friday evening to Monday morning. Why? Because the lawyers wouldn't hurry themselves, didn't spare a thought for us. Tell me, is anyone happy to be spending three nights and two days in a half-empty army camp?'

Jools thought Peter played to his gallery with skill, couldn't fault him. He had Corenza on side, all scratchy about her lost weekend. Where Peter the Moaner led, they followed with a chorus of dissent. Jools was far to the rear of the coach and kept quiet, but he glanced round at the detective, saw that the man seemed not to hear the simmerings of revolution in front of him, and had his eyes closed. Vicky was complaining – all flushed in the cheeks, which made her prettier, and her chest bounced, straining the buttons – about a lost pottery class. Jools thought it fun: he knew where he would be and what he would be doing at the weekend, and it would take more than a main battle tank and more than the guard-duty platoon to stop him being there and doing it.

'It's typical. It shows the complete lack of respect they have for us. They can't have a trial without us, but they play their games and do their fancy dress, and we're just the hired help that lets the show go on. They can all have a jolly weekend – but us? We don't matter. I reckon that Rob, as he's our foreman, has to let them know what we think. You going to do that, Rob?'

Jools saw their foreman writhe in discomfort. Probably, he thought, Rob dreaded the day the trial finished when his little trifle of status would be snatched away. He didn't know what Rob did – where he peddled his officious pomposity – but he might have been Inland Revenue or local-government housing or perhaps quality control in a factory. But Rob was in a corner, backed in. He wore that serious expression and nodded vigorous agreement.

'Well, go on, man. Do the business. Let them know we're not prepared to tolerate this treatment. We've had our fill of this lot, and that's what you're going to tell them – better than that, tell *him*. Or am I going to?'

A decisive moment, Jools could see it. The authority and dignity of the foreman was on the line. Back off and he'd lost the authority. Step forward and he maintained the dignity. Jools glanced back again at *him*. The detective was away, lost in his own thoughts, with his eyes closed, but was not asleep – must have heard each tinkle of complaint. The foreman left his seat, came up the aisle and passed Jools.

He paused, stood awkward, hesitated, then spouted: 'It's Mr Banks, isn't it? Mr Banks, you must be aware that there is deeply held annoyance among colleagues at our being locked up for the weekend at –'

'Tell my guv'nor tomorrow.'

'– at this camp. The general feeling is that more concern should have been shown for our welfare and –'

'I don't have the authority to swat a fly without an instruction. See my guv'nor in the morning.'

'– and there is resentment at the inconvenience being heaped on us. As the foreman I am protesting most strongly, and am representing the general view of colleagues, who feel—'

'It's against regulations to stand when the coach is moving. Please return to your seat.'

Bravo. Jools fancied he heard, almost, the hiss of escaping air – deflation. But regulations were the oxygen of a taxman, a housing officer or quality-control management. The foreman shrugged for his audience and returned to his seat, and Jools stole a glance behind him. The detective's eyes were closed – might not have opened them during the exchange – his head was tilted back and a frown furrowed his forehead, as if bigger matters were weighing in his mind than a jury's inconvenience.

He heard the dissent down the aisle, reckoned he'd lanced it but didn't care. In his mind he constructed the letter. In whatever form, he would write it that weekend in his room in the block where the jurors, grumbling, were housed.

Alone, swaying with the motion of the coach and hemmed in by the newspapers covering the windows, he thought it most likely that he would aim for the two lines, handwritten, what was left of his pride intact, and he would hand it to the REMF's outer-office assistant – and he would walk away. He would leave behind him the letter stating, 'After careful consideration, and bearing in mind

309

recent conversations, I am resigning from the Metropolitan Police Service, with immediate effect, Sincerely . . .' and on the assistant's desk would be his warrant card and his firearms-authorization ticket.

He thought of the short term, and the long term.

Short term, he would clear the bedsit in Ealing and load what he had into his suitcase and bin bags. He would drive them down to the bungalow on the Somerset and Wiltshire border, and dump what he did not need far at the back of his mother's garage . . . Long term, he might put it all behind him and forget his past, fly to Australia, New Zealand or Canada. He did not know which. Somewhere that had mountains and valleys and isolation. He could imagine the short term, his mother's anxiety at the direction change of his life, and could summon up a picture of the long term, the freedom from burdens – and the coach lurched to a stop.

They were at the barrier by the guard-house.

Banks went forward down the aisle, stood on the step, and the driver opened the door. He spoke to the sentry, saw the motorcycles that had escorted them peel away, and the barrier was raised. He would write the letter at the weekend, put failure behind him . . . and he would never again go to Isosceles stance and fire a weapon. It was for the best.

'I am not at liberty, even in this company, to divulge the source of this material.' The assistant director was loath to think of the circumstances in which it had been obtained. He had come down from his upper floor to what he liked to call the 'coal face', the open-plan area where a desk head analysed material, then passed taskings to surveillance, police liaison, the Internet watchers and those who trawled the financial records of suspects. His audience, perhaps twenty of them, was young and most were half his age.

'From an operation currently running, we understand that the Saudi citizen Ibrahim Hussein – you are familiar with the biographical details – will detonate himself *somewhere* in Birmingham, *some time* on Saturday. I regret this information is sketchy, but it's the way things pan out. That's all I have, all I can give you to work from. As we have done for the last several months, we all have to keep our fingers crossed and hope for a result, a satisfactory one. Thank you.'

He looked around him, hoped he wore an expression of suitable gravity and seniority. A rather bright little thing, a recent recruit from the Asian community in Bradford – working in the section that followed air journeys by Muslim boys from the UK to Pakistan and back – asked whether further intelligence could be expected, and added boldly, 'because this is pretty thin, Tristram, and gives little hope of interception'. He replied gruffly that he *hoped* for more but could not *guarantee* it. He had been sitting on the corner of the desk head's table, was shirt-sleeved with his tie loosened. The faces confronting him were grim, set, and he felt the sense of grievance. He slid off the table, was anxious to be gone before they found a mouth-piece. His shoes hit the floor. He gave them a fast smile and was on his way.

'Does this morsel have provenance, Tristram?'

He stopped, turned. She must have come in late, must have been standing beside him. 'I'm sorry, Mary, but I'd rather not . . .'

'It's a perfectly straightforward question, Tristram. Does the intelligence have provenance?'

It was asked with innocence. The assistant director had not reached his eminence without recognizing danger. He would have said that Mary Reakes – and it was why she had earned the pro-motion that would put her inside Dickie Naylor's cubicle first thing on Monday morning – had the innocence of a darting snake, a black mamba, and that reptile's venom in her sacs.

'It's an area of delicacy that I am not prepared to expand on, if you'll excuse me.'

'I don't think that's good enough, Tristram.'

There was silence around her – just the subdued bleep of computer screens and the stifled hack of a cough.

'It's what we have. It's where we are.'

'Would that be where Dickie is and where Joe – where the American is?'

'You're pushing me towards areas, Mary, that I'm not prepared to visit.'

He had taken two, three steps towards the door, then realized she was in front of him, blocked him.

'May I summarize, Tristram? A prisoner has explosive traces and is in police custody. The forensics are then denied, and the police are instructed to release the prisoner. He disappears into the night. Dickie is not at work today, and the American is off radar. I rang the Naylor home – no, he's not there, not off sick. I rang the American's hotel. He left at four this morning. I assume the two are involved in the gathering of this intelligence. Can you confirm that conclusion or do you deny it?'

She stood straight, shoulders back, legs slightly apart. At that moment, he thought her rather handsome. She was quiet-spoken but there was a spit in her voice. Every other head was turned towards her, as if she were their oracle, their soothsayer. The assistant director had been more than thirty years with the Service and had never before confronted anything that was remotely close to mutiny in the ranks. They were the future of the Service: it would be in their hands when he was gone and when Dickie Naylor was out of the door. He had no answer for her.

'Not confirm and not deny, and conclusions should not be drawn.'

'You see, Tristram, where I and colleagues stand. We stand insulted. We are all officers of the Security Service. The Service is our lives. It gobbles every waking moment available . . . I offer you a definition of an insult: I and colleagues are not trusted, are outside the loop. My problem is that I understand why you are content to insult us.'

He was close to her, his body and hers separated by a few short inches. What he noticed, her chest did not heave. She was in control and she spoke without bluster.

'Please stand aside, Mary. Please let us all get on with our busy lives.'

'What the Service is doing is a disgrace – a shameful, dishonest and illegal disgrace.'

'If, *if*, that were true, then I am sure you will be happy to shelter behind your ignorance.'

'A prisoner is undergoing torture. True or false?'

He could have reached out with his shirt-sleeved arm, could have caught her shoulder and shoved her away, cleared his path to the door. If he had touched her his job would have gone, and he would have had ten minutes to clear his desk – he would be history.

'I asked you, Mary, to stand aside.'

'A member of the Service has organized, has aided or abetted, the physical abuse of a prisoner. True or false?'

312

'I have nothing more to say. Please, get out of my way.'

'We have gone down into the gutter, have come off the high ground. True or false?'

The stiletto she had inserted into him, the blade she had twisted, had gone deep, had hurt. Her audience clung to her words. She held the stage, had held it too long. His temper broke. 'Mary, you can play an excellent imitation of a stupid, juvenile bitch. No, shut up and listen. I was at St Paul's, at that memorial service. I stood far to the back because the best seats were reserved, rightly, for those to whom the service mattered most. They were bereaved parents, widows, children who had been robbed of their mothers or fathers and who stood with shattered grandparents. They were the living – amputees in wheelchairs, faces scarred for eternity by fire, or destroyed psychologically by what they had endured and what they had seen. And for the dead and the living, little candles burned. I vowed, within sight of that altar, that on my watch it would not happen again if anything I could do would avoid it. If you wish to continue your rant I suggest you do so after first visiting the parents, the children and the mutilated, then come to me and preach. It's Birmingham, it's Saturday – you don't need to know any more. Just get on with it.'

She stepped back, gave him room to pass. At the door, Tristram turned and looked at the desk, saw the rows of heads poring over their screens ... all except Mary Reakes's. The assistant director knew then that an enemy had been made, one as implacable as any snake with poison in its fangs ... What were they supposed to *fucking* do? Stand on the high ground and lose? Lie in the gutter and win? He slammed the doors after him. God, his head was forfeit, would be on a pole, if Dickie Naylor and his increments did not come up with gold.

The mobile rang. Naylor was in the doorway of the little squat brick building, could not bring himself to come inside it, to be closer.

The screams came less frequently but were more piercing. The mobile shrilled in his pocket, and he was reaching for it. He sensed another shriek coming, and shut his eyes tightly as if that would be a defence against it. He had the mobile in his hand. In the moments after each shriek, a trifle more intelligence was gained, but the price of it wounded him. Did not appear to wound the American, who sat in his chair and had the small tape-recorder on his lap; the American seemed possessed with hearing acute enough to understand the grunted words that slipped from the prisoner's lips but Naylor, himself, needed them deciphered. The mobile was at his face. The prisoner was still suspended and the two men danced, shadow shapes, round him. They worked at his exposed genitals, and he saw the wretch writhe away from them as far as was possible; nothing of escape was possible.

He pressed the button. 'Yes?'

'It's me.'

'I can't speak, Anne, it's not convenient.'

'It wasn't convenient sitting up half the night wondering if you were coming home. You should make it convenient.'

'What is it you want? Be quick with it.'

'Have you forgotten it's your wife you're speaking to? Where on earth are you? Dickie? Right, I'll be quick. What time will you be home tonight?'

'Won't be.'

'What time in the morning will you be home?'

'Don't know.'

'Perhaps you'd forgotten what's happening tomorrow. Mary – she sounded particularly disagreeable – rang to say that a car will pick us up at five, bring us in and fetch us home . . . Have you written your speech? Daddy's, when he left, was a great success because he'd written it out and kept it short and remembered only happy times, nothing maudlin . . . I want you to promise me you won't drink, not like that Barney Weatherspoon who was pickled and made an ass of himself. Are you listening to me? Dickie, are you—?'

The scream ripped at his ears.

'My God, Dickie, what was that?'

'Nothing.'

And the scream came again, in agony.

'What's happening? Where are you, Dickie?'

'Nothing is happening. I'm nowhere. Can't talk. Sorry, dear.'

'Don't speak to me like—'

He closed the call. He strained to hear the grunts – damned if he could understand them but Hegner had his recorder switched on and scrawled longhand on a pad. He had never before, in forty-one years of married life – some happy, some miserable, some tolerable – cut off his wife in mid-sentence.

He heard the voices.

'Stubborn gentleman, Donald, isn't he?'

'Very stubborn, Xavier, a gentleman decently dedicated to his cause. But he's coming along, slow and steady.'

Hegner said, 'Here's where we're at, Dickie: no further down the road of a target, but the kid'll be walking, so it's not a car bomb. And we have, so far, three in the cell. No biog, brief on occupations, nothing on recruitment. Khalid is a cab driver. Syed serves up fast food. There's a girl, Faria. That's where we are. I think you should phone it in.'

He did not recognize it as dismissal.

Naylor gulped, said, 'Just stay with it, the cell and the target. He must know something of the target – the shopping centre, New Street station, the airport, the bus station. Damn it, that city has a population of a million souls. I must have a location in Birmingham and timing. That is the absolute priority, must have them.'

He hurried away into the night, into the rain.

He crossed the old concrete strip where Lancaster bombers had been armed and ghosts walked. He went into the big Nissen hangar where he assumed the aircraft had been repaired after flak damage, and where more ghosts roamed, and he groped for the car door.

Naylor shut himself inside and thought that there he would be safe from the wounds of the screams, and he rang the assistant director, told him of the little that had been extracted in the last hours: names and bare details of employment. He finished with, 'But you should know, Tristram, that I have emphasized to them both most forcefully that the priority – I called it an "absolute priority" – is the location and timing. That's it. Sorry it's not more.'

He did not know that Joe Hegner said, 'I'd like a drink. Make it coffee, black and no saccharine. I think, guys, that it's time to change tack. I don't give a rat's ass about foot-soldiers, meet up with them too many days of my life and they hold no interest for me. I reckin there was a man with them, and I don't have a name and don't have a photograph, who made their world go round, put the tick in the clock, a facilitator. I want to hear about him – don't often get close to him, but I am now and to lose the chance would piss me off . . . After coffee, and whatever you guys are having, I reckin it's appropriate to plug the wires into the juice.'

She lit the candle. Before the evening had come, and the darkness, she had worked alone at clearing a space for them in the back room of the semi-detached house. The boy had not helped her, had squatted down against a wall, his eyes glazed, vacant, and he had watched her but had done nothing. She had heaved aside the crumpled, dust-coated carpet and had made thick clouds of rising dirt. She had pushed, needed all her strength, to manoeuvre the settee to the room's centre. She had found a broom in the kitchen, without a handle, and a dustpan, and she had swept and made more clouds. The man was against the other wall, opposite the boy, and she had had to drag the edge of the carpet out from under him, and sweep round his feet. From him, also, there had been no assistance. She made a cleared, cleaned space in the house of her father's friend's cousin, who would not have visited it for a year since the doors and windows had been boarded up, plywood and planks nailed on to prevent access, and would not come – most likely – for another year. By then more dust would have settled and the traces of their presence would have gone. She had worked dutifully, as she would have done at home when she cleaned for her father, her brothers and her mother, who was an invalid confined to her bed. Last, secure inside its bag, which was knotted at the neck, she had laid out the waistcoat and had been careful not to bend it; she had left it near to the door on top of the crude carpet roll. For hours then, without speaking, without moving and without food to eat and water to drink, as the darkness had thickened round them, they had sat in their silence and their thoughts, and she had not been thanked for what she had done.

She had brought the candle from the cupboard under the cottage's kitchen unit. She struck the match and it blazed, and she lit the wick.

The flame burned upwards, brightly.

Faria saw the boy's face, blinking as if the light was an intrusion on his peace, and then there was confusion across it, and his eyes were dull, without life. She remembered what she had seen of his face when he had crawled – prodded forward by the man – through the loosened plank at the bottom of the back door. Then, on his face, she had seen despair, and she had tried not to look at it as she had worked on the room, but she saw it now and the same misery was closed over it . . . And she saw the man's face. It was cold and indifferent. She tried to smile, to match the faint warmth of the candle's flame.

The man asked quietly, 'Why did you light it?'

'Was I wrong to?'

'Did the dark frighten you?'

Was he laughing at her?

She bridled. 'No, I'm not afraid of it. Might have been when I was a child, but—'

He interrupted and his voice was distant, as if he talked to himself, not to her. 'The darkness is a friend. Throughout each day I pray for the darkness. The enemy has night-vision glasses and infrared that identifies a body's heat, but I can move with freedom in the darkness.' He looked away, as if the exchange of words was meaningless and the breath used on them wasted.

She had been kneeling by the candle, but she eased back and sat on the settee, its cushions, where a smell of age and damp reeked, sagged below her. She leaned on the arm and turned to the boy. Her smile was wider and making it cracked at the scar on her face. The knitted skin itched. What to say? He needed kindness, support. What was not hollow? She did not know.

'Are you all right, Ibrahim?' It was meant as kindness but its emptiness echoed round her.

He gazed at her and his eyes were wide open, stared at her. 'Is this where we stay, until . . . ?'

She glanced at the man, saw his shrug. She said softly, 'It is where we stay.'

'Where do I wash?'

'I'm sorry, where . . . ?'

He blurted, 'I have to wash, and to shave my body, spray on scents when it is clean and shaven. Where do I do that?'

She looked at the man. To Faria, he seemed to roll his eyes. Did it matter? She remembered what she had read: the bombers in Lebanon and Palestine, the martyrs, washed, shaved and put on perfumes before they walked to or drove a car at a checkpoint or a shopping mall. She saw it in the man's gestures and the backward toss of his head: in Iraq, the bombers were on a conveyor-belt and sometimes they were prepared – dressed in a belt or a waistcoat or handcuffed to the steering-wheel of a vehicle – in a grove of palm trees beside irrigated fields, and they had no opportunity to wash, shave and anoint themselves, and went to God and to Paradise dirty. They smelt of sweat when they died. The man did not care. She leaned further across the settee's arm and let her hand rest on the boy's.

She said, 'I will help you to wash. When I go out to buy food I will bring back a razor for you, and scents. I promise I will.'

Across the room from her, the shadows on his face, she saw the man nod – so briefly – as if he approved her answer. She thought she had played her part well, and she squirmed. If he had not been there, the man, she would have taken the boy in her arms, held him against her breast, and would have tried to give him comfort from her warmth . . . but he was there and watched. But she left her hand on the boy's. He was so far from his home, and so distant from what he knew, so long separated from the commitment made to his recruiters – and in the man's bag, beside his knee, was the video that condemned Ibrahim. The boy would die in a foreign land . . . Faria shuddered, and she held his hand tighter.

23 July 1938
In three hours we advance.

We are at the Ebro river. We have barges and rafts that have been brought up since dusk and they will take us across. We do not know if the enemy expects us or whether we will achieve surprise.

Our battalion has been given the target of taking Hill 421, and we have called it the Pimple. I looked across the width of the river at it this afternoon, when the sun was behind it and in my eyes, but I could see that it was well named. It is nothing: it is just a <u>target</u>. I cannot believe, if we take it, that the course of the war will be changed . . . but I have not said that, my <u>doubt</u>, because I no longer have friends that I would trust – to say it would be <u>treason</u>. Behind us are machine-guns . . . They will not fire at the enemy, but at us if we break and retreat, if we turn and run.

Opposite us is the Army of Africa, the Moors. Our commissars have told us that we cannot surrender to them, even if we have no ammunition left and are surrounded. The Moors – it is what the commissars say – have orders to _kill_ any prisoners who are volunteers of the International Brigade. They will slice off our genitals and then they will slit our throats. That is the _encouragement_ we have from the commissars: we cannot fall back and we cannot surrender. We must fight to the death, or be victorious.

So, we must take Hill 421, or it is over.

I wonder, dear Enid, if this will be the last entry in my diary.

All through this day, since we were moved forward to our start line, there has been a great quiet among our people. Are we doomed? Or damned? I believe so.

It is a clear night. When we advance to cross the Ebro river, we are promised that a mist will be over the water that will help us. This morning there was such a mist, but it was brief. The sun burned it away within two hours of dawn. When the mist has gone, the Moors will hit us with their artillery and mortars, and the German and Italian aircraft will fly against us, and the Pimple – should we have reached it – will be an easy place for them to find us.

I try to tell myself not to be afraid. I had no fear when Daniel and Ralph were with me. Without them, now, I have no friend to give me strength. I am not afraid of _death,_ nor am I afraid of a wound, however awful. I am, however, afraid of _fear._ There were men at Brunete, on Mosquito Hill, and at Suicide Hill, above the Jarama valley, who froze in fear; some lay on the ground and cried, and some threw away their rifles and ran back. We have seen the consequence of that fear. It is a post, it is a cigarette, it is a blind-fold, it is an order to aim and to shoot given to a squad of comrades – it is the most ignominious and shameful of deaths.

The light has gone out. None of us, I believe, has heart left in this war.

To end it against a post, with a cloth across my eyes, would be the worst.

I am thinking of Mr Rammage and his clerks at their ledgers – and of the members of my Poetry Group who will be meeting tomorrow evening – and of you, my dear Enid. Thinking of all that was secure in my life, where there is no Hill 421 . . . Better with them and with you than here? I cannot say that.

We are all destined to face challenges. Mine, after dawn, is the Pimple.

He closed the notebook. It was his rule, however great the provocation of what he had read, never to skip forward.

Precious few pages remained, but it was the discipline of David Banks that he had not – ever – turned to the last.

Overwhelmed by what he had read, he lay half dressed on the bed and gazed up at the ceiling light.

Obsession had hooked into him – the barbs of the triple hooks slung under a copper spoon that his father had tied to the line when they had gone together to find a pike in the big pool below the weir. Always that excitement when his father had made ready the tackle, always that massive sense of disappointment and shame when a fish had been dragged to the bank and was found to have taken the hooks too deep for them to be extracted, and his father had killed it with a hammer blow to the head, and the lustre had gone from the scales, and the carcass was left for the rats or for a heron's feast.

He reflected on the twisting moods his great-uncle's war had evoked in him: hatred of Cecil Darke and admiration. Loathing and fascination. Loyalty to the man and betrayal of him. Self-examination and self-destruction . . . At the weekend, incarcerated with the jurors in the barracks camp, he would read those last pages – from compulsion – and would curse again his great-uncle for what had been inflicted on him. Then he would write his letter of resignation.

In his mind was a man who was not a conscripted soldier, was a volunteer, was far from home . . . who had faced his enemy, yet was most afraid of fear.

Abruptly, Banks turned on his stomach, his head buried in the pillow. He sought to block out the images of Cecil Darke, who had no face to him, but all he saw was the river and beyond it a shallow hill on which howitzer shells fell, over which aircraft wheeled, into which bullets spattered, a killing ground . . . and he knew he would not sleep.

Another bloody day beckoned tomorrow. Another bloody day of his own worthlessness, and he thought respect was irretrievable.

Chapter 16: Friday, Day 16

An hour before, Mr Justice Herbert had closed his foolscap notepad
with finality, pushed it away across his desk, leaned forward, let his
elbows take the weight and said, with practised earnestness, 'It is
time now for us, ladies and gentlemen, to adjourn for the weekend.
You will be taken back to the location where you have, so very
patiently, stayed these last several nights. I am assured that
recreation and outings have been arranged for you. There are many
places, I imagine, that you would prefer to be but I want to put on
record that your maturity and dedication have been noted, and I am
confident that you will understand the necessity for the privations
that you are required to suffer. We will resume at ten o'clock on
Monday morning and then you will deliberate on your verdict. I
wish you well for a quiet and pleasant weekend. Thank you.'

'All rise,' the clerk had shouted, in an unnecessarily full voice.
Banks had stood, had seen the judge dive for his side door, had seen
the impotence and anger writ large on the brothers' faces, had
noted the sullen, helpless expressions creased on the jury's – all
except his Principal's, had filed out of court eighteen to oversee the
loading of the coach.

Wally had said, 'Quite envy you, Banksy. Me, I've a kid's birthday party to organize. Want to swap? Eighteen kids, twelve-year-olds, at Legoland. It'll be bloody chaos. You're a lucky sod, and don't forget it, tucked up with those deadbeats for, like the man said, "a quiet and pleasant weekend".'

He had stood in the yard, as the soft rain dribbled on his shoulders, and had watched the brothers led to the Belmarsh van, hemmed in with prison guards and the uniformed guns. When they had been loaded, and their convoy had pulled out through the opened gates, he had gone to round up and move his jurors.

Settled at the back of the coach, alone, he had closed his eyes, had started to think of being free.

'Mind if I sit here?'

A Protection Officer did not gripe – should not have scowled, but probably Banks did. He moved his coat off the seat beside him. He said curtly, the minimum of politeness, 'How can I be of help, Mr Wright.'

'It's just that I have a problem.'

Banks saw the smile and the shrug. His reply was brisk: 'Where we can, we try to sort them out – where's this one on the scale?'

The juror was beside him and Banks looked into his face. Wright's eyes did not meet his. The tongue skipped over the lips. He said, 'The problem's the weekend.'

'Everyone has a problem with the weekend.'

'I can't stay there, shut in, not this weekend.'

Banks was formal, distant: 'The instructions of the judge were pretty clear. You stay under guard together.'

'I am afraid that's not possible.' Wright had his arms folded tight across his chest, like that was a defence posture. 'It's my problem.'

'I'm sorry, but there's nothing I can do about it.'

'You see, Mr Banks,' the voice wheedled, 'it's about my parents. They're old and they're not well, and I have a routine of visiting each weekend. It's something that's really important to them.'

'You go out on Monday, do your bit in the jury room. From what I've heard in court, it shouldn't take too long – not that I'm suggesting how your decision on the case will go – and then you can visit your parents.'

'You're not hearing me, Mr Banks. I go each weekend to see my parents because they're old and ill.'

He'd attended a course when he was in CID, before going over to firearms, that dealt with interview techniques. There had been a whole morning's lecture on the recognition of evasion, the telling of lies and half-truths. Because it had been interesting, the lecture's lessons had stayed with him. Looking up to the right, not the left, was an indication that a lie was told. More compelling than the eyes was the mouth; a tongue smearing the lips was a giveaway of an untruth. Having arms close on the body and folded was the sure sign of evasion . . . Little things, all part of the body language, trifling but telling Banks that his Principal was playing games with him. Then Wright twisted away and presented his shoulder to Banks, which was confirmation: the lecturer had called it a 'liar's posture'. It was eleven years since he had been on that course, and everything that had been told him then was crystal sharp.

'I sympathize with your situation, Mr Wright, but cannot do anything about it.' He thought he had closed the matter, leaned back and faced the window, the newspaper covering it.

'So the consequences will be on your head.'

'What *consequences*, Mr Wright?'

'Pretty simple – the collapse of the trial.'

'What – what are you saying?'

'Arithmetic, Mr Banks. We are ten. Ten jurors make the minimum quorum. Nine, and the trial collapses. That's the consequence.'

'The judge – if you didn't know it – has very comprehensive powers to level against anyone, forgive me, who fucks with his court.'

'Stomach-ache, try that. Migraine. Twisted back, can't sit. I can think up a few others, and it's millions down the drain. Do I get to visit my parents or do I not?'

Alarm bells clamoured. Consequences battered in Banks's mind. He could hear the inquest in court eighteen. Defence submissions that the case had failed . . . The prisoners' smirk . . . What did it bloody matter to David Banks?

'Quite honestly,' Wright said, 'you'd have to lock me in a room and stand guard outside the door, because that's where I'm going. I'm going to see my parents, and if, Mr Banks, you prevent it, I will be handing in a sick note. What do you say?'

'Where are they, your parents?'

He was told. They lived in the Bedfordshire town of Luton.

Banks seemed then to shed the culture imposed by his warrant card. When his letter, two lines of it, was written and handed in, he would lose the card and his authorization to carry a firearm. It was ludicrous that, in the last hours of his service, he should play the pompous and dutiful servant of what he was about to reject. His career was gone, was in its last throes, and it concerned him not a damn that he had been lied to.

A final vestige of that culture remained. Banks said, matter-of-fact, 'Shouldn't be a difficulty, Mr Wright. Of course, I'll have to be with you. It'll be good to meet your parents. Don't mention it to the others.'

The juror sidled back up the aisle of the coach.

In the late afternoon, as dusk fell, Muhammad Ajaq crawled out through the gap in the back door, pulling his bag after him. For a moment he knelt on the wet concrete step, beside the base of the tilted rainwater butt, and looked back. She was there. He could see faintly that anxiety creased her forehead, and he reached through the hole, took her offered hand and squeezed it hard, then replaced the shifted plank. When he stood, he kicked it hard so that it was flush to the door. He left them, slipped away into the gloom and went out on to the road.

He had said to her, whispered in her ear so that the boy did not hear, 'Keep him strong. You alone can do that. He will weaken, will depend on you. You do what is necessary. They are all frightened at the last. You are with him tonight and he will lean on you, and you give him backbone. In the morning you will walk with him, and you will give him courage. The others were idiots, incapable, but you are the one who can help him. Walk with him as far as is sensible, until he has the smile on his face – we call it the *bassamat al-Farah*, which is the smile of joy – until he is within sight of the target area. When he smiles he is content that he is going to Paradise. Tell him, the last thing you say, that he does not look into the faces of those who are close to him, he must not. Must not gaze at the faces of the men, women and children who are around him because that is the source of failure. Then you are gone. You go home, return to your family. I think he will walk well. It is my judgement. Forget me, forget that we met, forget my face and my voice, forget everything of me, and sleep again.'

He went fast, with a good, confident stride.

He had the cap low on his bowed head and the scarf wrapped round his lower face. He did not look up – did not search for cameras high on lamp-posts. He went, in that early evening, where they would come in the morning.

The road was filled with streams of traffic, and he had to scythe through the pedestrians on the pavements. He passed the wide-fronted, brilliantly lit windows of the stores selling bright new consumer goods. He went by the wealth of his enemy, but emptiness gripped him. He felt the loneliness and it unnerved him. He was not looked at, not noticed, by the drivers of cars, lorries and vans, by the swarms of men, women and children who hurried towards him and passed him. It was as if he had no importance in their lives, and no fear of him. He swam among them. He heard laughter, raucous, and argument, and he was ignored as if he did not exist. He wanted to be clear, to be gone. Muhammad Ajaq, following the route she had given him, came down the long hill and into the town, into its soft belly.

He stopped, hesitated. He had reached the square. Around him, the day was ending, the shutters were coming down and office workers spilled out, jostling against him. He was anonymous. In front of him, dazzlingly lit, were the windows above the steps, and the signs for the sale starting the next morning. He stared at the target. A pushchair cannoned into his legs, and an Asian woman – in a *jilbab* robe – did not apologize but wheeled her child past him. When he stepped to the side, he was bounced by the shoulder of an Asian man whose beard was stained with the red henna dye, and again there was no apology. He went across the square and saw the sign for the bus station. When he advanced on a target in occupied Iraq – a mosque or street market of the Shi'as whom he detested, a convoy of the Crusaders whom he despised – he was satiated with commitment, and when he saw the bomb's blast he was consumed with pride. Here, he felt nothing.

He left the bus-station sign, the square, the steps and the sale posters behind him. He had said it so many times: he should never have come. He had yearned for it so often: he craved to be back where he believed he belonged.

Muhammad Ajaq stood in the queue – where she had told him to – and made a picture in his mind of the old men, in caves or in the compound of a tribal leader, and thought they crowded close to a battery-powered radio, and waited. He believed his name was on their lips.

The bus came. He boarded it and found a seat.

Muhammad Ajaq left behind him the target for a martyr bomb. He sat beside a young man who chewed gum incessantly. The bus drove away.

Naylor stood in the doorway, had not spoken but was noticed.

He was offered cake, compressed and fruit-filled, from a tinfoil sachet, then a mug of tea. To have regained control he should have refused both.

He ate and drank. His hand trembled and the mug dripped tea on to the crumbs at his feet. Control had passed, and he knew it.

He had lost control by introducing the American to the equation. The American sat easily in the chair given him. The notebook, pencil and tape-recorder were laid on his lap, and he ate heartily and drank, as if the circumstances were neither peculiar nor particular.

With his mouth still full, Naylor mumbled his question. So bloody anodyne, all the intensity of a chemist's pain-killer. 'So, how are we doing, boys? Where are we at?'

They did not answer. Both men glanced at each other, then – as if it were synchronized – gestured towards Hegner, their spokesman. The American took his time, cleared his throat and said softly, 'We're doing good. Getting there.'

'Where, specifically, are we getting?'

Droll: 'We're on to the subject of a ticket.'

The prisoner lay in deep shadow against the back wall. He had no shape, might have been a mass of half-filled, discarded sacks. Seemed not to move, was silent but for occasional wheezing groans. Naylor stared hard into the darkness and finally made out the hood and the shoulders, the feet that had no trainers on them or socks. Close to the feet a tangle of cables with bulldog clips lay loose, and he followed them to where they attached to the terminals of the floor plug.

It must have been four hours since Naylor had last evacuated himself from his car in the Nissen in answer to a fainter scream from the brick building. The last time he had come, like an intruder, Naylor had seen the prisoner suspended from the ceiling hook, his bound wrists over it, the wires clipped to his toes, and he had asked that same question: 'Where are we at?' The answers had been shrugs, and he had turned away. Not now. He searched for resurrected authority. 'The use of electricity was not sanctioned by me and –'

The easy drawl: 'Don't want to embarrass you, Dickie. Don't want to bring you down off your high horse.'

'– and I should be told how far forward we have come.'

'What I said was, we have a ticket. This is one obstinate man.'

'A ticket for whom, from where and where to?'

'Try making patience a virtue, Dickie. The man, right now, is more frightened of God's damnation, which comes with betrayal, than he is of us. He fancies that damnation will hurt him more than we can. We have to change his viewpoint, and that's where we're working.'

'Whose ticket?'

There had been something clinical, in the past, about the work of Boniface and Clydesdale . . . clinical and fast. A beaten Adeni Arab, from Sheikh Othman, with a split lip and bruised eye sockets, had been quick to tell where a safe-house was. An Irishman from Newtown Hamilton or Forkhill, without fingernails and pissing blood, was fast to spill where a fifty-calibre machine-gun was buried, and could then be released and would never reveal the pain inflicted for fear of his treachery becoming known. The face of a Bosnian Serb could be battered as a punchball – his testicles and kidneys too – and he would give up the secret of where an aid-worker was held in a makeshift gaol, a cellar . . . So why was this fucking man so bloody obstinate? He remembered the cockiness the prisoner had shown in the Paddington Green interview room . . . He had not believed that the confidence would translate to raw courage – hadn't another damn word for it, *courage* – in the face of the pain transmitted through the bulldog clips.

'Dickie, when I have something you can act on, I'll tell you about it.'

'That is hardly an acceptable reply. I need to know where we are.'

'You are getting in the way now. If you don't want to be here, you should get yourself somewhere else.'

Naylor snorted. 'Too damn right.'

He should have been in the front bedroom, with the curtains drawn, blocking out the late-afternoon early-evening view of the cherry trees coming into blossom. That was *somewhere else*. Should have been dressing in a new shirt and a best tie with the Service's discreet shield and motto embroidered on it, and the suit that was back from the dry-cleaner's. Should have been giving his shoes a last buff over the toecaps and round the heels. Should have been going bloody gracefully. It was his final day, and the last hours were being eked out, and the drawers of his desk were not emptied, or his safe, and the cubicle was not cleared for Mary bloody Reakes on Monday morning. But Dickie Naylor was not *somewhere else* – he was in the door of a shitty little building set among fields of growing pea-pods, and the chalice he sought that would make his career remembered was still denied him.

'I'll be in the car,' he said.

'Best place, Dickie. Have a seat and maybe play some music.'

'What I am concerned about – is *he* . . .' he motioned at the figure on the floor, then grimaced '. . . is he too weak to tell us what we have to know? You know what I mean.'

'All under control, Dickie. I'll tell you two things: he's fine, he's fighting, but he will lose. Second, this is not standard stuff. We don't have time to sit on our backsides, play mind games and hang on till next week or next month. We leave that to the Echoes. It's what we do at the Bagram cage outside Kabul. It's how it goes in Guantánamo. Maybe the Echo does six hours straight, and then he goes to the mess and eats a steak with fries, and he believes that next week, next month, his man will crack. Patience is a luxury, Dickie. My life and yours, and the boys' lives, are not luxury. I don't have next week and next month, I have the next hour. I have to learn in the next hour where a ticket will be presented. All I have is the word "ticket", but I have to have more or the time and the opportunity are wasted. So, do the decent thing, and go get yourself a seat in that car.'

Authority, once ceded, was not regained.

Naylor shuffled his feet, locked his hands and cracked the joints.

He saw mugs emptied of their dregs on to the concrete and the dirt, hands wiped on trouser thighs. Naylor saw the prisoner lifted up, inert. He saw Boniface and Clydesdale gasp, grunt, as they raised the weight to the hook, then let him sag. Naylor saw them scrabble for the ends of the cables where the clips were. He turned away, went out into the last light of his last day.

Naylor did not see Hegner screw his face in concentration as if the complexity of a mathematical formula exercised him, and did not hear his quiet voice.

'Guys, I reckin we need to up the voltage. Give the boy more juice.'

He was waiting for her in what had once been the chancel of the cathedral.

'Good to see you, Mary.'

'You look well, Simon, very well.'

She might have slept with him – gone to his room or him to hers in the hall of residence – but had not. He had been a theology student and quiet with his ambition, and they had been soulmates for three years, but never more than friends.

'It's been too long.'

'Too much water under a bridge.'

She might have married him – in white in the church near to her parents' home or in a town hall – but had not. She had gone to London and fast-tracked through the graduate entry into the Security Service, craving advancement. He had taken the route to ordination.

'I think of you, Mary, often enough.'

'Thanks for that last card. Took an age to reach me, but it arrived. I appreciated it.'

It had come, courtesy of the American military's postal service in the Green Zone of the Iraqi capital, and had shown a bland view of the river: 'Dear Mary, Can't say in truth that I wish you were here, but these are interesting times – and tragic times. Love, Simon.' The card was in the privacy of her bedroom, hooked under the frame of her dressing-table mirror. All his cards were there – from his three-times-a-year visits to Baghdad – and they made a ring round the mirror, and all showed the same view of the Tigris river. He was the only man that Mary Reakes, troubled and confused, would have thought of coming to speak with. She had left Thames House in mid-afternoon, having told her assistant that she could be reached on her mobile, had taken the train to Coventry and a taxi to bring her to the cathedral, had seen him waiting for her in the ruins where the chancel had been. She was a rising star in the ranks of the Security Service; he was an unknown junior priest in the cathedral's International Centre for Reconciliation. She had little belief; he lived by faith. She worked in a protected building in a supposed safe city; he travelled to Baghdad to support children's charities and a beleaguered church. She believed in the crushing of enemies; he strove to bring together adversaries in dialogue. Mary admired him, and Simon thought her beyond reach.

'Can't talk in a building – sorry and all that,' she said.

'Then we'll stand out here – I think the rain's easing. Forecast's good for tomorrow . . . Is it the Cross of Nails you need to touch?'

'I'll touch anything that gives me guidance.'

Mary Reakes told her friend of a suspicion. They stood, close to each other, inside the old lowering walls of the cathedral church of St Michael, which were retained as a reminder of the barbarity of war. On the night of 14 November 1940, fire bombs had rained on the city and a centuries-old building had been gutted. She told him of a plot identified, of a suicide-bomber loose on the streets, of a facilitator who had come from Iraq, of a prisoner who had been taken and brought south. A new cathedral, away to her left, had been built and dedicated to Forgiveness and Reconciliation, but she saw only the ruined walls and their stunted outline against the dusk. She told him of the release of the prisoner, of an argument with an assistant director, of the disappearance of her superior in the final and critical hours of the countdown, and of a blind American. In the days after the raid's destruction, a clergyman who was picking among the debris had found three long nails from the roofing beams and bound them together with wire to make a cross. She told him it was her belief that the prisoner was now abused, under torture . . . What should her posture be?

'You are, Mary, at the vitals of morality.'

'I don't know what to do.'

'You can be a whistleblower, or you can turn your cheek.'

'I am comfortable on the upper ground, not in the gutter.'

'Does it matter what is at stake?'

She told him of the morning at Thames House, the start of a July day, the sun's warmth on the streets, as the news had come in torrent blurts of four bombs targeting the capital's commuters. They started to walk, pacing on the sheen of the flagstones. She told him that in every office open area, as they rooted in their files and flashed them up on screens, television sets showed the images of the dead and injured, and some had wept at what they saw.

He wore a cassock of oatmeal brown and it swung like a frock as he moved. The rain glimmered on her suit's shoulders and in her hair, and her heels echoed beside him. She told him of that evening, and all through that week, of the numbing sense of failure that strangled life from her workplace.

'The motto of our Service is "Defender of the Kingdom". Our sole job now, for three thousand of us – and all the police agencies – is to defend our kingdom against a new atrocity. Simon, does that justify torture?'

He grinned. 'You know the answer for yourself.'

'I have to be given confirmation of it – I have to know I'm not walking alone.'

'But you will, Mary, you will walk alone. You will be shunned and ostracized. The career – so important to you – will wither. Brickbats and insults will be your reward. Or you can turn away and empty your mind of what you know.'

'When you were in Baghdad . . .'

'Morality is not a focus group – and I don't mean to mock you. The vision of morality is with the individual. Is torture ever justified? In Baghdad, daily, there are atrocities of indescribable evil, and many say that such evil should be confronted by measures that are extreme to the point of repugnance. If I go to the airport, where prisoners are screened, or to the Abu Graib gaol, and call for respect to be shown those who manufacture the bombs and plan their targeting, and talk of religion and the dignity of mankind, I will be shown the gate – probably pitched out of it on to my face. I see the problem from a different perspective. I look at the witness. If the witness keeps silent then he, or *she*, demeans himself, *herself*. That man, or *woman*, must live with the decision. I doubt, Mary, because you are my valued friend, that you could cross to the other side of the street, avert your eyes, erase what you have known and maintain your pride. But the sustenance of your pride will come at a price, a heavy one. You know that.'

She slipped her arm into his. Their steps had slowed and the darkness grew round them. Dulled lights lit the broken walls.

He told her of a man, implicated in the bomb plot to assassinate Hitler, called Pastor Bonhoeffer, who had been hanged in the Flossenbürg concentration camp a month before the final ceasefire of the Second World War. He told her of what the man had written, in his condemned cell, and apologized for his paraphrase. 'When they took the trade unionists, I did not protest because I was not a trade unionist. When they took the Communists, I did not protest because I was not a Communist. When they took the Jews, I did not protest because I was not a Jew. When they took me, no one protested because no one was left.' He lifted her hand from his arm and kissed it. She lifted her head, reached up, and kissed his cheek.

She saw only shadows. 'I have to get back.' She turned away, walked quickly towards the exit arch, away from the place where nails had been fashioned into a cross.

He called after her, 'I'd like to say that I'm here, Mary, always. Not true. I return to Baghdad in a week, will be there maybe three months. I urge you, pay the price, don't cross the street – don't look the other way. Hold your pride.'

'Look, I'm not picking a fight, but I'm entitled to an answer. Did you or did you not telephone the police?'

It was the fourth time she had asked the question, and three times the farmer had denied his wife a reply. Last evening he had shrugged and pleaded tiredness. At breakfast he had changed the subject to the latest ministry questionnaire on harvest yields. At lunch he had told her she nagged, had bolted his food and gone back to his tractor. He picked at his dinner, ate, swallowed and answered. 'No.'

'We agreed you were going to call the police.'

'I changed my mind. It's allowed.'

'So, there was a fire behind the Wilsons' barn. In the fire there were scraps of burned sheet, with patterns the same as Oakdene's, and towels. Together we went to the cottage. We found it empty and all trace of our guests gone. The cottage was cleaner – I'm not ashamed to say it – than from any scrub I've given it, and every room, the bathroom and loo, the bedrooms, living room and kitchen, stinks of bleach. Is that not something that should be reported to the police?'

'They paid for a month.'

'Paid cash, don't forget, in advance.'

'It was just bedding and towels.'

She grimaced. 'Can be replaced.'

'Which didn't go through the books, and wasn't paid into the bank,' he said.

She looked away, out through the darkened window and towards the shadow silhouette of the roof of Oakdene Cottage. 'Questions asked.'

'First thing Plod asks, "How did they pay? Before they thieved your sheets and vandalized your towels, did they pay by cheque? Cash in hand?" Maybe Plod wants to get his hands on the banknotes and run them through for tests, I don't know. Questions with difficult answers.'

'Best left alone?'

'Best left where the Revenue doesn't know. Not as though the bedding was new. Can of worms if I phone the police, that's my opinion.'

She said, 'I've done a nice plum crumble, your favourite.'

'That's grand, my love,' the farmer said. 'Can I take it that's the end of the matter?'

'The end.' She cleared his plate and hers off the table. Time now was short. That evening there was a meeting of the parish council. He was chair and she was the minutes' taker. At the sink, she turned. 'Actually, they were very pleasant, the ones I met. Particularly the girl, so well-mannered – and the man, the older one, very handsome, a real charmer . . .'

She heard it, then flicked the curtain and saw the car. Fury burned in Anne Naylor. She tried the number again. She heard his voice. In the metallic automated tone of the damn speaking clock, he told her that he was unable to take the call and urged that a message be left after the beep.

'I'm telling you, Dickie, that your behaviour today – no contact, not a word – is absolutely unforgivable. Where are you? Still running round like it's a Scouts' jamboree and you've to be there till the last tent's been taken down, the last campfire put out? I suppose you think the people at that damn place will admire you for working right up to the eleventh hour of the eleventh day – they won't. I just thank God that Daddy's not still with us and a witness to your pathetic behaviour. I promise you that tonight – and it won't be in a quiet corner – I'll bend your ear and not care who hears me. For Heaven's sake, what do you think you've achieved by this pitiful display of childish dedication? By Monday morning they'll have forgotten you. Me, I'm not in the forgetting business. Damn you, answer your bloody phone.'

She slammed down the receiver.

Her coat for the evening was silk. Her late mother had worn it at her father's farewell party, when the Service had been based at Leconfield House. A little dated, but elegant. In front of the mirror, she touched her hair – dabbed her fingers on it . . . and she remembered. Her mother had said, in the minutes before they had walked into the governor's formal salon, at the Aden residence, 'You don't have to do it, my dear. Pregnancy out of wedlock isn't the end of the world. Daddy and I will stand beside you . . . It's not as though he's a wonderful catch. I'm sure you can do better . . . All right, all right. Just promise me you won't snivel . . . And promise me you won't regret it.' God, that evening she regretted marrying Dickie Naylor. She closed the door behind her, double-locked it and hastened down the path.

The chauffeur held open the rear door for her. He looked puzzled. 'Just you, Mrs Naylor? Not your husband as well?'

'No, just me,' she said acidly. 'I'm meeting him there, but we'll be coming home together.'

'I suppose he's working,' the chauffeur said. 'Funny that. Most of those I take for their last party wish they'd quit a year ago.'

'I expect he'll get used to retirement, growing tomatoes in a new greenhouse.'

The chauffeur closed the door gently behind her, and drove off. God – see if she didn't – she'd bend his ear, then burn the bloody thing to a crisp.

'Give him more.'

'You sure, Mr Hegner?'

'It's what I said.'

'Never gone up that high before, Mr Hegner.'

Joe Hegner sat in his chair and asked the question in a clear voice, as if it didn't matter to him, like he was the schoolmarm talking to infants back near Big Porcupine Creek. 'The Engineer, my friend, will he be journeying with him?'

The prisoner hung from the hook, and his body had the look of an animal carcass that his grandfather had slaughtered and left to bleed. He could not see it, but was able to imagine it . . . The trousers were down to the ankles, crumpled and lodged there, along with the fouled underpants. The wires' clips were dug into the folds of the prisoner's lower stomach, near to the testicles but not on them. The bare feet swivelled. He expected the prisoner, when the question was put, to stiffen and writhe, try to summon resistance, but his body turned slowly half-way to the right and then half-way to the left – and Hegner knew it because of the creak of the weight on the hook. He strained to hear an answer, but there was nothing.

'Do it, guys.'

There was the gasp and the grunt, then more silence.

'Do it again, give him more.'

He heard the scream, shrill inside the walls and under the ceiling, and the strain on the hook whined.

'Every man has a breakpoint, eventually reaches the end of tolerance. Reckon we're near to it. What we have is good, but can get better. Hadn't thought he'd be so stubborn. He's stubborn, obstinate – but so am I. For me, it's all down to that moment of darkness. I'm in the mess hall, surrounded by good men. I'm queuing for food. I see this man – young, Arab, in big, bulky army fatigues, and he's a hand in a pouch pocket – standing by a table not twenty paces from me. I see him smile. I know then that he belongs to the Twentyman, have that sense of it. The shout's in my throat, and then the light's in my eyes. So bright, so vivid. I see men falling. I close my eyes – like closing them will protect them. And the blast of the scorched air knocks me down. I lie there, and there's men on top of me. I have pain so I know I'm alive and there's men shouting. I open my eyes. First, I think I can't see because of the men on me, but I push them off. My eyes are wide. That's the moment I realize why there's darkness. I blink, rub, scratch my damn face, where my eyes are, and there is only darkness. The Twentyman did it to me. I made the promise then, in that darkness and with other men's blood on me, the wetness of their guts, hearing them scream and moan, that I would get him or regard my life as a failure. What you've done, guys, is put me close to him and for that I am sincerely thankful. Do it again, up the juice.'

'Don't think there's any point, Mr Hegner.'

'There's not a pulse, Mr Hegner, no trace.'

'Do you know, Mr Hegner, it's the first time Xavier and I have ever lost a prisoner?'

'You're right there, Donald. He's gone, Mr Hegner.'

Behind him, deep in the darkness, feet on cracked glass. He heard the wheeze, air expelled between tight-set teeth, then, 'God, that is a bloody disaster.'

Hegner swung round sharply. 'Wrong, Dickie, wrong . . . We have a ticket, to and from and at what time. That is no disaster.'

The hoarse voice was raised to a shout. 'My remit – if you've damn well forgotten it, which I have not – is a bomb, a street, casualties spread across pavements. Where are we?'

'Go with the flow, Dickie, and they'll love you.' Joe Hegner laughed. 'All your people, who think you're yesterday's man, they'll be tossing garlands at you. Dickie, enjoy the ride. You're stressing on one bomb but I'm going to show you the big picture.'

She stood behind him. At her feet was the bucket, shiny and galvanized. In the bucket was the water she had taken from the rain butt, clouded with dirt. She used the soap to clean his body.

Faria believed that, without her, he could not have washed himself – could not even have undressed. He stood naked and trembled. She had not before seen the bare skin of a man's buttocks and the flatness of a man's belly. A lone candle lit them. She had started at the nape of his neck, from there to the bristle of his beard on his cheeks and jaw, and then her hands had gone down, slipping and sliding across his shoulders, and into his armpits, and on towards the small of his back and the shallow width of his hips. She washed him in the cavity of his buttocks, and she stretched her arms round to reach his groin . . . then down his legs. The shivers convulsing the body were not from the cold. She felt the hairs on his legs, finer and softer than those at the base of his stomach. He did not wriggle to be clear of her hands. She knew all of his body, had washed its secret places and had sensed the beat of his heart.

As the candle flickered, she left the bubbles on his skin, and bent down to pick up the cheap plastic razor. She lifted his right arm and ran the blade across the hair, then his left arm. She rinsed the razor in the bucket, and used her fingers to feel growth on his face, and he allowed it. Faria scraped the hair from his chest. She must have made a nick as blood stained her nails. But she dabbed the minute wound with water from the bucket and staunched it. She thought of the blood that would pour from him when the waistcoat tore him apart. By touch, she shaved away the matted hair low on his stomach, and held him so that she would not again cut him. Felt him stiffen, held him with gentleness, and made the skin smooth. She knelt and ran the razor's blade down his legs, on his thighs and shins.

It was how it had to be done . . . how it was done in Palestine, and in Chechnya, and in Iraq. A man, or a woman, going to Paradise must be cleaned – purified, if he or she were to sit at God's table.

She did not speak. What she had to say would keep till the morning, would be said when they walked.

Faria could not ask it. As the video had been, were the washing and shaving a further reinforcing of the pinions on him? Was he tied to death?

She dried him with an old T-shirt, wiped away the last of the soap and water, and her hands covered the softness of his skin. She squirted perfume over him, a popular brand that was advertised on television for girls to use.

She had tightened the noose on him . . . and she helped him to dress again, and still he shivered, trembled, and she hoped she gave him strength – as she had been told to.

The hours of the last night yawned in front of her, and of him.

Bloody awful traffic. Friday-evening traffic, going north, nose to tail, and so damned slow.

The car was from a pool left at the barracks for police use. David Banks drove but did not talk: his Principal would, soon enough. His Principal fidgeted in the seat beside him, seemed to wriggle for courage to spit out something. Banks was not minded to help him.

Banks had the radio on. A news bulletin droned on, then a weather forecast. Good for the morning but not yet, and his wipers sluiced rain off the windscreen and the spray that was thrown up ahead. He had called the chief inspector, told Wally that he'd be off the camp for the next several hours, that Tango One – Julian Wright – had a domestic emergency with his parents and he'd egged it, that he was escorting Tango One from the secure location, that there was plenty of uniform to tuck the others up in their accommodation. He knew he'd told a lie, the domestic emergency with the parents of Tango One, and didn't care.

He came off the dual-carriageway and Luton was signed bearing left, and the turning for the airport was right off the roundabout. The lights of the town, an amber glow nestling against the cloud base, were ahead. He had never been there. Knew it had a reputation for being as crap as the car he drove. Knew it had an airport, knew it had a car factory, knew it had a railway station where the four Seven-Seven bombers had taken the train into London.

'Go into the town. Keep the railway on your right. You'll see the shopping centre on the left. Sign will be for the town hall. We're off to the right, short of that. It's Inkerman Road.'

Banks did not reply, just nodded, as if he was staff and took instructions.

The spit came harder. 'There is – I'm afraid – Mr Banks, a small and inconsequential difficulty.'

Banks kept his eyes on the road in front.

'Not much point in putting it off, not sharing it . . .'

Banks saw the raised lights of the railway station to the right.

'I regret it, but I told you an untruth. Silly of me, but if I hadn't we wouldn't be here.'

The bulk of the shopping centre's outer wall was to his left. Banks followed the main route, and the town hall was arrowed from a sign.

'It's not my parents. They're in the pink – probably fitter, healthier, than I am . . . Sort of regular, you know, any weekend I can get away, I come up here and my parents are the excuse. It's where my wife thinks I am, and my kid. The sob story was a smokescreen – well, a lie. The answer? Of course, it's a woman . . .'

Did not answer, and saw a turn-off to the right: Inkerman Road.

'That's where we are. I told an untruth so I could get away for a weekend's shagging. And there's one more untruth, so don't be thinking shagging's due reward for a hero. I'm not. Personally, I would have taken the cash that was dumped on me. Would have done if my wife hadn't found it in the wardrobe. We're broke, in hock. We're in final-demand country, and that cash would have taken off the pressure. My wife found it. She said that if I didn't report the approach, she would – and I would have been up a creek with no paddle. My wife scuppered me, and I'm not a hero with a sense of civic duty . . . just so you know – but a louse, a cheat, a creep, not a hero. But, and I mean this very seriously, if you turn me round then I'm not in court on Monday. So, what's to do?'

Inkerman Road stretched away up a hill, and he saw the pub's sign, the squat block of flats below the pub and the line of houses past it. He could have told his Principal of a course for detectives that identified the body language of a liar . . . did not. Could have told his Principal that this Protection Officer was washed up, *useless*, and was putting in a resignation letter on the next working day . . . but didn't want to waste his breath. He changed down, eased his foot on to the brake pedal.

'Mr Wright, I really don't give a damn. Please, just tell me where to stop.'

Chapter 17: Friday, Day 16

Banks read a newspaper, learned the ground. Big print screamed at him. *'SAVAGES! A Man's Face Has to Be Rebuilt After Horrific Attack by Yob Gang'*. And *'Date Rape Warning on Drinks'*. And *'Drunk Yobs in Street Battle'*. Nothing here that was remarkable, that was not ordinary. And *'Woman Victim of Daylight Robbery Near Bus Stop'*. And *'Teen Yob Terror Hits Shop and Doc's Surgery'*. The same as anywhere. The streetlight above him blazed into the car.

Lucky, really, to have seen him in the mirror before he was past the car. A kid had bicycled up the pavement and had had the big bag on his shoulder with the town's *News/Gazette* logo on it. He'd lowered his window and asked if there was anything local. He'd been given a *News/Gazette* from the bottom of the bag, two days after publication. He'd given the kid a pound coin for it, when the price on the masthead was thirty-four pence. He'd sent him off happy.

He could have gone up the road to the pub, where live music played. Instead, he turned pages, moved on from crime, found another issue. The *News/Gazette* was big on race: *'Fresh Race Hate Probe'* and *'Police Chief in Race Plea'* and *'Town Muslims on the March for Moderation'* and *'Live Together or the Radical Groups Win'*, and he gutted the articles.

His man had rung the doorbell, given him a last glance and a grin, like the deceit was enjoyed, and a woman – attractive, middle thirties, bobbed brunette hair, strikingly similar in appearance to the Principal's wife – had opened the door. Wright must have given some sort of a curtailed explanation of a car in the street and a man left in it, and she'd gazed from the step at him, shrugged, and the door had closed on them. It was part of his life – a part that had less than seventy-two hours to run – to be left in cars outside doors. So, Luton had a crime problem with a race problem thrown in – so, Luton was pretty damn ordinary. He read about street muggings and the arguments over the appropriate dress for Muslim girls at school, and about a campaign to deface advertising nudity and about drug-addiction clinics that had opened in the town and were swamped. He wondered why the good folk who weren't thieves, activists or addicts bothered to shell out thirty-four pence and face that litany of misery, of hate. He turned the pages in search of something else.

Banks found another *'Overdose Death'* and skipped on. Better, so much better, *'Citizenship Classes'* were fully subscribed: *'New Citizens Queue Up to Take Oath of Allegiance'*. The football team was challenging for promotion, *'The Hatters March On'*. Most of what he knew of two dozen towns and a dozen cities had come from sitting in cars reading local newspapers. He'd gone through the misery of the first handful of grim news pages, and it was like the sunlit uplands beckoned him. A *'New Creche Opens'*, three bloody cheers. An *'Extra Budget Available for Town Square Clean-up'*, hip, hip bloody hurray. *'All Welcome at Saturday Town History Walk'* – worth throwing a cap into the air. Couldn't abide the small ads – dating agencies, televisions going cheap, rooms to let – and scrambled through them. Last was the two-page spread: *'Bargains, Give-Away Prices, Monster Sale, Come Early, Doors Opening At Nine, Shopping Centre Bonanza'*. It did not affect David Banks, but it humoured him as he sat in the car and the dark closed round his windows. He thought, at last, he had found a trifle of cheerfulness, and he pictured crowds gathering on a warm morning, tomorrow, with the forecast optimistic, and a lightening of the dreariness imposed by muggers, zealots and junkies.

The trouble with having the warrant card was that it placed a man outside the loop of normal life, and the Glock, 9mm calibre, in a pancake holster, at his hip was even further outside it. When the letter was in, with the card and the firearms authorization, and most of his possessions from the bedsit were gone to a skip or a charity shop, the rest to his mother's garage, and he was at the airport for the flight to Auckland, Sydney or Toronto, with a rucksack on his back, he would need nothing that a shopping centre, *Prices Slashed*, could offer him. He seemed to see those valleys and the tumbling streams, the endless expanses of desert, great inland seas, and he chucked the newspaper behind him. There, somewhere, he might find peace.

He reached into his jacket pocket, where it hung loose over the holster. His hand fastened on the notebook.

He lifted it out, felt the worn, roughened leather of its cover in his fingers. Only three pages remained to be read. He turned one.

David Banks, the streetlight spilling inside the car, saw that the writing was looser, a tiny scrawl – as if more laboured – and that the paper was tainted with a dried dark stain.

The newspaper had been an excuse, a diversion, a palliative as temporary as an aspirin. He was drawn to the page, a moth to a damned flame.

He read.

27 July 1938
I have been shot by a sniper.

I knew nothing.

I felt a weight hit me. A hammer blow. I was lifted up, then thrown down. There was no pain, not at first, only numbness.

Our officer had warned of the sniper three days ago. Then the sniper shot and killed a boy from Wolverhampton. He was not a friend – I have none left – but a good lad, and had been a factory machinist before he came to join the International Brigade volunteers, was always cheerful. He was going back to the latrine from the front-line trench when he was hit in the back of his head. But the sniper had not fired for three days. I had forgotten him. I was sent back to the rear to bring forward food, and there was a place where the parapet was lower, where I should have ducked to my knees, but then it would have been hard to carry all the food for our platoon. I did not duck.

I was hit in the chest.

Dear Enid, other men – some I have never spoken to, all to whom I have given no love – risked their own lives to come and carry me back to the second and third trenches, and safety.

I have been taken to a field hospital. At first, I was carried by two men, one holding my arms and one my legs. That was when the pain came.

Further back, I was put on to a cart that a donkey pulled. If I had been an officer, or a commissar, I would have been brought to the field hospital by lorry. I went all the way, several miles, on the cart.

This is a charnel house, it is a place of Hades. I think it was a place like this where Ralph died.

I must be thankful that I am able to write.

I am waiting to be examined. The doctors, one is Austrian and another is Polish, have a process that is called triage. Ralph told me about triage when the wounded were taken back from Suicide Hill. When the doctors come to me they will make an assessment of my condition. They decide, in triage, if I will live, or might live, or not. The priority goes to those who will live, and if they have the time and opportunity they will treat those who might live, and they put a black spot of dye on the forehead of those who will not live. There are many casualties here, and I believe it will be a long time before they reach me. A nurse – I think she was French – has put a new field dressing on my wound.

It is difficult to write. I am weaker, and breathing is harder. The effort of moving the pencil on the page is almost beyond me.

I think of the sniper. He did not choose me. It was an opportunity, my chest visible for two or three seconds where the parapet was low. I chose him, presented myself. But for those two or three seconds he would have seen my face, magnified in the lens of his rifle sight. When he saw me go down, did he rejoice? Or was shooting me meaningless to him? I do not know.

I cannot hate him.

He is a soldier, as am I. I do not think that, with my rifle, I have ever harmed an enemy, but I have tried.

I have thought of him . . . Perhaps he is a good man, perhaps he has a family, perhaps he has no hate for me . . . Perhaps, already, he has forgotten the image of my face.

Our officer said – when the boy from Wolverhampton was hit – that the sniper was likely to be German. I think of him as being as far from home as I am.

For now, dear Enid, I cannot write more.

*

There was one page remaining. He closed the notebook, slid it back into his pocket.

Stunned and quiet, not moving, David Banks was not aware that the outer door of the block had opened. He did not see the wash of light on the step and the pavement.

The window was rapped. He was jolted. His hand, instinct, dropped to the pistol's butt and he had half drawn it.

'Steady, you silly bugger, don't bloody shoot me.'

He loosed his grip.

'You hardly need that damn thing here. Where were you – Never-never Land?'

He shrugged.

'Put it down to my lady. She says it's ridiculous having you sat out here in the bollocks-numbing cold. She says you're to eat with us.'

'My thanks to her and to you, Mr Wright, but I'm fine.'

'She won't have any of that. And I'm to tell you that there's enough cooked for an extra plate.'

'I get an allowance for food, and I buy it.'

'God, Mr Banks, you make a virtue out of awkwardness. She also says that I'm not permitted back in her bed if you're stuck outside in a bloody car. Come on, shift yourself.'

'I suppose that tilts the argument. Just remember what I've said. I'm not a friend.'

'Made a good imitation of one this evening. I'm grateful.'

He checked his pockets, then the holster. Thought of the yob gangs of the *News/Gazette*. Climbed out and went to the boot, lifted out the holdall with the kit in it – magazines, the thunderclap grenades, the ballistic blanket and the first aid ... Not making it easy for the yob kids to get a bonus from a stolen joy-ride vehicle. He crossed the pavement, went up the steps and inside, heard soft music and felt the warmth.

Said, side of mouth, 'What does she know?'

Had the whisper back: 'There's been a jury scare. All of us have a Protection Officer, nothing particular about me.'

'Are you always so economical with the truth?'

'Offer it up when there's no alternative, only then. Story of my life, and it's worked so far.'

She'd had careful makeup on her face when he'd first seen her, her hair had been neat and brushed, and her blouse had been pristine.

In the living area, from the kitchenette alcove, she smiled with warmth and held out her hand. 'Good to meet you. I'm Hannah.'

The cosmetics at her eyes, the lipstick on her mouth, were smudged, the hair less neat. The white blouse was creased, and fewer buttons were fastened.

'My name's Banks. Detective Constable Banks.'

Wright grinned. 'Or, love, you can call him Mr Banks. In these matters we retain formality and he is not a *friend*, better believe it.'

'I've done a lasagne, there's plenty. A drink?'

'No, thank you.'

'He's on duty. Mr Banks is working.'

Her laughter trilled. 'I doubt organized crime – desperadoes – reaches this dump. Are you going to take your jacket off?'

He did, and gave it her. She hung it on a hook. She was staring at his waist, at the pancake holster and the butt of the Glock. 'But not that, you don't take that off?'

'No.'

She frowned, and mischief twinkled. 'I suppose you get asked it often – have you ever fired it, gone serious?'

'I get asked it very often. I haven't.'

A place was laid for him. They ate. The lasagne was excellent, and Banks told her so, felt a shyness. There was white wine on the table, Tuscan, and Wright drank but she drank more. Banks sipped a glass of tap water. They talked among themselves, the weather and the politics at her office, some more about the weather, heating problems in the block. He had no place there. Maybe he should have stayed in the cold of the car. Black coffee was brought him.

She leaned forward. Because of the undone buttons, he could see the shape and fall of her breasts. 'Jools said you'd told him your colleagues in a unit thought you were useless, that they'd bumped you.'

Banks wondered whether he'd been discussed before, during or after sex.

Wright flapped a hand. 'A bit below the belt, love. Christ, I was only—'

Banks said, 'Shouldn't have told him. But it's about right.'

'Why did they say it?'

Wright drained the last of his glass. 'You can't ask him that –
God . . .'

'Why?'

When would he speak of it again? Never. When would he meet
with this woman again? Never. He struggled to articulate the
words that jumbled in his mind. He said quietly, 'I don't think it's
anything covered by the Official Secrets Act. The team I was with
guarded the élite, the principal figures of the state. They're not
important in themselves, but as symbols . . . It's a sitting-on-your-
backside job, not one when you can judge whether you've done well
or badly – nothing happens . . . So, we talk. We talk about the threat
on the streets, talk about it every day since Seven-Seven. We talk
about suicide-bombers, have done every day since Twenty-two-
Seven and the tube killing. We talk about what we would do if
confronted with the reality, a bomber, face to face – or a *supposed*
bomber.

'If you're going to shoot a man, take his life – do something you've
never done before – you have to believe that your cause is good, that
his is evil. We talk about indoctrinated scum-bags and fanatics, and
put horns on them, scales and tails. We're in cars and canteens, hotel
foyers and restaurant kitchens, and we talk about us being right and
them being wrong, us being brave and them being cowards . . .
and we think that having doubt is weakness. To be weak is to be *useless*. If you pause, the half-second, and lose sight of scum-bags and
fanatics and cowards, the shot hasn't been fired and the street is full
of casualties. To doubt is unacceptable . . . I doubted. I spoke the
heresy, said that it was perfectly possible for a suicide-bomber to be
brave and principled. If the world hadn't caved in then, I would have
added, "But wrong." The caveat was never said. I lost the respect and
trust of my team, and didn't fight hard enough to get it back. There
you have it – I'm bumped and I'm going and I regret nothing.'

'Are you running away from making that judgement?'

'You could say that – going where I don't have to make the judgement, ever.' The silence hung round him, and he thought he'd
screwed their evening, but she poured him more coffee.

Many thoughts jangled in Dickie Naylor's head as he oversaw the
digging of the grave. He needn't have. He had waved a flashlight

and chosen a place a dozen steps behind the Nissen hut, but his men had gone to it, had rejected it, had pointed out politely that there would be concrete foundations skirting the building, and they wouldn't be able to go deep. They had moved further away, in an opposite direction, and the chosen place was where the weeks of rain had made the ground soft in the angle between the last surviving runway and the old aircraft stand. They had told him, again politely, that they did not need the flashlight. They were two indistinct shadowy figures. They grunted with the effort of their work, and talked quietly between themselves, as if he were not present.

He could have spewed up, bent, and coughed bile from his belly. A man had died under the excess of inflicted pain. His men, he believed, would go back to their island without a second thought.

Did the ghosts hear the two men, both in the pit – only their shoulders now visible in the half-light thrown down by a quarter-moon – hear them as they watched? The ghosts would have been of the young. There was a stone beside where the old camp gate had been, where the woman had walked her dogs and not known that what was done was in her name, and they'd gone past it fast, but he had seen the faded print of names carved there, and had not thought of them. Perhaps a bomb, a five-thousand-pound grotesque canister, had exploded as it was loaded into the undercarriage of a Lancaster. Perhaps an aircraft, cruelly damaged by the flak artillery on the way back from its target, had not been able to set down its wheels, belly-flopped and caught fire. Perhaps a pilot, navigator or rear-gunner, shattered by the stress of a never-ending tour, had drawn a Webley pistol from the armoury, walked to the trees and put the barrel into his mouth.

He thought the ghosts watched as dirty work was done under the cloak of darkness. Would they have approved? Naylor had been told long ago, by a one-time squadron leader who had transferred in the peace years to the Service, that the crews were always briefed on the military importance of targets, never told of the civilians who would be in the cellars when the bombs fell and the firestorms were lit. Had they cared about the civilians, now called 'collateral damage'? Would they have said, 'I just obey orders,' as he had? Would the ghosts have said that the firestorms were justified in the interest of ultimate victory, as he had?

'You happy with that, Xavier?'

'Very happy, Donald.'

'It's a nice job we've done.'

'The best that was possible.'

They came out of the pit, helping each other clear of it. He thought it meant about as much to them as digging down to a blocked sewer drain, and gulped again to hold back the bile. They left him. Naylor shivered. They tramped away, were lost to him. He thought of the American. When he had last seen him, the man who'd usurped Dickie Naylor was sitting in his chair, impassive like a sphinx, the body at his feet, wrapped in old, tossed-away plastic agricultural sacks. His phone rang.

He saw the lit screen, saw the number that called him, put it back unanswered in his pocket.

They brought the body, labouring under its weight, and tipped it into the pit. An animal would have been buried with greater dignity. They heaved sections of concrete on top, then refilled the pit with earth, relaid the turf and smacked it down with the spade, then carried away the rotting plywood on which the excess earth lay and scattered it among the growing pea plants.

'Done nicely, Donald.'

'Done a treat, Xavier.'

'I think we'll make good time.'

'No problem. Clear roads, and we'll have a decent run.'

The two cars, on side-lights, drove down the runway at speed. He saw the memorial stone where the gate had once been, but he did not slow and swept past it. Naylor had no more business with ghosts and their place. On the main road, he snapped on his headlights and saw in his mirror those of the car behind him.

'You all right, Joe?'

'You bet I'm all right. And in the next several hours it'll get better, believe me.'

On the dashboard was the lit clock. He knew where he should have been and would not be.

As an assistant director, Tristram was host to the party.

It was a wedding without a groom, a play without Denmark's prince.

He thought her magnificent – she was the bride and Ophelia in one. More to the point, Anne Naylor was a trouper of the old school. He eased towards her. If her temper was foul, if she was bottling her anger, she guarded it closely. Canapés were being handed round on plates, and little sandwich triangles. It was a fine dress she wore, obviously new, purchased for the occasion, and if she was mad with fury she hid it successfully. What he would have expected from the daughter of a Cold War legend: the woman had pedigree. He thought they could make do with two glasses of wine each – maybe a splatter of a refill for the toast after his speech, but there would not be much drinking done. As soon as was proper, he would escort Anne Naylor to the Embankment entrance, with the envelope of vouchers in her handbag, see her into the car and wave her off . . . There was still work to be done that night.

And quite a good turnout, considering the pressure of that work. An older group of Dickie Naylor's contemporaries, and the younger ones who sat in his office . . . Mary Reakes among them. Within ten minutes of Anne Naylor leaving, the car barely over Lambeth Bridge, the room would have emptied. Would he have walked those last miles, trudged through those last hours, up to the last chime of the damned clock? Would he hell. Damn right, he would not. But it was in his speech: Dickie Naylor was 'a shining example to all of dedication and commitment and duty, a safe pair of hands'. It was not in his speech that the man was, in Tristram's opinion, a bloody fool and a pliant one.

He was at the wife's shoulder. His hand on her elbow, he eased her from the group. He led her to a quieter corner. 'Anne, you're putting up such a terrific show.'

'I'll bloody well murder him.'

'And taking it so well.'

'He'll regret the day he was ever bloody born.'

'It's a moment when he, dear Dickie, has more to contribute than any of us.'

'Bullshit. I'll bloody swing for him.'

'There's a heavy flap on, Anne. Dangerous times, you know, and all that. Right now, he's rather a crucial cog in the works – can't say where those wheels are turning. He'll be home in the morning.'

'Likely to find the bloody locks changed.'

'Then you can go out together, everything forgotten, and buy that greenhouse.'

'Then barricade him into it.'

'I knew you'd understand, Anne. Well done.'

He slipped away. Tristram was now in hourly contact with Dickie Naylor and the motley elements he travelled with – the increments from the Inner Hebrides and the Riyadh agent. There were, of course, no written records of past conversations and he thought of Dickie as a kitchen rag hung out on a line at the mercy of the elements. Himself, no damn way would he have offered up so many hostages . . . Himself, he was near completion of an illustrious career, not one of mediocrity. He saw glasses being refilled, but not liberally, and moved to the side. He looked around, at the table from which the wine came, checked that the envelope was there, searched for a spoon with which to rap a glass and win attention . . . and saw Mary Reakes advance on him.

She said, as crisp and cold as frozen snow, 'At a personal level, I want you to know I'm not happy with our handling of events. I'm asking, which is my privilege, for a one-on-one with the director general.'

'It's not the time, Mary, and not the place for us to discuss your happiness.'

'Just thought you should know of my intentions before you dig yourself deeper into this cess-pit.'

'Always better if we stay on the same song sheet . . . Because of the nature of things, the DG's in tomorrow morning – I'm sure he'll fit you and your conscience into his schedule. Thank you for taking me into your confidence. Please excuse me, I've a speech to make.'

He lifted a spoon off the table and rapped the glass.

She laid out the clothes he would wear, placed each item on the plastic bag that held the waistcoat.

His eyes were on her, duller and without the brightness of the low candle's flame.

Last on the pile was the white T-shirt with the spitting swan on the front, where he would see its anger and defiance.

She sensed his weakness and knew what she must do.

She bent, cupped a hand on the flame, blew once, sharply, on it.

The flame wavered and was gone. She groped across the floor and crawled over the rumpled roll of the carpet, smelt it and gagged. Her fingers touched him. He flinched from her. It must be done or the weakness would overwhelm him.

It was where Faria had never been before, and she thought neither had he.

Her fingers were on his face, then caught at the back of his neck and she eased a knee over his legs. He did not struggle against her. She kissed him, his mouth against hers, his lips moist against hers. She pushed her tongue on to his teeth, forced his mouth wider. Her tongue licked the inside of him and she tasted the food she had brought back with the bucket. She wriggled tighter against him.

If it were not done, in the morning he might turn, or freeze, or run. It was to strengthen him.

Her hands came from his neck and slid down his body, so slight and frail, and across the bones that made the cage of his ribs, and came to his belt. She unfastened the belt, then the upper button of his trousers and drew down the zip. Her hands climbed again. She pulled the jersey off him and the shirt. She had to lift each arm because he did not help her. It was done so slowly, but the layers came off and then she could touch the expanse of the skin, and she sensed his heart pounding. She used her nails to make patterns on his now hairless chest – the same patterns that had been made on her skin by the man, and into the navel, as the man had done. She had said then: *It is never the leaders who make the sacrifice.* Had said in anger: *He is the one with true courage.* Her breath came faster, as the man had made it.

She broke the patterns. Faria took his hands and guided them under her upper clothing to her breasts. She bared herself and led his hands to the fastening clips on her back. He did not know how to do it. There were girls, white girls, on the streets near to the Dallow Road, not aged fifteen, who knew how to undress for a few seconds of writhing, and boys from near to the Dallow Road, not yet at their fifteenth birthday, who could have stripped her and unfastened each clip and each stud within moments . . . and she was twenty-four and the boy, she thought, was past twenty . . . and neither of them knew how. So they learned.

They learned. Her purpose in learning was that he would walk better in the morning – not stop, not cringe, not reject what was asked of him.

They fumbled, the one as inexpert as the other.

Clothing was taken off, dumped beside them. Her weight on her knees, her hips rose so that he could ease down her jeans, then her knickers. She took him in her hands, stroked him, felt the hardness grow, then pulled down his trousers. He was so hesitant, but so gentle. She guided him, placed him at the lips, then thrust down on to him. He gasped. He had his hands up now, on her small, shallow breasts, and they found the nipples and squeezed softly. He was deep in her and moved slowly under her. She felt the confidence, his and hers. She thought he moved slowly so as he might prolong the glory of it, make it last. She squirmed to tighten her muscles on him . . . It could not last for ever, not beyond the morning. He spoke words – little guttural cries – in a language she did not understand. She panted louder, abandoned the shyness that had been drilled into her youth, gasped and yelled. He drove up into her, heaved her body up, and she felt the strength, knew she had given it to him. At the end there was a shout. Faria could not have said if it was his or hers. Then a long sigh, hers and his.

She held him close. She felt his hands locked round her back.

His sweat was slick on her body, and hers on his.

It played in Faria's mind. Was it merely a mechanism to give him strength? Was it the same, the equivalent, of making a speech that inspired, as the recruiter had to her? She did not know . . . She heard his breathing soften and calm. She felt, inside her, that he shrank. In the morning, as she had been told to, she would walk with him and lead him to the place of his death – she would not see it. She would have gone from his side as he took the last several paces, and would head for the Dallow Road, and her home. Long before she reached the side-street off that road, she would have heard the explosion, the silence, then the scream of sirens. She would open the front door, greet her father – and tell him nothing. She would start to prepare lunch for her parents – as if she had not been away for sixteen days. She would tell them nothing and they would ask nothing, and she would go upstairs, sit with her mother and concoct lying anecdotes of days spent on the computer course. She would ask dutifully if there was news of her brothers, in Islamabad, students of religious studies. From the kitchen, she would hear the television baying out the news of an atrocity, and she would have returned to her sleep . . . She did not know if, ever again, she would be woken. That day, and the next, and the next week and the next month, she would be back at the drudgery of caring for her parents and . . . perhaps, one dawn, when she was in her bed and alone, she would hear the door cave in below her, and her room would be filled with masked, armed policemen, and rifles would be aimed at her, or perhaps she would be left to sleep.

She lay on him. His breathing was even and regular.

She could not stop the coming of the morning when she would help him to dress. Would she be damned by God, or praised for giving strength to him? She shivered, but felt his warmth.

The boy slept in her arms . . . and she wondered if the man thought of her and of where his hands had been, and if he would remember her.

He sat on a bench with the stars for company, and the moon's light. A man had come to the bench an hour before, had sat with him for less than two minutes, had gone. The man had come to the bench, past the hour of midnight. Would have come on each of three previous evenings. There had been relief on his face that the rendezvous was successful. He had been asked if it had gone well – he had shrugged, replied that the morning would give the answer. He had thought the man was perplexed that he displayed no enthusiasm . . . He had given the man the video-cassette, had seen it pocketed, had been promised that it would be moved on at speed. The man had kissed his cheek and left him. Muhammad Ajaq had shown no enthusiasm because he felt none . . . His work was elsewhere, and those he had been with had slipped from his mind – were worthless.

In front of him was the sea. He heard the rumble of the waves against the pillars of a pier, and beyond the quay was the harbour into which the ferry would sail. Ajaq dreamed because he felt himself free, already beyond reach.

Beside him, Naylor did not speak.

They were on big roads, empty freeways, and Hegner sat easily.

Near to the end – near enough for him to have rung far away Riyadh, to have roused Cindy from her bed, to have heard her voice, first drowsy, then alert, to have asked her to make the reservation for him to return the next evening. And she'd asked him, was it going well? 'Just fine,' he'd said, and had not cared that Naylor heard him. They went south. There was a phrase impregnated in his mind from child-hood. It was his grandfather's, used in the smithy where the community's ironwork was repaired, and where the bellows heated a fire for the shoeing of horses. He'd been a kid then, still near to Big Porcupine Creek, and had not yet gone to the high school at Forsyth, and his grandfather had softened the iron of the shoes in the bright charcoal, and had used the phrase for a certain type of horse. A horse that was not for riding but for dragging a cart or a light harrow, that was not pretty and not loved, was a 'useful beast'. A 'useful beast' had a purpose, and was willing. The car took him at speed towards the Twentyman.

It was his good fortune – and when he was back with Cindy he would tell her – to have met up with a 'useful beast'.

It was better fortune than laying the woman in Naylor's office, good but not great . . . It was his best good fortune to have met up with a 'useful beast' and harnessed him.

The farmer lay on his back and snored, and his wife had turned away from him. The clock in the hallway below, a fine piece handed down by his grandfather, struck the quarter-hour after midnight.

She allowed him to sleep because the evening's dispute was resolved. The stolen, burned bedding and towels would be replaced. Straight after breakfast he would do what he hated most and what she had coerced him into. They would take the Land Rover into town and go to the shopping centre, be there good and early, and would buy new sets at sale prices. Maybe she would beat him with the rod and make him try on new trousers.

Odd, what had happened, and no answer she could put to it.

The handler came off duty late.

The clock on the wall showed half past midnight. His dog was the only one allowed access to the canteen, and it sat expectantly by his chair and begged titbits.

A sergeant carried a tray to the table, sat, pulled a face. 'Reckon your Midge isn't the celebrity we thought.'

'What you mean?'

'Didn't you hear?'

'I didn't hear nothing.'

'Your joker – he walked.'

'Can't have.'

'Did. The swabs off the joker's hands went to the forensics laboratory. First they came up positive . . .'

'Of course they did . . . The dog was going bloody mad.'

'Second load of tests was done – came up negative.'

'That's not possible.'

'Heard it from the Branch office. The joker had no traces of explosive on his hands or on his clothes, so he walked. Your dog had it wrong.'

'What you telling me? You telling me my dog's no good? I won't have it. God, there's a year's training gone into Midge. The reaction didn't leave any room for it, not for a doubter. I can't credit it. That dog's alpha sharp. I'm not selling Midge short. If some smart-arse is telling me I don't know my job, that my dog gets explosives wrong, then I'm saying that something pretty damn bloody funny's abroad.'

'Maybe you're right, but I'm not expecting to hear what's funny.'

He lay stretched out on the settee.

He had been given a blanket, but Banks couldn't sleep.

The sounds from behind a thin wall reverberated round him.

He had been lied to but had not made a judgement. Nor did he make a judgement on the cries from beyond the wall or the squeak of the mattress. Served up to him on the same day: an untruth, a confession and a damned act of adultery – what the Delta guys called a bit of 'playing away', what his wife had done to him – but he thought of himself as too flawed to condemn . . . A man was shot in the chest, a man lay in the filth of a casualty clearing station, a man waited for the triage verdict, a man wrote in tiny halting script of the sniper who had shot him down: *I cannot hate him . . . Perhaps he is a good man . . . I think of him as being as far from home as I am,* a man's notebook diary, with one more page to be read. David Banks did not criticize his Principal, did not dare to.

They climaxed, the second time, noisier than the first.

Would they now, please, bloody well sleep?

He drifted . . . The weekend had arrived, tugged him towards Monday morning when he would be gone, forgotten and the loss of him unmourned . . . What stayed with him, tossed him awkward on the settee, was the charity for an enemy: *I think of him as being as far from home as I am*. Banks thought the charity of Cecil Darke showed true humility and courage, was that of a man who was brave and principled.

He knew he wouldn't sleep, would be exhausted – fit for nothing – when the new day dawned . . . and that was fine because he didn't have anything to be fit for.

Chapter 18: Saturday, Day 17

The sight was locked. The shape of the man's upper body, chest and head filled the telescopic lens. The finger was off the guard and on to the trigger bar. The squeeze started, with gentle pressure . . . The man had no face. At the base of the lens' view was a cardboard box. Perhaps the man paused for a moment to gather breath, perhaps had forgotten that the parapet of sandbags was lower there, that he was exposed. The sniper prepared himself for the recoil at his shoulder, and its bruising power. The man he would shoot had no face.

His mobile rang.

The sniper had been with him through the night. If he had slipped towards sleep, escaped from the marksman, the clock's chimes in the town had shaken him back to the image. On the settee, with the blanket rucked up and scarcely covering him, he had lived with the sniper in the darkness hours.

Reaching down, Banks fumbled for his mobile and found it underneath his trousers and the belt that held the pancake holster. He answered.

'Right, found you. Wally here. Banksy, where the hell are you?'

He said the name of the town.

'Banksy, what's going on? I can't sleep, got an itch in my bum. I call the location, just a check and just doing my job – not intending to wake you. The location night-duty bugger tells me all's quiet, then adds you're not there, or the top Tango . . . What, in God's name, are you doing off camp with no clearance from me? I gave an OK for a few hours, not an overnight. What's going on? Am I asking something unreasonable? I don't think so.'

He lied, and it didn't seem a big deal. The lie was that the ailments of his Principal 's sick mother and father had worsened. A mercy call, and really necessary to be there through the night.

They'd started up again in the bedroom. Banks could hear them through the thin wall and the thinner door – grunts, groans, a mattress heaving – and he cupped his hand round the mouthpiece of the mobile so that his chief inspector would hear only the quiet of a house of the sick and the ill. He said he hadn't telephoned because he hadn't wanted to distract his superior from the planning of a kid's birthday party.

'If that's not impertinent, Banksy, I don't know what is. That's bloody cheek. If I don't know where my people are, it reflects on me. It makes me a prat, which I don't like, an inefficient prat.'

He said that he took responsibility for his decision, and that this morning the patients seemed in better health and that he hoped the kid's birthday party would go well.

'You have an attitude problem, Banksy. That's what I was told, that's what I've found out for myself. Here's a fact of life: you were assigned to us because you weren't wanted on serious business. There's a major bloody alert on. Every gun in the goddamn force is out on the streets, that's the word, but not you. You were not wanted because you have a problem. Don't think this won't be reported. I gave you support and my reward is that you've shat on me . . . Go back to your bloody beauty sleep and, when it's *convenient,* take your Tango back where he's supposed to be – and don't move a bloody inch without my say-so . . . You there, Banksy?'

The groans of the mattress had become squeals, shrieks. He lied again, said a doctor was due to call when the working day started and would give Mr Wright an all-clear on his parents. Then he would take the Tango back to the location. Again he wished the chief inspector well for the kid's party.

'You're a plonker, Banksy, a useless plonker and a—'

He cut the call, dropped the mobile back on to his trousers, on to the holster. And they finished. A last gasp, a final shout, and bloody finished. He lay on his back and his thoughts returned to where they had been previously.

He was with the sniper.

What had been with him through the night were the calculations the marksman would have made . . . Four years back, they'd done a course with paratroops out on the Brecon Beacons, and there had been a sergeant instructor who'd talked them through a sniper's skills. Wasn't relevant to Banks, but he'd listened. It was more for SO19 gun people who might carry a rifle and be put on rooftops for a state occasion or be tasked into a siege situation. He'd thought, before he listened, that a sniper had a damn great 'scope on the barrel that did the work. He'd heard about the mathematics of 'wind deflection' and 'bullet drop', and he'd been shown the little laminated charts that listed the equations. The sergeant had talked about the need to watch a flag's motion or the bend of trees, and how an aim might be at a roof gutter when the target was lounged by a ground-floor door, or by sunshine or snow. He had learned of the experience and skills of the sniper, which overrode a pocket calculator . . . and a target could be hit at a thousand paces. During the night he had set himself behind the 'scope sight and had seen the last of the autumn's dead leaves blowing between the pocked shell-holes of Hill 421 across the Ebro valley, and paper scraps carried by the summer wind. The sniper had used his skills and experiences, the same as the sergeant instructor's, to fire the bullet into the chest of Cecil Darke. He could not see his great-uncle's face. The sniper had. The sergeant instructor, men quiet around him and listening to an expert, said that the sniper – among his own – was a hated man. Shrapnel from an artillery shell, a mortar bomb's splinters or the bullets from a traversing machine-gun carried random death. The sniper looked into the features of his target, saw the magnified eyes, saw the chest where a heart beat and where a photograph of a loved one was pocketed, made a judgement and fired. Could he? Could he look into the face, through the 'scope, of a stranger and make him familiar and take the time to know him, then kill him?

Play God – could he?

He rolled off the settee.

The apartment was still. Beyond the thin wall and the thinner door, they were spent.

He found, at last, a way to lose the image of the finger on the rifle's trigger bar.

Banks took the magazine from the Glock, then the magazines that were housed in the holdall. He began, carefully and methodically, to empty them. He laid the bullets out on the back of his shirt, beside his trousers, made four little piles of them. It was a therapy, of no purpose but to clear his mind. Then he reloaded the magazines, pressed each bullet down against the spring. It was the routine of his working life, what he did each morning before going on duty. Unthinking, hands moving mechanically, Banks filled the four magazines and placed three in his holdall, and one in his pistol. He worked a bullet into the breach, checked the safety, put the Glock into the holster.

It was worth doing. The procedure was not so that he was proof against a jam of the firing mechanism but to clear his mind. Through the curtains, not closed completely, the dawn was coming. Later he would read the last page of the notebook, but he had succeeded, had lost sight of the sniper's finger that whitened as the pressure on the trigger grew.

The room was lighter, but Banks slept.

Also waking that morning and preparing for the coming day . . .

In the second bedroom of his mother's housing-association home, out in the Leagrave district of the town, Lee Donkin shivered as he dressed. The tremors were not from the cold: he had not injected brown into his veins last night, or the last day, not for fucking near a week. He did not pad to the bathroom, did not wash and had not run a brush across his teeth. He dragged on yesterday's sweatshirt over yesterday's vest, and yesterday's jeans over yesterday's pants, and yesterday's socks. From the floor he took his anorak with the hood and slipped into it, then prised his feet into his trainers. He could not control the shake and shouted an obscenity, but was not heard. He did not know where his mother was, from which pub she had been taken home by a punter. If she had been there she would have yelled back a curse from her room for waking her . . . She was not often there. He went to the kitchen, took bread from the bin, ignored the pale green mould on the crusts, and wolfed it down, but it had little effect on the shivering. He heard the couple who lived above them already rowing, and the baby next door was crying. He lifted up a chair from beside the kitchen table, and banged against the ceiling with its legs. Now he went to the bathroom and wrapped his hand in his anorak's sleeve. He stood on the lavatory seat and stretched himself up to the old cistern high on the wall and reached inside. He retrieved a short-bladed knife from the hiding-place in which it was taped. It went into his pocket. Later, before he left, he would rummage in the debris – clothing, fast-food plastic plates and syringes – on the floor of his room for his gloves, lightweight leather. His hands would never touch the handle of his favoured knife. He was too smart, too switched on, to give prints or DNA if he was done on the street with a stop-and-search. Just found it, hadn't he, just picked it up in the street and just going to hand it in, wasn't he? They had an operation going, the police had, and called it Failsafe, but they hadn't netted him, too smart and switched on. Because he craved the brown, Lee Donkin needed a snatch that morning – on the way to the shopping centre in the square and the sale when purses were loaded – needed it bad.

Avril Harris crawled from her bed, stumbled to the bathroom. All through the night, she had festered the anger that she had been sold short, had bought a car that was already broken. She had been out the previous evening for a curry with three of the other girls from A and E, and she'd been the one who hadn't drunk a beer or three and had given two of them a lift back. Every time she'd slowed at the damn lights, the backfire had gone. A hell of a noise. Hadn't frightened the others, with beer inside them, but had made them laugh hysterically. They had laughed at her car, when it should have been her pride and joy. In the bathroom, under the shower, her anger slackened. She thought through her day ahead ... Up and out and into the car, bloody thing. A drive into the town and at the multi-storey car park around nine, and into the shopping centre a few minutes after ... Wasn't going to hit the mad rush for the opening of the doors. Into work by eleven. If it hadn't been for the car – sluicing herself under the shower's rose – it would have been a day to look forward to.

His alarm, old-fashioned with a clapper bell, woke Steve Vickers. His had been a good, dreamless sleep. Off to the bathroom and he ran the piping-hot water. He was content, as close to happiness other than when he had an attentive audience round him. Without his daily bath he would have been – his opinion – a lesser, unfulfilled man. Living alone, he had no queue outside the door, no one to bang it and urge him to hurry. He lay among the suds and talked to himself, aloud, of the history he would impart that morning. He believed that what he did in bringing history alive was valuable, couldn't imagine anything else he might achieve had greater value. He lingered, ran more hot water, had time enough before he met his audience in the town square.

George Marriot's sister shook him awake. She gazed down at him and he recognized the affection that linked them. He assumed that at the pub – could not be otherwise – his life with his spinster sister was a source of sniggering amusement. She was already dressed. They would laugh in the pub, when he had gone out through the door and had started on his walk home with his sticks to aid him, that they were two lonely, misplaced souls, the flotsam rejects of ordinary life . . . They knew sod all . . . She was always up at five and she always woke him at six. He could get to the bathroom without the support of the sticks. There was a line made by his hands along his room's wallpaper, along the corridor and into the bathroom. In former times, it was him that would have risen at five, but they were gone. He used the shower, always cold water falling on him. It took him back to the days of the camps at Kandahar and Jalalabad, when the dawn peeped up over the mountains and fighting men prepared for their day . . . and the scars on his legs still puckered and were deep blue where the surgeons had probed for detritus. The chill of the shower invigorated him, gave scope to his memories of the best of days . . . One cloud, always one bloody cloud in a sky of clear blue. The petty remarks about his shirt – true, but should not have been said – had hurt, were wounds. When he had eaten his breakfast of kedgeree – egg, fish and rice, she cooked it for him every day of the week – he would go down to the village, take the bus to the town, buy three shirts in the sale and, with luck, still have change from a twenty-pound note and bring flowers for her back with him. The water ran on his skin, as it had done when it had dripped from an elevated oil drum and he'd hunted men for bounty, when his life had had purpose. The long-nurtured memories gave him comfort.

362

'He'll have slept rough,' Hegner said.

'Joe, I'm already about a light year's miles beyond any authority I once owned. I'm outside. Hours back, the card I swipe at the door of Riverside Villas will have been made invalid. If we lose this, I'm done for.' Dickie Naylor would be anyway, and he knew it.

He heard the snort of derision. 'I've gotten the feeling you're a man who sees his glass as always half empty. Buck up, Dickie, tell me where we are.'

His boys, the elderly Boniface and Clydesdale, were in their car and the glow of their cigarettes lit their faces, so passive and calm, as if what had gone before was past history, worthless. Not so with Naylor. He seemed to hear the screams, had heard them while he drove south and west. They were the same, piercing, as those of the gulls that had flown from the water when the first of the dawn's smear was on the horizon.

Naylor said, 'We're facing the sea.'

'I feel it on me.'

'About two hundred yards to the right of us is the entrance to the ferry terminal. Two entrances, for vehicles and foot-passengers. Nearest to us is the foot-passengers' gate. Going on from the terminal is the commercial area, warehouses and company offices, but that's all fenced off. Then there are cliffs that go out to the big headland. We're on the esplanade, that's the walkway between the road and the beach. The road is well lit, but not the walkway. The lights are aimed away from it. There are benches and—'

'Not a tourist brochure, Dickie, stick with the programme.'

Asked, with acid, 'What time is your flight?'

'Time enough for this to have finished – and don't you worry, Dickie, you're going to be a hero. Take me left.'

There was a low mist on the beach, hovering at the edge of the esplanade. He described it. He could see a pier, supported by pillars against which waves broke, a haze clinging round it.

'Am I getting on your nerves, Dickie? Don't mean to. I would have traded my right ball, right anything, in exchange for the sight of two good eyes. You're a friend to me. How far is the pier and what's beyond it?'

Naylor softened. He realized it now: the American's hand was loose on his arm. He could not imagine it, the darkness that was for always, and shuddered. He peered down the esplanade, squinted – damn tired from the drive and he hadn't slept in a bed for so bloody long, and tomorrow was his sixty-fifth birthday, and then he was as washed up as the weed the waves lifted – and said that there were more benches and a shelter hut. He told of all he saw.

Naylor's arm was held in a firmer grip. The voice rattled, as if the cold was in Hegner's throat. 'He'll have slept rough, depend on it, but stayed in sight of the sea. He has to see the boat come in, unload its people. Then he's within sight of safety. Don't reckon he's gone to the right, where you say it's commercial, because there'll be cameras there and security men and it won't be a place he can loiter. He'll want to seem like a vagrant, a drifter, and that's a bench or a shelter. Go into his mind. Right at this moment the ferry coming in is the single most important item in his life. The boat is freedom. He will be travelling alone . . . That kind of man, trusting damn near nobody, believes he is safest when solitary – on foot. Will see the boat come in, see it disembark its people, will come walking . . . Dickie, take my advice and I'll promise the red carpet out in front of you, except there'll be a fence round it so nobody sees you.'

He was beyond fighting, went with the flow. He was the bureaucrat who accepted orders. Had done all his life, could not change on the eve of a birthday.

'You don't have a photograph, don't even have a description.'

'It'll be the way he walks. How many male foot-passengers? A dozen or twenty? How many of them in the demographic window? Five or ten? But only he, the Twentyman, will walk in a way that betrays him.'

'Shuffling? Nervous, hesitant?'

'You're a mile off, Dickie. He's a leader. He's a man who has come, done his business. He's a captain of war, and is going back to familiar territory. He'll think not as a fugitive but as the guy who fucked you over. He'll walk as a leader does, like a captain. We go down from here towards that pier. We sit there and we wait. Each man who comes, you tell me how he walks. That'll be good enough for me.'

The gulls came over Naylor, and the wind freshened on his face. He searched the sea's horizon for the ferry-boat but saw only the pink of the sky on the grey of the sea. The car started up, U-turned in the road beyond the esplanade and headed off past the empty benches and the shelter hut. It stopped level with the pier. Naylor strode after them, and the beat of the waves against the pillars grew in his ears.

The lights, when Ajaq first saw them, were blurred in the mist.

The dawn grew bolder. A wetness from the night hours had settled on him and the damp hung on his face and hands. It was too soon for him to move, to leave the bench. He would have preferred rain and cloud low over the shoreline and the harbour because grey gloom dulled men's senses. He wanted them dulled when he reached the queue for the foot-passengers, when his passport was examined by men who yawned, fidgeted and shivered. A cleaning cart came behind him, the brushes scouring up rubbish from the gutter beside the esplanade's kerb. The first cars of the morning were on the road. A woman crossed it with a dog on a leash and took the animal down to the shingle and sand below him; he watched the dog squat close to the surf.

Now he could see the ferry clearly. Its decks were floodlit, its navigation lights flashed, its portholes and picture windows blazed. It came steadily on towards the harbour's marker buoys.

Twisting, as he had often done in the night since the man had come to him and taken the video-cassette, Ajaq stared up the straight road at his back. He was able to see, from the bench, the brilliantly illuminated sign and the wash of light round it at the harbour's entrance. If the place was staked out, if they watched for him, he would have noted columns of men disgorged from vans. When the Americans came to raid a safe-house, half of a battalion was deployed. Each time he had turned to look, he had seen only a few cars and more long-distance lorries tugging trailers behind them . . . and they did not have his photograph, he knew it.

The boat ploughed past the nearer buoy, where a red light showed. Then it turned on its own length and began to reverse towards a low light at the extreme end of a breakwater. He reached into his pocket, as he had many times, and felt reassurance as his fingers touched the slim shape of the ticket. He stretched on the bench, arched his back. It was nearly time, a few minutes more, for him to move.

He felt regrets.

Regret that he had not taken more time to toughen the mind of the Saudi boy, to prepare him better. In the country where he fought – and the boat would take him on the first step of his journey to return there – he had satisfied himself that a cuff on the shoulder and the murmur, always the same, of 'God waits for you, God loves you, God will give you virgins', the briefest of brush kisses on the cheeks was enough. And the Engineer, checking the wiring on a belt or to a switch on the dashboard, would have told the idiot that failure would mean torture by the Americans and worse torture from the collaborators, the Shi'a Iraqis. Should he have done more?

Regret that he had not organized classes in the cottage for the cell. Not classes in indoctrination and Faith, but on resistance to inter-rogation, of the procedures to counter surveillance, of the making of explosive devices, of the chemicals to be mixed if commercial and military dynamite could not be obtained, of the selection of targets . . . but he had thought them imbeciles and not to be trusted, except the girl with the scar on her face and the smooth skin on her belly.

And regret that he had not gone far to the north and found a man alive or dead, that he had not gone to the door of a small retirement house and confronted, with fury and violence, his father, or had gone to a cemetery and kicked down a gravestone, had not, on the step or by the grave, spoken the name of his mother. It would never happen now, and that was the most wounding of the regrets.

The hull of the boat rose over the breakwater, dwarfed it. When he was on board, when the coastline – and there would be sunshine on it – faded, he would be on a remote corner of a deck. He would not use the canteen self-service or sit in a public area. He would find a place where the wind blustered cold and where passengers did not come, sit alone there with his thoughts, and the regrets would be gone. It would be two hours after the sailing that the boy walked into the square, went towards the crowds waiting for the doors to be opened. He would be on the deck, with the boat's wake stretching out behind him and the dark line of land barely seen, when the boy died.

The woman with her dog came off the shingle and sand, used steps that were close to him. She walked past him, then stopped, smiled. 'I think it's going to be a fine day,' she said. 'The sort of day it makes one glad to be alive.'

And she walked away.

Ajaq killed more minutes, and the light brightened the paving slabs of the esplanade, glimmered prettily on the sea's waves, and he felt the first traces of the sun's warmth.

Pricks of light, and zebra lines of it, crept through the holes in the plywood over the windows and the gaps between the planks nailed across the door.

She had not slept. She had held him.

She did not want to move, to wake him.

He had cried out in the night, twice. He had used the Arabic language that she could not understand. She did not know whether he called for God, or for his family, but it was not for her. Each time, to calm him, she had wrapped her arms tighter round him and had let her nakedness warm him.

He was still now and his breathing was quiet. His head was against her, cradled in her arms. Faria did not know whether she would be cursed or praised. She had been told to give him love and had done so. He was at peace.

She did not want him to wake, but could lie there no longer. She extricated herself.

Ashamed of deceit, no glow of pride, she moved first the arm that was above her shoulder and round her neck. Then the arm that reached across the small of her back, and the hand over her hair. His eyes did not open. So slowly, she eased away from him. She rolled on to the floor, felt the bare boards and a protruding nail gouged her buttock. She went on to her hands and knees and crawled clear of him.

He did not stir, slept on. He had not touched her scar – had never gazed at it. He had shown no sign that the scar – a motor accident in a cousin's van, on early-morning ice – frightened or disgusted him. Every other man she had known in the Dallow Road, and all those in the cottage, had stared so blatantly at it, as if it repelled them. He, in spite of the scar, had loved her. For that, she believed she owed him more than he owed her.

Tears came to her eyes. She convulsed, wept . . . She was a whore, she betrayed him ... The *imam* who had recruited her, twenty months ago, had said before she was sent away to sleep, 'Much may be asked of you. Only the most strong and dedicated are capable of doing what is asked of them. Are you?' She had sworn she was. Her strength and dedication was to sleep, body to body, him inside her, until she had given what was asked of her. She swallowed hard, and used her wrist fiercely against her face to wipe the tears. She had been, through one night, loved.

Light, spots and lines, lay on his body.

She dressed, then rooted in her bag. She lifted clear from it the black robe, the *jilbab*, that would cover her from neck to ankles, then searched for and found a deep grey scarf, the *dupatta*, that would mask her neck and hair and would be drawn across her face. But Faria did not yet dress in the *jilbab* and the *dupatta*, would not make them filthy.

He slept and her movements threw glancing shadows on to his skin. He seemed to reach out for her, not find her, and his arm subsided, but he did not wake. In two hours his life would be over – finished, destroyed – and she thought it good that he slept. She slid on her shoes. What should she tell him at the last? What were the last words she would speak to him before she slipped away, left him? Awake, him holding her and her holding him, she had rehearsed what she would say ... She took the new bucket and went to the door.

Faria heaved open the loose plank. It groaned. She thought he must wake, but he did not.

She crawled through the hole. The back of her T-shirt caught a wood splinter, and she wriggled to free herself.

Looking around her, up at the windows of the houses on either side, out into the gardens beyond the broken fencing, Faria saw that she was not watched. She took the top from the rain butt, lowered the bucket into it, filled it and saw the swirling scum. She replaced the top, and went back into the dark and the damp of the room, through the hole and worked the bucket after her.

He slept, but soon she would wake him – must.

'Tell me about the way men walk, describe to me every inch of their faces.'

368

'Yes, Joe – same as the last time you asked me.'

The low sunlight made jewels on the wave caps, but Naylor sat beside Joe Hegner in the recesses of the shelter hut where the sun did not penetrate. It was more than an hour since he had last rung his assistant director . . . Nothing to add that was new. Neither had he rung home . . . Nothing to say. They were in place as the American had demanded. A hundred yards west along the esplanade was the pier, and the tide must have reached its high point: the sea lapped the top of the pillars then fell back and tossed up weed. Set in the middle of the esplanade, level with the pier, was a foot-high brick square in which Parks and Gardens had planted shrubs and along-side it were the boys, Boniface and Clydesdale, in their car. A further thousand yards, Naylor's approximation, down the esplanade was the entrance to the ferry-port, where the big boat now unloaded articulated lorries from its bow ramp. A man came towards them, pushing a pram in which a baby yelled.

'He's fifty. A grandfather, maybe. Caucasian. It'll be the daughter's kid and howling.'

'Thank you, Dickie. I'm not deaf as well.'

A minute passed. He had no conversation, nor did it seem expected of him. Hegner sat beside him, hunched, alert, and he had the stick upright between his legs and leaned his chin on it. Another man came.

'Little chap, could be forties, but he's all wrapped up. Has a fishing bag on his shoulder and—'

'Thank you, Dickie.'

Another minute slipped. No, Dickie Naylor would not have said he was near to panic, would have denied *panic*. But his gut was tightening and his hands clasped and unclasped, and he shifted his weight continually on the slats of the shelter seat, and his eyes ached from peering ahead. Not yet panic, but closing on it. Thoughts raced, jumbled, in his mind. A bomber would strike and he didn't know where – a cell member, a junior, under torture, had supposedly spoken of a ticket and where it would be used and at what time – a gamut of arrogance and egocentricity and the chase for a career's legacy had put him, Dickie bloody Naylor, into the palm of the American.

'Two lads, around twenty. Big rucksacks. One is Caucasian and one is Afro-Caribbean. Look to be half pissed . . . students.'

'Thank you, Dickie.'

If Hegner was close to a similar state of panic, he showed none of it. Not even apprehension. He had started to hum a tune. One of those sickly sweet, sentimental songs that were played on the radio at this time, as Anne cooked his breakfast with that station on her radio. Irritation swarmed in Naylor, was kept with difficulty in check. The humming lilted on. He imagined consequences. Men and women of the Internal Investigation Branch, grim-faced and no understanding of the reality of pressures, would come out of the dark burrows, would examine the logs for details of the release of a prisoner, would confiscate mobile telephones and locate the source place of calls, would dig down into the earth, drag away concrete debris and uncover a body wrapped tight in plastic, would check the tasking of an RAF helicopter and . . . God, it was a bloody nightmare. He saw himself confronted in a police station's interview room by Branch officers – probably would know them, but no damn chance they'd acknowledge previous association. Heard the caution given. A bloody nightmare like no other. The American had said that a red carpet would be unrolled for him. Naylor doubted it. He gazed away, as far as his eyes could focus, along the length of the esplanade. Didn't believe in red bloody carpets. Saw emptiness, no one coming. He stamped his feet, beat a tattoo with his shoes. He flinched as the first of the sun's strength slid into that corner of the shelter hut and the light bounced on Hegner's darkened spectacles. He shifted again and let the breath, his frustration, whistle in his teeth.

The humming stopped. 'Calm yourself, Dickie. He'll come.'

'There's no one coming.'

'Think of the glass as half full. Just keep describing the faces and the walk.'

'Time is cut fine, they'll be starting to board. Where you said, there's no man coming.'

Naylor saw the wide smile, thought it was meant to belittle him. 'Your problem, Dickie, is that you let your worries get on top of you. Believe me, he will come, right here and right past us.'

They were approaching the last turn-off from the motorway. Then, with their sirens and lights, they would have a clear run into Birmingham's city centre.

'I mean, it's like Daff said when we were back there and drawing the gear . . . It's a pin in a damn haystack. He's God's definition of a great comforter.'

'Maybe they should have closed up the whole damn place.'

'Can't lock down an entire city. So the centre's closed and *he*, slimy little sod, goes somewhere else, where people are.'

'Don't see how we can win.'

Some talked quietly, some read their magazines but interjected. There was no bravado, no joshing and crack.

'We have the photograph, and we have this daft bloody bird on the T-shirt. But *he*'ll wear a baseball cap, and have something over the T-shirt, stands to reason, to hide the belt.'

'Remember that briefing last year – I'm not trying to be funny – that business about the smile? The Israelis say they all seem to smile. They're smiling before they go off to screw those virgins.'

'Can't shoot every Asian lad who's in the city centre and bloody smiling. Bloody ridiculous.'

The Delta team were in the lead Transit and behind them were Golf and Kilo.

'Got to be a head shot, double tap and hollow nose rounds. Only place where there isn't a spasm is the head. Chest, even straight through the heart, and *his* hand's on the button switch, and up the shebang goes.'

'A head shot with a Glock at ten paces – it's a miracle. How you going to use the H&K, a crowded street and all that crap? *He* sees you aim, and you have to, and presses the tit, and it's curtains time.'

'At ten paces, if you don't drop *him*, blow *his* effing head off – and *his* finger's on the switch, you go with *him* – but you don't get the women like *he* does.'

'Best thing to hope for, pray for, *he's* not on my bit of pavement.'

They would be on the streets, along with every gun from West Midlands and Mercia, Warwick, Greater Manchester and South Yorkshire, before the shops and offices opened. The big man of Delta, the nick on his earlobe well healed, tried with gallows humour to break the Transit's pessimistic mood. 'You got it all wrong, guys, you haven't figured it. What to do is get out a bloody great bullhorn and shout into it. What you shout is: "Anyone here with a rucksack or a big belt that's heavy, take your hands out of your pockets, and raise

371

them over your head if you're brave and principled" . . . How's that?'

'Don't mention that jammy bastard, just don't.'

'Because he's history.'

The sirens and the lights took them fast through the traffic, and into the city's suburbs.

The first of the management and shop staff were let in through the side door.

There had been a bad Christmas and a dead New Year of trading. Few did not appreciate the importance of the sale as a way of jacking up the turnover of the brand-name stores at the centre.

Lights flickered on, lit the shelves and counters, piers and interior window displays.

The managers began to check the tags with old prices crossed out and new prices highlighted. The shop staff started to tidy the stock they had dumped in place after closing the previous evening.

A commercial-radio DJ, from a local station, was booked to declare the sale open.

Although it was more than an hour before the outer doors would be unlocked, a small knot of customers was already gathered on the steps that led up from the square, but the feeling, and the hope, of management and staff was that, by the magic hour, the steps would be packed tight and the queues would stretch away towards the town hall.

'I'm feeling good,' the centre's chief executive told whoever had time to listen to him as he walked the aisles. 'Quite honestly, I don't reckon the start of the Third World War would keep them away.'

He had been to the bathroom, had used the shower and found a razor in the cupboard over the basin.

He'd dressed. Always carried with him in the holdall a clean shirt in a plastic bag and a pair of clean socks. Had to rifle deep down among his gear for them. The shirt was crumpled from burial under the grenade canisters, the first-aid box and the ballistic blanket, but hadn't been ironed anyway after its wash at the launderette in the high street near his bedsit. Trousers on and belt buckled, he'd touched the holster with the pistol in it, as a man did to be certain he had his wallet or a handkerchief in his pocket, or his cigarettes and lighter ... had knotted his tie. He'd felt decent, like he could face another day. Banks punched the settee cushions back to shape and folded the blanket he'd been given, made it neat.

There was movement behind the thin wall, and he heard their low voices beyond the thinner door.

She came out, closed the door behind her. 'Morning, Mr Banks. Looks like a nice one. You sleep well?'

'Thank you, yes. Can't remember when I slept better.'

She was coy, rolled her eyes. 'We didn't disturb you?'

'No, not at all. A big battle wouldn't have, slept great.'

She wore only an old rugby shirt, faded red hoops on a faded blue background, a trophy, he assumed, and it stretched down to her upper thighs. Oh, yes, and flip-flops on her feet. It was too long for him to remember when he had last seen Mandy with that same satisfied, well-screwed look – and tired eyes that still held mischief, and the grin ... There had not been another woman since his wife had gone.

'I was just going to make a pot of tea.'

'Thank you, I'd like that.'

'And do some breakfast, the full works.'

'Brilliant.'

'And what's the rest of your day?'

'Take him back where we came from.' He added, his voice dry but his expression impassive, 'Take him back after he's been to visit his sick parents ...'

'He's a lying bastard,' she said.

'... then field the flak about escorting him away from the location for an overnight, put my feet up, then we're all off on a bus outing for the afternoon. It's an all right sort of day.'

'Actually, he's a complete shit,' she said, matter-of-fact.

She went to the bathroom. He sat on the settee and reached to take a magazine from a side-table. He started to read about a film star he'd not heard of, and the making of a film he'd never see. The toilet flushed. So bored, so unfulfilled, so wrecked. She went from the bathroom to the kitchen, and he doubted she regretted calling her bed-partner a shit. Turned more pages and started to scan a profile on a couple who had renovated a castle in west Wales, and were younger than him, and had spent a half-million on consultants and

373

builders. So worthless, so inadequate. He heard the whistle of a kettle and the clink of crockery. Read about a seashore holiday let in Barbados, with guest chalets, that cost for a week's rental – without flights – what he was paid for seven months' work. Felt so bloody *useless*, washed up and a spare part that had been discarded. The mug was placed on the table beside him. Sausages had started to sizzle and hiss in the kitchen. Carelessly, he chucked the magazine on to the side-table and a little of the tea slopped from the mug on to its surface. He wiped it clean with his handkerchief.

'And a very good morning to you, Mr Banks. Sleep well?'

His Principal was behind him, in the doorway, wore only his underpants.

'Very well.'

No drop in the pitch of his voice. 'I tell you, no messing, she goes at it like a bloody tiger. Right, first I'm off for a crap and a bath and a scrape.'

'What's second?'

'Second I go for my little walk.'

'Where to?'

'Into the town.'

'What for?'

'God, are we playing the professional? I go into town, after a night of shagging – always the same routine – for a packet of fags and the day's newspaper. Then, if you want to know, she has my breakfast ready and I eat it and read my newspaper. Then it's over for another week. It's not all bad, you know.'

'Just tell me when you're ready.'

'You don't have to come with me into town. I'll be fine. Five minutes there and five minutes back, not a big deal. It's only to a newsagent's on the square.'

'If you didn't know it,' Banks said, irritation rising, 'it's why I'm here.'

'Christ, aren't we dedicated?'

Chapter 19: Saturday, Day 17

He waited for his Principal to be dressed, to appear.

Banks paced the living room, could hear the breakfast cooking.

He had opened a window and freshened the room.

He strode the length of the carpet, or the width of it, varied his steps, did the settee to the hallway door and the window to the kitchen. Sunlight came in off Inkerman Road, and he wanted to be outside where there was cleanness, not the old smell of his body that still hung in the room. No, he had no objection to walking into the town and stretching himself; it was what he often did from the bed-sit, tramped the streets round the green in Ealing to settle himself before taking the Underground into work. It was the habit of long ago, of childhood, to take the collie out and walk the perimeter of a couple of fields, have the dog sniff at fox holes and badgers' setts before collecting his satchel and going up the lane to the stop and the school bus ... When it was over, next Monday morning, and his letter, his card and his authorization were dumped on his superior's desk, he would be gone and free to walk till he dropped in mountain valleys and beside great lakes and across desert spaces. He stopped, and could not have said why.

On one side of him the breakfast cooked and he heard her washing up the last night's meal; on the other, behind the door, his Principal whistled to himself and was dressing.

Banks was alone, unseen.

Not for much longer, maybe for the last time, he did the drills.

Jacket on, coins and pebbles and the notebook in the right-side pocket that hung heavily. The target was the door into the hallway.

Swung on his hips, threw back the weight of his pocket, right hand dropping to the Glock. The Glock out of the pancake. Weight on his toes, feet apart, went to Isosceles. Arms outstretched, hands clamped together on the Glock's butt, the right hand's forefinger on the trigger guard. Over the needle sight and V sight was the door – was a bank thief, an assassin, a guy holding a kid in his arms. Did it again and again, and – heard her.

'For Heaven's sake, is it that serious?'

Slapped the Glock back into the pancake, felt the glow of his blush. 'Sorry – did I frighten you? I was just grandstanding. Is there that much danger?'

He felt the tension ooze away, and the blood from his cheeks. 'It's only a precaution. I apologize, you shouldn't have seen that.'

'I'm not a fool, please. I know what things cost. I assume, and you'll not deny it, that you don't come cheap – that the danger's real, and the threat.'

'We try to minimize them.'

'You're telling me that people would want to kill Jools.'

Banks said, 'Money was proffered, was taken, and people believed that a promise was given in return. The promise was broken and the payment was reported to the judge. Mr Wright has made lifelong enemies and their aim now will be to track him down, hurt him a great deal, then murder him. The two brothers involved will receive, if they are convicted, exceptionally heavy terms of imprisonment, locked away in maximum-security cells. Mr Wright will be the target of their demand for revenge, and they'll be obsessed by it. They have money and they have contacts. They will ensure that Mr Wright is hunted down. I have to tell you, Miss, that your association with him puts you into the front line. We're around, mob-handed, till the verdict and, hopefully, the sentence. After that, Mr Wright and his family, and you, become increasingly vulnerable – budgets are assessed and are not bottomless pits. That's what it's about.'

'Actually, I'm throwing him out.'

'I told it like it is.'

'It's over, nothing to do with you.'

'That, Miss, is not my business.' Banks shrugged.

'Good sex and going nowhere. I have a transfer, a chance to start something new. Like I said, he's a lying bastard and more fool me for hanging on too long. I'm going to tell him after breakfast. Would you shoot to protect him, knowing what he is?'

He paused, turned away from her, faced the window and the sun dazzled him. 'While I draw my wages, I do what is necessary in my job.'

Ajaq moved, left the bench behind him.

He did not walk on the open esplanade, but went down the steps where the woman and her dog had gone.

His head was level with the top of the retaining wall that separated the walkway from the beach. The dried stones of the shingle, above where the tide pushed the surf, crackled, crunched, under his feet.

Caution was inbred in him. He cursed the noise he made, but went quickly, had estimated how long it would take him to walk the beach, go past the shelter ahead, then climb back to skirt the pier, descend again for the kilometre to the harbour's entrance. He would arrive when the checks took place for foot-passengers' tickets and passports in the last five minutes before the gates closed on the ferry's sailing schedule. Going this way, on the shingle and with the wall alongside him, he minimized the chance of being observed. If men sitting in a car on the far side of the road beyond the esplanade, or in the back of a van, were waiting for him, he did not think he would be seen. He had no reason to believe that surveillance teams were in place, but suspicion was a habit he would not break.

He smelt the tang from the sea. His feet crushed brittle shells. He checked the luminous face of his watch to see how many minutes remained to him to reach the harbour's gates . . . not to know how many minutes remained before the boy jostled for a position among the queue on the steps he had been shown. His mind was focused, clear of detritus.

In front of him he saw the roof of the shelter, and bright sunlight played on the faces of two elderly men. One had darkened spectacles, and they sat in silence. He dismissed them. Further ahead, beyond the shelter, was the black outline of the pier, and the waves broke against the pillars to which weed was attached. Near to the pier were more steps that he must climb.

Sudden fear caught him. He wanted to run. It was the sight of the pier and the shadowed depths below it, the slurp of the water against the pillars. He could not see under it because none of the sun's low brilliance reached there. Further out, at the end of the pier, the waves broke with force and tossed spume. He had no knowledge of the sea. In childhood, in northern Jordan and at the home of his grand-parents, he had never been taken to the resort town of Aqaba far to the south. The sea and its force – its power as it broke against the pier's pillars – were alien to him. He checked himself.

Muhammad Ajaq despised fear in others.

Fear was corrupting.

He was so far from what he knew.

Coming closer to the pier, near to level with the shelter above him, he could no longer see the shape of the ferry, moored and awaiting him. It was his target and he craved to see it. With fear there was chaos. He had shot men who showed fear. Fear turned a man's mind. He had kicked the legs from under men who trembled, had the pallor of fear on their faces, aimed a rifle at the back of their heads and killed them. Fear destroyed a man. Now it captured him.

He knew it, he must not run. If he ran, submitted to the fear, he would reach the harbour checks with sweat on his forehead and hands, and he would not be able to meet the eyes of men who stared back at him from behind a cubicle desk . . . Fear would betray him. He had not shown fear when he had been in the brief captivity of the Americans and had used the bogus limp and the bogus papers to extricate himself. He gulped air to calm himself.

For a moment he stopped dead. He shook himself, tried to loosen the stress that tied his muscles and loosened his gut. He took a deliberate, steadying step forward.

He saw only what was ahead of him, the shelter where two men sat and the darkness of the pier. His mind was blurred.

Each step forward was harder than the last, but he did not run.

*

'He's coming.'

'No one's coming.'

'And I'm telling you, he's coming.'

'Don't you listen? No one,' Naylor said, with snapping impatience. 'I hear him.'

'The last time I tell you – I can see four hundred yards away, and it is *empty*. Is that clear to you? No one is coming. What I reckon is, you've made a major error of judgement.'

Dickie Naylor stared up the length of the esplanade, past street-lights and past benches. He saw gulls and blowing plastic bags. Surprising, really, with the sun out, but not a living soul was there. He scratched round his eyes, blinked, looked again. Of course the American *wanted* to believe his man was coming: a bloody reputation hinged on it. Two reputations in reality. He glanced down at his watch, did the mathematics.

'I'm as sorry as you are, Joe. I can't conjure a man up when he's not there. That boat's going to sail without him. I've as much to lose as you, maybe more.'

'You don't hear him, but I do. I'm just going to sit and listen for the both of us.'

As if to humour a child: 'What can you hear, Joe?'

He was jabbed hard in the ribs with the stick's curved handle. 'I can hear feet on loose stones.'

Naylor stiffened and straightened. He heard the gulls' cries, the wind against the lamp-posts and the surf rumbling. He heard the feet slip and dislodge shingle and fracture shells. He stood. He stared down at the beach, at a man's head and the shoulders where the straps of a bag were hitched.

'There, Joe . . .' A panted whisper. 'On the beach, almost level, coming to us.'

'Description? Quickly.'

'Middle thirties, Arab but pale. Might be half-caste. Has a bag.'

'More.'

'Like he's in a trance, far away, doesn't see me.'

'Focus now, get me close.'

Naylor took Hegner's arm and pulled him up. Dragged him. The stick caught Hegner's legs, but Naylor steadied him. He led him away from the shelter and to the knee-high wall on the esplanade. The man was below them, level with them.

'You're close, Joe.'

It seemed to Naylor an age, but it was not. In his ear, Hegner murmured soft and private, 'I've come a long way to find you. Now I've found you and I'm going to fuck you. You are the Scorpion . . .'

The head turned. Naylor realized that Hegner had spoken in guttural Arabic. The head twisted as if it was tugged round.

'Reacted,' Naylor muttered at Hegner. 'Bloody poleaxed.'

The man took two paces, but shingle scattered under his feet and he stumbled. Naylor saw the confusion spreading on his face, then the head shaking – as if he was clearing it, his mind going at flywheel speed. Such a damned simple trick, so bloody basic, and Naylor had seen the reaction of hesitation at the Arabic language, in quiet talk, and the jerk of the head at the word that was 'Scorpion'. He would run – yes, of course – towards the pier . . . but he didn't.

His hands on to the wall.

The heave and the push, the scrape of smoothed stones flying from under him.

The man came up and over the wall. Naylor saw the power of him, saw him coil his body, as if he would break out. What threatened him? Naylor thrust Hegner back behind him, heard the sharp cry, and Hegner fell . . . What threatened the man, blocked his escape, was Dickie Naylor, who might or might not get to celebrate his sixty-fifth birthday the next day, and blind Joe Hegner, who was on the ground behind him. The man came near, crouched, was on the balls of his feet, poised, launched his bloody self.

They might do survival and self-defence with recruits, these days, might not . . . but they didn't do refreshers for old warriors.

Fists into Naylor's head and upper body, a knee into his groin, savage kicks at his shins and ankles. He had never before faced a beating – not in his youth, in his middle years, not now that he was old. He felt his breath wheeze out of his lips, he could not see and the pain surged. He collapsed. Going down made him an easier target. The fists beat at his upper head as he sank on to the paving, and the knee hit under his chin and the kicks were now in his stomach. He couldn't protect himself. He toppled further, felt the softness of Hegner's body under him, and the broken glass of spectacles slash his cheek, added to the blood that came from his mouth. Naylor thought it was where he would die. Old school, old chap, old warrior and saw duty. Made sure he was over Hegner. Cried out once, not again – had no wind left in him. More blows battered him. Scrabbled with his hand – not bloody ready to die. Felt anger.

The stick was in his hand, its glossed white paint in his fist.

Remembered little of what had gone before, but remembered the tapping hard beat of a stick, the story of a blind man's stick being removed from him – at the main door's security check – because its tip would set off the metal detector alarm. Remembered that.

Naylor had the stick, drove it up. Smelt the breath over him, imagined the moment that the man readied himself for the chop blow to the neck. Not bloody ready to die. He pushed up with the stick in one violent thrust and felt it catch softness. Heard a gasp, then a choke. Somewhere soft, maybe in the throat. He braced himself, but the next kick did not come.

He heard a hacking, coarse cough, then the stamp of feet running away fast.

And he heard, 'You all right, Dickie?'

'Not really.' The pain throbbed in him.

He looked up. Saw the back of the man, the pier and the parked car.

He tried to push himself up, failed, tried again, was on his feet and staggered, like a drunk does, and tasted blood. The man ran towards the pier. Without the stick he would have toppled. The man careered away, and Naylor saw that he had a hand raised to his throat, as if he had been badly hurt there. Who had seen it? Nobody. A milk cart went by. Two children scurried for the beach, kicking a ball ahead of them. A dog ran into the surf in pursuit of a thrown toy. Nobody had seen him made into a punchsack.

'If you can, get me up . . .'

Naylor dragged Hegner to his feet, then leaned on him.

'. . . and give me my goddamn stick. Has Twentyman gone where I said he would?'

'He's getting there.'

'Talk to me. I've waited so damn long, Dickie. Tell me what's going on.'

They followed the man slowly. Hegner had the stick and took

Naylor's weight. The sunshine was on his face and he used his tongue to lick the blood from his lips. He said what he saw.

The man ran in full flight, approaching the car. Suddenly its doors opened fast. Boniface and Clydesdale came out of the car. Their view would have been blocked by the shelter and they would not have known that he was down, and Hegner, would have known nothing until they saw the man charge on the esplanade towards them with Naylor and the American in hobbling pursuit: but they'd reacted. The man swerved to avoid the near side door, and lost his footing as it smacked against him. He fell against the little brick wall that held ornamental shrubs. Boniface and Clydesdale were on him; one at the upper body and one at the knees. The cluster of them dropped. He saw the fight. Arms, legs, buttocks heaved up, down, and writhed, as if it was a haphazard playground scrap. Naylor could not tell whose body was uppermost, but he saw punches flail. He pulled Hegner after him, gripping his arm. Far beyond the pier, two young women pushed prams and talked, never looked ahead. And then it was over. He saw the pinions go on to lifted arms and on to the ankles. They knelt on him, and the man's bag lay discarded.

Naylor took Hegner close. He looked down into the face and thought it that of a wild creature. The eyes, burning, stared back, raged. There was discolouration already in the centre of the throat, near the chin. The mouth was open and the breath rasped. The plastic binding was tight on the wrists and ankles, and the two men's weight was squatted down on him . . . yet Naylor could not believe, not completely, that the man no longer represented a danger to him. It filtered into his mind: it was an old poem from school, and a grievously wounded naval captain – an Elizabethan hero – was on the deck of a Spanish galleon, helpless, but his captors would not go close to him, still feared him. He told Hegner what he saw, what was in his mind. But Hegner broke the grip restraining his sleeve, and reached out. It was Boniface who took Hegner's wrist, seemed to know what he wanted, and guided the hand down. Clydesdale had his fist in the man's hair, ensured his head could not move. Hegner's fingers were taken down, so gently, by Boniface, and came to rest on the man's forehead. The fingers slid on the skin from the forehead to the eye sockets, from the eyes across the cheeks and over the shape of the nose. They skirted the mouth and rambled over the stubble on the chin. Naylor understood. Hegner learned the man, as if his fingers on the features made a photograph for him.

Hegner rocked back, and Naylor pulled him upright.

Not to Naylor, Hegner said, 'I want his bag and his documents, and I want him weighted.'

It was done. Boniface searched pockets, produced a ticket, a passport and a slim wallet, then threw the bag at Naylor's feet. Clydesdale did not loose the hair, but kicked hard and backwards with heavy boots and broke the side of the shrub bed to loosen the bricks.

To Naylor, Hegner said, 'Don't you countermand what I ask of them.'

Naylor said, vomit in his mouth, 'I'll not describe it, damn well won't.'

To Boniface and Clydesdale, Hegner said, 'Weight him well and put him over, where it's deep.'

He saw whole bricks and broken bricks shoved into pockets and down the trouser waist, knew they would be held in place by the ankle pinions. He wondered whether the man would cry out, beg, plead, at the last. He gazed into the face of an enemy, at the features over which Hegner's fingers had moved. Saw contempt and defiance. It struck him then, worse than any kick or knee blow or punch, the power of that enemy. Could it ever be bloody beaten? They had him up. One on each arm, in a shuffling run, they dragged him on to the pier. Naylor turned away.

He watched the approach of the young women. He held a handkerchief over his face and hoped to hide the split lips, the blood and the bruising. They never looked at him, did not break step, or their conversation. He heard the babble of their talk as they passed him. Was it done in their name, to keep them safe, and the babies they pushed? He listened for a splash but heard only the waves, above deep, dark water, pounding the pillars.

Naylor said, 'Joe, if it is for vengeance, then that is a shaming motive. It does no credit . . .'

Hegner said, 'Put him in the legal chain and he has a lawyer, and he doesn't speak during human-rights-controlled interrogation, and he becomes an icon of resistance, and kids all over speak his name. My way, he disappears. He's gone from view, from sight –

where to? Confusion is created. Men move, men make calls, men hit the email. They have to know where he is. And if they don't? Then it's disruption and chaos. It hurts them, hurts them so bad, because they don't know. I live off mistakes made. Do they change codes, change safe-houses, change the membership of cells? They're in ignorance and they flounder . . . Think about it. Now, can we go find some coffee, Dickie?'

He saw Boniface and Clydesdale walk back from the pier, short lengths of the plastic ties in their hands. They would have cut them at the moment they stunned him with a blow, then pitched him over . . . Could be a week, or two weeks, longer, before the nameless body was found, and he thought of the scientists and engineers – the new soldiers of the front line in the new war – scouring air waves for messages sent by an enemy who was confused and disrupted . . . and thought also of a boy in a white T-shirt with an angry bloody swan on it.

'You forgot that damned Saudi kid.'

'Didn't forget him, but I prioritized. Please, I'd like to go back and look for my glasses, what's left of them, then I want some coffee. Dickie, you let the kid take his chance and you don't know, and I don't, what might happen. All I'm saying is, the glass is half full – believe in the bright side.'

Lee Donkin's targets were those who hoarded a bus fare in their purses, didn't have a car available to them and would walk all the way down the main road into the town and would not fritter what money they had collected for the sale in the shopping centre.

The sun was on his pale face.

His hood was up and, drawstring tied, none of his hair and little of his features, vindictive and cold, were visible. His gloves were on, and those of his right hand were in his pocket and on the handle of the short, double-edged knife. Because it was too many days since he had last injected himself, it was difficult for him to walk and more difficult for him to concentrate on a target. Once, he went forward, increased his speed sharply and came near to a woman with a buggy, but she must have heard the hiss of his breath: she turned abruptly and confronted him. She had an umbrella, folded and concertinaed, in her fist as a weapon, and he backed off.

The aches in his chest and stomach were not from hunger or thirst, but from the craving.

He saw another woman, ahead and on the pavement, and again stretched his stride, but he saw a police car crawling in traffic towards him, and the chance was lost.

He looked ahead and behind and could not see a lone prey, without people close. He swore . . . He reached a favoured place. Had struck there three times in the last two months, and there were boarded-up toilets beside the pavement that were surrounded by an overgrown evergreen hedge, then a school's playing-fields. He leaned against a lamp-post.

Must wait – and desperation swam in him.

What did he need food for? He did not need food, and she had none to give him.

She had heard his stomach growl as he had prayed.

He had knelt and faced a wall barely visible in the dull, dark room. She did not know what his mind saw but there was content on his face when he had finished. Her own lips moved, spoke the rehearsed speech, but in silence. She weighed it, the decision as to when she would make the speech, and whether it was necessary . . . There was no need for him to eat, and Faria knew the time had come.

She took the bucket to him, and the damp, sodden T-shirt she had used the night before. She washed him again. In his armpits and round the neck where sweat had gathered in the night and his arms, legs and face. She squirted the scent on him. He looked down at her as she crouched on her haunches in front of him, but she could not read him.

He lifted his feet and allowed her to manoeuvre the pants and trousers over them, and she pushed them up and pulled the zipper high, then buckled his belt. She put on his socks and trainers, tightened the laces and knotted them, and her hands fumbled it. He was impassive; she did not know whether he felt fear, whether the strength she had tried to give sustained him. She stood, then bent to lift the T-shirt from the careful pile she had made. He held out his arms and she threaded it over them. Faria saw the swan, and its open beak, its wide, outstretched wings: did the bird, in its anger, curse her? She gazed into his face, then sucked breath into her lungs.

She took the waistcoat from the plastic sack, felt its weight. She swatted at the flies crawling over the bags of shit tied to it. Nothing in her life had prepared her for this. Nothing at home, nursing her sick, demented mother, nothing in keeping house for her father and brothers before they left for the religious schools of Pakistan, nothing at school, where she had passed with distinction all the examinations she had sat, nothing in the room above the house that had become a cultural centre, where she had watched the videos of smiling women making declarations of Faith and then had seen buses, military convoys and street markets erupt in fire, where she had been recruited . . . nothing in the long months as a sleeper, and the call . . . nothing in the cottage.

Its weight sagged in her fingers. He held out his arms, and she slipped one through the space, then went behind him and guided the second through. She saw the pressure from the waistcoat settle evenly on his shoulders, and almost drag him down – but he straightened his back, took the weight. He had the button switch – which she had bought in the hardware shop and might have been used on the light beside her bed at home – in the palm of his hand, pulled the guard cover off it, and she saw the routing of the wires to the detonators, the taping that fastened them to the sticks in the waistcoat's pouches.

The hand that held the button switch was inserted into the sleeve of the leather jacket, then emerged and disappeared again into the side pocket. When his hand was there, inside the pocket, the wire was hidden.

She wanted to be gone. She hurried. Stepped back from him. Left him standing statue still. Threw the *jilbab* over her head, wriggled and let it fall, wrapped the *dupatta* round her neck, over her hair and across her face. Needed to be gone from the stink of the place, its darkness, the sweet sickly stench of the perfume.

She went to the door, crouched at it. He was by the bucket. She had seen his nakedness, but now he was turned away from her. She heard the tinkle against its side before he drew up the zip. He would not kiss her, as he had done in the night – lips on lips, tongues into mouths, teeth gentle on the hardness of her nipples – he had turned away from her so that she would not see it, and his dignity would not be lost . . . It was over. She had done what she had been told to, had made him strong.

Faria said brusquely, without love, 'Time to go. Come on.'

She moved the plank, went first into the gap. He followed, eased himself through and was careful not to jar the waistcoat under the heavy jacket, blinked in the bright sunlight. She led him up the side of the house. At the end of the wall, Faria looked right, then left, was satisfied and walked quickly to the pavement.

They were a young man and a young woman, unexceptional, unremarkable, on an empty road, heading for its end. At the top of a hill they turned right and began the walk towards the town centre.

The crowds had filled the steps to the doors. Ragged queues stretched across the square, and were already level with the library entrance.

Cheerful – eating chocolate, smoking, gossiping – anticipation grew, and the sun had climbed above the town-hall clock tower and warmed them.

'It's Mary, isn't it? There's tea or coffee, whichever you prefer. And as of this morning you have taken over stewardship of a section particularly important to us, am I correct? Do help yourself to biscuits or a croissant. I'm told you have grave personal concerns as to the legality and morality of Service actions in this current time of crisis. Those are the fundamentals? Please, take a seat. You asked specifically to see me this morning when, sadly, the dictate of events gives me little time to lay at your disposal, but you should know – and I emphasize it – I take most seriously any such anxieties from the brightest and best of our staff. You know that? Mary, you have my full attention.'

Light poured into the room, pierced the bombproof glass of the windows . . . and she knew already she was wasting her time. On the upper floor, in the director general's sanctum where she had never been before one on one, he had waved her to a chair that faced the window. While she had nervously cluttered herself with a cup of tea and a saucer, he had taken a position where he leaned easily against the window-sill. To look at him, to hold his eye, she must peer into the full force of the sun. She was disadvantaged, and understood that nothing was by chance.

She said that a prisoner with proven explosives traces had been wrongly freed from Paddington Green's cells.

'I followed the matter, personally, very closely. I was told subsequent forensics disproved earlier conclusions . . . but please continue.'

She said it was her belief that the prisoner had been freed, then abducted by her superior – who acted in concert with an American, a liaison agent of the Federal Bureau of Investigation . . . and she remembered the hands on her and the way they had explored not only her body but her face, and she stumbled on what she said – for the purpose of illegal torture and abuse.

'That is a most desperately serious allegation, Mary, but – in your own words – a *belief*, not substantiated with evidence. For all that, I assure you I will follow this trail with the utmost rigour. What else, Mary, do you have for me?'

She was about to speak when his red telephone, in a bank of three, rang. He grimaced, as if to tell her that he was obliged to answer, a tacit apology for the interruption. He showed no elation or satisfaction that she could see. He repeated the short bullet phrases he heard: 'a facilitator' and 'resisting arrest and broke free' and 'lost in the sea' and 'presumed drowned' and 'a treasure trove of documentation recovered' and 'nothing on the bomber'. He listened closely for a few more moments, then replaced the receiver.

'Where were we, Mary?'

She had no more heart for it. She said that she had told him what she knew.

'May I freshen your cup, no? Another biscuit, no? I think, forgive me, it was that you *believed* you knew, but could not swear to . . . but don't doubt that I will follow this through as soon as our present difficult time is played out . . . May I remind you, Mary, that Dickie Naylor has been a most loyal and devoted servant of our organization for thirty-nine years, a stickler for rectitude, and I find it hard to imagine he would have entered the realms of illegality. The presence of the American is something we welcome, a man of great experience in his field, but I would remind you of last year's speech by his government's secretary of state when she championed the rule of law in dealing with prisoners and most categorically denied they were subject to maltreatment. I quote, "use every *lawful* weapon to defeat these terrorists" . . . Even if well-intentioned, Mary, innuendo cannot be permitted to blacken the names of good men.'

She stood up, put down her empty cup, thought herself a chastised schoolgirl.

He said, 'You will, of course, be pleased to hear that early this morning the facilitator, a senior organizer in that murderous gang of zealots, was intercepted as he tried to flee the United Kingdom, broke free but went into the sea and is presumed drowned – good riddance – but he left his travel papers behind him. That information, Mary, is UK Eyes Only and it would do extreme damage to the war against terror should his people learn of his loss and what we have recovered . . . But, Mary, it goes without saying that you have my complete trust.'

Her head was down. She thanked him for his time. She was at the door.

'Oh, a final thought, Mary. The vernacular for such a person is "whistleblower". It is not, in my opinion, a wise route for anyone to follow. It leads inevitably to resignation, the end of a bright, prospering career, and to denigration from previously valued colleagues. New friends might appear to lionize the blower, but it's short-termism in the extreme. Their usefulness past, the blower is discarded, left lonely and unemployable. I hope you have found our talk helpful.'

She said brightly, 'I have and I'm grateful. Thank you.'

It had been helpful, she reflected, and disguised her rampant bitterness, because she was not a *trade unionist*, or a *Communist*, or a *Jew*.

She closed the door after her.

They were walking along the pavement towards him, towards the boarded-up toilets and the shadows thrown by the hedge where Lee Donkin waited.

Tremors shook his arms and legs, and he bit down hard on his tongue, his lower lip.

There was heavy traffic going both ways on the road, but still moving. Not another pedestrian within a hundred yards of them, behind them. He checked the sports field: kids booted a ball towards goalposts that had no net, but there were no adults with them. Lee Donkin thought his patience rewarded. His escape run was clear.

The man wore a heavy leather jacket, his body bulging under it, and his hands were in the pockets. The expression on his face was vacant, as if he was distracted, but he had a slight smile on his face. The woman alongside him was dressed in the black robe – what Lee Donkin called 'binbag gear' – had a scarf across her face, and a bag hooked up on her shoulder. They were not talking. They didn't look right or left, just walked. He would have said, Lee Donkin would have, that they saw nothing . . . would not see him until he hit them. He readied himself, which made the shaking worse, tensed and flexed.

They came level with the hedge.

Lee Donkin was out fast from the shadow, was on them before he was seen. He hit the woman with his shoulder, heard her gasp, saw the shock. She reeled away, nearly fell into the road as a lorry went by. He had his hand on the strap of the bag and tried to drag it clear of her, but she clung on. A kick slashed at the muscle on the back of his shin. His hand went into his pocket, clasped the knife handle – should have had it out at the start. The man grappled him. The woman held on to her bag and used her free hand to pound him. He was vicious but not strong. Was bloody losing . . . Wouldn't have realized it, but the addiction had sapped him. He had a grip on the leather jacket and tried to pull it closer to him to make the stab thrust shorter. Tugged and ripped at the jacket and was poised to strike with the knife. Lee Donkin felt his arm twisted back – like it would break, and loosed the knife, lost it. Heard the knife fall . . . He broke free and fled.

Lee Donkin ran, slipping, sliding, across the mud of the sports field. Past the kids and their bloody ball. Didn't look back, didn't know what he had done. Ran until he dropped, couldn't breathe, then slumped.

She bent, picked up the knife. Crouching, she dropped it into her bag – couldn't have said why.

'You all right, Miss?'

She looked up, saw the driver high in the lorry's cab. She nodded, and stood. Ibrahim was beside her, and seemed detached from it, far away, still smiling, one hand in a pocket.

The lorry pulled away.

They went on together, walking down the hill towards the town.

*

It was a busy road, no different on a Saturday morning from any other day and it led to a chosen battlefield of the new war . . . There were no defiles and crag peaks, as in the mountains outside Jalalabad, no high-walled compounds that could be defended, as in the remote villages of Waziristan, no culvert drains into which improvised explosive devices were packed, as under the route from the Green Zone to Baghdad International Airport.

The new war had found a fresh fighting ground where people gathered in a square, and did not concern themselves that they paid the wages of soldiers and airmen, paid for the bullets, shells and bombs that were used in their name, did not think of the consequences, and considered themselves far removed. The news on the radio that morning, if anybody had listened, reported a new operation by American troops in difficult mountain country, a raid by Pakistani military against an Al Qaeda leadership target, a bomb in Baghdad that had killed three South African security guards . . . but it was all a long, long way away.

He heard the breakfast cooking, heard the whistled anthem through the bedroom door, waited to go with his Principal to buy a newspaper and a packet of cigarettes.

David Banks opened the notebook, turned to the last page.

2 August 1938
To: Miss Enid Darke, Bermondsey, London
From: Nurse Angelina Calvi, 38th Field Hospital, Ebro River Front

I regret to report to you the death of Cecil Darke, volunteer of the XV International Brigade.

He passed from us three hours ago. He had been hit by a single high-velocity bullet in the upper chest, which caused a Pneumo Thorax condition, the collapse of the right lung. Inevitably there was also internal bleeding into that lung, which had deflated. The original wound was bandaged on the instructions of the doctor i/c, and a trocar was inserted into the lung, a procedure that allows excess blood to be drained. Regrettably, in the conditions of the field hospital – there were many casualties admitted at that time – he was subject to infection. Bacteria would have been introduced through the nasal air passage, and from his uniform particles carried into the wound by the bullet. His temperature rose to 101 deg. F, and his pulse rate and respiratory rate had also risen. To alleviate pain, morphine was injected. At the time of death he was unconscious.

With comrades, he was buried one hour ago. The grave will not have been marked. We withdraw tonight, and tomorrow the Fascists will hold this place; they would destroy, defile, any grave they identified.

I talked to him this morning, before he went to unconsciousness. He was calm, able to speak in a whisper. You should know that, at the end, he had courage and was dedicated to the cause he had joined. He told me that he wished, when he was buried, that the words of Psalm Number 137 should be spoken over his grave: it is not permitted that Christian prayers be said, the commissars forbid it. He had this diary in his hand when he passed. We have an amputee who is being repatriated and he will take the diary to London.

I think he was a man for whom you should feel pride.

Sincerely, Angelina Calvi.

'You ready, Mr Banks? God, you look like you've seen a ghost.'

Low on the settee, his body hid the movement as he closed the notebook, slid it back into his pocket and let it fall on the loose coins and the two pebbles. He said curtly, 'Yes, I'm ready and have been for half an hour.'

'No need to be scratchy.' His Principal grinned. 'Looks like rather a nice day out there.'

She called from the kitchen that they should get a move on or the sausages would be charcoal. He touched the Glock in the holster on his hip, shrugged into his coat and followed Wright out.

Banks walked a pace behind his Principal, and a stride to his Principal's left, held the outer section of pavement. He wondered if an Italian nurse, sixty-nine years, less a few weeks, before, had written the truth of a man's death. Banks raked his eyes over the road ahead and the cars approaching, the people on the pavement, as his training had taught him. He wondered if a man with a hole in his chest and his lung collapsed still felt courageous. Banks saw the ordinariness around him, and sensed no danger.

He thought of betrayal. It would be a big day for betrayal. His, because he had been dumped by the team he should have been with.

Cecil Darke's, because he had been fooled by the cause he'd followed. Julian Wright's, because of what would be said to him after the burned sausages had been served. He thought betrayal made a bad start to a day – to any day.

'Are you always so damn miserable, Mr Banks?'

Ignored him, walked a pace behind and a stride to the side. Saw the cars, saw the faces, saw the square opening out in front of him. Saw the crowds in the far distance.

'All right, what's the story? What's going to happen to me?'

Banks said quietly, as if it was a conversation piece, 'The trial ends and you go into protective custody. You make a statement, which has not yet been done for fear of prejudicing the case you're hearing. If you're lucky you won't be called as a witness in subsequent proceedings because there's a stack of first-hand evidence of arson. You are then let go. You go, if you have an ounce of sense, about as far as is possible. Change your name, change your identity. You forget everything of your past – including your wife and your daughter because they make for the weak link. Only thing you remember is to look over your shoulder, keep looking. Never stop looking into shadows, into darkness, into the faces of strangers. Never think, for what you did, that you're forgotten. How's that, Mr Wright, for a reason to be cheerful?'

'I don't fathom you. I'll miss you, been good having you alongside, does the ego wonders. Yes, I'll miss you – but I don't understand you.'

'You shouldn't try to.'

He saw the rise of the packed steps, heard the clock ahead strike the quarter-hour, saw the snaking lines of the queues in the square. He thought of betrayal and death, and what a sniper had done, and of a psalm not spoken.

Chapter 20: Saturday, Day 17

The square opened out to their left. Nothing was said between them, and his Principal led, Banks following. Every eye that passed him, men and women who bustled forward as if delay were a crime, was fixed on the steps and the great monolith that was the shopping centre; rock music played loudly. He studied each front display window – used the reflections off them to check his rear – and each business doorway and each alleyway between them, because that was his training.

He reckoned his training protected him. It was not his business how one stranger ended a relationship with another. Should worry about himself, not about others, should lock himself in a cocoon of selfishness. He noticed, because he was trained to, each front window and each narrow cut where rubbish bins were stored, where there were the bottles, shit and cardboard sheets of vagrants.

The music, beating down from the centre's loudspeakers, grew in intensity. He took in faces, but none was important to him . . . He felt cold. Realized he was in shadow thrown down by the tower of the town hall. Shivered. Quickened his stride. In shadow, sensed a threat. Came to his Principal's shoulder, then burst back into the sunshine. But it stayed with him, lingered on the skin of his face, and his hand had flipped, without reason, to the weighted pocket of his jacket – no cause – and his fingers had dropped to the hardness held in the pancake holster. Could not have explained it.

But David Banks had been told he was useless, had told himself he had no future.

He snapped, 'Are we nearly bloody there?'

Wright stopped, turned, gazed at him, a grin on his face. 'You seeing ghosts again, Mr Banks?'

'I just want to know if we're nearly there.'

'You're white as a damn sheet. Breakfast's what you need. Yes, we're nearly there.'

He could not have explained, to a stranger or to himself, the chill that had come to him when he had walked through the shadow cast on the pavement.

They were 'nearly there'. He should have seen it, but hadn't. There was an alley with a big wheeled rubbish bin half across its entrance, then the A-shaped hoarding outside the newsagent's door and window that announced the grand opening of the bonanza sale in the town, as if it was the biggest, most vital and critical matter in the whole wide world. Now, breaking the training, his glance came off his Principal and flitted to the crowds on his left, dense and close, with the murmur of excitement given off like hot breath.

'Patience, Mr Banks, patience . . . We're there.' Then the mocking laugh. 'Did you really see a ghost?'

Banks snarled, couldn't help himself, 'Just bloody get on with it.'

The bell rang as his Principal opened the door. He saw that the shop was full, that it would be an age before Wright was served. The door closed after his man and Banks turned away from it, looked back up the street where they had come, and waited.

Now she spoke, said what she had rehearsed. 'There, in front of you, is the crowd. You go close to it, into it. Push hard among it. But look at nobody.'

They had come down the hill and had walked past places she had known all of her life. Had left the big stores far behind. And the turning into the road where the mosque dominated – she had prayed there before moving to the smaller mosque where she had seen the videos and been recruited – and they had gone along a road with stalls, on which were laid out the fruit and vegetables, from which she shopped. The scent of spices had billowed at her from the open doors of the edge of the ghetto where her society lived, and soft silks for clothing had danced in the sunlight from racks. She had brought him to the square. As they had walked, there had been silence between them. What had happened at the top of the hill, the attack, was gone, irrelevant; all that remained of it was the knife in her bag. The square was wide in front of her. She could not fathom his mind, but the smile on his face – spread and open – was childlike. She thought him at peace, but did not believe she could be certain of it, not when he walked the last steps.

'There are women there, and children, and men of our Faith – many others. Do not see their faces. Look at them and you will, want it or not want it, identify with them and hesitate. Do not join your eyes to theirs. Promise me.'

No answer was given her. He had been in step with her, had matched her stride. If she stopped, he had stopped. If she had gone quicker, so had he. She realized her power over him, his dependence on her. She checked her step, and he slowed.

'You do not look at them . . . You think, when you are with them, when you have the button in your hand, of God and of your Faith – of where you will go and who you will be with, and of the pride of your family. Hear, as God welcomes you, the praise of your family, and of all those who love you.'

She did not know if it was enough, but had nothing more to say.

Most days, Faria walked through that square. Most weeks she climbed those steps and entered the shopping centre. She pointed to it, had no reason to but did. Her arm, loose in the folds of the *jilbab*, gestured towards it. Her vision was blurred, clouded by the enormity of what she did. She did not see, misted in her eyes, the shape of the man in the old raincoat who held the clipboard and gazed round him, or the expectation and pleasure on his features. What she saw, as she directed him with her arm, were the images from the videos that had been shown to her: the statements to camera of martyrs, the movement of crowds in street markets, the passing of convoys of Humvee personnel carriers, the guns of the enemy . . . did not see the man in the raincoat turn, break away from the little cluster close to him and advance towards her.

'You're just in time. I had started but it doesn't matter,' Steve Vickers chattered. 'You've come for the inner town's historic tour . . . Well, you've found it. I've done the Roman period, but we can do that again – no one will mind. Now, if you could just follow me . . .'

They were rooted. Oh, people were so strange. The young woman had waved at him, clearly. Had seen him, had waved – he had explained that repeating what he'd already said did not make a difficulty for him, had asked them to follow, but they stood stock still. It would be shyness, perhaps embarrassment.

Vickers, the amateur historian, saw the smile on the young man's face. So many of them, so often – and absolutely he rejected prejudice and would have thought stereotyping beneath him – were so defensive, so withdrawn and uninterested in learning the heritage of the society they had become part of. It was a fine smile, so filled with youth, almost with happiness. The woman was different, had a chill in her eyes – and he thought he saw a gleam of anger there. It dawned on him.

'Are we at cross purposes? I'm Stephen Vickers. I take parties of interested people round the town so that they may better understand what happened here, where we are now, in the generations and centuries before. I assumed you'd seen my advertisements in the local paper and are intent on joining us. Am I wrong?'

'Yes, wrong,' the woman spat.

He saw the livid scar on her face and the blaze in her eyes, but the young man beside her merely smiled, like some sort of idiot, and seemed decent enough if detached.

'Then I'm sorry to have intruded . . . Of course, should you wish to join us, not having intended to, please do. It's a fascinating story, the town's. We walk where Romans did, where Saxons, Vikings and Normans made their lives and—'

'Leave us alone,' the woman hissed.

He would have said that she was on the point of tears, but her rudeness was extraordinary. Vickers said, 'Another time, then, perhaps.'

He strode, annoyed, back to his group. Rejection came badly to him. He did not realize, could not have, the consequences of his approach to the woman and the young man, the importance of those moments lost to them. Nor what would be the result of his delaying them for not more than a minute and a half. His face was flushed from the rebuff when he again addressed his audience.

'My apologies for abandoning you. As I was saying, the Saxons from the Elbe river liked what they saw and found the alluvial valley of the river Lea a most suitable place to settle. Right here, where we are now, they made their first encampment . . .'

The woman was talking urgently to the young man. Steve Vickers ignored them, forgot them.

'You are ready, it is the time. The man was a fool . . . It is you who will make history.'

She did not know whether he listened to her, understood her. She had her hand on his arm, near to his wrist, close to where his hand was hidden in the pocket of the leather jacket.

'I am with you, not beside you but close to you. We are together. I will remember you always. We are going to start to walk. One day we will meet again.'

She cursed the wetness in her eyes. Blinked to squeeze away the tears. She felt the hard shape of the waistcoat under the jacket, and could smell the perfume, and the filth from the field. The music screamed in her ears and a metallic voice shouted a welcome to the crowds. She looked back and up, saw the clock face, four minutes to the hour, and she did not consider the time lost in the spit and hiss to get rid of the fool.

'We are going to start to walk. I am with you, but never look back – and do not see the faces. You are in my prayers.'

If she had not done it, he would not have moved. She used the strength of her arm, her hand on his sleeve, and pushed him forward.

He stood outside the newsagent's. So bloody slow. A few came out and a few went in, not his damn Principal. His eyeline traversed.

He saw the centre and the crowd on the steps, the spread of the queues into the square. Saw a man doing a tour with an audience and shouting to compete against the loudspeakers and the music's clamour. Saw an Asian couple linger on the pavement, and the woman wanted to go forward, and the young man looked reluctant, but she shoved him. Saw an older guy on hospital sticks, coming behind them ... and the older guy lurched round them, as if it were a difficult manoeuvre with his sticks, then stopped to gawp. Banks stamped his foot impatiently ... For God's sake, even with a life history thrown in, how bloody long could it take to buy a newspaper and a packet of cigarettes? Saw the scar on the woman's face and the old guy, weight on his sticks, staring. Saw the young man respond to her shove – he had a dumb smile like he was manic – and start to move ... but the old guy stood four-square in their path.

Banks felt the cold again, but the sun dappled through the trees' branches, and he was far from the town hall tower's shadow.

The bounty-hunter from Afghanistan, George Marriot – he had the wounds to prove it, and shrapnel still embedded – knew what he saw and was knackered.

He was exhausted because he had walked from home into the village, then stumbled along on his sticks to the bus stop. He had stood on the bus, too proud to take a woman's offer of her seat, then lumbered from the bus station into the square. The strength had dripped out of him, but not the keenness of clear thought in his mind.

George Marriot was laughed at, behind his back, when the door closed after him, by the customers in the pub where complacent arse-holes drank. He had hunted proud and able fighters in the Tora Bora mountains. He had taken, dead or alive, the best men of the enemy. But George Marriot had stayed alive. He recognized danger.

George Marriot might not have recognized what confronted him, had he not met a German in the camp at Jalalabad. The German had been GSG9, special forces and their élite, and had talked of the unit's training. Bust into a building, hurl the stun grenades ahead, see the enemy cowering in shock, identify the women – kill them: 'No god-damn messing, Georgie, put half a magazine into them. Shoot the women first, is what we're taught. The women, Georgie, are deadly.' She had the set face and pursed lips and there was, he thought, contempt in her eyes, as she pushed the boy. The boy wore that damn smile ... had cause to smile. George Marriot knew what the *muftis*, *mullahs* and *imams* told them, the martyrs. Absolved of sins, a seat in Paradise. No torture in the grave, and up alongside seventy-two dark-eyed women. Can take seventy relatives to Paradise, and earn the Crown of Glory. A kid had walked in Kabul and another in Herat, and both had walked, sweaty, nervous, but people near enough to see – who had survived – had said those kids were still smiling.

This one had a blown-out chest and a heavy gut under his coat, but spindle-thin legs from the outline of his trousers, and a hand deep in a pocket, which did not come out when he was shoved – it made sufficient of an equation for George Marriot.

His balance unsure on one stick, he lunged at the kid with the other, but the woman came across him. Her hand was in her bag, and then he felt pain running in torrents.

David Banks saw the old man lurch towards a couple, as a drunk did when incapable. He targeted the boy, but the woman had intervened with her body, and her robe swirled as she moved. The old man fell against her, then crumpled, went down on his stomach, was slumped flat.

A mother with a push-chair, and other parents with children, pushed past heedlessly because it was none of their business.

On training days, they drilled into Protection Officers that they were not to move off-station. A traffic pile-up – drive round it and head on. A fight in a street or a snatched bag – keep moving with the Principal and leave it to the uniforms. He stayed put, his back to the newsagent's door.

He might have thought it pathetic for an old man to be pissed-up that early in the morning ... but his life was past making judgements. He looked away, made his eyeline traverse again and off the pavement where the sticks lay crazily and the old man was sprawled. Last thing he noted was the woman and the young man step over him, and start to come up the pavement. He looked behind him, through the shop-door glass, and saw that Wright was next in line to be served.

She felt no love; nothing of it remained.

Together, they had stepped over the body where the knife was. A little trickle of blood seeped from under the chest, and from the mouth.

'You should walk. I am behind you, but do not turn to find me ... Know that I am with you.'

For a moment, with his free hand he held hers. Then Faria pushed into his shoulder, shoved him away. She thought, at that moment and as he seemed to skip to regain his footing, that his smile had gone.

She followed him for three or four paces, no more, and saw him meander down the pavement . . . She was satisfied that he would not look back, would not search for her.

Everything that was asked of her, she had done.

She turned and started to walk away, back where she had come from. In front of the Tasty Fried Chicken and its steel shutters she did what she had forbidden to him, and stared after him. He went slowly, as if he walked asleep, and was near to a newsagent's and an alleyway with a rubbish bin, and beyond it he would cross the road, through the traffic, and join the queue at the base of the steps. She was not with him, was not close. She ran.

She ran until she was round the corner, close to the town hall – saw the clock that showed two minutes to the hour – then she snatched breath and walked.

It was done.

She slipped into a cut-through lane. She was alone. She heaved off the *jilbab* and dumped it with the headscarf, shook loose her hair and went out of the far end of the lane.

Faria, with a good stride, started for home. And she felt the emptiness, and the choke in her throat.

'God, look.'

'Can't, bloody traffic.'

'It's that girl.'

'What girl?'

The farmer's wife swivelled in her seat to look behind, out through the Land Rover's back window. 'The girl we had.'

'Had where?'

'You can be damned thick, dear. The girl we had in the cottage.'

'I'm not stopping or we'll be shunted.'

'Gone now anyway. You know what, she—'

'What?'

'Don't interrupt me, dear. She was crying her eyes out.'

'I haven't any idea where we'll get to park.'

'Listen, dear, she was sobbing, like her world had ended. Well, I

401

think it was her. No, she was so composed, couldn't have been. It was *like* her.'

He saw the loop of the wire.

David Banks had seen the drunk veer against the couple, then smack at them with a stick, lurch into them, then collapse, and he had seen him ignored on the pavement. The couple had parted, the woman had scuttled away and the young man had walked on towards him ... and the crowds heaved against the line of security men who were across the top of the steps.

Thoughts raced in the mind of Banks. It was a bright day, and sweat glistened on the skin of the young man's face, made a sheen there. There had been a smile, vacuous, where the sweat now dribbled – but not any longer. The smile had gone, was replaced by the tremble of lips, his eyes scattering glances ahead of him. His movement was slow. With each step, a loop of flex – three inches or so – bounced below the hem of the leather jacket. He saw a thin face, pinched at the cheeks, and a neck without flesh. One hand was deep in a pocket, but the other hung limply at his side. The legs, where the flex showed, were narrow and insubstantial, and the trainers were small ... Yet the body was so large, as if it had been built with a weightlifter's pills, like layers of sweaters were under the jacket. The rest of the body did not match the size and bulk of the chest. And there was the loop of wire.

Banks remembered a zephyr of sneering laughter in a briefing room, the day before the American president's arrival on his last visit to the UK capital. A photograph pumped up on to a screen by the boss of the Rear Echelon Mother Fucker. A Secret Service guard, his arms thrown aside, gripping a machine pistol that was aimed at the heavens, waistcoat buttons bulging under strain, mouth open, as his president was collapsing, shot, on the pavement, and the caption across the screen's base was the guard's incredulous shout: *Christ, it's actually happening*. Yes it was, Christ, actually happening.

Clothes weren't right, were too full and too cumbersome for the upper body, too heavy in that morning's sunshine, and there was the loop of wire.

Remembered the cold on the neck, and the hackles up in the Alley where they practised. Saw the window and the cardboard figure in

it. It spun and might show him the gun or a child in arms ...
Remembered the age-long inquest after a Brazilian was shot dead in
a train carriage: a guy working for a better life, not a terrorist bomber
... Remembered an officer who had faced a charge of murder for
killing when there was no cause to kill ... Remembered a marksman
who had fired with justification, and was now a stressed-out shell.
The memories careered in his mind.

There was a target behind him, a moving, flowing mass, an ants'
nest of activity on the steps and in the square. There was a young
man with sweat on his face, a body that was not to scale, and a loop
of wire that was too thick for a personal stereo's cables.

Knew it, and could not escape from it – it was *actually* happening.

He looked into the face of the stranger, the young man. Saw it as a
sniper would have. Saw the shake of the chin and the fear in the eyes.
Made a judgement, as a sniper had. Passed the sentence, condemned.
He smelt, for the first time, the perfume – what a teenage girl would
have worn – and the sentence was confirmed, no appeal.

Banks wondered, then, if the young man struggled to be brave –
tried to summon up the principles that had sent him – but was now
frightened, his brain fogged ... He reverted to his training, long
hours in long years of it, because it was actually *happening*. The
young man was coming level with the alleyway, crabbing sideways
to avoid the rubbish bin on wheels. Banks's hand flicked against his
jacket, and the weight of a notebook, loose coins and pebbles flapped
it back. The hand went, one movement, to the butt of the Glock, and
as it was snatched out a finger slid the safety.

The weapon came up, and his feet splayed out.

The young man had stopped dead, and stared.

Banks went to the shooting posture, Isosceles stance. Fast enough?
Could not be. Aimed for the head, forehead and temples, but the
head seemed to shake as if it sought to remove the reality of
the moment. Couldn't, in the time that was a second's fraction,
lock the aim over the needle. Gasped in the breath. Saw the pocket,
where the hand was, writhe, and knew the button was pressed ...
and nothing ... His finger squeezed, and the target backed away
into the alley, and bounced off the rubbish bin. Kept the squeeze
on.

*

She changed down, then stamped on the brake.

The damn thing did it again. Had had to brake or would have hit the van in front. Like two shots fired, the damn car that Avril Harris had bought seemed to explode with noise. It rang in her ears. She blushed, would have gone scarlet, and a man in a car beside her – in an outer lane – leaned clear of his window, grimaced, grinned and called to her, 'You want to have that seen to, Miss. It'll be the crank-shaft and timing belt that need adjusting and—'

'Thank you. I know what the sodding thing needs.'

The van in front had pulled forward and she drove on after it, past the square and the great swaying crowd. She heard the town hall's clock strike, and saw the big doors at the top of the steps open, the surge that engulfed the security men.

He dropped the Glock back into the pancake holster, pushed it down so that it was secured. His arms quivered from the recoil of the firing, and cordite stench was in his nose.

His target had been thrown back. Could not see the head or chest because they were lodged behind the rubbish bin, but the frail-built legs and feet – and the loop of wire – were visible to Banks. He felt no emotion, did not know whether he should. He looked behind him, expected to see a crowd gathering in a half-moon, but people walked on the pavement, a pensioner couple, a family, youths with their hoods up, and all hurried towards the steps to the shopping centre, and the traffic cruised by.

He went into the alleyway. The rubbish bin stank of old refuse. He thought it as good a place to die as a forward trench where rats roamed. He looked down, through the shadow light, into the face. Yes, two good shots. Yes, the best a double tap could do. The holes, wide enough for a pencil to be inserted into – or a cheap ballpoint-pen tip – were an inch or so apart and their median point was the centre of the forehead, half-way between the top of the bridge of the nose and the lowest curls of the young man's hair. They oozed blood. He didn't need to, but Banks crouched, felt for a pulse and found none.

Should not have done, but he lifted carefully the hand from the pocket, found a fist round a lamp switch, and knew the last intention of his target. He unbuttoned the jacket – the training work was done, the double tap, and he was separated from it. He knelt. He revealed the waistcoat, the careful stitching, the line of the sticks, and the pouches where nails, screws and ball-bearings were . . . and he saw where the taped binding had come loose, and wondered how and by whom it had been torn free. There was more tape at the end of the flex wire, and he understood why the device had not fired, why the switch had not linked with the batteries and the detonators. Banks had no training for it, but it seemed as simple to him as when he was at home at his mother's and she requested some small repair to an electrical device. Methodically, he made it safe. He unwound more tape and broke the connection between the batteries and the explosives. He stood, and behind him the entrance to the alleyway was empty and he was not watched.

On his mobile, he dialled the number of his REMF, heard it ring, heard it answered.

He said quietly, but composed, 'This is Yankee 4971, Delta 12, two shots discharged and one X-ray down. One IED made safe . . .' He gave his location, heard the babble of questions thrown at him and answered none. Banks finished, 'Over, out,' and rang off. He was 'Yankee', code for 'a good guy', and did not feel it. The face now hidden from his view was that of an 'X-ray', who was in Delta speak 'a bad guy' – but it had been his promise that he did not make judgements. He imagined the chaos pursuing the news he had laconically telephoned in, that a suicide-bomber was dead and an improvised explosive device had been disarmed.

He went back into the alleyway a last time, and dragged the body deeper into the shadows. Then he pushed the rubbish bin, moved it so that the entry was better blocked and the corpse better hidden.

Banks stood beside it, his feet close to the waistcoat. Soft words spoken, those of a psalm. He stepped back, was on the pavement again.

His Principal said, behind him, 'God, wondered where the hell you were. Pretty little bit of totty in there, makes a good start to the day. Then they had to go out the back and bring in more papers . . . Then the cash machine jammed. Breakfast'll be screwed. Time to leg it.'

'Yes, let's get clear of this bloody place.'

They went fast. Had to go out into the road because paramedics, on the pavement, were lifting on to a stretcher the man he'd thought to be a drunk, and he saw the bright blood smear on the pavement dirt ... and Banks reflected, hurrying, that nothing was what it seemed to be.

Afterwards, it was a time for tangles to be unravelled, and loose ends tied, and for the lives of the living to be regained and the dead to be forgotten.

'The chief constable up there is a very good man, sound – but he's short of a knighthood. I think such a deserved award is in order, if he's co-operative.'

The assistant director sat in the comfortable chair of his director general's wide office, sipped coffee, and nodded agreement.

'You see, Tris, there's no call to trumpet this affair. By the skin of our teeth, we've avoided a catastrophe that could have brought the roof down on us, on all of us in the Service, but that's past now. What concerns me most acutely is that delicate knife edge on which racial relations exist in these days. Take that town, Luton. Ethnic prejudices bubble barely beneath the surface on a daily basis. This is the sort of business, if shouted from the rooftops, that could fracture what little harmony exists, excite the bigots and therefore drive that Muslim minority – most of whose young people are utterly decent and totally law-abiding citizens – into the welcoming arms of the fanatics ... and the same goes for a score of other communities the length and breadth of the land. I'll work at full stretch, and demand the same of the whole Service, to keep matters quiet, as quiet as the grave.'

'Very wise, if I might say so ... Dickie Naylor's at home, getting some sleep, but he'll be taking that American to the airport later. What he did fits well with your ideas.'

'I don't think it appropriate for me to speak personally with him ... I think we can just leave him to get on with, and enjoy, the start of his retirement.'

'The officer who fired the shots – reacted so fast that this murderous Saudi did not have the chance to detonate himself – is, I am told, a steady fellow and not one to make waves.'

'A first-class man, Tris, and I hope with a bright future. If those dunderheads at Great Victoria Street have a modicum of sense, he'll be tracked for fast promotion. He's saved us from acute embarrassment.'

'I'll pass the word, with discretion – nothing happened.'

'Excellent, and come and have a little wet with me tonight, a sherry or three. There's cause for quiet celebration. Oh, the Reakes woman, she won't be silly, will she?'

'A level-headed girl.'

'Thank you, Tris. We were so near to being trampled and broken reeds ... A most satisfactory beginning to a day when nothing happened – make sure you come and see me at the end of it.'

A purser said to a steward, 'There's a blind gentleman in business class, American, third row back and by the port-side window. Looks pretty helpless, keep an eye out for him.'

'Sad, must blight a life being so dependent. My imagination, or are his glasses stuck together with tape? Probably walked into a door. Of course, I will.'

A detective from Special Branch, briefed and regarded as reliable, had been admitted to a terraced home in an East Midlands city.

He sat in a small living room opposite a mother and daughter, and there was a framed photograph of a son, a brother, behind them. He said, with practised sympathy, 'The problem was that Ramzi formed associations with dangerous people. We released him and sent him home and know that he reached very near to here. The rest is surmise ... We believe he made contact with those people. They may have concluded that we had turned him after his arrest, then freed him so that he could inform on them. It's not true, but they may have thought it. There are, now, two possibilities: they may have murdered him, or he may have fled beyond their reach. We will be, you have my promise, working day and night to ascertain which, and I most strongly advise you to leave these matters in our capable hands. If he is still living, your own enquiries could jeopardize his safety ... I think you understand, and we'll hope for the best.'

'Oswald Curtis, for this heinous and disgusting crime, you will serve twenty-two years' imprisonment. Oliver Curtis, a younger brother and undoubtedly under the influence of your elder sibling, you will serve eighteen years' imprisonment. Take them down.'

Mr Justice Wilbur Herbert, well satisfied with the trial's outcome and with the quality of his address, watched them escorted from court eighteen, their faces flushed in impotence and anger. He did not know of the chain of events begun when the brothers had employed Benny Edwards, the Nobbler – and the links of that chain that had put, with inevitability, a Protection Officer on to a pavement outside a newsagent's that fronted on to a town square.

He congratulated all of the jury on their courage, but his eye was on the bearded man who wore sandals, the school teacher.

'All rise,' his clerk shouted.

The golf team's secretary was first back at the bar, the churchyard's mud on his polished shoes, and the darts team's treasurer was at his shoulder. He ordered for them and waited for the drinks, doubles of Scotch, to be given him.

'That's something I'll never forget,' the secretary said. 'I mean, all those Americans there, Rangers and Green Berets, and that unit pennant on old GG's coffin, and that big sergeant singing the "Battle Hymn" over the grave. Don't mind admitting it, I was crying fit to bust.'

The empty stool was beside them.

'Sort of humbling,' the treasurer said. 'How wrong can you get? Thought he was just a sad old beggar who lived with his fantasies, and it was all real and we took the piss. You just never know a man, do you? God, we'll miss Gorgeous George . . .'

They raised their glasses and toasted the vacant stool.

Longer *afterwards*, the tangles were tidied and the ends knotted.

From behind a desk, Mary Reakes worked with driven energy for the cathedral's International Centre for Reconciliation.

Other ladies with whom she shared office space in the building beside the new cathedral had considered, lightly, opening a sweep-stake – with a prize of a tin of chocolates – to be won by the first who saw the incomer smile. They did not know where she had come from, or why – each day her face was set with an undisguised chill –

and her cubicle had no decoration except old and new postcards from the Iraqi capital, Baghdad. She did not share.

The head teacher of a secondary school said to her deputy, 'I think Julian's settled in well. Don't understand him. Can't imagine why a man with his qualifications wants to make his life here, the back end of Adelaide – must have been something of an earthquake that dropped him down on us.'

'And you don't get anything of explanation from him, or from his partner.'

'She's nice. Vicky's a bit scatterbrain, but the heart's there – she's doing good things in year five's craft class. I hope they stay.'

'I think they will. Most of the new migrants who've had – what did you call it, an earthquake? – some damn great upheaval, they don't have anywhere further to run. Mr Wright and his lady are here to stay.'

Faria looked after her invalid mother and never went further from home than the Khans' corner shop.

Khalid drove a mini-cab in west London, Syed worked in the family's fast-food take-away, and Jamal had started the second year of his business-studies course.

None of them would again be sleepers, or willing to be woken.

Two elderly men, one a retired power-company engineer, the other a retired quantity surveyor studied the stands on which the Horticultural Society's show entries were displayed, and eyed where the judges had laid the prize-winning rosettes.

The engineer said, 'That man, Anne's husband, he's never been seen here before – never put anything in before – and first time up he's taken the gold with his tomatoes . . .'

'I've the impression that he's lived with them since they were two-inch plants, cosseted them and fussed over them, probably slept with them each night. It takes an utter obsession to produce tomatoes of that quality, totally life-consuming.'

'What did he do before taking his pension?'

'She's never said, Anne hasn't. Some dreary job in Whitehall, I suppose – and exchanged it for a greenhouse. He's so damned aloof, has the manner of someone who used to think himself important, but it was probably only pushing paper . . . Maybe I'm wrong, maybe it was life-and-death stuff, but the knife came down and it's exchanged for tomatoes.'

'And that's your Englishman?'
'That's him.'
'Your stranger?'
'Less of a stranger now. He came to us in the spring, now it's the autumn.'

It was only once a year that the bishop visited the village and its priest. It was near the end of the day and a cool wind came from the north, chilled by the high points of the Pyrenees. Leaves fluttered down around them. After the heat of summer, a cruel winter was usual at this lonely, unlovely cluster of homes and its church, which lay between the larger communities of Calacete and Maella.

'And he spends his days here?'
'And his evenings writing letters – which is why you are visiting and can see him for yourself.'

The bishop's body threw a long shadow and the chill wind blustered the cloak he wore. He stared across a slight ravine over bare, fallen rocks and past a long cattle barn that was now broken into disrepair. Beyond it there was a flat space of dull sun-scorched earth where weeds grew high. There the man sat, his back to them. If their voices carried to him he showed no sign of caring that they intruded on the privacy of his space.

'The hospital was in that barn?'
'It was.'
'And the dead were buried where the weeds grow?'
'They were . . . but it is difficult to be exact about where the graves lie. There are no witnesses in the village. Everyone had been evacuated before the battle for the Ebro began. They were forcibly removed or fled. The village was a shell. When people came back, they had too many bitter memories and they did not believe it correct to relive those dark days . . . They had chosen the wrong side, they had supported the losers. It is natural that the dead of the defeated should not be honoured.'

'They were difficult times.'

The bishop saw a man, lit by the last of the day's sun, sitting motionless on the hard ground. The man, he thought, was well built in an athletic way and had none of the flab of middle age. His hair was tousled in the wind. Too young a man to be so captured by the dead: a man of an age at which life still stretched ahead and where ambition for the future should not be denied. In the files at his office, the bishop had seven translated letters from this man, all signed 'Respectfully, David Banks', and all written in a clear, strong hand.

'And he has been to other battlefields before coming and staying in your village?'

'He went to the old barracks at Albacete, then to Madrid. He has walked in the Jarama valley and at Brunete, and he has been down to the Ebro river . . . He did all of that before he came to us and took a lodging in the village. He has lived here very simply. He does not take alcohol and he is polite in all his dealings with us. Each day he leaves the village and walks up – past where we are now – to the barn where the wounded were treated, and where some died, and then he goes to the place where it is said the graves were dug. He has been there when the sun was fierce on him, without shade, and when the rain has tipped on him, without shelter . . . and he has written those letters to you.'

'And I, alone, have the power to free him?'

'I believe so.'

'Then it has to be done . . .'

The bishop grimaced, then hitched up the hem of his robe and strode away. The priest hurried after him. Helping each other, they scrambled down the loose stones and the dried dirt of the ravine. In its pit were old and rusted tins that might have held rations issued to combatants. There were three aged shell cases with lichen surviving on them. On their hands and knees they scaled the far edge of the ravine. They came to the barn where the walls of stone still bore the pockmarks of bullets. The bishop paused there, at a doorway that had no door, gazed inside, and his eyes peeled away the interior's darkness. He imagined he looked into the hell of an abattoir, and he murmured a prayer for those who had died there close to seven decades before. He seemed to hear the moaning of the wounded and the cries of those who were past saving. On the flat ground, the priest hung back, but the bishop tramped on, crushing weeds under his feet. He came to the man, walked round him, then lowered himself, placed his weight on a rock and was in front of him.

'You are David Banks?'

'I am.' He was answered in halting Spanish.

'You have written many letters to me.'

'I have.'

'And you carry a diary of old times.'

'I do.'

He saw a youthfulness but it had no peace. He sensed the restlessness of a troubled mind, perhaps tortured. The letters had been blunt, to the point, and the bishop had no stomach for excuses, or procrastination. He thought it time to free a spirit.

'There is little appetite in our modern society to relive the harsh scars of days gone by. The lessons of history, as I have learned them, are that ancient wounds can be healed by time ... Atrocities and savagery are passing things, and quickly forgotten. My grandfather was bayoneted to death by the Communists, but I have forgiven them and their heirs ... I cannot enter the minds of those who did it, the hatred they harboured. I seek now only the passing of black days. You have asked that a stone be put here, that a name should be carved on it, that a prayer – a psalm – should be said here. That recognition should be given to those who died for a cause they believed in, for which they volunteered their lives, that they should have dignity in death. I promise, it will be done.'

'Thank you.'

He believed he took a burden from the shoulders, gave them back their strength. A wad of banknotes from David Banks's hip pocket was given him. He was told it was to pay for the stone and it was requested that a mason should carve on it the silhouette outline of a bird, a swan, with the name of Cecil Darke and the dates of his life. He put the notes into his wallet. And he was also asked if some several items could be buried in the earth under the stone when it was laid down: an old book, with a frayed leather cover was handed to him – almost with reluctance – and then from a pocket two small pebbles, each with seams of quartz running through them, and last a few coins of a currency he did not recognize, but they had weight.

'As you have asked it, so it will happen. Will it help you? Does that free you?'

'I will stay here for the night, and in the morning I will be gone.'

'Where to?'

'I don't know, it doesn't matter . . .'

The bishop backed away. He walked fast, the priest at his side, and the barn and the ravine were behind him. He was anxious to be on the road for Barcelona before the darkness came. He looked once over his shoulder and saw faintly, a last time, the man who was squatted low among the weeds, bathed in the brilliance of late sunshine, and believed he had brought peace to a troubled soul. He held the old notebook tightly, and the pebbles rattled with the coins in his pocket . . . He did not understand what was asked of him, or why, and thought few would have.

The bishop shook the hand of his priest and drove hurriedly away from a place where, he thought, old scars had lain open and untreated wounds had festered, but he trusted his promise would have healed the scars and cleaned the wounds. On his journey, ghosts danced in his mind. They were those of the dead in their lost graves, and of the living man who had watched over them and who – he hoped – was now freed, and at liberty.